TEXAS FAITH

ANDREW ROTH

ELK LAKE PUBLISHING INC

PUBLISHING THE POSITIVE
Plymouth, Massachusetts

A Christian Company

COPYRIGHT NOTICE

Cover and Interior Design: Derinda Babcock, Deb Haggerty
Editor(s): Cristel Phelps, Deb Haggerty

PUBLISHED BY: Elk Lake Publishing, Inc., 35 Dogwood Drive, Plymouth, MA 02360, 2022

Library Cataloging Data

Names: Roth, Andrew (Andrew Roth)

Texas Faith / Andrew Roth

374 p. 23cm × 15cm (9in × 6 in.)

ISBN-13: 978-1-64949-667-6 (paperback) | 978-1-64949-668-3 (trade hardcover) | 978-1-64949-669-0 (trade paperback) | 978-1-64949-670-6 (e-book)

Key Words: Western, post-Civil War, helping others, sacrifice, belief in God, survival, friendship

Library of Congress Control Number: 2022943986 Fiction

DEDICATION

To all the faith-filled pioneers who helped shape this
glorious country. God bless America.

CHAPTER 1

When the war broke out, and Pa left to join up, I thought things couldn't get much tougher for Ma and me. I was wrong.

Dust clouds lifted above the trail that led past our ranch, and I leaned on my pitchfork and shielded my eyes as I watched the rider approach. Although the war had ended a few months back, we still were unused to the increased travel on the trail near our place.

A man on a tired bay gelding loped into the yard, and I glanced toward the house, knowing Ma would be just inside the door, the old shotgun at hand. Returning soldiers naturally stopped at our house, our place being on the main trail from the Indian Nation into Texas. Although the panhandle wasn't a good place to be in the summer of 1865, this was my home and all we had left.

I studied the rider as he leaned back in his saddle while the bay drank thirstily from the water trough beside the barn. His piercing stare bore into me from beneath his battered hat, and I shifted. I'd grown accustomed to passing strangers, but sensed something different about this one.

I peered past him to the cattle dotting the hills, frowning as I remembered the branding we'd left undone these past years. But everyone had cattle, and we hoped stealing would have little effect on our herd, filled with countless unbranded mavericks anyone could claim.

During the war, the vast herds had been left unattended. Huge bulls with wide horns wandered the open lands, but no market existed for them in Texas. Except for the occasional need for fresh beef, the thousands of wild cattle held no real value.

After Pa and the hands left to sign up, Ma and I hunkered down to simply maintain the ranch. Before long, we were working from before sunup to well after sundown to feed the riding stock and keep up the barn and the house. We let the bunkhouse fall into disrepair first and soon, corral by corral, the outlying pens and sheds. Ma worked day after day on our big garden, and we sometimes traded at Anderson's store in town for things we couldn't grow ourselves. Or we did without.

Again, I glanced quickly toward the silent house and fidgeted. Ma had forgotten today was my birthday, but I didn't blame her. She had a lot on her mind. Besides, she couldn't make me a cake even if she wanted to. We hadn't seen sugar in years.

The bay nickered as he lifted his nose, drops of water shimmering like jewels as they dribbled back into the trough. I studied the stranger's tattered gray uniform and brown slouch hat, common enough on the occasional riders who stopped by. He carried no gun I could see, but he wore tall cavalry boots, gleaming black despite a layer of dust. An old coat lay bundled behind his saddle. By the look of them, both rider and horse had come a long way.

He sat his horse, looking around as I walked from the barn, his sharp scrutiny missing nothing. The rider rested a hand on his thigh and nodded. "Howdy, boy. Is this the Garret place?"

I blinked, startled and curious. How'd he know us?

"Yes, sir. I'm John Garret." I'd always been Johnny, but now I was seventeen and figured to be a John. The soldier didn't seem impressed, though, as he narrowed his eyes against the bright sun and surveyed the weathered buildings behind me.

I wondered if he blamed me for the poor condition of the dilapidated ranch, and I bristled, defensive and embarrassed. I was the man of the place, after all.

The saddle creaked as he shifted, and I grew restless, wondering at his purpose. Was he here only for water, a passing traveler? Again, something nagged at me, and I suspected there was more to his visit.

"You have new boots," I ventured, impatience prodding me as I gestured to his stirrups. I didn't like the look of disappointment I sensed in him as he scanned the graying house, the dirt yard, and the quiet barn.

His gaze dropped to his boots, and he chuckled, the laugh never reaching his eyes. "I shot this Yankee officer and was pulling off his boots when three blue bellies jumped out of the brush and caught me. I went to prison camp after that." He paused, and then added quietly, "I ain't had new shoes since the war began."

"How long were you in prison?" Sheer curiosity forced my question, but I didn't want him looking over our ranch again and shaming me. Most of the soldiers didn't want to talk when they stopped for water, and I dearly longed to hear another's voice.

But he looked at me and didn't reply, his eyes staring blankly. I leaned back on my run-down heels and glanced over my shoulder toward the house where a slight breeze stirred the curtains at the open window.

The man shifted again. "Is your ma home?"

I nodded and walked across the hard-packed dirt yard to step onto the porch, speaking quietly as I kept an eye on the stranger. "He wants to talk to you. He knew our name."

The shotgun thumped on the wooden floor when she leaned the weapon against the wall. A moment later, Ma came outside and stood beside me. The man on the horse removed his hat, his eyes widening when she stepped to the edge of the porch, her light brown hair blowing in the ceaseless wind. She swiped at the rebellious strands as they waved across her pale cheeks.

"Ma'am? Are you Annie Garret?"

Ma nodded, lips tight, as if she knew what was coming. She squeezed my shoulder.

"I served with your husband, Vince. He was a good man. He made me promise I would come by here and tell you. He died at Fort Fisher, under General Bragg. I was with him, ma'am, and a few days later, I was captured." He paused to let his words sink in. Ma didn't say anything.

"I'm sorry, ma'am." He put his hat back on, tugged on the reins, and rode from our yard, leaving only a lingering smell of dust behind him.

Silence hung between us like a wet blanket, only the wind making a mournful sound as the prairie grass leaned and swayed before its force. I heard the gelding's hooves retreating down the trail. The bright afternoon sun seemed to dull and blur, and my shoulders slumped.

We stood there a moment longer, and then, Ma patted my shoulder before she went inside, closing the door behind her, so I knew she wanted some time alone.

I shoved my hands into my pockets and watched the stranger disappear down the trail. So, there it was. Pa was dead. I'd kind of figured as much when he hadn't come home right after the surrender, and we hadn't received any letters from him since last fall. Ma had tried to keep a little hope of his return, but now the story was told.

That evening at supper, we spoke only of stock and weather and how the vegetables were doing in the garden, the weeding never completed. But later that night, I heard her crying softly in her room.

Lying in the dark, I stared up at the unseen ceiling, my hands threaded behind my head. I knew things were bad, no doubt about that. We'd been trying to keep things going, trying to make it through the war, waiting for Pa to come home. But like Pa, that slim hope was dead now.

Responsibility weighed on me like a heavy stone. I would miss Pa—he was a good man, but I would miss his leadership even more. What were Ma and me going to do? Of course, we couldn't keep up the ranch any longer. We'd been hanging on, barely surviving, waiting for Pa's return. Now clearly, we needed to move on, give up the land, locate a place we could settle again. Someplace where we could afford a simple existence. We still owed money we couldn't pay at Anderson's, and we'd heard rumors of back taxes coming due now the war was over.

I'd heard immigrants were finding work in the factories of the northern cities. Wrinkling my nose, I squinted into the dark, hating the idea of leaving Texas for the stinking, overcrowded Yankee cities. But we couldn't stay here any longer.

The next morning, Ma stood at the cupboard, her back to me, when I pulled a chair to the breakfast table. "Johnny, your pa worked hard to give us this ranch, and we're going to keep it."

I tilted my head, surprised by her spunk after such crushing news. Did she guess the worries that kept me up last night? I studied her ramrod stiff back and clenched my teeth, knowing better than to argue with her when she was like this. Surely, she knew in her heart we couldn't stay on here.

Without looking at me, she added, "God is good, even when we don't understand him. Things will work out."

I couldn't tell if she was trying to convince me or herself. I just chewed the inside of my cheek and didn't reply. What for? God would do what he was going to do, whether I liked the outcome or not. But I knew we'd have to pack soon and vacate the property. I felt sorry Ma thought her prayers mattered.

She clung to her faith, but I arched an eyebrow, recalling how difficult things had been for so long. Yet Ma had the uncanny ability to find good in a bad situation. She'd always been a strong woman. I guess she had to be to live on the plains of Texas.

Me, I was remembering these last five years. Ma could make soup out of anything and stretch the broth for days by just adding more water. Beef and eggs were plentiful, but any item we needed from the store was scarce, like coffee and flour. The two of us barely squeezed a living from our garden.

She never complained, but I always wondered at God's plan. If it weren't for bad luck, I figured we'd have no luck at all. And now we needed to go somewhere else, start fresh, like thousands of others were doing. The war had been hard on everyone.

Hurrying through my meager breakfast, I stole glances at her as she stood at the kitchen window. I wished we could sell out, but there were no buyers. Our land was good, so our cattle hadn't strayed far, but they were of little concern to us—other than when we butchered the random steer. Our riding stock, however, we kept close to home. With the war over, horses were suddenly in demand, although there was little cash money. Also, with the scarcity of men around, some strangers weren't overly particular whose horse they threw a saddle on.

Knowing this, we were constantly watchful and slept lightly, one of us always keeping the shotgun close by.

I knew we'd have to face facts now and pack what we wanted for the impending move, but Ma deserved her grief. Vowing to give her a little time, I trudged through normal movements, keeping my distance as I performed the usual chores, ignoring the inevitable as long as I could. Besides, I felt reluctant to saddle her with more, and this had been my home my whole life.

For the next two weeks, Ma kept her own counsel. Quiet except for a few words at mealtimes, she walked a lonely vigil. Often, I heard her pacing the floor at night, and I knew she prayed unceasingly. I thought she was grieving for Pa, but sometimes I saw her staring skyward with a look of expectancy etched on her face, and I knew who she wrestled with.

I thought of Jacob in the Old Testament and frowned. Things were bad enough without wrenching Ma's hip out of joint. I hoped God would remember that.

Me, I just did my chores, left Ma alone, and ignored God. Yet, I noticed a sense of suspense hovered around her as she peered anxiously out the window when she heard sounds in the yard or studied the ceiling as if words were written there for her alone to read. As the days passed, she ate little, always on edge, as if waiting for something.

I made mental notes of what gear we would need and what we could do without when we abandoned the ranch. We couldn't stay here much longer, that fact was clear to me. We would need a place to settle before snow fell this winter.

A gentle breeze buffeted me as another hot summer day passed, the sound of a cow bawling from the nearby hills. My axe bit deep, slicing the log, and I bent to retrieve the firewood, tossing the pieces onto the woodpile as movement on the trail caught my attention. Watching out of the corner of my eye, I straightened, squinting as I studied him walking from the south.

I chewed my lip, thinking most of our visitors came from the north, returning home.

Selecting another log, I placed the wood just right on the stump and split the log with the axe. I wondered at the traveler's slow progress, still a long way off, and kept working.

Finally, he neared, and I guessed he'd been a slave, freed after the war, his ragged clothing barely hanging on his thin frame. A glance toward the garden revealed the leaning scarecrow dressed in better clothing than this man.

I drove the axe into the stump and turned to watch him, wiping my sweaty face on my sleeve. He halted a short distance from me, staring with his dark eyes like he expected me to throw rocks at him.

"Hello, sir." I was shocked at his well-spoken words.

"Howdy, yourself," I replied. "Can I help you?" I knew Ma would never turn away a hungry man, so I waited for him to reply. He would get fed at this house, if that was what he wanted.

He looked at me and then at the house. He straightened a little taller, and I turned, following his gaze.

Ma stood on the porch, hands on her hips, a deep scowl over her usually soft features. She looked disappointed, as if she'd expected someone else.

"Ma'am, I would appreciate any work you might have so I could earn a bite of grub. I haven't eaten in three days. I'll do any manner of work."

Ma stared at him, seeming to measure him with a sharp and critical evaluation. What she was thinking, I couldn't guess, but her frown deepened as I saw her lips move silently. Was she *praying*?

She pursed her lips as her gaze lifted to the clouds. Then she looked again at the stranger.

"I wouldn't be a Christian to work a man who looks about to drop. You wash your hands here at the pump and then come on in. I'll fix supper."

She paused, her face set in stern lines, before reaching for the door. She hesitated again and glanced over her shoulder. "I need to ask you something."

With another scan of the sky, Ma walked into the house.

CHAPTER 2

The stranger stood rooted in place, as if unable to comprehend Ma's words. He peered at me, his eyes begging for confirmation, and I nodded.

"She's serious," I told him. "Wash up and come on in. You're welcome here."

The man hesitated before he shuffled to the old pump. Metal squealed as he worked the rusty handle and water gushed from the spigot. Eyeing me the entire time, he washed his hands with the bar of soap on the platform. Then he dunked his head under the stream and scrubbed his face.

The sun leaned far west when I opened the back door, beckoning him to follow. Shadows stretched across the barnyard, where a few chickens scratched listlessly in the dirt. He looked around, eyes wide, as he entered our home.

Ma worked at the stove. She turned brusquely to the stranger and ordered him sit down. He eyed me for permission, and I gestured to a seat at the table. The lantern had been lit and that surprised me. We usually did without the lamp, using homemade tallow candles to save the precious oil.

Ma scooped beef stew, cut a thick slice of fresh bread, and placed the bowl in front of our guest. Then she poured him coffee and placed the cup in front of his plate. He didn't move, looking from Ma to me as I took my seat beside him.

"Is something wrong? Do you not like coffee? Perhaps it's too strong?" Ma indicated the steaming cup.

He looked at her directly. "I've never had coffee."

She scowled again, as if this wasn't expected, as if something else was supposed to happen. "Well, I can give you buttermilk or water, if you prefer," she snapped as she reached to take his cup away.

"No." He covered his cup quickly. "I'd like very much to have coffee. Slaves never had coffee on our farm." He gingerly picked up the cup and held the mug to his lips, watching us over the rim as he tasted the hot brew before he wrinkled his nose with disgust. I laughed, and a smile seemed to tug at the corners of Ma's mouth.

"Well, we never had slaves, and you don't have to drink coffee if you don't like it." Ma smiled as she again reached to take his cup from him. He gripped the mug with both hands.

"I'd like to keep the coffee, if it's all the same to you, ma'am."

Ma nodded as I leaned my elbows on the table. "I'm John. John Garret."

"Paul."

I grinned, leaning back and gesturing to Ma. "This is Annie Garret."

He nodded at Ma, and she pointed at his bowl. "Eat up, Paul, and then we'll talk."

He lowered his head, and using the spoon with some difficulty, started to eat his soup. Despite his clumsy handling of the utensil, he ate with haste, as if at any moment he expected someone to snatch the food from him. He stuffed the bread into his mouth, barely chewing. When Ma filled his bowl for a second time, he continued his assault, only slowing as the last of the seconds disappeared. Paul inhaled deeply as he looked up, a satisfied look in his eyes.

I still ate my supper, but Ma stood near the stove and tilted her head when she saw Paul had finished. "Would you like another piece of bread?"

He shook his head. "No, ma'am, but I'll take it with me, if it's all right."

Ma cut into the loaf and handed him a thick slice. He sat there, looking uneasy, as fear settled once more on his features. Ma refilled Paul's coffee cup, along with ours, and then sat down at the table. She leaned back, hands folded in her lap, bunching her apron as she stared at the ceiling, a pensive look on her face. Then, as if coming to a decision, her gaze fixed on Paul.

"It's nice to meet you. I'm Annie, like Johnny said."

I glowered at her for not calling me John, but she ignored me. Then I frowned as I wondered why she reintroduced us, like she was beginning an important meeting.

"As you can see, we don't have much. The war has taken its toll—on everyone—and we're trying to put the old place back together again." She paused and seemed to consult the ceiling once more, and I chose not to contradict her. Of course, we were considering nothing of the kind. We needed to be planning our move out of here. But for now, I allowed her to go on, as if we intended on staying put at the ranch.

She pursed her lips before peering intently at him. "Paul, I need help. I know you're a Christian."

He sat up just a mite straighter, but then simply nodded. I, too, was taken aback. He couldn't have been more surprised than me. What was Ma getting at? Always uncommonly wise and strong, she seemed a little rattled, as if this unexpected man were not so unexpected.

"Yes, ma'am, I have the Holy Spirit," Paul confirmed as he leaned forward, a gleam in his eyes where the fear had rested before.

"Good. That'll make it easier. I've been praying the Lord would bring a Christian man to the ranch to work the land and help us out." She paused again, stuffing a loose strand of hair behind her ear with a trembling hand, and I could see she was losing her nerve. She shrugged and rallied her wits.

"Not just any man," she added quickly, as if to qualify her brazen request of the Lord. "I asked for someone kind and wise, willing to work hard, but also able to give wise counsel, help point us in a spiritual direction."

She hesitated, arching an eyebrow. With a lopsided grin, she pointed at him. "You're the answer to my prayers."

Paul stared at her without saying a word. My chest tightened as I worried she might make a bigger fool of herself if I didn't interrupt. The time for help had passed, my unanswered prayers telling me the time had come to flee. We needed to prepare for departure, not get this man's hopes up. I could see the light shine in Paul's eyes as he contemplated Ma's speech. My chair creaked as I leaned toward her, reaching to grip her arm. "Ma?"

She pushed my hand from her and then shook her head, making her loose hair shimmer in the lamp light. "I know what this sounds like, but I'm not crazy." She lowered her voice and rushed on. "I've known a few women driven crazy by the endless wind out here, but I can assure you I'm rational. I've nothing else, Paul, and I'm leaning into the Lord. I have to trust God for whatever he brings us, and he's brought you."

An eerie quiet settled upon the room, and still Paul didn't move or reply. No doubt he was wondering if he should make a run for the door, get away while he could.

A mixture of pity and apprehension swept over me as I glanced at Ma, uncertain how to feel at her startling words.

She went on, her tone flat. "I can't pay you, but I can feed you and give you a place to live." She leaped to her feet, fumbling at the sink where she poured Paul a glass of water and tried to remove his cup of coffee, but again he reached out and stopped her.

"You're not drinking it," she protested, but he lifted the mug and sipped.

"I'd like to try, ma'am, if you don't mind." But he grimaced at the now cold brew just the same, unsure.

He licked his lips as he studied the mug of dark liquid. "I don't know about that. No, I surely don't." He looked at me and then back at Ma. "I've been praying too," he whispered. "And I feel the Spirit moving. Something drew me to this place, I know it, and now I'm certain the Lord guided me here."

I rolled my eyes at this, but he hurried on. "If you're willing, I'll stay and work for you. I'm a hard worker, but I cannot ride a horse."

"Can you read?"

"No, ma'am. But with the war over, I aim to learn."

"Then we will teach you. For tonight, you sleep in the barn. But tomorrow, we'll fix up the foreman's cabin for you." She paused, her brow furrowing. "You are not what I expected, but I believe you were sent here, the answer to my prayers. God is going to do a mighty work here, and you'll be a part. Now get some sleep, Paul, and we'll see you in the morning."

The interview concluded, Ma rose and walked to her room, closing the door softly behind her.

"Goodnight, ma'am." Paul stood, his piece of bread clutched in one hand, and I frowned at his tattered clothes. Perhaps tomorrow, we might find him a better shirt and trousers. I felt certain Ma would address his thin frame, as she loved to see a man eat hearty.

Then I shook my head, remembering. We were not staying. With a huff, I turned to the back door. Carrying the lantern, I led the way to the barn, a pair of blankets slung over my shoulder.

He thanked me twice, and then began asking questions.

"Why are you all so nice to me? I was trying to find a little food, and now I have a job."

I bit my lip, wondering how much to say. "Pa didn't come home from the war, and Ma is a praying woman." I paused, watching in the dim lamp light as he spread the blankets over the hay of an empty stall. I shrugged, not sure what else to say. "She feels God sent you."

He stared at me, a blanket gripped in both hands. "What do you think?"

We'd been going to church all my life, and we read the Bible a lot and enjoyed discussing what Scripture said about life, history, laws, and relationships. I was brought up believing the Bible was the perfect guide for every soul on earth, and we lived by God's teaching. Plain and simple. But lately, I'd had my doubts.

I shrugged, divided by loyalty and common sense. "She's in charge," I mumbled. I wanted to tell him to make a break for the open road, that surely he would find a better place than ours.

He grinned. "But you don't agree with her, I can tell."

I didn't reply and he went on. "You folks never had slaves, but your pa went off to fight for the South?"

"Yes. He didn't hold with slavery, but when everyone was signing up and going off to fight, Pa figured he was a Texan and had to go. He said it was a matter of self-respect. He wrote in one of his letters that General Lee felt the same way. Ma did not agree, and they quarreled, but Pa was a stubborn man. He said Texans always step up when time comes to fight."

I recalled the heated debates that raged around the bunkhouse table over Lincoln's election and the Constitution and states' rights. After the Confederates shelled Fort Sumter, Pa and the hands had all left.

Ma had pointed out our governor himself, old Sam Houston, had argued against joining the War Between the States, but Texas ignored him. Pa said it was easy for Houston to say this because he'd done his fighting already, and everyone respected him. Houston had nothing to prove to anybody.

Now here we were with Pa gone, and the ranch falling around our ears. A shiver slithered down my spine as I recalled the whispered warning from neighbors of the impending taxes. Ma kept telling me God would provide and take care of us, and I tried hard to believe and stay faithful, but the Lord sure was taking his time. So long, I'd wondered if he'd forgotten us.

Paul eyed me again. "I feel the Lord around me. He hovers over this ranch."

I bit back a chuckle and tried to smile, to reassure him, but I couldn't make myself line up with Ma. We were in a fix, and no amount of prayer was going to solve our problems, but I wanted to hope. Only I had none.

I walked from the barn and left him alone with the animals. Returning to the house, I blew the lantern out and went to my room. It wasn't late, so I lit a candle and reached for my Bible, then hesitated, not wanting to read tonight. Instead, I prayed, but I felt my pleas bounce off the ceiling. Usually, I felt a measure of peace after studying Scripture and praying, but lately I found only questions I couldn't answer and worries that weighed on me. What were we going to do? Fear gripped me when I thought of

the scarce food in the pantry, our debt at Anderson's store,
and now Ma taking on a stranger, another mouth to feed.
I blew out the candle and went to bed.

CHAPTER 3

The next morning after breakfast, where Paul insisted on having his own cup of coffee again, Ma followed us out to the back porch and handed him a stack of neatly folded clothes.

"Burn those rags you're wearing. Here are some of my husband's. Go down to the creek and wash up." I noticed a cloud in her eyes as she handed over the clothes, a reluctance to give up something of Pa's. I felt it too, as if memories were passing away, making room for something new.

I hated the unfamiliar sensation and wished things could go back to the way they'd been when Pa still ran the ranch, and we had all we needed. But things were different now, and no use crying over spilled milk. Yet I knew we were finished here, as if the land had turned on us. Or perhaps God.

Paul took the clothes with trembling hands, his eyes wide. I almost grinned at his astonishment, and I drew a deep breath, proud of Ma's generosity when we had so little to give. Her kindness seemed still more than Paul expected.

"Ma'am, I'll clean up and get right to work, don't you worry."

"No, you won't. You've had a hard time. After you and Johnny tidy up the foreman's cabin, take the rest of the day off. We'll work you enough starting tomorrow." She turned and walked back into the kitchen. Appreciation glowing on his face, Paul could have been knocked over with a feather.

"Is your ma an angel?"

His whispered query startled me, and I narrowed my eyes as I watched Ma disappear inside.

I indicated the path to the creek, and when I saw him next, Paul stood straighter in clean clothes, with a determined look on his face. He'd tied a piece of rope around his waist to keep up his pants, and holes peeked through his old shoes.

The foreman's cabin was small and sparsely furnished with a bed, table, and chair. A pitcher and basin sat on a bench near the door. A solidly built rock fireplace took up most of one wall while a glass window centered upon another. Together we cleaned the cabin. Dust covered everything as nobody had lived here in years. Yet Paul seemed excited as he shook his head, muttering under his breath. "I can't believe this."

After we swept and dusted the rafters and ledges, Paul fetched water and mopped. I brought fresh bedding, and we filled the wood bin beside the fireplace—Paul muttering the whole time.

I wanted to warn him not to get too comfortable. Surely we would be leaving soon. But his evident joy made me hold my tongue. There'd be plenty of time to crush his dreams, like mine, later when we moved away.

His busy hands stilled as he stepped to the mantel where a few books lined the rough timber set into the stones. Reverently, he hefted a book, peering at the cover. "Will you help me learn to read?"

"Of course, if you want me to," I said, hoping I wasn't misleading him. Dusting my hands on my pants, I reached for the book. "Hand it here."

Paul passed the book to me. I nodded when I read the title, *Skeletons on the Sahara*. "This is a good story, one of my favorites, a true story about a trading ship that wrecked off the coast of Africa. The sailors were made slaves by the wandering desert people of the Sahara Desert, but some later escaped."

"Were those sailors white men?" His face wrinkled.

"Yes," I answered.

"I've never heard of white slaves," Paul countered, shaking his head.

I pointed to another book on the mantel. "This one's the Bible."

The thin black man stiffened and stared at me. "The Bible?" he whispered as he reached for the thick book. "I want to read God's Word. I've loved him most of my life. He's been my constant companion, giving me hope in dark times. I used to drive the family of the plantation to church every Sunday and sit outside beneath the open window to hear the preacher."

He pulled the book from the mantel, and I shifted as he lovingly caressed the leather cover. Then he opened the book, gingerly turning the thin pages.

"We will start later." I touched his arm. "You enjoy the rest of the day. I need to get the milking done."

He gazed at me then, a warm glow coming to his eyes. "John, you are the first folks I've met who've treated me kindly. I think your ma might be an angel. No way am I going to rest in this beautiful cabin while you work. Let me help you with the milking."

We walked to the barn, and I saw right off he was first rate at milking cows. He helped me feed the stock and then we repaired one of the old corrals where some bars had fallen. Guiltily, I watched him work, knowing our upkeep was for naught.

By dinner time, we were hungry. "Where will I be eating my meals?" Paul asked.

"Why, at the table, of course." I led the way into the kitchen.

Ma had prepared extra food that night for supper, and we did the bounteous spread justice, Paul eating the most. As Ma cleared dirty dishes from the table, Paul asked her how he should address her.

"You can call me Mrs. Garret. Or, if you want, just Annie. It doesn't matter to me."

I could tell by the look on his face that this informal title would be too much for him to attempt. From that moment on, he usually referred to my mother as "Miss Annie."

Paul proved to be a great asset on the ranch, although I saw little sense in his dedication. He did everything around the house, including repairs, tending the garden, and taking care of the stock. This freed me to get back to riding the range and tending the cattle, which was unnecessary since we'd be leaving soon. But it gave me time to think, to plan. In the evenings, he and I would work on reading, or we'd play checkers. He never tired of playing checkers.

He was a good student to teach because he was such a hard worker. Paul would wrestle over words and try hard to remember the rules, like *i* before *e* except after *c*. Not easy to remember so many rules all at once, but he grasped the concepts quickly.

Paul's greatest contribution to the ranch—or to Ma—was his gift of prayer. The first time Ma asked him to give the blessing at supper, we stared amazed at the intimate words he lifted to the Savior. As if speaking to a close and special friend, he conversed with Jesus in a way that filled me with envy, thus confirming Ma's unorthodox acceptance of him onto the ranch.

As for his age, he didn't know how old he was. But he'd been told he was born in the summer of 1840. He was eight years older than me, but always listened to me and asked my advice on matters. His respect made me feel grown up.

I headed out each morning in a different direction than the previous day. Our range was big, and we hadn't been able to keep up on the branding and castrating. Too many cows and only me to work them. Now we had Paul, but he couldn't ride a horse. I thought that was funny because everyone I knew learned how to ride at about the same time they learned to walk.

Each day I worked on improving our ranch, a habit I couldn't break even though it seemed so senseless. I'd given Ma time to grieve, to accept Pa wasn't coming home. Yet she moved through each day as if she were committed to some measure of success, as if the Lord weren't done with us.

As I cleaned out water holes, gauged grazing areas, tallied numbers of stock, and watched for signs of predators, two- and four-legged, I wrestled with a destination. Where would we go? I loved the Texas plains, bleak and relentless, but like the Lord, the land had forsaken us. There was nothing more we could do here.

Although I worked tirelessly—old habits die hard—I drew the line at branding mavericks. The work seemed so useless now we were throwing in the towel. Or I should say, *I* was quitting. Ma didn't show any indication she'd come to her senses and realized we needed to move before we were evicted. The ranch was ours, but we hadn't paid taxes in years. Sooner or later, a day of reckoning was coming.

I felt reluctant to leave my home too. But I was the man of the house now, like it or not, responsible yet abandoned. I pitied Ma's last-ditch effort at building the ranch, but I knew the futility of her attempt. And I felt sorry for Paul.

He'd only just joined us, and our leaving would be difficult for him.

Still, I rode the ranch, doing what I could, unable to stay still while Ma healed. Loss is a worrisome thing, but I'd expected Pa was dead before we received word. Perhaps she needed more time, but I refused to brand the unclaimed cattle that roamed the range.

Surveying the open prairie around our home, I shielded my eyes from the sun as I studied the near worthless cattle. A maverick is a cow with no brand, and anyone could claim the animal. Not that claiming cows made any money. But they were our cows, and I used to brand them when I came across them.

We had a passel of wolves in our corner of Texas, but we also had a bunch of Comanche Indians that lived west of us about twenty miles. We first found them six years ago when we had a tough winter, and Pa was out hunting strayed stock after a big blizzard. He stumbled upon this starved bunch of Indians and raced back home to fetch me and a few head of cows.

We pushed those steers to the Indian camp which sprawled in a creek bottom, out of the wind. They'd been eating starvation rations for weeks, and were in bad shape. We gave them those three cows and they seemed grateful, although they watched us with skeptical looks, reserved and uneasy.

A month later, three Indian braves and a young girl stood in our yard one morning when we woke. Ma put together breakfast for them, and we sat on the porch and talked. I should say Pa talked with that young girl.

Her name was Hannah Tall Basket. She was about my age and spoke English. She'd been sent to a mission school north of us in Indian Territory because her father, their chief, had been told in a vision to educate her in the white man's tongue. This education had paid off many times, and she proved an excellent interpreter. And, I felt impressed how the older braves deferred to Hannah with her long black pigtails and small round face.

The braves wanted to know why Pa had given the Indians beef. Pa explained it was because our God wanted us to help people. Hannah interpreted, and those braves chattered among themselves like magpies, apparently impressed with a spiritual response. Somehow, they felt indebted to us for saving them, and they wanted to form an alliance, respecting Pa's connection with God. They believed we'd been sent by the Creator to feed them.

This started quite a bit of back-and-forth talk, and it seemed we'd made some progress, as a friendship based on spiritual understanding had been formed. "Leave them alone and they will probably leave us alone," Pa advised after the Indians had left, and he was right. The Comanche raided other ranches and killed some settlers, but they never bothered us.

I saw Hannah a few times each year, and she always had lots of questions about white people's culture. I also had questions for her, and we struck up a friendship. I enjoyed any opportunity to see her.

On one such visit, I explained the purpose of brands on an animal, displaying ownership. An unbranded cow technically could be claimed by anyone.

This band of Comanche promised to never take cattle wearing our brand. The problem, of course, was we then needed to brand all our cows or the Indians believed they were fair game.

On this particular morning, I'd headed toward Old Woman Mountain, which sprawled on the southern border of our range. Puffy clouds drifted like fat sheep across the blue Texas sky, and another hot summer day spread before me. I carried my canteen and a bite of grub Ma had packed because I figured to be away from the ranch all day.

I explored many draws where cattle had moved into the thickets, looking for water. I counted much stock, some with our brand burned on their flank, the Bar G, but many mavericks too. I kept accurate count of animals and made mental note we needed to start branding these cattle if we didn't want to lose them to other ranchers or to the Comanche. Then I'd remember we were not staying on, the branding a waste of time.

Cattle in Texas, after the war, were not worth anything. Rumors had spread among neighbors of a demand in the east, where urban centers needed beef for swelled populations of immigrants and refugees from the South. Many had lost everything and moved north, searching for work and new homes. Apparently, we would soon be among them.

A man could buy cattle cheap, if he had cash money, which no one seemed to have. Most folks traded for what they needed or ran a tab at the general store and then paid with chickens, eggs, or vegetables in summer.

The farther south I rode, the fewer Bar G cattle I found. The grass grew thinner and coarse, and those cows just naturally liked to stay where the feed was best. The good grazing on our range had kept most of our stock from straying.

Late in the day, I turned my tired mount homeward. A roadrunner raced ahead of me as I trotted up the trail, the huge red sun just dropping over the horizon when I entered our yard. I put my horse in the barn and spent a few minutes fussing over the gelding with a curry brush before trudging to the house.

Ma was placing food on the table as I entered, while Paul squinted at a book. The chair dragged on the worn floor, and I dropped to a seat beside him. We ate in silence while they waited, sensing the worries I hated to share.

Finally, I pushed my empty plate away. "Saw a lot of stock today," I began as Ma poured me another cup of coffee. Most folks had blended mesquite beans or chicory to stretch their supply of coffee or did without. I felt pleased we still had the real stuff, a credit to Ma's resourcefulness and tenacity.

I leaned back in my chair, and Paul nodded. He listed his accomplished tasks as if he wanted to make sure we knew all he'd done that day. The farm he'd worked on before coming to us must've been demanding.

A glance out the window revealed clean laundry hung on the clothesline, waving in the evening breeze, and I knew Ma would appreciate a hand taking down the linens before dark. Jars of fresh preserves lined the counter, our small orchard providing a little variety to our mostly beef and potato diet. The canned fruit also gave us something to barter with at Anderson's store in town.

She filled Paul's empty cup as I sighed, not wanting to start the difficult conversation, but knowing I must.

"See many mavericks?"

Her unexpected query gave me the opening I needed, and I took it. "Ma, we would need more hands. There's a lot of stock with no brands. We're asking for trouble."

The implication was clear, at least to me. We'd need more hands if we intended on staying. Obviously, that wasn't an option.

A tired, weary look came into Ma's eyes as she pulled a chair from the table and gripped its back, peering down at me in the dim candlelight. I was getting more and more used to that look, knowing what she was going to say before she opened her mouth. My plan was to use this against her.

"Johnny, there's no money for more hands. And there hasn't been anyone along here for months looking for work, even if I had money to pay them. Every now and then a rider passes us on his way to the Nation to hide. You know we can never hire such men. They're outlaws and thieves, escaping from Texas into the Indian Territory, or they're passing by on their way from the Nation into Texas to commit a crime. I don't have any answers to our problems, Son, except to have faith and be patient. The Lord has a plan for us, and he'll reveal his ideas in time." She sat down abruptly as if her legs weakened.

Paul did not say anything, but his eyes widened. Ma placed a hand on his arm and tried to smile. "We know you can't ride, Paul. You need not worry about this."

"I can try," he ventured with a skeptical look.

"We need cowboys, riders who've been on horses since they were little boys," I growled impatiently. Then I shook my head, relenting. "You do enough around here," I added, hoping I hadn't hurt his feelings, but knowing the help we needed wouldn't really help anyway.

He nodded as relief flitted across his features, but my shoulders sagged. I hated being the bearer of bad news, as if Ma hadn't already known we'd be forced now to leave.

"We need to figure out a place to go," I snapped, not letting the subject drop. "Things are rough with no relief in sight." I hesitated, my gaze narrowing as I studied Ma. "If the Lord wanted us to stay here, he'd have done something, right?"

She widened her eyes and blinked before gesturing at Paul. "The Lord is doing something, Son. He's brought help."

I shook my head. "Paul can help around the barn, but we need riders. We need a market for cattle. We need money."

No one said anything to disrupt the silence that filled the room, and then I added, "We need to leave."

She stiffened as Paul shifted on his chair. "We are not leaving. I am confident this is where we're to stay. He hasn't opened any other doors for us. Trust, Johnny, this is where he wants us."

Paul cleared his throat, drawing my attention. "I know I have no right to interfere, but I sense the Spirit brought me here for something. Something particular."

Ma gestured at Paul again, a wide smile creasing her anxious features. "See?"

I didn't want to contradict her resolve, but I was not so sure. The Lord certainly hadn't said anything to me, and things had been bad for so long. And now that we knew Pa wasn't coming home, how could she stay so confident? How could she know we were meant to stay here? Of course, we had no money to move anywhere else, but I sensed the wolf at the door, waiting to catch us unaware. Yet her faith puzzled and angered me.

My chair scraped as I pushed away from the table and rose to my feet. Wearily, I plodded to my room, a sense of desperation swelling within me. Our deplorable situation nagged at me, urging me to get out while we could. How could I guess things were only going to get worse?

CHAPTER 4

We heard a buggy coming into the yard the next morning as I pitched hay from the loft down to Paul, who fed the stock. Buggies weren't commonplace out here. Most folks rode horseback.

I shoved my pitchfork into a pile of hay and scrambled down the ladder. Paul shot me a quizzical glance as I stalked into the bright sunlight of the dirt yard. The sun beat down cruelly as it had for the last week or so, and I shielded my eyes with a hand to see who approached. My chest tightened when I saw three men in a buggy, two of them on the rear seat wearing nice suit clothes. Although I didn't recognize them, I knew exactly who they were.

Dust hovered as they came to a stop before me. Their eyes were on the house, and they jolted when I spoke.

"Morning. I'm John Garret. Can I help you?" It was as if I played a role in a school play, talking and acting as if this visit were the most expected thing in the world, which it was.

Their heads swiveled fast, and they faced me. I could hear Paul coming up behind me. Not recognizing them, I figured they weren't from around here, yet I guessed their purpose.

The driver looked away, not making eye contact as he held the reins still. One of the well-dressed men smiled.

"Well, good morning, young man. I am Ruben Richards and I'm with the County Tax Commission. This is Mr. Dalrymple from New Hampshire. He is here as an investor."

Ruben Richards had a pencil for a neck, and his slicked hair—held stiffly in place with some kind of paste—glistened in the sunlight. His thin face looked like a hatchet, and his pale cheeks lacked tan.

Dalrymple took up most of the back seat and had a wide, florid face, making me not want to trust him. His eyes seemed too close together, but he nodded courteously.

The kitchen door opened, and Ma stepped outside, lifting a hand against the glaring sun.

"Ma," I called, "these gents are from the County Tax Commission." I introduced them, but they didn't get out of the buggy to shake hands. Their first mistake.

"Ma'am, are you Mrs. Annie Garret?" Mr. Richards asked with a toothy smile that reminded me of a wolf.

"Yes, sir." Ma dried her hands on her apron as a worried shadow stretched across her face.

"Ma'am, let me begin by saying how sorry we are for your loss. We heard in town that Mr. Garret didn't return from the war."

Ma's face pinched. "Thank you, Mr. Richards. Right kind of you." I could tell by the look on Ma's face she didn't trust these slickers any more than I did.

Mr. Dalrymple had seen Paul approaching behind me. "Hey, boy, the war's over and slavery is gone. You are free. You don't have to do as these folks say anymore."

Paul pursed his lips. "These are good folks. I was never their slave."

Mr. Dalrymple ignored him and turned back to my mother, the buggy lurching as he shifted. "Mrs. Garret, the nature of our visit is to inform you that taxes have come due on your ranch. In support of the war effort, the great state of Texas had not collected property taxes for the past four years. Now with the war over and the late Mr. Garret unable to pay what is owed on his property, the land will be confiscated by the county and put up for public auction."

The land speculator dug in his pocket for a notebook, flipped a few pages, and wet the end of a pencil with his tongue before looking around at the buildings, appraising their condition. After making a few notes, he turned to me.

"John, wasn't it? Do you have a tally for the amount of stock you are currently running? Horses as well? The place could use a little work," he said as he surveyed the buildings. He seemed to only want information at this juncture, but I peered at Ma—her face gone white—and knew he'd get no satisfaction today.

Ignoring his question, I asked, "Mr. Richards, how much tax money is due on the place?" I had to know what we were up against, even though I knew we couldn't pay any amount. This information surely would make Ma see we needed to leave. No matter how much I disliked these men, the fact remained we had to move on.

Mr. Richards turned to Dalrymple. "Dal, how much is owed on the Garret land?" Dalrymple quickly put aside his notebook and lifted a register, thumbing through the thick book until he came to the right page. He held the book up for Mr. Richards to read. "Exactly three hundred and eighty-seven dollars." The thin man jerked his head up suddenly. "You don't have that much, do you, young man?" he asked quickly, a look of fear crossing his face.

"No, sir, we don't." I replied honestly enough. I could see Ma was in no shape to talk to these swindlers.

Mr. Richards relaxed, his tense shoulders sagging. In control again, he went on. "Well, then, we are sad to inform you that you must vacate these premises within seven days. Auction will be a week from Thursday at noon in town."

I heard a small gasp from my mother, and all heads turned. She held her apron to her mouth, staring hollowly at the men in the buggy.

Mr. Dalrymple added, "Of course, you will have the week to come up with the money, if you can. Just bring the necessary funds to town and pay at the hotel. We will be staying there for a while, completing land acquisitions for this region."

"We wish you good day," Mr. Ruben Richards said. With a nod to the driver, the buggy turned around and headed out of the yard.

The three of us stood for a minute longer, the dust from the retreating buggy filtering gently to the ground. Ma turned slowly and retraced her steps into the kitchen. Paul had wisely gone to the barn on some pretext of a task, but I followed my mother into the house. As the door closed behind me, I saw her drop into a chair and bury her face in her hands.

Taking the chair opposite her, I waited, unsure what to do. She'd always been the strong one for both of us. Perhaps the time had come for me to help carry the load, old as I was now.

"Ma, that man says we owe back taxes on the ranch. We don't have any money. Do you see what needs to happen now?" I was pleading, searching for the right words to give wise direction.

Ma suddenly came back to herself. She lifted her head and saw me then, though I don't believe she heard anything I'd said. "Johnny, we serve an awesome God. This is not our problem, it is his. If he wants us to leave here, there is nothing we can do. But if he wants us to stay, there is nothing he can't do." She reached across the table and took my hands in her own trembling ones. "Johnny, have faith. I need to spend some time in prayer."

She rose stiffly and, with a straight back, walked into her room and quietly closed the door.

I sat there alone for a time, digesting her response, not surprised by her stubborn defiance. But I knew there was nothing we could do. Ma only needed time to realize we were finished here. Finally, heaving from my seat, I made my way to the sink, noticing the unfinished dishes. Plunging my hands into the lukewarm, soapy water, I scrubbed pots and pans, keeping my hands busy while I pondered. When I finished the dishes, I swept the floor. It felt good to keep moving.

Ma still hadn't shown herself, so I went out to the barn. Paul stood in a stall, currying a horse's mane. He looked up when I entered.

"I knew this was too good to be true," he lamented with a long face. "You all are the first folks to be real nice to me, and I surely thought the Lord had brought me here for a little piece of heaven. This is the best job I've ever had, with all the food I can eat and my own place with no leaks. I have plenty of blankets and my own fireplace. I sure thought God had confused me with someone else. Now it's all over."

I didn't say a word as I considered his observation. He was right, of course. Compared to what he was used to, we had a lot of food, if you could stand beef and eggs and potatoes for almost every meal. He'd have to leave as well, find a new job. But this had always been my home, and I would miss the ranch dearly. Sadly, there was nothing left to do. We had no money for those taxes. Come to think of it, we had no money for supplies either, and I worried about our travel plans. We already had an outstanding bill at Anderson's store.

Turning on my heel, I walked out to the corrals. I wanted to be alone too.

Supper time came and went. We didn't feel like making a meal, so Paul and I just ate bread and honey and made coffee while we glanced covertly at Ma's closed door. I went to bed that night with a lump in my throat.

The ranch had been a pure nightmare for Ma and me to manage for those four years of the war, but we'd held on, hoping Pa would return and set things right. But I'd kind of expected something like this to happen. Things had been rough for so long, I knew we couldn't keep hope alive forever. The time had come to give up and get out. Texas took its toll on folks, I guess.

But where would we go? We had no kin I knew of, and certainly no travel money to get there. I felt empty and sick to my stomach.

I lay awake a long time, thinking how bad things had gotten, and I cried some. Now, for a seventeen-year-old boy to cry was embarrassing, but I felt miserable and didn't care. We'd been dealt an unfair hand. Ma didn't deserve this, but neither did all the other ranchers and farmers who would have their land taken by the County Tax Commission.

My anger homed in on the one who'd done this, or at least allowed such bad things. "Why, Jesus? Why do this to Ma when she loves you so much?"

I fell asleep along then, and my dreams were filled with images of me and Ma walking the cold prairie, searching for shelter and something to eat.

CHAPTER 5

No matter how rough things were, or how terrible I felt, the new day dawned with a bright sun, and work that had to be completed. Summer in Texas is predictable that way. Stock had to be fed. Crops had to be tended and gathered.

I rolled out of bed and dressed, a little chagrined at sleeping in, which was not my common practice. Opening the grate on the stove, I searched for signs of red embers, surprised at the neglected fire. Clearly, Ma hadn't been up yet either, and I wondered at her tardiness. Nudging some coals into flame, I put coffee on and then went outside to help Paul with the morning milking and feeding. We didn't even greet each other when we met in the barn. A heavy, somber cloud had descended, and it was like moving through a gray fog. I felt numb and angry and helpless. Apparently, Paul too sensed we'd be leaving soon.

The endless day wore on with no sign of Ma, and Paul and I did the chores like machines, our thoughts elsewhere.

Finally, hunger drove us into the kitchen. I shot Paul a stunned glance when we found Ma sitting at the table. She seemed composed and her features reflected a real peaceful look. I tensed when I saw her Bible lay open before her.

She didn't look up when we entered, just sat there gazing down at the thick book. A change had come over her, and a peace filled the room, as if whatever she'd decided had caused the worry and anxiety to be pushed from the house.

"Ma, are you all right?" I asked, somewhat afraid at the way she sat so calm. "I'll bet you're hungry. Let me get you something to eat." Before I could move to the stove, Paul had beaten me to it and started coaxing the cooking fire into a blaze. Then he started cracking eggs into a skillet.

Ma looked up. "Thank you, Paul. That's right nice of you," she said in a soft voice.

Paul peered at me over his shoulder, an unspoken message passing between us before he looked at Ma. "Yes, ma'am. My pleasure."

"Ma?" I started again, not really wanting to discuss the subject. "Ma, you heard what those men said. We only have a few days to get our stuff together and leave the ranch. Where do you think we should go?"

The look she drilled into me caused me to shuffle back a step. "Nowhere, Johnny. We're going nowhere unless the Lord wills it. We are going to stay right here until he tells us otherwise."

I glanced at Paul again. He blinked and stirred the eggs.

"Ma? You heard those men," I repeated, speaking in a soft voice, as if speaking to a child. "We have to leave."

"Johnny, this is our place. Your pa and I believe the Lord led us to this spot, and I do not see he has changed his mind. Our God is the same yesterday, today, and tomorrow. Until he speaks to me and says leave, I'm going nowhere." Her voice sounded like a strong wind, steady and constant, as if these words were stone and could be counted on. I shifted and tried again.

"Okay, Ma," I said, playing the devil's advocate. "What do you propose to do?"

She smiled, but her bravery confused me. "I believe we serve an awesome God. This," she gestured around her, indicating all our troubles rolled together. "This is not our battle. This is not what God wants for us. He is testing us. We need only have faith." She looked down at her Bible. "Listen, I was reading the story where Peter spoke to the Jewish leaders boldly in Jerusalem and they beat him and told him not to speak any more about Jesus, and then they released him. Peter left there praising God, counting himself blessed to be crushed for the Lord's name's sake." She paused and looked up at me, as if waiting for a response.

"So?" Frustration surged within me, but I pushed the angry emotion down, wanting to be kind to Ma. Had she snapped? I didn't understand her point, yet I tried to be patient.

"So, we should count ourselves blessed that God has found us worthy to be tested." She sat back against the chair and smiled. A shudder crept down my back.

"That Scripture is in reference to Peter sharing the Gospel of Christ. We are not being persecuted for sharing Jesus." I hoped she could understand. Her actions were scaring me.

"Yes, Johnny, I see that, but the point I'm making is that God has found us worthy, like Abraham and Job. I also read in James that trials build our character and perseverance. God is shaping us. That means all we have to do is be patient and wait to see how the Lord will help us out of this. If God is with us, who can stand against us? This is not too much for him." She sat up straight once more and flipped through her Bible. "I also read in Romans that we are not to compare our present sufferings to the glory that awaits us. This is nothing for God to handle. We need to wait and see how this adventure will unfold."

"An adventure?" We both turned to look at Paul where he stood near the stove, a spoon in one hand, his eyes shining with excitement. "I feel that is what the Lord wants. A spiritual adventure for us," he said as he nodded.

Ma turned back to me. "Don't you see? If God wants us to stay here, he'll work this out. If he wants us to leave, there is nothing we can do. It's all in his hands. We have only to wait and see what he does while we remain patient and faithful, praying all the time. Will you share this adventure with me, Paul? We have a week."

Paul glanced at me, and I could read his longing. I gritted my teeth. "Paul, don't do this. We need to be realistic and prepare for leaving."

He shrugged. "The Lord brought me here for something. Maybe this is it."

I shook my head. "We need to plan," I argued.

"Paul, Johnny, let's pray." Ma held out her hands to me as if she hadn't heard my plea. "Let's pray for a miracle."

I crossed my arms over my chest and frowned as Paul scooped eggs onto plates and delivered the food to the table. Ma dropped her hands, and they ate in silence while I fumed. Our time would be better spent preparing for the imminent departure, not just hoping and praying to an intangible helper. We needed to figure out some place to go, and I worried Ma would be no help in her present condition. And now she'd roped Paul into her crazy scheme.

Ma pushed her plate aside and looked up, taking a deep breath as she leaned back in her chair. "Yes, the Lord is with us and wants good things for his children. If we walk with him, he will disclose his will. Draw nigh to God and he will draw nigh to you. I have no doubt we can remain faithful for a single week, don't you agree?"

A wide smile creased her face, and I felt ashamed I'd turned against her. Of course, I could be faithful for a week, but that wasn't what was happening here.

"A week is easy, Ma," I began again. "But we've already lost the battle. It's time to pack what we can save and find a place to move our belongings."

Ma tilted her head, as if she were finally listening to me. Then Paul leaned forward, bowing his head as he clasped his hands together. I turned on him, my anger mounting.

"What are you doing?"

He glanced at Ma and nodded. "I'm with Miss Annie. The Lord brought me here for something, and I'm willing to give this a try. It's only a week, and I have nowhere else to go." He pursed his lips and stared at me. "Join us, John. The Lord is mighty. Taste and see he is good. There is something about this that draws me, and I feel the Spirit moving."

"I do too," Ma agreed happily, beaming at Paul across the table.

I fumed as the two bowed their heads. I still refused to give in and felt silly sitting here while they prepared to pray over a lost cause. Couldn't they see God had left us alone on these empty Texas plains? Pa was dead, and we owed money we could never pay. Why couldn't they see the time had come to give up?

Ma cleared her throat and glanced at me from the corner of her eyes, as if willing me to join them. I squinted at her and leaned my elbows on the table, pressed my hands together loosely, and bowed my head, my thoughts dark and unwavering. God had abandoned us, and I felt angry he teased Ma and Paul this way, putting false ideas in their heads. There was nothing we could do to change the situation, but I didn't want to hurt Ma's feelings. She'd suffered enough. Yet I would have to figure out some way to save Ma, and I would have to do it alone.

"Lord," Ma began quietly. "I pray for answers. I pray you bring a solution to our problem. I'm sorry we're pushed for time, but you can do anything. If it's your will, please save our ranch. You have a week to figure it out, although I suspect you already know the answer. Please let us believe you have us in your hands and will take care of us, whatever happens. But we want to believe you have good things for us."

She paused and I felt my anger slip. She genuinely wanted to see if God heard her prayers. A mixture of doubt and challenge wrestled within me. Could God do anything for us? Did he hear Ma's prayers?

"Lord, help us come up with the money we need for our taxes," she went on. "This is a huge dilemma for us, but not for you. Let us have faith and watch how your mighty hand provides. You love your people, and we will wait on the Lord."

Paul's voice boomed next, making me flinch. "Lordy, you've brought me to this house, and I believe it was no accident. I've heard the tale of Jonah fleeing from you, but we're running into your arms, throwing ourselves at your feet. Now, hear our prayer. We wait with faithful hearts to see how your hand answers. Bless you, Lord, be forever praised."

He went on in an eloquent manner, beseeching God's intervention and proclaiming the Lord's goodness. His earnestness rivaled Ma's own confidence, yet I confess I had nothing to say. I loved God, but I thought these two were simply praying out of desperation. There was no way God was going to reach down from heaven and right this situation. But I couldn't say this out loud. I could see the incredible faith Ma and Paul possessed, and I could not crush their zeal.

"Amen," I said when Paul finished. I studied the look of peace and quiet resignation on their faces. Whatever happened, I knew they believed it was the Lord's will.

That night, the atmosphere in the house changed. Gone was the feeling of fear and doubt and failure. Paul and Ma chatted as if the problem was already solved, as if the money had already been paid. They talked of normal things, the vegetables in the garden, the need to protect the crops from rabbits, the milking of the cows, and the churning of the butter.

I sat silent, amazed at their assurance. But I did not share this poise, as I thought of the mere six days we had to vacate this land.

The next day Paul and Ma moved through the day as if the back taxes had been paid and our troubles were over. I heard them singing praise songs under their breath and caught silent lips trembling in prayer more than once. I felt embarrassed for them. They were waiting for something that wouldn't happen. A miracle was not going to save us. Taxes were a normal fact of life, and we didn't have any money. They were ignoring reality.

My annoyance returned, burning and seething in my chest. They were acting as if everything was fine when it wasn't. Things were far from fine.

That night at supper, Ma could sense my uneasy mood. She studied me as she passed the biscuits.

"Johnny, what's wrong? You seem upset."

I sighed. "Ma, it's over. You must see that. We need money and we have none. Let it go. Help me make a decision about what to do next, where to go."

She smiled at me, but I read the disappointment in her eyes. "I have made a decision. I have decided to trust the Lord."

I could feel my blood boiling. "You're simply putting off the inevitable. We must pack and get out of here. We have five days."

"What makes you so sure the Lord will not answer our prayer?" Paul asked. I hadn't expected an attack from this quarter and turned on him.

"Not you too? You know this is foolish. God is not going to answer this prayer with a time limit on him. He doesn't work that way. You two have pushed him into a corner and demanded he respond within five days. That's not fair."

"Fair to God?" Ma chuckled as she passed the biscuits to Paul. "God can do anything, even in five days, if he chooses. No one pushes God anywhere."

Paul nodded. "John, when I left the farm where I'd been a slave, I prayed God would lead me to a place he wanted me, where he wanted me to *do* something. He brought me here. God didn't bring me here just to get kicked out. Let's watch with excitement and eagerness how he will answer this need."

Ma lifted a hand, pointing at me, and I knew they were ganging up on me.

"Have faith. Believe God has good things in store for you. God loves us, and even though things have been hard, I feel in my soul God wants to do a mighty work in us. Let's have faith and see his power."

I sat mute for a minute, stunned by their silly expectancy. Hadn't the Lord showed his face was turned against us? What purpose could there be in the rough treatment Ma and I had endured? Or Paul? I excused myself, leaving the kitchen and plodding to the barn to check the stock.

Paul and Ma had shamed me with their trust. At seventeen, I wanted folks to look on me as a man, a man responsible for his family, but I doubted God could save us. Ma and Paul encouraged me to have faith, but I thought they prayed over a lost cause.

A tug on my soul made me peer up at the rafters above me, shrouded in darkness and barely visible in the dusk.

A chicken cackled as the hens moved to evening roosts, and a horse swished a tail. I felt a muscle twitch along my jaw, and I scratched my chin, wondering what would happen if I threw in with the others? Could God really do anything to help us?

My irritation vanished and turned to resignation. Surely nothing would happen to help us in such a short time. But ... what if something *could* happen? What if my prayers mattered? Not that I really believed I had any real power or sway in this matter, but what if I tried to believe?

I glanced over my shoulder before moving to a dark corner and kneeling in the hay.

"God, you know the trouble I face. You know when I sit and when I stand, and you have counted the hairs on my head, so you know my doubts. I can't hide anything from you. Yet, I want to believe. Develop me into the man of God you want me to be. Let me be strong and believe you will do a mighty work on this ranch. I love you, Jesus, but you've crushed us. Please help. Please hear my prayer."

I hung my head, wanting so desperately to believe, but memories haunted me of the crushing years we'd suffered. And now Pa wasn't coming home. Hope waned, and I worried my faith was too small for miracles. What could God have in mind for us?

Anxiety and fear threatened, bubbling up within me, but I pushed them aside and shook my head. No, I would try and believe the Lord had this. I would try and be faithful like Ma and Paul. I shrugged. What could the attempt hurt? Besides, I had no other solution.

Slowly, I stood, my gaze scanning the darkening interior, sensing I was not alone. Brushing loose hay from my knees, I peered into the shadowed corners and nodded, hoping the Lord knew the sincerity of my heartfelt prayer.

A shiver raced down my back as I strode from the barn, feeling unseen eyes upon me as I headed for the house.

That night, I slept soundly for the first time in days. I awoke totally rested with the sense that something was going to happen. An anticipation filled me, and I looked eagerly toward the new day. Perhaps Ma and Paul had something to their hopes, and I wondered if I were strong enough to stand with them in confidence.

Despite my new acceptance that God might help us, I never expected what happened next.

CHAPTER 6

I blinked my eyes against dawn's dim sunlight peeking through my open window and immediately thought of the Lord.

"Good morning, God. What are you going to do today?" I half expected to hear a voice respond, but none did. Instead, I heard a horse whinny from the front yard.

Surprised, I rolled out of bed and swiftly dressed. The screen door slammed behind me as I studied the saddled, yet rider less horse standing near the water trough. Not a cowboy pony, that was certain. Tall, the handsome limbed bay looked like a racer. Cowboys preferred rangy stock horses that were good cutting animals, ones that could stop on a dime. Whoever owned this horse was no cowboy. Also, a rifle sheath hung from the saddle, and cowboys did not like extra weight cluttering up their work space. A long gun got in the way when roping. A pair of saddlebags also drooped over the animal's flanks.

The bay stamped an impatient hoof, wanting grain. I approached him slowly, grabbing his bridle with a quick hand as I observed a bloody crease along one shoulder. I led the animal to the barn and unsaddled him, a crimson smear marring the smooth leather. Taking my time and speaking soothingly, I fed the bay and pondered the strange horse. The minor injury in the shoulder bothered me, and I frowned as I saddled my own mount.

"Bullet wound?" Paul appeared at my elbow, staring at the furrow in the horse's shoulder.

"Maybe. And maybe the owner of this horse is lying nearby, hurt," I suggested.

"What do you want me to do?" I know his question meant he worried about accompanying me when we both knew he couldn't ride.

"Stay close to home. This shouldn't take long. I expect to be back for breakfast." I turned to go then hesitated, pulling the stranger's rifle from the scabbard and handing the weapon to Paul. "Do you know how to use this?"

He shook his head and I grinned, patting his shoulder as I led my horse from the barn and into the yard. "Give it to Ma." With a step into the stirrup, I swung aboard my gelding. Ma hadn't made an appearance before I rode from the yard.

The sun felt warm on my back as I trotted into the road, following the prints in the dust. The trail was easy enough for a boy who'd grown up around stock, but I scowled at my foolishness when I realized I hadn't even brought a canteen along. Pa had taught me to always carry a canteen, even when I thought the errand wouldn't take long. A man never knew when he would need water. Or a gun. I pursed my lips. Should I have brought the stranger's rifle?

Having turned seventeen, I liked to think I was pretty smart. But I promised to consider more the next time I left the ranch. My eagerness to get going sometimes trumped wisdom and caution, but I wasn't a little boy anymore.

The road that passed our house led to the Indian Nation to the north. This easy thoroughfare was used by Indians raiding into Texas or outlaws trying to escape to the Nation. A lawman had no or limited jurisdiction in the

Indian Territory, so a number of outlaws hid up there and often rode this trail. Sometimes Comanche or Kiowa raiding or hunting parties would run into travelers on the trail, looking for scalps and guns.

I back-trailed that horse a good three miles before I found the man, lying face down in the trail with two Comanche arrows sticking in his back. No other tracks indicated he was probably alone when he tumbled from the saddle. I glanced up the trail, musing if he'd been shot far away and then rode hard to put some distance between him and his attackers. Trouble was, he didn't get far before he died and fell from his saddle. His horse had continued running, probably looking for familiar sights and smells. That fresh hay in our barn must've been what drew the bay to our place.

Drawing rein, I peered down at the dead man, watching a fly buzz around the wounds. Then I swung my gaze to scan the surrounding area, looking for clues, but I was alone. It paid to be careful, and I was trying hard to be careful now.

Saddle leather creaked as I cautiously dismounted. Were the Indians nearby? Kneeling beside the corpse, I studied the feathered shafts of the arrows, confirming my first suspicion as I fingered the Comanche weapons. Only a short section protruded from the body, indicating a deep piercing.

As I leaned over the dead rider, not recognizing him, rapid hoof beats sounded farther up the trail. I looked up to see four Indian warriors bearing down on me. I stood quickly, watching their black hair streaming in the wind as they whooped and raised weapons. I remembered the man's rifle and scolded myself for not bringing a gun with me.

As the young braves approached at breakneck speed, I faced them with a sense of stupidity filling me. I could do nothing against these braves, and they would kill me.

The one in the lead lowered a lance to run me through when another warrior shouted a warning. The brave with the lance pulled his spear up and rode past me, his horse nearly brushing my shoulder.

The three other braves pulled reins, horses skidding to a halt as the lancer galloped on to wheel farther along the trail. A cloud of dust drifted over me as the brave who'd yelled a warning stared hard at me and then chattered and pointed at me as the first rider joined his comrades. They all seemed to be debating, and the one with the lance was growing angrier as the tense moments passed. He had a fierce, proud face and gestured like he had some influence over the other braves. A young chief, I wondered? The one who'd shouted the warning argued with the lancer for another minute while I stood rooted in place, my heart lodged in my throat.

I shifted as the hullaballoo continued, not knowing what to do next. The other two Indians seemed just as stunned as I. They sat their ponies, silently watching the dialog between their companions.

Finally, the brave who'd wanted to spear me turned his horse away, and with a menacing glance at me, raced back up the trail. The other three braves took up positions on both sides of the trail from me and sat their ragged ponies, their stoic faces disclosing nothing.

After realizing they weren't going to kill me outright, I moved to mount my horse, but one of the riders blocked me, not allowing me to depart. A stern glance from the silent warrior warned me to stay where I stood.

I shifted nervously in the warm sun and glanced again at the dead man, trying to be patient as sweat rolled slowly down my back. The Indians were waiting for something.

I decided to turn my focus back to the dead man. Who was he? I nudged him onto his side with my toe. He was not a young man by any means, probably in his mid-forties. Grizzled and dirty, he had a tough look about his features. The thin line of an old scar ran down one cheek and a small trickle of dried blood in the corner of his mouth revealed a possible lung wound. One of the arrows must've nicked vital organs. A bright red scarf wound around his neck, and he wore a Yankee cavalry pistol and belt. I could still read the US stamped in the black leather and noticed the holster flap had been neatly cut away.

I squinted at the sun, perched high now in the cloudless sky. Sweat darkened my shirt, and I licked my lips, wanting a drink. But any move toward my horse met with more blocking from the three mounted warriors, all of them silently watching me, and I hadn't brought a canteen anyway.

I'm not ashamed to admit my fear at that moment. I'd be a fool not to dread what these Indians could do to a man alone. But I vowed to meet my end with what bravery I could muster, whatever that might be. Our days on earth are numbered, and maybe my time had come. I felt more worried for Ma if something should happen to me. She surely needed all the help she could get.

An hour passed, and then another before I heard the sound of approaching horses. Lifting a hand against the sun's glare, I watched a dozen Indians ride toward me, the mean one leading the pack. His snarling face was set in harsh lines, but I squared my shoulders and faced them, accepting my fate.

A muscle twitched along my jaw, and I glanced up. "Well, Lord, if this is part of your plan to save our ranch, it doesn't look like it'll work."

A smugness roiled in my guts, like I'd been proven right. The Lord wasn't going to help us, and in fact, might not even help me now. I knew my doubts were justified, but little good that did Ma. I gritted my teeth and stared down the new arrivals, waiting.

The bunch of riders split as they neared, and a female Indian galloped forward, a wide smile splitting her smooth face. An electric shock raced through me when I recognized Hannah Tall Basket. But where were her braids and lanky form?

Bronzed legs flashed in the sun as she slid gracefully from her horse, and I turned away, startled by the beautiful girl's supple figure and flowing raven hair. The last time we'd met, Hannah seemed like such a young girl. She straightened her buckskin dress, and I felt my eyes widen as she held her hands to me. An amused glint danced in her dark eyes at my startled look, and she laughed, the musical lilt a discordant melody amidst the tense situation.

She studied me as she gripped my hands. "Johnny? You act as if you've seen a ghost. Don't you recognize me?"

I mumbled a greeting, still stunned by her unexpected presence. What was she doing here?

"I'm glad it is you. One of the braves recognized you and stopped Dark Cloud from killing you. He called you 'the spirit-filled boy who brings cows.'" She laughed at this description, but I didn't see what was so funny.

Her smile faded as she released my hands and glanced at the congregated warriors around us. "He also told me you stood and faced your enemies without a weapon. Big medicine, Johnny," she whispered as she faced me again. "These men respect that. But Dark Cloud says you are taking his right to the dead man's scalp. He demands his prize. Will you let him scalp the dead man? They killed him and deserve their reward."

Together, our gaze shifted to the dead man at our feet. My stomach tightened at the arrows protruding the still form, and Hannah looked at me, a questioning expression in her eyes.

I peered at Dark Cloud, the young brave who'd almost speared me. He wore a mask of stern features and sat his horse proudly. His face purpled as I studied him, but he stared, narrowing his eyes, and our gaze locked. I had the feeling he would've enjoyed killing me just for the sport, but something about the Indian's description of me stayed his hand, and he scowled, not liking me or the situation.

Although Hannah had spoken to me like an old friend, I felt amazed at her appearance out here on the trail, looking grown up and lovely. By the way Dark Cloud nudged his horse closer to her, I suspected the cantankerous brave believed he had a claim on her she didn't acknowledge, or at least ignored. This might account for his surly mood. I grinned, realizing he thought there was more between Hannah and me than there was.

Hannah said something, and my gaze returned to her. "What's that?" I didn't trust Dark Cloud, but he was forgotten when I looked into her eyes, feeling like I was seeing her for the first time.

"It is good to see you, Hannah. What do the brave Comanche need of me?"

Her white teeth flashed as she smiled anew, and she tilted her head. "You act strangely. Are you not hearing me? I said this warrior demands the right of the dead man's hair. It is only fair."

Gathering my wits, I realized I had nothing to fear from them. My glance dropped once more to the dead man in the trail, and my mind whirled with possibilities. His horse, his gear, his weapons. What were they worth?

I shrugged an affirmative to the mounted Dark Cloud. "Sure, go ahead. But I lay claim to what I have found on the trail. The kill belongs to Dark Cloud, but the body and gear belong to me."

Hannah interpreted to the listening warrior, and he threw a leg over his horse's head and slid to the ground. With one more glance at me, he pulled a rusty knife from his belt and knelt beside the dead man. Grasping the shock of hair and then dragging the knife's blade under the skin, he removed the scalp.

My stomach turned as Dark Cloud thrust the tuft of hair into the sky and whooped. A number of the mounted braves echoed his shriek of victory. Then, he shoved the bloody mass into his belt and looked at me. I could tell he wasn't impressed with what he saw. A young boy of seventeen with no weapon. I could tell by his expression he wanted to add my scalp to his belt too, but I straightened and stared him down.

Without another word, Dark Cloud vaulted to his shaggy pony and rode away in a whirl of dust and a pound of hooves.

All the other warriors turned to follow, and soon I stood in the trail above a scalped stranger. Hannah seemed unaffected by the dead man as she gripped her pony's hackamore and stilled the horse's impatient prancing. I wondered if she'd seen such things before.

I gestured at the corpse at my feet and the veil of dust that lingered in the air. "I'm glad you came here to figure out this mess. I back-trailed this man's horse and found him at the same time as your braves. They wanted to take my scalp, too, I think." I smiled at Hannah, recalling all of our years of friendship. We'd known each other for a long time, yet suddenly I looked at her in a different way.

She nodded, a long strand of black hair blowing across her copper cheek. "Yes, Dark Cloud wanted to kill you. But when they discovered who you are, they were afraid to harm you. My father says you are protected by the Great Spirit, a blessed man among my people."

I nodded, remembering the stories the Comanche told of my family. My throat tightened, suddenly missing Pa.

As if reading my thoughts, Hannah placed a hand on my arm. "We do not forget the kindness your family showed my people in the big snow."

I wanted to say something, to tell her how grateful I was to her, but memories of Pa crowded my mind, reminding me we were all alone on the Texas prairie. What were we going to do?

A shy smile tugged at the corner of her mouth as Hannah stepped back and leaped onto her pony's back, settling herself as bare legs peeked below her long dress. With a strong hand, she held the fidgeting pony in place. "When I rode up here, you acted like you didn't know me. Didn't you recognize your Hannah Tall Basket? Have we not been friends for many years?"

I shifted in the hot sun, trying to order my thoughts. "Well, it's been a while since I last saw you. You've grown up." I hoped she heard the sincerity in my stammered reply. I certainly appreciated seeing her again.

Her dark eyes danced, and her smile widened. "Many of the braves in camp have told me I have grown up. I am glad you noticed too."

With a kick to her pony's sides, Hannah rode away, dust lingering in the air as I watched her go.

CHAPTER 7

My thoughts curled—and not only about the heavy corpse—as I slung the dead man over my horse. Although I didn't know the man, he deserved a decent burial. The animal shied a little from the smell of blood, but when I calmed him with a firm hand, he took the weight readily enough.

I reached for the drooping reins and then paused and stripped the man's gun and holster. Slinging the belt around my hips, I loosely cinched the leather, allowing the gun to rest easy. Being a cavalry holster, it lay on my left hip with the pistol butt forward, ready to hand while in the saddle.

I pulled that Colt dragoon out and inspected the loaded pistol. I held the gun aloft, liking the solid feel of the weapon in my hand. With the sound of metal on leather, I slid the pistol back into place, feeling a little better for being armed.

Living in Texas, growing up with guns was normal. I'd used them plenty of times and felt comfortable with firearms. When Pa went away to the war, he and the hired riders had taken all of their guns except the shotgun.

Starting back down the trail I'd come from, I led the horse and walked. I knew I was an hour from the ranch. Having had no breakfast and forgetting a canteen, my stomach grumbled something awful, and my mouth felt like cotton. I pushed forward despite the discomfort.

Walking along like that gave me time to think. This predicament was not what I'd expected when I prayed to be open to God's plan. I did not know really what to expect, but a scalped man on the back of my horse was not it. Yet I felt a little better having a gun. This man didn't have any further need of the pistol.

My mind concentrated on fleeing the ranch, although I confess my reluctance. We had only four more days to come up with the three hundred and eighty-seven dollars, and I doubted that would happen. I chuckled dryly when I imagined the money falling suddenly from the sky, like Ma and Paul hoped. And what if the money fell from heaven? That would only save the ranch for now. What about the future?

God had many details to work out, I figured. But he's God and I'm not. At least he'd provided this man's guns and gear. I pondered my troubles as the sun broiled me like a piece of meat over a fire, slowly cooking.

Abruptly, my thoughts turned to Hannah. I was not used to girls, especially pretty girls. She seemed to be flirting with me at the end of our conversation, but how could I know? We'd known each other for years, and I'd never noticed she was so pretty. I scowled when I considered she'd seemed to want me to notice.

I shook my head. *Don't be a fool*, I told myself, not allowing my fanciful thoughts to run away with me. She was a beautiful woman, daughter of a chief, and I was just a poor rancher, rich in cattle no one wanted, but nothing else. Besides, we would be leaving soon. I would do well to keep focused on my problems.

Later, I trudged into the ranch yard. I felt hungry, thirsty, and footsore but needed to talk to Ma. Seeing me first, Paul called to my mother in the kitchen as he ran from the barn.

"Good Lord, John, what happened to this man?" He clucked his tongue and muttered darkly as he examined the scalped man draped over my saddle. We both turned when Ma approached.

My horse gulped water from the trough as I accepted the tin cup Ma handed me. Water spilled down my throat as I tipped the cup and slurped, allowing the coolness to satisfy. I wiped my mouth with the back of my hand before I spoke.

"I trailed his horse back about three or four miles and found him dead in the trail, a pair of Comanche arrows in his back. They rode up then, wanting to kill me, but they didn't. They made me wait until Hannah Tall Basket arrived and sorted things out."

"Hannah?" Ma echoed, peering closely at me. I felt like she could see into my soul, and I squirmed, worried what she might see. "She's about your own age," she murmured, still watching me.

I shifted and glanced toward the barn. "They wanted his scalp and gave the rest of him to me."

Ma nodded, all business once again. "You did right, bringing him here. And I'm glad nothing happened to you." She gave me a hug and then turned to watch Paul lower the dead man from my saddle.

"I'll take care of this." He dragged the lifeless body to the empty bunkhouse while I stepped into the house for something to eat and drink.

Paul came in while I was finishing my second cup of coffee. "He had some money on him." He placed the crumpled bills on the table.

"Did you go through his pockets?" Ma looked at him sharply with a disapproving look, but I quickly interjected.

"We don't know who this man is." I shrugged, dismissing Paul's invasive search of the dead man. "We're in a bind here. Maybe God wanted us to use this gent's stuff for our needs. The Lord does provide in mysterious ways."

"That's not funny," Ma snapped, fingering the soiled bills on the table. "And I don't like the way you bandy the Lord's provision about so easily. Everything he does has purpose."

She pushed the money aside and rose to fetch the coffeepot. I glanced at Paul, indicating the pile of money with my chin. "How much?"

He shrugged. "I don't know anything about money."

Shooting a glance at Ma, I reached for the bills, smoothing the rumpled paper in a neat stack as I counted. Ma cast a curious look at me over her shoulder but said nothing. I saw her look to the ceiling, her mouth moving wordlessly as I laid the final bill on the table. Ma's curiosity must've burned inside her, but she said nary a word as I leaned back in my chair, contemplating the amount. Not much in the scheme of things, but more money than we'd seen in years. I wondered how much we owed Anderson and what supplies we might purchase for our departure.

"I want to see him." Her words made me lean forward and I glanced at Paul with the same astonishment I read in his eyes.

"And who would that be, Miss Annie?" Paul said, eyes still locked on my own.

"You know very well who I'm talking about," she whispered, not bothering to look at us. "I want to see the dead man."

Paul shrugged again and our chairs scraped as we pushed away from the table, leading Ma across the sunbaked yard to the bunkhouse. The low building had been unlived in since the hands left for the war, but now a corpse stretched upon the long table. My eyes adjusted to the dim room as the three of us entered and stared down at him.

Paul had placed a ground sheet over the table and laid the corpse out, placing his arms alongside his body as if he only rested and was not as dead as a stone. The dead man was a gruesome sight nonetheless, and I avoided looking closely at his violated head wound as we went through his belongings.

"Well, there's nothing on him, that's certain," Ma quipped sharply with a glance at the dead man's turned-out pockets.

Paul dumped the rider's saddlebags on the bench before giving Ma an apologetic look. "Everything he had in his pockets, except the money, is on the table." A folded jackknife, two short lengths of rawhide string, and a small, polished rock heaped between the man's boots. He surely didn't have much. We left the bright red scarf wound around his neck.

"There was a dirty coat tied behind his saddle, along with an old slicker," Paul added. He hesitated and then rushed on, tugging on the rope around his waist as he studied the man with a longing look in his eye. "What of his boots and belt?"

My boots shifted under the bench, feeling a little uneasy at the hasty appeal. But was the request so inappropriate? After all, the dead man's gun hung at my waist, and I considered laying claim to his rifle as well.

Ma looked thoughtfully at the prone body before she responded. "His things are his own for now." She caught the disappointment on Paul's face and shrugged "We'll see."

Paul nodded, yet I could tell his disappointment didn't diminish.

Together, we examined the contents of his saddlebags. A dirty towel wrapped around shaving gear and a small brick of soap, a ripped shirt, a few camp utensils, a slicker, and some food stuff. Behind his saddle had been tied a blanket roll and a worn coat.

"How much money did he have?" Ma's inquiry made me scowl. Her curiosity could not be contained, which I didn't blame her, but I wondered if she were considering how the Lord was providing. I choked back a smirk as I could see the Lord's hand was almighty small if this were his idea of provision.

I'd spent time last night earnestly praying to God for help, promising to be faithful as I watched him work in our dilemma. Yet doubts assailed me, surrounded me at every turn, and I confess my faith had crumbled in the brutal light of day as I frowned down at the dead man before me. And time was running out.

"Thirty-seven dollars," I reported with a sad note, feeling an unaccountable sorrow for the stranger's meager belongings and the worthless aid his unexpected corpse offered us.

With no papers revealing his identity, we stared at the dead man, wishing we could put the pieces together. Who was he? Did he leave a family behind? What accomplishments could his life boast?

I shifted again, wondering if his soul was in heaven. Did he know the Lord? Did I? My faith had taken a real blow with the struggles we faced, but I wanted to believe God was still with us, hadn't abandoned us.

An image of last night's prayer in the barn darted across my mind again and I snorted, angered this was how God answered prayer.

Ma looked at me. "What?"

"This is the Lord's idea of help?" I indicated the still form on the table and didn't try to keep the scorn from my words.

"You can never tell how God will answer a prayer or the way he chooses to do things," Paul testified philosophically.

I glared at him and then pointed at the dead man, a bloody gash where his hair had been. "This is no answer to prayer. This man had little enough to go around. He was just a saddle tramp," I concluded, sick of trying to paint this grim picture any other way, and impatient to consider our demanding need to vacate the ranch. We had only a few more days with no destination in mind.

I shot Ma an accusing glance, but she ignored me, rubbing her chin as she studied the corpse. "This man was no cowboy. Chances are he was riding the old trail from the Indian Nation when the Comanche jumped him and gave chase."

I pressed my lips together until they hurt, not understanding her stalling. I'd noticed earlier the stranger's horse didn't belong to a cowboy, but the time had come to give up and accept defeat. We needed to pack and be moving somewhere, not wasting any more time on this dead rider. His time was over, but we still had a life to live … somewhere. But Ma spoke on, thinking aloud and tapping her chin.

"They probably shot him last evening, lost him in the dark, and waited until dawn to pick up his trail."

"Pure coincidence I happened upon him," I agreed, eager to speed up her pondering.

Paul and Ma exchanged glances. "Was it?" Paul narrowed his eyes.

I frowned at his remark. "What does that mean?"

Ma inhaled deeply. "It means the Lord is at work. There are no coincidences, only hidden meanings. There must be a purpose in this."

I tilted my head. "Why? I mean, if this is God's work, why use hidden meaning? Why not shout it from the roof top how he intends to help us?"

Paul chuckled and waved a hand in the air. "That would be too easy. There's no challenge in that. The faithful will wait on the Lord and search for his hand." A tight grin played on his lips as he looked at me. "And the faithful will see his works and praise him."

My boots made a dull scraping sound as I shifted once more, feeling guilty at his comment. Was I unfaithful? Was I not seeking God's hand in all of this?

"You were lucky those Indians didn't kill you too," Paul added, observing the arrows in the man's back.

"It was not luck. God was protecting you, Son." Ma always saw God's involvement in every situation, and this time I wondered. Those Indians did not kill me because they thought me spiritual, connected to a Christian family. Had the Lord protected me?

"What do we do with him now? Bury him?" I suggested, thinking again of his guns. It would be helpful to have them.

"No," Ma replied. "No, we will take him tomorrow to the sheriff." Of course, that made sense. I hadn't even considered that.

We wrapped the man in the ground sheet and left him in the bunkhouse for the night, but I slept fitfully, still bothered at the responsibility thrust upon me. Pa was not coming home, and I was the man of the place, yet I knew Ma and even Paul didn't think my opinion held much weight. I looked at things with a practical eye while they looked at our struggles with a spiritual bent I couldn't grasp. Perhaps the trip to town with the corpse would help them see the necessity of making a decision. Despite my prayers of the previous night, I felt convinced God was silent, and we needed to get moving.

It took me a long time to learn that prayer was not inactivity.

CHAPTER 8

The next day, Paul helped me load the corpse into our heavy farm wagon. The former slave wore a hangdog look on his face and muttered as we pushed the stiff form deeper into the wagon. "It's a waste to not keep his boots. He doesn't need them anymore," he lamented sourly.

I'd stuffed his thirty-seven dollars into my pocket and still wore the man's gun when Ma and I drove to town. She hadn't said anything about the big pistol in the black holster. We needed guns and she knew it, yet I wondered if she would let me keep the pistol.

We traveled the four miles into town without talking, each of us lost in our own thoughts. With only three more days to get off our ranch, we both stewed silently, and I sensed she shared my unease, but for different reasons. This thought lay heavy on me, and I knew it haunted my mother, but she seemed unwavering to see this ludicrous waste of time through to its end. I on the other hand, clung to reason.

I gripped the leather reins tighter. Where would we go? There was no one to take us in. We simply had to find a place to move to, and soon. Winter loomed only a few months away. We would need shelter before the snow flew.

Ma insisted we bring all the man's gear, including his long-legged bay gelding. Even his rifle lay on the floorboards next to him. I would be reluctant to give up his handgun.

Town was not much to speak of. A dozen buildings squatted along both sides of the wide street, and a scattering of homes dotting the surrounding prairie made up the village, merely a speck on the vast empty plains. The general store was the biggest building, serving as post office as well. The hotel, bank, and sheriff's office were all connected in a long brick structure while the blacksmith's shop and the livery stood across the street. The café served as the center of the small metropolis.

We pulled up in front of the sheriff's office and I wiped sweat from my brow with my sleeve before wrapping the reins around the brake handle. Jumping from the wagon, I opened the office door and peered in, my gaze scanning the empty room.

"Stay here, Ma. I'll find him," I called over my shoulder as I stalked up the main street. I moved toward the café, figuring if the sheriff wasn't inside, someone there would know his whereabouts.

I felt Ma's eyes upon my back as I covered the short distance to the café. Did she think of me as a man, or was I still her little boy?

Leaping lightly onto the boardwalk, I adjusted the holster around my waist before opening the café door. The sheriff sat at a corner table with the blacksmith, coffee mugs stilling as they glanced my way. Both men's gaze dropped to the gun on my hip. I could feel the heat tingle in my cheeks as I maneuvered the empty tables toward them.

"Sheriff? I just rode in with my mother, and we would like a word with you."

The thickset man leaned back in his seat and grinned. Mort Caffrey had fought in the War Between the States and lived to return, though many had not. "Johnny Garret, I haven't seen you in a while. How's the ranch? How is your ma doing?"

I bristled at the name he used for me, but nodded respectfully at Sorenson, the blacksmith. Facing the sheriff, I drew in a deep breath. "We got word Pa isn't coming home."

A muscle twitched in his jaw and he nodded, his eyes darting to his boots before he spoke. "I'm sorry to hear that. Your pa was a good man."

With a grunt, he shoved himself erect and clamped a firm hand on my shoulder before leading the way to the door. I glanced at the silent Sorenson, appreciating the look of support on the blacksmith's face, and followed the sheriff across the room, our boots thudding in the near vacant space.

He paused at the door and held it open for me, a rare show of respect I figured my news of Pa brought from him.

Walking beside me back across the dusty street, Sheriff Caffrey greeted Ma warmly and helped her down. As he swung her to the ground, he stepped back, a wide grin creasing his leathery face. "You're still as light as a young girl, Annie."

Ma reddened and blinked as she shot me a quick glance. "It's been almost twenty years since we went to school together, Mort."

"Time flies," he agreed as he pushed his office door wide and walked around his desk while indicating a chair for Ma. I stood behind her, thumbs tucked into my belt. Caffrey seated himself and studied us across the scarred wooden desk. Abruptly, he frowned. "Johnny told me about Vince. Sorry to hear, Annie."

Ma said nothing to this, only waited a polite moment before she spoke. "Johnny found a dead man on the trail near our ranch."

Caffrey squinted up at me. "A dead man? What's this?"

Chairs scraped as I led the way through the open door to the end of the wagon, where I pulled the canvas tarp aside, revealing the corpse. Mort shouldered past me, taking in the ghastly sight with a quick survey. He turned on me, his bushy eyebrows bunching.

"A saddle horse came into the yard yesterday morning, searching water," I began as I dropped the canvas over the man's face, shielding it from the bright sun. "I back-trailed the gelding to this." I pointed to the concealed corpse and waved a noisy fly away.

Mort stepped into the shade of the awning. Ma stood with her back to the adobe office, and I felt pleased she allowed me to handle this.

"This man is scalped," Mort announced brusquely, as if I should've noticed.

"I know that," I snapped. "I was there when the Comanche scalped him."

Mort peered from me to Ma and shook his head. "The Comanche can be all fired handy with a scalping knife." He studied me again. "They let you go?"

I briefly explained my role in the situation and Hannah Tall Basket's intervention. Caffrey nodded and jerked a thumb toward the wagon, an agitated look on his face. "I think I've seen this man before."

Once again, the three of us stepped into the small, sparsely furnished office. It felt cool in the shadow of the room, a welcome relief from the glaring sun of the street. The adobe walls did well to keep most of the heat outside, especially this early in the day.

My gaze swept the little room as Caffrey and Ma resumed their seats. A potbellied stove filled one corner, but there weren't even cells in the office. I wondered what the sheriff did when he needed to keep someone locked up. A pair of fetters on a long chain dangled from a hook and I scowled.

My attention was drawn to Ma as she nodded at me, indicating the gear I carried. Depositing the saddlebags and rifle on the desk, I stepped back. "That's everything he owns, except his gelding tied behind the wagon."

I paused and caught Ma's concerned glance. Frowning, I pulled the money from my pocket and tossed the bills on the desk. "And his money. Thirty-seven dollars."

Ma's eyebrows arched and I knew what she wanted, but I balked, slapping the pistol on my hip. "And his belt gun," I announced shortly, making no attempt to unbuckle the belt around my waist.

Without looking at me, Ma spoke. "Johnny, leave his gun on the sheriff's desk." I scowled but knew better than to argue with my mother. Slowly, I unbuckled the leather belt and dropped the heavy handgun on the desk.

"You will have to leave it here with his gear," Mort said simply.

"What will you do with his horse and gear?" Ma's question startled me. I thought we were done, our good deed coming to an end. We'd delivered the body to the sheriff and now I expected to leave town, empty-handed and bitter.

"They are to be sold to pay for his burial and any expenses that might occur in capturing his killers," Mort replied, as if reciting rules printed in a book somewhere.

Ma held up a hand. "Now wait a minute, Mort Caffrey. You're telling me that the county is going to sell this man's outfit to pay for a four-dollar burial? Johnny risked his very life to bring this man in. I believe that, in a way, he did your job for you. It is only fair that he is compensated for the work provided this office."

Mort blinked, no more surprised than me, and I could tell he'd not expected this. Shuffling his feet beneath his desk, he scratched the side of his head. "Well, uh, it is customary to relinquish all personal belongings to the county." He was trying to find firm footing with some difficulty, and Ma hedged, not letting him get set.

"He is dead and has no more use for his gear. We do. I'm being kicked off my land in three days for not paying taxes, and we will need these guns for defense or hunting. We will keep his guns and saddle horse to compensate Johnny's risk in bringing the body to town."

A scowl darkened Caffrey's features, but Ma talked fast. I sensed Mort was backing up and she just kept prodding, seeing how far he'd let her go. We didn't need his horse, so I knew Ma mentioned the animal only as a bargaining chip.

The sheriff lifted both hands, almost appearing to surrender. "Now see here, Annie. I will need to sell his horse to pay for burial. You have plenty of saddle stock on the ranch. You don't need another." The sheriff scrambled to keep his head above water, but Ma was a shrewd horse trader. She'd gotten the better of this deal, and we all knew it.

She reached for the thin wad of bills on Mort's desk and held the money aloft. Then she handed the gun belt to me, and I strapped the leather holster on again while she lifted the saddlebags, the neatly folded bills in the other as she eyed the sheriff.

"We found thirty-seven dollars on him. The county will bury him after selling his horse. I figure my son taking this man from the Comanche to bring him to you is worth something. We are taking everything but the gelding and going home after you unload the body."

"We will also have need of his boots and belt," I added softly, not quite wanting to join the argument.

Mort shot me a disgusted look. "Well, you are taking everything but his body and his horse, aren't you? Anything else I can do for you?" Sarcasm edged his words and I felt embarrassed, but not too embarrassed to gather all the equipment and gear we could. Desperate times called for desperate measures.

Ma arched her eyebrows. "Mort, we're not trying to be callous, but we did bring him in. This man is finished with these items, but we still have need of them. If there was anything else we could get from him, I'm not too proud to ask for it."

I ducked my head. Ma might not be too proud, but I felt the last of any pride I owned slip away as we stood in that sheriff's office and pleaded for the dead man's gear. Shame washed over me, and I felt galled to beg. What would Pa have said?

Mort narrowed his eyes and leaned back again, his face softening. "I know, Annie. Lots of other folks around here are in the same situation as you. Taxes are due, and others are losing their ranches and farms. Those blasted carpetbaggers from up north ..." His voice trailed off and he paused, another muscle twitching in his jaw as he considered. "You're right—the county does appreciate Johnny's effort to bring this outlaw in. You can have his trappings."

With that, Mort ran a hand across his chin, a gleam coming to his eyes. "Well, now, you make me recall something. I *have* seen this man before." Reaching across the desk, he rifled a stack of papers on the corner. He mumbled for a minute and then grunted, pulling a paper from the pile.

"Yep, here it is." He waved the paper and smiled. "I knew I'd seen this, Annie. Listen." He cleared his throat and then slowly read aloud. "Wanted. Dead or alive. Red Bill Jenkins. Three hundred fifty dollars reward."

CHAPTER 9

Ma gasped, and I stared at her. A gentle gust of wind blew in the open door, a dust devil dancing across the street as I tilted my head at Mort's words. I was not quick enough to grasp what Caffrey's comment truly meant, but the stunned look on Ma's face made me tense.

"You mean this man is worth three hundred and fifty dollars to whoever brings him in?" Ma whispered, clarifying what I was too thick to comprehend.

Mort nodded. "Yes, Annie. You also get the gratitude of this county. He would've been a bad man to have around." Mort turned to me. "Thanks, Johnny, for bringing him in." He looked down at the flyer in his hand, reading it again in subdued tones.

I could see Ma putting all the pieces together in her head, her thoughts falling into order. She looked at me, a bright gleam in her eye, and I saw tears pool in the corners as she gripped my hand and squeezed.

Mort continued. "Says here this man killed a teller in Fort Smith while trying to rob the bank. He's also wanted for a few other things. They'll be happy to hear my report."

"Is this a feather in your cap?" Ma's question revealed she'd not been completely bamboozled by the unexpected news.

Mort shrugged. "Doesn't do me any harm, that's sure."

Ma squirmed. "Not to seem too impatient, but when do we get the reward money?" My mother was always a practical woman, and I had to admit, I was wondering the same thing.

"I have to verify his identity and get word to Fort Smith by telegraph. I know of two men in town who can identify Red Bill. He never went anywhere without that red scarf around his neck. When I get authorization, I'll write a draft receipt and you can take the check to the bank and cash it."

"How long will this process take?" I could tell Ma was now worried about the time table for our taxes.

"A day or two, I reckon. Let me get started and we'll see." The sheriff motioned to me to follow him outside.

"Johnny, take the body to the livery and we'll keep him there for now. You can help me unload him." He spoke as he climbed heavily into the wagon and seated himself. Climbing to the place beside him, I drove the wagon into the wide-open door of the livery. It was dark and cool in the old barn. A few horses munched their hay, but there was no one around. A pair of doves fluttered above the loft, their wings flapping loudly in the quiet.

First, I untied that long-legged bay and put him in a stall. Then I helped carry the body near the grain bins where the horses wouldn't be bothered by the smell of blood.

Sheriff Caffrey wiped sweat from his brow as I knelt and took the boots and belt from the dead man. After tossing them into the wagon bed, I climbed up onto the seat, staring straight ahead and trying to conceal my humiliation. I hoped keeping the boots and belt would not anger God. It seemed disrespectful to the dead man, but Paul would have more use for them than Red Bill.

Mort clambered up beside me and shot me a sharp, sidelong glance, not saying anything. Yet I felt his scorn and I tensed, hating being so impoverished. I knew what he was thinking, how unfitting it seemed to take a dead man's gear. But Mort had no idea how needy we were.

With a slap of the reins, we went the short distance to the sheriff's office where Ma waited. I was eager to talk privately to her about the reward money.

Mort climbed down and then helped my mother into his vacated place on the seat after she'd loaded the rifle and saddlebags into the bed. As she settled herself on the hard wooden bench, I glanced over my shoulder at the goods strewn across the wagon boards. I dearly wanted to check the rifle but forced myself to be patient. There would be time later.

As I gathered the reins, Ma looked down at Mort where he stood on the boardwalk. "Sheriff," she began stiffly. No one could miss the formality in her address. "Thank you for the news of the reward. I will be in tomorrow to check on the progress of that bank receipt. Have a good day." I slapped the reins over the horses, and we sped from town, a trail of dust lifting in our wake.

We didn't speak for a few minutes, letting the wind whip around us as town stretched behind. With the body taken from the wagon and the bay gelding no longer tied to the tailgate, the team stepped out, as if sensing the gruesome weight they'd carried was gone now.

And as the vast plains spread before us, my palms moistened. What had just happened? In the twinkling of an eye, we had sizeable money coming to us. I glanced up at the azure blue sky and marveled, stunned by our good fortune and the way things had turned out—certainly better than I ever hoped for. Despite my lack of faith, God had been faithful. There was no way I could deny his involvement, my gaze scanning the road ahead before lifting once more to the few wisps of clouds drifting above. I nodded, pleased my tiny sense of expectancy had not been fruitless. I felt the gates of his storehouses had been opened just for us, and I praised him, grateful he rode our trail with us.

"Johnny, did you hear that?" Ma breathed near my ear as she gripped my arm. "The reward money plus the thirty-seven dollars makes the whole three hundred and eighty-seven dollars we owe the county. We are not losing our ranch. I understand what King David meant when he said goodness and mercy would follow him all of his days." She gave a squeal of delight I hadn't heard in years, and hugged me tighter still, my chest constricting as I felt the swell in my own throat. "God knew this would help us pay our back taxes, and now we're able to stay. God is so good to us, Johnny, and we need to thank him."

I shifted and pulled away from her, wanting to put some distance between us. "Well, uh," I began. "I agree the Lord has done this. Surely God gave us the money. But maybe not to pay the taxes and stay at the ranch."

Her eyebrows arched. "No? What then?"

I drew a deep breath and rushed on. "Ma, we need to move. We can't keep the ranch going with no riders and no market for our cattle. I think the Lord gave us this money as a road stake, to help us settle somewhere else."

She shook her head. "Are you kidding? This is the exact amount we need for the taxes. This is from God, a precise answer to our prayers. I feel encouraged. We need to praise him and wait for what is next. The adventure has only begun."

My heart sank. With Pa gone, the ranch was more than I could manage alone. Couldn't she see that? And our cattle were as good as worthless. Where would more money come from?

"If we pay the taxes, we still have nothing," I argued, hoping she might see reason.

"Manna in the desert."

I looked at her. "Huh?"

She laughed, eyes glowing with excitement. "You know the story of the Israelites in the desert. God gave them manna to eat, just enough for today. Nothing left over. He wanted them to trust him for tomorrow's provision."

"No, no," I stammered, trying to ignore her biblical illustration. "Ma, you have to realize we can't go on."

"That's right," she agreed. "We can't go on with only our strength. But we can continue if we lean on Jesus. Trust God, Johnny," she said and patted my arm.

She hummed softly to herself, the argument completed—at least in her mind. But I worried about the future, to the inevitable new challenges that were sure to come. Pa would say "crisis averted" when a problem had been solved, but he always prepared for the next one, sure to descend when least expected.

My sour attitude had been circumvented—this time. Ma had been right, and my sense of expectancy had been merited. But would the Lord linger to handle our next dilemma? Our taxes would be paid, yet worry would not leave me. Anxiety pressed in upon me at every turn, and I wondered if God would stick around and walk with us through the troubles of our Texas home.

We quickly covered the short distance to our ranch, Ma's giddy droning making the miles swiftly pass, but I scowled as doubts assailed me. Why couldn't I just be happy like Ma? She saw God's hand and praised him with joy and thanksgiving, but I felt my frustration mount as the weathered, faded buildings of our ranch came into view.

Halting in front of the barn, I glanced over my shoulder to the scattered treasures that littered the wagon bed. My spirits lifted when I remembered we were not completely left with nothing after the taxes were paid.

Paul came out to help unhitch the team and his stern features melted into a wide smile when he saw the pile of gear. He turned inquisitive eyes upon Ma, and she beamed. I caught the glint of moisture in her gaze, but pressed my lips tight, holding my tongue against ruining this moment of celebration.

"You boys unhitch the team and then come in for lunch. We'll be spending some time in prayer, I think."

Paul helped her down from the high seat, and she moved for the kitchen door. I watched her go, somehow disquieted at her eagerness to give the Lord thanks. Yet, the taxes would be paid, and we didn't have to move away immediately. Resigned, I knew we'd be staying on, thanks to God, but a restless spirit still wiggled within me.

While unhitching the team, I explained to Paul what happened. At first, he didn't understand the significance of the reward money, but he crowed like a kid at Christmas when I told how the money was the exact amount we owed the county.

"John, it was the Good Lord who brought me here, to be a witness to these amazing events. God is here, and wants to do a mighty work for this family. I'm glad to be a part."

White teeth flashed as he broke into song while he rubbed the horses down with a piece of burlap sack. I draped the harness on pegs before retrieving the boots and belt from the wagon. His singing stopped as he reached for the leather items, his hands trembling.

"For me?" I almost didn't catch his whispered inquiry.

My humiliation at pleading with Sheriff Caffrey for these objects soon to be planted uselessly in the earth melted away as I observed the pure joy that swept over Paul. He sat in the dust and pushed away his tattered, shabby shoes and pulled on the dead man's boots. Like a rooster strutting proudly across the barnyard, Paul scrambled to his feet and paraded the worn boots.

"I've only had cast offs, but these are the best I've ever owned. And I've never owned a real belt." He tugged the rope from around his waist and threaded the belt through the loops on Pa's old pants. Slinging the length of cord across a low wall, he faced me, standing tall in the shadows of the noonday barn.

Speechless now, he stared at me, his eyes unnaturally large. I clapped him on the shoulder before lifting the rifle and saddlebags from the wagon. Together, we made our way to the kitchen, stopping only long enough to wash up before entering. But as I dried my hands on my pants, I caught Paul studying his new boots again, a look of sheer appreciation on his face. Why didn't I feel as content as him? He'd only received worn boots and a stretched belt, but our back taxes would be paid. I knew God had done this, yet I felt as if I waited for the other boot to drop, as if good things were not for us and something terrible loomed on the horizon.

I held the door open for Paul and we passed into the kitchen. Ma had prepared quite a spread with cold beef sandwiches and potatoes. The smell of baked bread from the morning meal still lingered in the small room, and I sat at the table as Ma poured coffee. Paul sat beside me, watching carefully as Ma filled a cup for him, steam rising. Ma nodded at me as a restful smile touched her lips, a look of pleasure that reminded me of Paul's look I'd seen in the barn. "Johnny, will you say grace?"

I almost begged off, then read the gratitude in her eyes and relented, bowing my head as I clasped my hands together. Guiltily, I wished she'd asked Paul to pray or done it herself. But this seemed like a day to celebrate, and I knew the Lord had blessed us, even if temporarily.

"God, you know how hard things have been here. You've asked a lot of us, demanded a heavy price. Your yoke has not been light. Having Paul come along has been a real help, and surely finding Red Bill on the trail was no accident." I paused, not anxious to blame the Lord for all our difficulties. But hadn't he been with us through the duration of the war, allowing Pa to die and us to suffer, barely making ends meet?

"The Lord giveth, and the Lord taketh away," I quoted, recalling Scripture. "Thanks for this respite, and I hope good things for this ranch. Thanks for our daily food," I mumbled at the last, keen to conclude.

Ma shot me a confused glance, but the three of us dug in, eager to enjoy our simple fare and call the meager meal a bountiful feast. There had been no break from tough times for so long and now we knew God was with us, but only I wondered for how long.

"An adventure, that's what I call it," Paul said jubilantly as he smeared butter on another slice of bread.

Ma nodded. "Jesus has a plan for us, and it's starting to unfold in very unexpected ways." She laughed, pleasure shining in her eyes, and I disdained my treacherous heart. Why couldn't I share their strong faith? Why did doubts assail me and steal my joy?

A scowl crept across my face as I watched Ma's infectious conviction draw Paul in. Or had he already been a part of the team without me? Regardless, their iron clad belief put me to shame somehow, although I wondered how long they could stand against a wave of impending troubles. We'd been saved from immediate eviction from our home, but what now? How long could we live here without an income?

As if my battles were against unseen foes, not made of flesh and bone, I squinted into the distance, wanting to rely on the Lord. But a war waged within me, whispering in my ear that my inadequacies held me back from experiencing all that God had for me. As if gripped by an invisible hand, I felt restrained. Although my desire was to seek the Lord and do his will, a resistance like a heavy stone weighed me down. The blossoming courage I'd experienced in the barn a few nights ago seemed to vanish with the light of day, and I felt weaker than ever. Attacked by an unknown enemy, I'd already lost the war before the battle had a chance to begin.

CHAPTER 10

After lunch, Ma removed the dishes from the table before seating herself again. She leaned her elbows on the table, eyes glowing. "God has shown us his provision, and he deserves praise. I think we should spend some time thanking him for this reward money and for letting us stay here. Also, we need to ask for guidance as we seek his will. Surely, he has something in mind for us to pursue. Let us wait on the Lord and see how this adventure will work out. With faith, we'll seek his favor."

We sat around the table, heads bowed. I kept stealing covert glances at Ma and Paul. Their apparent reverence uneased me, and I gritted my teeth. Why did we have to seek God's favor? Didn't he want to always do good things for his people?

"Wait," I said as I leaned away from them. The pair looked up, startled glances making their eyebrows arch. Crossing my arms over my chest, I glowered. "Isn't the Lord on our side? Why do we have to ask? He knows our problems, our troubles. Surely, they are no secret to him."

Paul nodded and licked his lips before reaching for his cooling coffee mug. "He knows everything, but we don't."

"What's that supposed to mean?" I challenged, demanding to understand something about God I couldn't grasp. "He loves us, so why torture us? Why not just give us good things all the time?"

Ma chuckled and I swung my glaring gaze on her. "What's so funny? We barely evaded getting kicked off our own land. I don't think it's funny."

Ma's eyebrows bunched at my brusque rebuke, but it was Paul who spoke. "He sees everything while we see only a piece of the situation. We are unable to comprehend all that is happening while he knows every detail."

"Then why pray? Or praise him? He knows what we're going to do before we do it. We're surprised by our scrapes, but he's not, right? Shouldn't he fix them without making us pray or struggle or fail?" I felt pensive as they pondered my accusations.

Ma chuckled again, and I could feel my stomach tighten. She pressed a hand to my arm when she read the disapproval in my glower. "We're not children, Johnny. We don't need simple reassurances or sugar sweets to make us feel better. We're adults who want to understand God, to lean into him for understanding and provision. Our desire to grow in our faith is what makes us seek his will. With understanding, we grow closer to our Lord."

I waved a hand in the air, hearing all of this before. "But why not simply speak and tell us what to do? Why not make it easy on us, especially those who truly want to live for Christ? Why make everything so difficult?"

Paul spread his hands wide. "What's the fun in that? Life is to be lived, not conquered."

I shook my head, not understanding and not wishing to hear pat responses that held little meaning. "Why?" I pleaded, needing to know what God was up to.

Ma smiled a sad, somber smile, and I saw her lips tremble as her eyes darkened. "That's not how the Lord does things.

He stretches his children, teaching them lessons that grow their faith. That grow *our* faith."

I exhaled slowly and leaned my elbows on my knees, still staring at them. "I don't like how he does things. He makes life too demanding." My mind darted back to the bleak years during the war when Ma and I barely survived. Then Pa died, and now we didn't know which way to turn.

But then new images of Paul's arrival and finding the dead outlaw on the trail shoved the dismal times aside, reminding me that God was with us.

Paul chuckled now. "You said it, John. Life is far too difficult, especially without Jesus. It is easy to get beaten down." He paused and his eyes seemed to glisten as he continued, his gaze lifting to an unseen point above me.

"But with Jesus," he whispered, not really speaking to me anymore. "Life is a journey that tests us, grows us, shapes us. The adventure doesn't end until we're dead. Every day brings new challenges, and new lessons, new blessings."

Ma drew in a deep breath, and I saw her eyes glistened too. "We need Christ. No matter where our faith is, we need him. His help, his guidance, and his love."

"New mercies each day," Paul agreed softly.

"But I prayed," I confessed with a quivering voice. My lungs hurt and I could feel the strain working in my chest. "I prayed in the barn that I wanted to submit to him, to allow his hand to work in our problems. But I feel he has already turned away again."

"Or have you?" Ma's challenge made my head snap.

"Don't I need only the faith of a mustard seed?" I lifted my chin, my hands gripping my knees as I straightened in my chair. "The burden is on God to do something, right? I need only to pray, to tell him what is on my heart."

"You need to be faithful," Ma countered. "God already knows your heart. And he doesn't just give things to petulant children who demand good things. He is a perfect Father, giving when he determines the merit of such a gift. He wants rather to shape your beliefs and to teach you how to be more like his Son Jesus—caring, forgiving, faithful, merciful, obedient, a servant. Jesus died for our sins, so we can know God fully, without our sins getting in the way of a healthy relationship."

The room stilled as Ma's words faltered, and I felt we'd talked it out. But I felt no better. I knew God wanted to grow my faith, to mature me, but why did it have to be so hard?

Air whistled through my teeth as I filled my lungs, my gaze softening as I studied my companions. "I just want to be a good man. I'm in charge of this ranch now, and I don't want to fail."

"Then pray again," Paul suggested. "Like I said, God already knows your heart. But pray relentlessly. Show the Lord your determination and diligence. You cannot work hard enough to impress God, but he loves to see his children's commitment."

I frowned but said nothing more. Perhaps they were right.

Ma leaned forward again and closed her eyes. Paul grinned at me and then closed his eyes while I watched them connect with the Creator.

Ma whispered her prayers, her voice rising and falling as she praised God and asked for his hand to guide us through whatever the Lord had for us. She also prayed Jesus would guide my own faith journey and develop me into the man of God he desired. Paul prayed for strength and integrity while we waited on the Lord's direction, his intimate and eloquent petitions making me marvel at his deep relationship with God. He couldn't read, yet he used unfamiliar words I remembered from the Bible, and he quoted Scripture he obviously had memorized, reciting passages he'd heard while crouching below the church window during services.

The room grew quiet as they finished, both waiting on me to take up the thread of prayers and pour out my heart to the Lord. But I bit my tongue, still resistant to openly share my frustration and my hopes. If he could read my heart, he knew what I was thinking.

Silently, I promised to spend more time with Jesus, revealing everything that troubled me and asking for his help, but I worried at being a negative Nancy in front of these two faithful servants.

Finally, Paul sighed, signaling the end of the prayer time. He slapped his hands on the table and smiled. "I am renewed," he exclaimed as he rose to his feet. "I feel his peace course through my veins like rainwater on crops." With a nod at Ma, he pushed through the door and onto the back stoop. With a sheepish nod to Ma, I followed.

We spent a quiet afternoon completing our chores, Paul striding taller in Red Bill's boots. Yet anxiety rode me like a tick on a cow's ear. Our taxes would be paid, but what then? What did the Lord have in store for us now? Had we surmounted one obstacle only to be faced with the next?

Part of me—a big part—wanted to accuse God of never-ending challenges ahead for us. We were used to tough times, but was this to be our lot?

That night, I prayed again, alone in my room. My prayers flowed like prairie fire roaring across the plains, leaping one over another as each concern sprawled before the Lord. I felt full of dread and worry as I lay in bed and clasped my hands behind my head, staring pensively up at the unseen ceiling in the darkness.

"All right, here's the truth. I read that when John the Baptist was in prison, he sent word to Jesus and asked if he was the one they'd waited for or should they look for another. Jesus replied to John that he should see what Christ had done. The blind see and the lame walk, lepers are cleansed, and the poor hear good news."

I paused and licked my lips. "Well, Lord, what I'm saying is, I want to see you do things. Bringing Paul was a good beginning, and finding Red Bill certainly helped, but what now? Paul and Ma think we're on a grand adventure, but I'm not so sure. My doubts drag at me like stones, and I want to believe, but I'm overwhelmed with worry."

I paused again, not wanting to test God but desperately wanting to know he was with us. I'd been alone with Ma for too long and we'd suffered. Although I sensed something happening on the ranch, I wanted the Lord to know exactly where I stood.

"I love you," I breathed, my chest tightening. "I love you so much, but I need your help. Grow my faith."

Eventually, exhausted and spent, I tried to sleep. Yet I tossed uneasily in my blankets, realizing I lacked the satisfaction Paul shared at lunch. His renewed energy and faith did not extend to me, and I still felt frightened. In the morning, I rose bleary-eyed to face a new day.

Having far too many tasks around the ranch, I felt relieved when Paul volunteered to accompany Ma to town. I stewed and muttered my complaints to God as I went about my chores, demanding results and wondering when things would get better. The pitchfork stilled in my hands when I heard the wagon's return. Watching from the shadows within the barn, I thought Ma nearly leaped from the high seat when Paul slowed before the house, her skirts swishing as she stormed inside.

Leaning the fork against a stall, I helped Paul unhitch the winded team. He scowled a great deal but didn't say anything for a while, his lips pressed into a tight line. Vindication bubbled within me, and I just knew I'd been right to question our short-lived victory. Surely, more calamity had come upon us. I shivered with anticipation when Paul lifted his eyes over the horse's back where he curried the animal.

"Mr. Anderson at the general store wants his money. He says the Garret family owes him a good deal."

My own curry brush stilled as I worked on the other horse. Justification flooded over me, and I nodded, knowing only struggles loomed on the horizon for the Garrets. I quirked an eyebrow when I considered Paul. Surely the Lord had brought him here, but for what? To help or to witness our demise? Taxes were paid, but would we have done better to save that money and gone elsewhere? Perhaps Ma was premature in paying our debt to the county when that reward money might've given us a solid road stake.

I met Paul's gaze and nodded again, not knowing what to say. But he stared at me, an expectant expression on his features.

"Well?"

I straightened at his question and shrugged. "Well, what?"

He narrowed his eyes. "Well, what're you going to do about it?"

I felt my eyes widen. "Me?"

Paul dropped behind the horse once more, his hand moving swiftly over the horse's side. "Yes, you, John Garret. You said yourself the ranch is your responsibility. The Lord has asked you to lead, now lead."

I laughed at his reproving remark, but he didn't lift his head again or say anything as he continued to brush the horse. Something niggled at me, and I hated the way his words made me think. Pa wasn't coming home, and I wanted folks to think of me as the man of the place. But what kind of man doesn't take charge or take responsibility for the difficulties his family faces?

I heard Paul finish his work and move away from the stalls, yet I lingered, not wanting to speak with him. My brief feeling of vindication had turned to ash in my mouth as I realized we were in yet another fix and I should do something about it.

"I knew this was going to happen," I crowed aloud in the silent barn after Paul left, blaming the Lord. "Everything is against us and where are you? Nowhere to be found," I grumbled as I completed my task and set the brush on the shelf.

Slapping the horse on the rump, I reached for the pitchfork and started forking hay to the horses. "What can I do?" My gaze scanned the empty barn, searching for solutions, yet I felt so alone.

"I am a man, but what can I do when you've pitted life against us?" I demanded, pleading with God, but not truly expecting a response.

My thoughts wandered to when Pa and the hands went away to war, the bitter winters and blistering hot summers when Ma and I struggled to keep things together on the rundown ranch, barely eking out a living. And now I was to fix things? Alone?

Again, something niggled the edges of my mind, making me wonder if I were truly alone. "Then where are you?" My voice rose, demanding an answer.

My loud words scattered the frightened chickens, and I scowled in the shadows, worry plaguing me all the more. "I want to help Ma, and she believes you brought Paul, but what now? I'm no leader."

I speared the pitchfork into the hay pile and threw grain into a bucket. The chickens scattered again, feathers flying as I tossed the grain across the barn floor, pelting them absently.

"I know you want something from me, but what?"

No answer came to me, no lightning streaks from heaven or peals of thunder that prompted enlightenment. What did God want me to do?

Dismayed, I dropped the empty bucket and stalked to the kitchen, wanting to hear Ma's take on her trip to town. The taxes were paid, and we were poor once again, debts piling at Anderson's store. And wouldn't we have to pay the taxes again next year? How was that going to happen?

The door slammed behind me, louder than I intended. I hesitated, looking at Ma where she stood beside the sink, washing dishes.

"Sorry," I mumbled. I pulled a chair from the table and dropped into the seat. Stretching my worn boots before me, I studied them, wondering how long they might last. I'd traded fresh vegetables with Mr. Anderson only a year ago for these boots, but already my toes touched the tips.

"I got supplies while I was in town," Ma said abruptly, breaking into my thoughts. "Mr. Anderson wants us to pay some of what we owe him. He's been mighty nice to us, Johnny, giving us credit and allowing us to trade for goods."

I knew all this, so I also knew she was speaking aloud to herself, processing the storekeeper's requests. "What'd you tell him?"

She leaned against the sink, her gaze peering to the distant hills through the open window as she straightened her shoulders. "I told him to be patient just a little longer. I told him God was doing a great work on our place, and we'd pay him soon enough."

I just stared, wondering if the strain had finally made her snap. "What'd he say to that?"

Ma shrugged, still not meeting my gaze. "He said all right." I could imagine Mr. Anderson giving Ma a courteous nod, always one to give the benefit of a doubt. But did he worry like me? Did he wonder where the money would come from?

CHAPTER 11

In the past, merchants at Galveston on the coast had purchased cattle, providing leather for the tanners and tallow for candles. But those unreliable markets had dried up years ago, and now, our range seemed overrun with cattle. Yet I felt a sense of anticipation swell within me, building like a storm on the horizon. Something told me to work our cattle, slap our brand on as many head of stock I could, and be ready. Ready for what? Had Ma's faith challenged me to tag along? Despite my resolve that the Lord was not with us, something made me hope I was wrong.

Ma had paid the back taxes, and we were committed to our ranch for at least a while longer. However, as my faith struggled to develop, I wasn't sure she'd made the right decision. Yet here we were, and for better or worse, the cattle remained ours. I would continue branding mavericks.

Perhaps the time had come to give in, see what God would do when we released control and quit getting in his way.

I rode the prairie daily, searching for cattle to brand or to clean water holes or to shoot wolves. Although there was no real market for cattle locally, they were our cattle, and I treasured ownership of them. Besides, our brand did seem to protect our cows from the Comanche taking them for food.

Every day, I practiced with the guns too. I shot at every rabbit, coyote, and prairie wolf I saw. I wasn't bad with the rifle where I could steady my aim with two hands, but the handgun was another matter. The pistol seemed easy to just point and shoot, though it took a while to perfect my accuracy.

I tugged that old pistol from the backward holster, sitting right handy for a man astride a horse. Designed for the cavalry, the pistol grips pointed forward, ready to grab quickly, and I had to admit I fancied Red Bill's gun.

My gaze roamed our spread while I rested beneath a cottonwood tree, my horse swishing its tail at flies while I held the handgun. Lifting the gun, I aimed at various targets, pretending to draw a bead. Shoving the heavy pistol back in the holster, I leaned my forearms on the pommel and pondered.

Paul accomplished a sight of work around the house and barn while I looked after our stock. It took no great shakes to see he was a better carpenter, roofer, and blacksmith than me. He fixed many things that'd fallen apart from disuse or needing repair. The ranch house and buildings were looking better than ever as autumn approached, yet I felt more uneasy as time passed. We still hadn't paid Mr. Anderson.

The four months Paul had been with us had flown by, his eagerness to serve and to learn encouraged me to do the same. He took to reading like a duck to water, and our Bible lessons had done a lot to teach me about God's faithfulness and his desire to grow his people. Yet famous men like Abraham, Job, and David showed me life could be cruel. Still, the Lord worked, stretching a person's faith and preparing them.

Those faithful men of God inspired me, making me want to be more than I am. But what was the Lord preparing me for? Could God use me as he'd used others before me? Could I relinquish control and allow myself to *believe*, hope in God's goodness even when staring despair in the face?

I wanted to, I really did. But my worries made me pause, and I scanned our land for more mavericks, searching for another cow to brand.

I sighed, realizing sometimes, it felt easier to just keep moving rather than wait on the Lord. Yet I felt he was working on me, challenging my way of thinking.

That night during supper, I peered over my second cup of coffee and watched as Paul squirmed on his seat, not meeting my curious gaze. I glanced at Ma and could tell by the concerned look on her face she'd seen his unease too. Something bothered the usually never flummoxed Paul.

"Paul, what's on your mind?" Ma cleared dishes before bringing the coffeepot back to the table. I watched steam rise as she filled his cup. He wrapped his hands around the mug and frowned before he spoke.

"Miss Annie, John, when I first came here, you two were mighty nice to me, and I have begun believing this is my home."

"It is your home, Paul," Ma said, gripping his shoulder before returning the blackened pot to the stove. "For as long as you want, this is your home. You are a godly man and a hard worker and our friend." She sat down again as silence settled around us, but Paul shifted, and I knew he wasn't through.

"Thank you kindly, Miss Annie. You and John have become very important to me too." He paused and took a sip of his too hot coffee, scowling as he burned his tongue. "I'm grateful for all you've done for me, and I considered just being happy here with the two of you, but I know that's not right. I made a promise to someone special, a girl on our farm I promised I'd return for if I ever found a better place. I believe the Lord has led me to one," he finished, eyes wide as he waited for our response.

I felt my own eyes widen. "You have a girlfriend?" I glanced at Ma, but she only smiled.

"We have plenty of room," she said casually, as if discussing the weather. Astonished, I stared again at Paul, stunned to learn this fascinating information.

"I promised to come back for her if I ever settled," Paul explained.

Ma nodded, not saying anything more, but I admired Paul's openness. A girl? Paul had a girl?

There weren't any unmarried girls my age around, not even in town. Except for the nearby Indians, women folks were scarce in Texas and married young on the prairie. I had nothing to offer a girl. Although our ranch had become more mine than I wished, we still had no money or nice things that might entice a girl to join our failing ranch. Still, the idea of a girl intrigued me.

"When will you go for her?"

Ma's question startled me, reminding me that some kind of action was required to bring the girl here. I looked at Paul, studying him like a newly discovered creature.

"Me and Lydia planned to jump the broom over a year ago, but I knew the war was ending. We heard the folks discussing war news often, and I wanted to wait and marry free. Then I left the farm. She wanted me to stay, but I couldn't. I just had to leave. Now I feel settled, and I want to fetch her here." His eyebrows arched when he recalled some additional information he'd obviously rehearsed. "She's a hard worker and will do all the cooking and cleaning and laundry. She'll not be a burden in any way."

Ma laughed at his recommendation. "You don't have to convince us. She's welcome here, Paul."

Yet he tensed and then slumped and then straightened in his seat, never allowing his gaze to meet ours as he restlessly scanned the walls and the ceiling, as if he wanted to say more but couldn't find the words.

Ma smiled one of her warmest smiles. "Paul, you are free to do what you want. You can bring Lydia here, if you choose, whatever you want to do." She sipped her coffee again and glanced at me before she went on. "It is not good for man to be alone," Ma quoted, and I wondered who that tidbit was for.

Paul exhaled slowly, letting her words sink in.

Ma added, "It will be very cold soon enough. If you want to fetch her before winter, you'll have to think on going soon."

"I'll leave in a day or two," Paul said with a faraway look.

"Is she a believer, Paul?" Ma wanted to know. With her questions about Paul's girl, I thought of Hannah, not sure why.

"Lydia taught me about Jesus." I smiled at the note of pride in his voice.

Ma gave him her blessing, and the matter seemed settled. Later that night, Paul told me he and Lydia had been house slaves together and so were expected to speak and dress better than the field hands. But if help was needed outside, Paul had been expected to work hard anywhere.

Two days later, Paul shook my hand as he waited on the back stoop for the pack Ma filled. Still dark, only a dim gray tinged the eastern horizon as dawn prepared to bloom.

"John, you folks had no cause to take a broken down, starving scarecrow like me in but you did, and I'll never forget. You've been mighty kind to me, and I aim to return and make my home here forever." His earnestness touched me, yet I sensed an anxiety too.

"You're a good man, Paul. We appreciate you." I tried to allay his fears, but he shifted, glanced to the dimming stars overhead, and looked at me again. I didn't quite understand his point.

He studied me in the low lantern light drifting from the kitchen. Then his gaze drifted over the ranch yard to where the sun would rise in the next hour or so. He turned back to me. "It's not easy for an ex-slave to travel in Texas. If something should happen to me and I don't return, I want you to know I'm grateful for what you've done. Thanks, John."

Ma stepped through the door and thrust the pack into his hands. "You're one of us. We need you to continue this adventure we're on." She shot me a curious look and I squinted in the darkness, trying to decipher her glance. Did I read disappointment in her eyes?

"You be careful now," she added.

He tried to smile, but his fear remained. Then he walked out of the yard, his figure vanishing in the morning gloom.

Ma returned to the kitchen while I remained on the back stoop, straining to catch a sound of his going. I know Ma didn't think it much to feed a starving man, but Paul surely did, and I felt proud Ma was my mother. Yet the adventure she mentioned seemed a private affair between the two of them, as if I were not included. Had my lack of faith excluded me from spiritual insights and situations? And how could their adventure continue with Paul gone?

I took a deep breath, feeling the welcome chill in the morning air. Far from winter, the mornings had grown cold of late, and much appreciated after the searing heat of summer. I filled the wood box beside the stove before eating a quick breakfast and hurrying to the barn. With Paul gone,

I would have to return earlier than I liked to help Ma with outside chores.

I fed the stock and gathered eggs before saddling a horse. Leading the gelding to the hitching rail, I walked into the kitchen for a final cup of coffee before hitting the trail, the wide range demanding my attention if we were to ever grow our herd.

Paul would be sorely missed, and I started thinking. If the Lord wanted to do amazing things here, he would have to step up his game.

I paused on the back stoop to wash up, the rusty pump creaking in the still morning light as water gushed over my dirty hands. I watched for the sun, hovering just out of sight below the horizon. A sunrise always tugged at my heart strings, making me see God's creativity and provision. But I balked this morning, knowing with Paul gone, I could grumble more easily about the hard work that awaited me.

"I can't stop from praising you, Lord, when I see the morning sun. A new day dawns, clean and bright, as if there's a chance for good things. But you've laid a heavy load on Ma and me. Do what you will. I love you, although sometimes I feel you could think of us a little more. You know we still owe money at the store."

The Lord brought Paul at a crucial time and the former slave fit in nicely here. Now we still needed help to run the ranch. Would God provide? How much longer could we stay here if we didn't figure out a way to make an income?

The sky had turned a vivid pink where clouds bunched in the east, capturing the early rays of the rising sun. My breath caught as I glimpsed the last star of night wink from view as the sun topped the hills, casting light across the rutted barnyard. I gripped the kitchen door and stared, a feeling of freshness and possibility welling within me. A sense of expectancy surprised me as I tugged the door open, not wanting to expect too much from God. What if he didn't meet our needs?

Unlike Paul and Ma, I hated to be disappointed day after day, waiting on things that never happened. They called it patience, I called it neglect.

"You'll ride the range?" Ma's question caught me unprepared. Of course, she knew I had to take care of the ranch, but with Paul gone, she'd be alone at home. Did she feel safe?

"Is that all right? I can stay close to home, if need be," I replied hastily, wanting to relieve any fears.

"Don't you worry. I'm not afraid." Ma hummed as she worked over the stove, reminding me of long-ago times. She used to be so full of life and excited about every little thing I discovered on the prairie. I'd bring home bird's nests and wildflowers and unique stones. She'd beam at me and share my interest, making me feel I could do anything. Everything I touched fascinated her. But these last few years, I'd watched her worn down with weariness and strain. Her humming today made me think.

"Are *you* all right?" Worry niggled at me, and I wondered if she'd expected too much again, pushing God to provide something he didn't want to. I hated to see her struggle with the disappointment that weighed me down.

She smiled. "I'm fine." Perhaps she sensed my doubts, for her smile widened. "Johnny, I'm fine, really. The Lord is with us." I felt my face pinch and her smile lurched. "You don't think so?"

Her query made me scowl even more and I shifted. "Well, we're not making money, and Mr. Anderson still needs to be paid. He won't extend credit forever."

She shook her head as she reached for a mug, filling the cup with coffee before handing it to me. "He brought Paul and the dead outlaw you found on the trail. I feel God is working with us, providing as we need."

I scoffed as I accepted the steaming mug. "Maybe God should work faster. I mean, how do you figure to pay our way? We couldn't even push cattle to Galveston without a dozen hands, even if the merchants were still buying hides and tallow. What do you think we can do to make money?"

I sipped the hot drink while I watched her over the rim of the cup. She shook her head again and I hated the feeling of vindication that filled me. I didn't want to win arguments, I just wanted to find a way to make money.

"Have faith, Son. I feel God is working. Be patient and let him work."

"Patience?" I took another sip as she nodded, eyes bright with an excitement I didn't share. "Ma, I'm praying all the time. I pray and nothing happens. We can't live here without money, and you know it."

This time her smile seemed strained, as if my misgivings irked her somehow. Then she blinked and the tension left her features as she drew a deep breath. "Have faith. Everything will work out in the end."

I ground my teeth and handed the empty cup to her. Faith? Faith didn't pay the bills, and I was growing desperate for help. Who knew how long Paul would be gone, and we needed more help than I could even imagine. The ranch, house, bills, and even Ma was beginning to make me worry.

The door closed softly behind me as I stepped once more onto the stoop and eyed the risen sun. "I do have faith," I muttered as I stepped from the stoop and reached for the gelding's reins.

I hesitated, convicted and chastised by Ma's belief God would do *something* in his timing. Ashamed, I stepped into the saddle, wishing I didn't believe my timing felt more important.

CHAPTER 12

The day passed slowly, and I became acutely aware how much I had come to enjoy Paul's company around the place. He always had an encouraging word for me and was quick to help in any situation.

Regardless of Paul's absence, something else made me stay close to home. I circled, keeping one eye on the old house as I scouted for mavericks and repaired watering holes, never straying more than a couple of miles from the ranch.

Weeks of pouring over Scripture with Paul had sharpened my biblical memories and I mulled over various passages, pondering faithfulness and prayer and blessings. Sadly, I found myself delinquent when it came to diligence and hope. To hope in the unseen, to wait and be patient, and to persevere, these virtues about drove me mad as I wanted action—now. Why wouldn't God work a miracle?

As I contemplated my own shortcomings, I considered the faithful ways of Ma and Paul. Even though I might be found lacking, surely these two godly servants deserved the Lord's intervention.

My thoughts returned to Paul and our spiritual conversations. Although I'd been teaching him to read, he'd been teaching me to dive deeper into the Bible, to search for truth, meaning, and righteous guidance. Jesus came alive to me in the Gospels. I realized I enjoyed learning and deepening my knowledge. Paul had become a good friend, and I didn't take him for granted, hoping he'd return soon.

That evening, a gentle breeze blew from the west, a welcome relief to a warm afternoon. I watched the sunset while scattering grain to the chickens, the sky a light blue where the sun dipped behind the western hills.

As I turned to enter the barn, the distant report of a gunshot drifted on the evening wind. I paused, straining to hear another. Or had I heard one at all? Not sure, I continued into the barn and replaced the feeding pail on a shelf before checking the horses once more, listening to them chew hay as their tails swished restlessly in the gloomy barn.

Tired yet pleased with the day's work, I strode to the house, looking ahead to supper. My boot thumped on the stoop just as another shot drifted to my ears, distant and faint. I paused, one hand on the door, waiting, but no more sound came to me. Shaking my head, I entered the dimly lit kitchen, a candle glowing on the table where Ma placed dishes.

We ate mostly in silence, my hunger not allowing for casual table talk. After supper, I helped Ma clear the table. She washed while I dried, putting the few plates away in the orderly fashion Ma liked. She lit another candle as we sat to play cards. Tallow candles were much cheaper than lamp oil.

Card games were a pleasant diversion after Paul's unending checker games, and I sat back with my third cup of coffee, tired yet relaxed, recalling similar evenings with Ma during the war.

"The hay needs cutting," she remarked while shuffling the deck.

"I'll help Paul when he returns." I took another sip, my gaze on the sliding cards Ma held.

"Winter's coming," she warned, and I grinned, knowing she wanted me to start soon.

"I'll ride west tomorrow and check that pasture near the creek." I narrowed my eyes, remembering. "Thought I heard a shot earlier, over west of here."

She glanced up, the cards stilling in her hands. I tried to smile when I read the fear in her eyes. "Probably nothing," I soothed. "Hunters likely." But like her, I knew our nearest neighbors, the small band of Comanche Hannah belonged to, lived over thataway.

She dealt seven cards to each of us and placed the deck between us. "There's a shingle lifting along the edge of the roof."

I nodded, studying my cards. "I'll take a look."

She frowned when she studied her own hand. "Ranch work never ends."

"I know that," I replied tersely. Why'd she say that? Was she not pleased with my work? I eyed her while pretending to check my cards. "Something on your mind?"

She shifted, the chair creaking. "I know better than most how lonely ranch life can be. I just want you to consider all options before you settle in here forever. I never want you to feel stuck."

I stared at her. This was our land and my home. Even if we couldn't pay the taxes next year, I would still find a piece of land to ranch. Moving north and finding work in the urban factories seemed foolish now. Running cattle was all I knew. Confused even more, I tilted my head. "What are you getting at?"

Ma shrugged. "Just a lonely life, that's all. A man will need a wife, lots of children to help with the work. You'll be having to think on such things now that the ranch is yours."

You could've knocked me over with a twig. I squinted, my chest tightening as her words sunk in. "Ma, I thought we were discussing cutting hay and fixing the roof. How did we jump to a wife and kids?"

Ma mumbled something from behind her cards, her face hidden. I scowled, my relaxed feelings vanishing with the sudden inquisition.

"Well," she continued, lowering her cards to peer at me over them. "Your pa and I married at about your age. He was nineteen and I was seventeen. My parents were all for it, eager to get me out of their house. One less mouth to feed. Your pa had no parents. You were born less than a year later." She glanced at her cards. "Any sevens?"

"Go fish." I shifted uneasily, glancing covertly at her from behind my cards. We never talked like this before, always sticking to ranch business and future goals. It felt strange to hear her discuss my life as if I were a man, able to make my own decision. My scowl deepened as I felt caught somewhere between a boy and an adult. Now, suddenly, I felt on the hot seat. "Any threes?"

"Go fish." Silence hung, and I wondered if she were finished with her interrogation when she cleared her throat. "You're not a boy anymore. This ranch will be all yours one day, and you'll need a family. Hannah Tall Basket is pretty and close to your age. Do you have any jacks?"

I choked at her not-so-subtle attack. "She's an Indian," I sputtered in protest. "Besides, she doesn't like me." I held my cards high, hiding my guilt. Did Ma guess my thoughts about Hannah? I'd thought too much lately about our recent encounter on the trail. She'd grown up since I'd seen her last.

"We've known her and her family for years. Your pa always said she was bright, raised by a loving and kind man. Her pa was chief of that band and sent her to the mission to be educated. He acted honorably with us. Why do you think she doesn't like you?"

I shifted again, growing increasingly uncomfortable.

"Did I ask you for jacks?" Her repeat question allowed me time to collect my thoughts.

I handed her my jack and stifled a yawn. "I'm tired. It's been a long day." I folded my cards and tossed them on the table. My chair scraped as I pushed away from the table, stretching to emphasize my fatigue. "Goodnight, Ma." I pretended not to notice the smirk on her face as I shuffled to my bedroom.

"Goodnight, Son. I love you. Sleep well."

Undressing in the dark, I worried over the strange conversation. How could Ma know what I felt for Hannah? I'd never said a thing to her. Hannah had always been my friend, and now she'd become something more. Her grown-up beauty had caused me to think of her more than I should.

I crawled into bed and clasped my hands behind my head, staring at the unseen ceiling. What did God have in store for my future? Was there to be a girl for me, a family? Perhaps it was time to start going to the church socials or dances. Yet I couldn't get Hannah out of my mind.

Rolling over, I punched my pillow as I pushed the nagging thoughts away. That fence by the bunkhouse needed a new board. Winter would be here soon, the hay needed cutting, and there was the shingle Ma pointed out. Would the store let us continue adding to our tab? My head swam with ranch demands.

Concerns swirling, I began to drift off to sleep.

The whinny of a horse outside my window brought me full awake. How long had I slept? My stomach clenched and I knew something was wrong.

CHAPTER 13

Tense, taut like a whipcord, I strained my ears into the night. Nothing. My shoulders relaxed and I felt my eyes squeeze closed, my body drifting off to sleep once more when I heard the horse again. Hooves stamped the hard-packed yard as the horse whinnied again softly.

Throwing back the covers, I slipped into pants and shucked the Colt from its holster before easing the door open and padding quietly across the kitchen to join Ma where she stood peering out the window over the sink.

"It looks like a saddled horse," she whispered. "Be careful, Johnny. It might be a trick to draw you from the house." She was thinking like me, and I felt better when I noticed she held the shotgun. I always worried that someone who'd lost everything in the war would try and take what was ours.

Fading back down the short hallway, I crossed the living room and slowly opened the front door. Glancing all around, I eased myself out the door, deep shadows concealing me.

The horse blew again, weariness evident in its stiff-legged stance and hung head. Stepping cautiously from the porch, I grasped the gelding's reins while scanning the yard for invaders, my blood chilling in my veins. Were Indians or a veteran of the war, beaten and desperate, watching me?

The gelding nuzzled my arm, looking for food. I balked when I noticed the military saddle, a blanket rolled neatly behind the cantle.

With no fight left in him, the horse allowed me to lead him to the barn where I unsaddled him by candlelight and rubbed him down while he devoured some hay. The lathered sides of the horse indicated hard riding, but how far had he come?

Working in the dim light, I listened to the night. In a nearby stall, a horse swished a tail while the milk cow lowed inquisitively, wondering if I'd come early for milking.

Returning to the house, Ma glanced at the heavy Colt thrust into my waistband but said nothing. Maybe she felt better having an armed man on the place. She chewed her lip as she pulled her worn and faded robe around her shoulders.

"Get dressed," she ordered as I swept dirt from my bare feet. "I'll put coffee on. It'll be dawn soon."

It didn't take me long to dress and I swung the cavalry belt around my waist as I walked back into the kitchen, the pistol riding backward on my left side. The lantern glowed dimly on the table, revealing Ma at the stove, still in her nightclothes.

"That horse came from nearby, Johnny. I remembered you said you heard shots last evening."

I nodded, recalling the dull report of distant gunfire. Was someone hurt? Were they signal shots, calling for help, or the sounds of battle?

"The gelding wore a military saddle," I blurted. "With a blue blanket."

Ma's back stiffened as her head lifted. "Could be returning soldiers with Yankee gear."

"Or Yankees," I said with scorn heavy in my words. Right or wrong, we were Texans, and Pa had died in the war. Yankees would not be welcome around here.

I watched as she nodded. "Still, the Lord would have us do the right thing. Ride his back trail and discover what you can."

A frown settled over me, not liking her response. "But Pa—"

"Pa would have us do the right thing," she snapped, not brooking any opposition. "Go saddle your horse."

Slowly I stood, feeling as if Ma needed time alone. I surely didn't need to saddle my horse while she finished breakfast preparations. Yet I made my way to the barn, checking on the new addition before throwing a saddle on my gelding.

A sudden thought flashed across my mind, and I wondered at the second stray horse to come to me in the night. Red Bill's horse had led to an interesting situation, and my hands quickened with the tack as I pondered at any possible significance with a second stray horse.

Not even a dull glow appeared in the east, yet I felt wide awake. The mystery of the unfamiliar horse's arrival made me curious, and I eagerly wanted to head up the trail and learn what I might.

Tying my horse to the hitch, I turned to find Ma at my elbow, a steaming mug in one hand and a towel covered bundle in the other. Startled, I stared as she thrust the parcel into my hands. "Drink this and get going. Let me know what you find."

Without waiting for word from me, she walked back to the kitchen, the lamp dimming as she trimmed the wick. The kitchen plunged into darkness.

A star hung low in the sky, and I choked my coffee in the pale glow of the heavenly body. My insides warmed, I stepped into the saddle and rode from the yard, eating a biscuit as I went. I paused to glance back after topping a low rise on the trail north. Only the lone star gave light, dully illuminating the empty yard and outlining the darker shadows around the house and barn with no sign of Ma.

Sometimes, I feel Ma is so tough, like old shoe leather. Her faith makes her tough too, allowing her something to cling to, something to hope for. But other times, like now, I know she remembers the tough days and misses Pa.

Gratefully, she'd have the canning to keep her busy today, maybe keep her out of her head. For the hundredth time, I wished Paul were still here to help bring all the crop in from the garden. With our ever-increasing debt at Anderson's, we'd planted even more potatoes last spring, along with more wheat and corn. The preserved vegetable stores would be greatly appreciated this winter.

A faint glow in the east allowed me to pick up my pace, and I nudged the gelding into a trot. An unexpected chill filled the air and I wondered if we'd have early winter, making me worry anew about cutting hay.

As the sun rose, I rode uneasy in the early morning light. The back trail of the unknown horse wasn't hard to follow. A bird whistled from the thickets, and I squinted at the noise maker, wondering if Indians lurked behind every bush.

When I passed the place where I'd found Red Bill Jenkins, I slowed, peering all around. My hand gripped the pistol butt near my hip, and I felt better as I loosened the gun in the holster. This time I was armed, ready for anything. Or so I told myself.

I halted after another mile to drink from my canteen, recalling the last stray horse that wandered into our yard and the dead outlaw that netted us the unexpected reward money. God sure worked in funny ways.

I glanced at the hoof tracks in the dust before letting my gaze drift far ahead. With Pa gone, there was no one else to trail the lost horse, and that rankled me. I liked being the man of the place, but I lacked experience. Surely other boys had lost their fathers in war, but my deficits haunted me, filling me with apprehension.

A rabbit leaped into the trail and zigzagged away from my startled horse before darting into a bush. When I passed the thicket, I slowed, leaning from the saddle to locate the rabbit's den in the deeper shadows of the undergrowth. Finding nothing, I nudged my horse on to the nearby ridge. As I topped the rise, I tugged on the reins, my eyes widening as I watched the Indians below, one snaking through the grass toward an old buffalo wallow.

That long-eared rabbit had surely saved my life, slowing me as it'd done. Or was that the Lord, knowing what awaited me farther along the trail?

Moving back down the trail, I slipped from my saddle and crawled forward to get a better view, my rifle pushed ahead of me across the turf, cutting a narrow path through the tall prairie grass. I wormed to the crest of the ridge and peered down into the little valley.

Three Indians were in sight, their bare, bronzed bodies barely glimpsed in the concealing grass. One lay motionless on his back, eyes staring at the blue sky. Another sprawled about forty yards from a distant buffalo wallow, not moving. A third brave crawled in broken drags toward a copse of trees. Was he wounded? I studied the green grove, shimmering willows indicating a seep. Were the Indians retreating?

I chewed my lip, wondering what I should do. The horse I'd discovered in my yard harkened to Red Bill's stray horse. Good things had come from that unexpected event. Was there something here for me to do, something God wanted me to do?

As I considered the layout below, a fourth brave leaped from the copse of trees and pulled his wounded comrade into the brush. A pair of gunshots whistled from the buffalo wallow, alerting the Indians their quarry still lived.

Who was he? Obviously, a tough man pinned down by a bunch of Comanche, his horse gone. The military saddle on his horse irked me, but I shook off the nagging sensation. Did he have water? Was he wounded? Now I knew those shots I'd heard last evening had come from this small battle playing out on the endless plains. How long had the man been stuck? The shot I'd heard had been hours ago. Whatever the answer might be, my heart went out to this brave man, and I knew what I had to do.

Returning to my horse, I mounted, holding the nervous horse in place as I checked my weapons. My gelding had heard those shots and knew something was happening just over this little rise. Shoving the rifle into the saddle sheath, I tugged my hat low as I drew my pistol and gripped the reins tighter. Facing the ridge, I pictured the layout on the other side and gritted my teeth, planning on how to ride to the buffalo wallow without getting myself killed.

"All right, boy," I whispered to my prancing horse. "Let's go."

CHAPTER 14

Coming over the ridge at a gallop, I prayed the sound of my horse's pounding hooves would be masked by the thick prairie grass. No such luck rode with me when I saw an Indian step from the copse of trees and lift a bow. With a shout, another Indian rose from the grass almost beneath me, a rifle coming to his shoulder as my gelding struck him, knocking him aside as we raced for the low mound around the hollow at the far end of the meadow.

The trapped rider within the buffalo wallow tried to cover my approach, and I ducked as gunshots filled the morning air. I heard another Indian whoop cut short with a hideous scream as one of the rider's shots hit true.

Sweat stung my eyes, but I ignored the bite as I looked at the trees where I suspected the main body of the attackers lurked. An arrow streaked past my head, and I ducked again, wondering where the missile had come from. Firing at the trees with blurred vision, I emptied my handgun as I sped through the grass to the slight rise where an arm extended, pistol firing at those around me. Ears ringing with war cries and gunfire, I leaned over my saddle as the gelding leaped the rise and thudded into the center of the buffalo wallow. Pulling the horse to a halt, the animal skidded on its haunches. I leaped from the saddle, only glancing at the arrow shaft that protruded from the rider's shoulder as I pulled my rifle from my saddle and threw myself onto the rim of the hollow.

Aiming along the barrel, I waited. Silence. I blinked the sweat from my eyes and gripped my rifle tighter, but nothing moved on the prairie, and it was as if my sudden dash into the valley had quieted the hullabaloo of a moment ago.

"Are you bad hit?" My query brought no response and I cringed, fearing the worst. If his final act was to cover my rescue attempt, I was in a lot of trouble. Trapped here with a dead man would not help my situation.

"Mister?" I tried again, not risking a glance over my shoulder lest the Indians rush our position.

"Water," he croaked from half a dozen yards away. Scowling, I hesitated only a moment before lunging to my feet. Securing my horse with a ground hitch, I retrieved my canteen and crouched as I ran to the wounded rider.

The arrows had stopped as quickly as they had started. As he drank, a breeze pushed gently at the tall buffalo grass, but nothing moved. Only a lone cloud kept us company.

An arrow had gone through his sweat-stained and faded blue shirt. I tried not to think of his uniform as he took the canteen and tilted his head, water spilling down his throat as he drank.

Bareheaded, his face covered in ragged beard, he smelled of blood, sweat, and horses. A scarf wound around his leg, blood staining the edges, and I noticed a discarded arrow on the ground some feet away. Another arrow quivered in his shoulder as he pulled on the canteen, his throat working as he chugged thirstily.

When he finished, he dragged the back of a hand across his mouth and scanned the silent prairie. "You got here just in time. I figure they were tired of waiting and were about to charge."

He dropped the canteen between us as he leaned on his side and took up his position once more on the grassy rim. "Lucky for me you showed up."

"Not luck." I chuckled grimly. "I felt the Lord lead me here." I wanted to laugh at my outlandish statement, the words dripping with Paul and Ma's backing.

He squinted as he studied me and then peered toward the trees. My abrupt remark made me wonder. Did I really believe God had brought me here? Surely the second stray horse in our yard had influenced my curiosity. I recalled praying as I rode down the hill, guns blasting away as I hoped the Lord would protect me. Suddenly, I felt pleased I'd remembered God as I thrust myself into danger. Was Ma and Paul's inspiration rubbing off?

Licking my lips, I blinked, watching the gently swaying grass as wind teased the prairie. "Your horse came to our ranch. I back trailed him this morning." I paused, awaiting a response. "Are you bad hit? I see the arrow and the leg wound. Any others?"

"No," he grumbled. "But they're enough. I can't walk, and this arrow needs to come out."

The rider opened the cylinder of his pistol and ejected spent cartridges. Pulling fresh bullets from his belt, he reloaded, never taking his eyes from the surrounding meadow. "I'm a dispatch rider, coming south from the Nation. These Comanche got an arrow in my leg first off. This one in my shoulder I can't pull out. I've lost blood."

I wanted to help him with his wounds, I surely did. But his Union uniform made me tense. Pa had died in the war. "Dispatch rider? Union Army?"

My comment must've made him consider, for he cleared his throat. "I fought for the South, but I needed work when the war ended. Figured I could ride a horse for the victorious blue devils, delivering dispatches from fort to fort."

I nodded, knowing how difficult it was to make ends meet. He didn't allow me to ponder further as he continued. "You're a mite young to be saving lone riders from the Comanche."

A sigh escaped me as I shrugged. "You're not the only one with tough stories." I didn't feel like elaborating, and he didn't push for an explanation. "What are we going to do with that arrow in you?"

He shifted, pistol still pointed at the trees. "I've been thinking on that. I want you to break the shaft and push the arrow on through."

I scrambled to my knees and crouched beside him. Then I recalled my pistol had been emptied on the field, and I drew the weapon free once more and quickly reloaded.

The rider struggled to his knees and my stomach turned when I grasped the arrow shaft protruding from his chest. Thank God the tip stuck from his back, the arrow going through the meaty muscle of his broad shoulder. I didn't see any red froth on his lips, so I figured the arrow had missed the lungs.

As I hesitated, he growled between clenched teeth. "Come on, break it."

It took both hands to snap the shaft. The rider gasped but didn't cry out. Using the bottom of my palm, I shoved the broken arrow through him, then braced a hand against his back as I tugged the other end, pulling the arrow free. A shudder ran through him, and he dropped his head. I feared he'd pass out, but then he looked up, his gaze darting to the silent prairie beyond. "Wrap the wound. Quick now, boy."

"I'm John Garret." Wrapping my scarf around the wound, I tied the ends beneath his arm and shucked my gun out once more. "I don't know what else to do, mister," I said as I took my position on the grassy rim again.

Nothing stirred on the meadow, not even a bird. That made me wonder if the Indians were still there, simply waiting for a better opportunity to renew their attack. Or were they waiting for us to die? Surely, they knew they'd wounded the dispatch rider and we were effectively pinned down. Perhaps if they waited long enough, we would not be able to escape.

When I voiced my concerns, the rider shook his head. "I don't think so. I got a couple of them before you came along. Now they think we're too strong. I think they might try another quick attack, or they'll pull out altogether."

"Well, your wounds need attention. Ma is handy with wounds. We need to get home where Ma can look after you."

He nodded. Sweat sheened on his brow, and I worried fever had already set in. He hadn't had water for a day when I arrived, and I knew he needed medical attention soon if he were to have any chance to survive.

"When your horse came into our yard, I knew I had to back trail him. That wasn't the first stray horse I've found in my yard." I don't know why I baited the hook, hinting about Red Bill's horse. Maybe I hoped he'd ask about the other stray that came to our place. He didn't ask me anything though, just stared out across the meadow, watching. But as I continued to peer at him occasionally from the corner of my eyes, I saw he dozed, his head jerking now and then as he struggled to stay alert.

"Get some rest, mister. I'll keep watch."

He pursed his lips and studied me before nodding. When he stretched out on the side of the grassy hollow, he retrieved his blue cavalry hat from where it'd tumbled and pulled it low as he relaxed. Almost immediately, his snores drifted to me.

Wounds on a ranch were fairly common, and I'd seen my mother treat more than one cowboy gored from a cow's horn or an axe cutting or a knife wound. I'd even seen the occasional bullet wound.

For no good reason, I picked up the arrow he'd pulled from his leg and studied the long shaft in the sunlight. The rider had been asleep for a couple of hours before I risked rising and shoving the arrow beneath my saddle blanket. Nothing stirred but a gentle breeze, and there hadn't been a sound from the distant copse of trees in a long while.

"Well, John Garret, what do you see?" He lay on the grass, hat pushed back as he watched me. Sweat beaded his pale face, and I knew he needed more help than I could give here.

Handing him the canteen again, I studied the prairie as he drank. "I don't see anything. Maybe they've pulled out." My suggestion sounded wistful, and he shook his head, struggling to brace himself on one arm as he shifted to a sitting position. He closed his eyes against the pain and paused, allowing the sharp discomfort to pass.

"I don't think so," he said after a long pause. "I got at least one of their friends, and they'll want my scalp. No, I think they're still out there, not sure what to do now you've joined the scuffle."

Crouching low, I moved around the perimeter of the buffalo wallow, checking the prairie from every angle. He'd chosen his position wisely and my respect grew for the tough dispatch rider in spite of the uniform he wore. No more than ten yards across from rim to rim, the hollow proved first-rate cover from the attacking Comanche while providing an excellent field of fire. Yet, worry rode heavy on me. I knew the rider was not doing well, and his wounds were taking a toll on his endurance. How much longer could he withstand before he succumbed to his injuries? I had to get him home where Ma could take a look at him.

My roving gaze halted on the dead Indian, the brave staring up at the blue sky. My stomach tightened as I thought of him giving his life in pursuit of taking another man's life. Could I kill a man who attacked me? I hoped I would not have to.

Retrieving the food Ma had packed, I scanned the silent plains as the rider ate and explained how he'd gotten here.

"After they got the arrow in my chest, I knew I couldn't stay in the saddle and out run them, so I looked for a spot to defend. But I was bleeding like a stuck pig and knew I'd fall from the saddle soon if I didn't take what offered. I slipped from my saddle and almost passed out when I tumbled to the grass here. Before I could get my bearings, my horse had vanished, still galloping down the trail."

I nodded as I squinted at the stand of trees near the luxuriant grass across the meadow. Did something move within the copse?

"Good thing you found my horse," he went on. "Guess the Lord's not done with me yet."

I glanced over my shoulder, surprised at his reference to God's intervention. Like the outlaw's body I found on the trail, was this part of Ma's grand adventure? I narrowed my eyes and peered out at the prairie again. For the hundredth time, I asked myself why God would care about us, a few believers stuck on the Texas plains. Although Ma and Paul surely had more faith than me, I wanted to believe, to see the hand of God working in our lives. But we'd suffered for so long, all alone while Pa was away at war. Could my skepticism be turned around?

"I didn't say my thanks for coming. I am now. I was in a bad fix. Still am, but at least I've been fed and watered and don't have any arrows in me." He grinned and the smile softened his rugged features. Judging by his ragged, faded clothes and his unkempt beard, he looked like he was used to doing with mighty little. Times were hard for everyone, I figured.

"You're welcome," I muttered, still trying to comprehend God's plan. "I wonder how you fit into Ma's notion." I stared at the rider, wondering, when his eyes widened, and he straightened.

"I've been praying," he whispered, eyes shining in the slanting, late afternoon sunlight. Had his fever worsened? "I've prayed about something new, something different," he went on, his words tumbling over one another as if he were excited. "I can tell you and your ma are Christian folk."

My jaw twitched and I felt my lips press into a tight line. What did this rider know of the Lord?

"I guess God is in control of all things. It's no accident my horse went to your house. No accident at all," he hurried on, a note of desperation in his voice that concerned me, and I thought again of his fever. I'd taken a peek at his wounds and the inflamed, angry skin around each puncture made me worry anew. I knew I needed to get him home as soon as I could.

"Well, John Garret, I think we should slip out of here when it gets real dark. The Indians seem bunched in those trees over yonder. With your horse, we should be able to head off into the prairie and then go 'round to meet the trail farther on."

His speech sounded flighty now, and I nodded, trying to conceal my anxiety about his worsening condition. With luck, we'd give the Comanche the slip and be home by dawn. Would the rider make it that long?

The man shifted his position, trying to make his hurt leg comfortable. I could see he was in considerable pain, but there was nothing to do about it. I also noticed he didn't complain.

The evening hours dragged by, and I saw no Indians. We were in a good position where no one could sneak up on us without being detected. Yet I feared the coming night, although I felt reluctant to share my worries with the wounded man. He seemed to have enough on his mind with his two arrow wounds.

A whippoorwill called plaintively, and I heard the movement of quail in the grass as the twilight deepened. Only a faint breeze stirred the grass, and I shivered, my gaze darting to the coat bunched behind my saddle, yet I knew I wasn't cold.

"We'll wait an hour and move out. You'll have to lead your horse, me not able to walk," he grumbled. He hung his head as he said this, and I could tell he did not like the idea of not being fit for travel or battle.

When stars twinkled overhead, I moved my horse beside the wounded rider, and he grunted as I wrestled him into the saddle. He didn't cry out as I pushed him into place, but his pale face shone brightly in the dim light.

"Ready?" I gathered the reins with one hand while I held my pistol with the other. If we bumped into opposition in the dark, I wanted to be prepared.

The saddle creaked as he settled himself, and I could see his white knuckles where he gripped the pommel. "Let's go," he breathed through clenched teeth.

CHAPTER 15

"Are you sure you can stay in the saddle?" My doubtful whisper made the wounded dispatch rider look up and, by the dim starlight, I read the pain in his sweat-covered face.

But he nodded as he made a gesture with one hand. "Keep going," he growled. "I'll stick."

We'd gone less than a mile when I took our first break. I'd pause occasionally and try to listen into the night, not hearing anything but the sounds I expected. A coyote howled on a distant hill, and I wondered if it were really a coyote. Were the Comanche after us? Even now, did they surround us, slowly moving in for the kill?

My eyes had grown accustomed to the dark and I couldn't see anything moving. Yet, could a Comanche be seen in the dark?

I gripped my pistol tighter and tugged on the reins, my gelding trailing me as I made a roundabout way to the yonder trail. If we could give the Indians the slip, I felt confident I could locate our house by dawn.

With infinite care, we circled far away from the buffalo wallow and the trail to home. Our first goal was to escape the Comanche.

Despite the chilled night air, warmth filled me as I walked, either from the constant exertion or the anxiety that nagged at me. I stopped constantly to listen for pursuit and prayed for the wounded man to keep his seat in the saddle.

It took us a few hours to come around again to the trail. Sometimes, I halted and checked on the wounded man. Teeth clenched and eyes feverish, he stared at me each time I looked at him, a hint of defiance or courage etched in his features. I could only guess how much the pain of his wounds tormented him.

The moon had risen, making things appear easier to see while making the shadows even deeper and darker. Yet not even a faint gray glow hovered in the east when our huge barn loomed out of the gloom. Relief flooded my bones as I tossed the reins over the hitching rail and wearily marched up the steps to the front door. I'd been gone an entire day and a night and wondered how Ma fared in my absence.

The door creaked open a crack and then Ma threw the door wide. When she saw the man straddling my saddle, limp and quiet, she leaned the shotgun against the wall and ran to help me carry—or, I should say drag—the unconscious rider into the house. With a grunt, we dropped him on the cowhide-covered couch and stood back to survey him.

In the glow of the lantern, I could tell Ma had been sitting up, waiting for my return. Her long brown hair lay in a braid down her back, the way she wore it to bed, but now loose strands had escaped and ringed her oval face.

"Arrow wounds in his leg and chest, high up near the shoulder," I explained, my voice sounding tired even to me. I felt exhausted and wanted to get my horse into the barn before I collapsed from being awake for more than twenty-four hours.

As I stepped to the door, the rider moved restlessly and Ma bent to place a hand on his arm, peering down at him. His eyes blinked open and then widened as he studied Ma in the low lantern light. "You're beautiful," he breathed hoarsely. "Are you an angel?"

His eyes closed once more and Ma leaned back, her hand going to her throat as she glanced at me over her shoulder. I shrugged and went out to the porch.

A dull light seemed to hover in the east, and a couple reluctant stars still hung in the velvety blue sky, refusing to depart. The rider's flighty comment made me grin as I led my horse to the barn, pondering Ma along the way.

Working swiftly, I stripped the saddle from the gelding. I'd forgotten the arrow I'd brought along until it tumbled to the ground. Grabbing it behind the blood-stained tip, I thrust the arrow onto a shelf above the stall. I hurried back to the house, where a pan of water and a pot of coffee boiled on the stove.

As I returned to the front room, I noticed a pair of dusty, worn-down boots standing neatly beside the couch. The rider's cavalry hat adorned a hook on the wall, and his silent form lay beneath a familiar quilt. Ma looked up when I entered, a blush creeping up her neck as she kept her face averted from me while she fussed over the injured rider.

"I cleaned his wounds. I think he'll heal," she said softly. Then, in a lower tone, she whispered, "Johnny, did you hear what he said?" She wouldn't meet my gaze as she spoke, and I sipped coffee, watching her in the dim light, feeling something significant happening. I tilted my head at the catch in her voice.

"I sure did, Ma." I felt more surprised than angry or offended at his offhand remark. Surely the man was out of his head with fever.

With a hand that trembled, she swept the hair back from his brow. "What a fool thing to say. He must be out of his head," she muttered brusquely, but I caught the wistful note in her words.

In the soft light of the lantern, Ma looked like a young girl rather than the mother of a seventeen-year-old. Life had taken some of her youth and made her hard and lonely, but she was still an attractive woman. I turned away, embarrassed.

Strangely, the last person on my mind before I finally fell asleep was Ma. A lump rose in my throat as I recognized she was still a young woman, and I chewed my lip wondering just how old she was. She and Pa had me right off when she was about my age. With wonder, I realized she probably wasn't even thirty-five.

Lacing my fingers behind my head, I stared up at the dark planks above, pondering the adventure God had thrown us into. What lesson was God trying to teach me? With Pa gone and not returning, the ranch barely provided a meager existence for the three of us. And now Paul had gone after his girl, and a wounded man lay on the couch in the parlor. Could God provide for all of us?

Hannah Tall Basket flitted across my mind, and I shifted uneasily, not wanting to think on her and yet struggling to push her from my mind. The beautiful Indian princess was never far from my thoughts, yet we had bigger problems to consider, and a chief's daughter didn't figure into the challenges we faced.

My thoughts returned to Ma. Why had she fidgeted when the dispatch rider mumbled something about her looks? And what did God expect from my floundering faith as I bounced between doubt and belief? Did he even care about us way out here on the Texas plains?

CHAPTER 16

Sunlight streamed through my open window, and I stretched in the late morning rays. Never one to sleep in, I felt embarrassed as I hurriedly dressed, remiss at missing early chores around the barn.

Tucking my shirt into my pants, I stepped into the kitchen. My socks made no sound on the plank floor as I passed through the empty room and then stood frozen in the parlor doorway, watching Ma spoon soup to the strange rider.

Despite the four days' growth of beard along his jawline, he seemed well off to me, sitting pretty as you please propped against pillows as Ma fed him. His cheeks bloomed, and I noticed a similar stain on Ma's cheeks.

Clearing my throat, the pair looked up at me with guilty expressions. They both glanced away quickly and I narrowed my eyes. "Everything all right?" I took a step into the room, sensing something afoot. Had I interrupted a private conversation?

Ma turned at my question, her chin lifting. "Morning, Johnny. I can't recall the last time you slept so late, though no one deserved rest as much as you. James and I were just having some soup. He's been telling me how you saved him."

I stared at her, suddenly noticing her normally tight bun pinned above the nape of her neck replaced by a ponytail of wavy chestnut hair. Golden strands in her locks gleamed in the sun from the front window. I felt surprised how much younger she appeared.

"James?" I realized the stranger had never offered me his name. A faint smile touched his lips as he turned from Ma to glance at me.

"James Casey, dispatch rider for the army. A bunch of young braves jumped me while I was en route to Fort Marcy, near Santa Fe. Your ma and I have been having a nice conversation and getting better acquainted."

He had an easy way about him, but my anger stirred. Something warned me to protect Ma from this man, yet I felt he was no threat. At least no threat to me, although Ma's shining eyes worried me.

Ma shifted on her seat beside the injured man, her cheeks brightening even redder. "James is very lucky his fever didn't hold. I believe he will get better."

He tried to chuckle, but a short cough emitted instead. Ma moved swiftly to prop pillows in place and hold a cup of water to his mouth.   You'd never guess we hadn't entertained visitors in years by the way Ma fussed over this stranger.

James leaned back, his face paling. "I was going to say that no Comanche arrow would keep me down, but I guess I'm not as fit as I'd like to think."

"Well, of course not," Ma agreed hastily and lifted the bowl of soup once more. "You need to rest and eat nourishing food to regain your strength." Without a protest, James nodded, never taking his eyes off his nurse.

A cloud of uncertainty hovered around me, and I retreated into the kitchen, needing coffee. "Can I get anyone anything?" I called over my shoulder, doubtful if the two in the parlor would even hear.

"Coffee, please," James called after me. I pressed my lips tight and scowled against the rising steam as I filled two mugs and returned to the parlor.

"So, is that why you were on that trail? Carrying dispatches for ... for the ..." Ma's voice trailed off as I handed the rider the hot mug. He shot me an appreciative grin as he accepted the cup.

"Yes, ma'am." James shot me another glance before he continued. "I wore the gray uniform in the war, but I needed work when I came home. Seems my land went for back taxes, so I went to work for the Yank army, doing the only thing I'm good for. I guess I'll always feel most comfortable in a saddle, no matter what color the saddle blanket."

Ma nodded, her gaze dropping as she spooned more soup to the invalid.

"Was your man in the war, ma'am?" I took a seat on a low bench against the wall and watched as James interrogated Ma, as if the two of them were the only people in the room, unaware of my presence.

"He died at the end," Ma whispered. "Can you believe that? He almost made it through the entire war." She drew a deep breath, letting it out slowly. "Johnny and I've been alone for so long."

She lifted her face and peered at the wounded man, a glow in her eyes I'd come to recognize when she spoke of the Lord. "Only by God's grace are we still here. He is faithful, Mr. Casey. He brought Paul to help tend the place so Johnny can brand our stock, and now God has brought you."

She paused and tilted her head, studying him soberly in the late morning sunlight that brightened the parlor. "Why has God brought you here, James?"

He shrugged and tried to grin, but her serious inquiry made him shake his head. "I'm wounded, ma'am. I'm here because your boy brought me here for you to tend."

She squinted at him as if trying to perceive a cleverly concealed secret. "No, there is another reason. One that eludes me at the present, but I am convinced the Lord brought you here for a purpose. You see, we are on a grand adventure, and the Lord is doing something mighty in our little corner of Texas."

She spoke with a confidence that annoyed me, and I scowled when I read the pity on James's countenance as he considered Ma. He shot me a worried glance, a muscle twitching along his unshaven jaw, and I knew what he was thinking.

Many folks had broken from the trauma of the war. Poverty, starvation, financial demands, loneliness, and deep sorrow had descended like a heavy fog over the country, and people needed to find a way to cope with their troubles and shock. Some moved west for a new start, many turned to drink or crime, taking what others had worked for. But Ma turned to the Lord, kneeling at God's feet with a faith that eluded me.

Is it possible God is doing something that I don't recognize? What am I missing? My beliefs—the faith passed down to me from my parents—feel shaken and challenged.

Ma continued. "Between Paul and the dead outlaw Johnny found, we're still here, guided by the right hand of God. Don't you see? God has provided for us to stay on this property. And now he has brought you."

I choked on my coffee, burning my throat. Listening to Ma, I saw how my faithlessness had not stopped God's faithfulness. Despite my flip-flopping beliefs, the Lord had worked among us, delivering good things when I least expected.

James ignored my sputtering. "Me?" He laughed softly. "I doubt if the good Lord has anything to do with me. During the war, I saw ... well, and I did ... never mind that now. Leave it alone, ma'am. I'm here because I'm injured and nothing else."

An uncomfortable silence filled the room, and I sipped my coffee. Although I knew Ma watched for God's hand in everything, I doubted this rider had been delivered to our ranch for any particular reason other than he needed medical attention, and Ma was the best attention we could provide.

I shook my head and stood, padding softly toward the kitchen for another cup of coffee before attending to the demands of the day. I wished Ma were right, for it would be wonderful to relinquish the burdens I wrestled, but I believed chance—and nothing more—led this wounded man to our house. I felt like tumbleweeds on the prairie, blown by sporadic winds without meaning, not by divine intervention. Yet, I still longed to witness God's action in our lives.

"Once my wounds heal," James went on as I paused by the door, listening, "I'll be moving on. I have to get these dispatches to Fort Marcy."

Ma smiled, a fierce gleam in her eye that frightened me. "You will do what the Lord directs, Mr. Casey. Perhaps it will be to continue to Fort Marcy, working for the blue devils. Perhaps it will be to work here, discovering God's will for your life as you experience a deepening of your faith."

James dropped his gaze. Ma pushed the spoon into the cold soup and rose, smoothing her skirts as she brushed past me and entered the kitchen. I glanced once more at the injured rider as James looked at me.

"Your ma is a determined woman."

"You have no idea," I muttered before following Ma into the other room.

Ma stood with her hands not moving in the sink water as she gazed out the window. I walked to the stove and gripped the coffeepot.

"He's wrong, Johnny," she said in a low tone that stilled my hand. "There are no accidents when you submit to the Lord. He guides us and maneuvers everything for those who sincerely obey him."

I moved forward and dropped my empty cup into the sink, no longer wanting more as my gaze locked on her profile. "You can't make God do what you want him to. He moves like the wind, unseen and from anywhere, sometimes with no rhyme or reason. He does what he wants."

She whirled on me, and I stepped back as her face pinched. "He loves us, Johnny. With a depth we can't understand or fathom, he loves us and wants good things for us. Not to harm us but to grow us, instructing us as a loving father does a child. I find my strength in him, and I will not lose heart because of a lost soul who doesn't understand the Lord's purpose for trials. Mr. Casey has something to contribute to this adventure, and I will wait on the Lord until he reveals why Mr. Casey is here."

Not wishing to argue, I backed away, squinting at her fierce defense, and retreated to the parlor once more. James looked up as I entered, a slow tendril of steam rising from his coffee cup.

"You rescued me, for which I am grateful. But the Lord had nothing to do with those braves filling me with arrows like a pin cushion. Just bad luck."

I held up a hand. "You don't have to convince me. I can't see the Lord's hand in this either."

He stared at me, his knuckles turning white on the mug he held. He licked his lips and blinked. "Problem is, I'm having some doubts," he whispered.

"Doubts?" I shifted, not sure I'd heard correctly.

He nodded. "Ever since the war, well, even during the war, I felt my faith slipping. As if God were hiding from me, making me search for him. Now, your ma makes me ponder. What if God *did* bring me here? What if he is answering my prayers?"

I felt my chest tighten as I studied him. Despite his assertions that he acted independently of the Lord, I sensed his misgivings. Perhaps Ma's speech had rattled him and made him consider another option for his presence on our ranch. Perhaps he felt the conviction of the Holy Spirit like Paul had said would prompt true believers.

I exhaled loudly. "Mister, you're just a wounded man, tied up here until you heal. Soon, you'll be on your way."

He said nothing but his scowl deepened, and I suddenly wanted to be elsewhere. If Ma's predictions were starting to frighten him, I wanted no part of their unreality. God had left us alone for years, stuck out here to struggle and suffer. Ma believed the trial had shaped her faith while I just felt God had been mean, forcing us to walk through the fire. What good could come from such pressure and tribulation?

As I turned to depart, Mr. Casey stopped me with a question. "Why haven't the Comanche killed you or burned you out? According to your ma, you've been alone out here for five years."

I paused, eager to escape, yet pleased to have someone other than Ma to speak with. Again, I realized how much I missed Paul. "We give them beef occasionally, and they admired my pa."

"Well, having met your mother, I admire your pa too." He spoke with a note of respect. Then, placing his empty cup on a table, he sank into the pillows and closed his eyes. Within a minute, his low snores filled the room, his even breathing telling me he'd fallen asleep.

Our conversation had probably tired him. Although he appeared a tough and capable man, his wounds and his ordeal with the Indians had fatigued him.

As I picked up his empty cup, I glanced at the sleeping rider, surprised how much I appreciated having a man in the house again, even if only for a short time.

CHAPTER 17

Not wanting to hear more from Ma, I avoided her as I deposited the rider's cup on the counter on my way out the back door. I felt grateful when she didn't try to stop me to continue our conversation.

After quickly taking care of the morning chores, I curried Mr. Cascy's gelding and my horse, the animals still looking a bit done in. Saddling a smaller paint mare, I left the heavy rifle behind and rode west, checking stock and scouting possible hay meadows. Snow would arrive soon enough, and I didn't want to be caught unprepared. Although our cattle mostly grazed in wind-swept places where the snow didn't drift, I felt the need to contemplate, to get away and consider.

Wandering westward over the plains, I let the paint choose her way as I searched for likely grazing land and investigated the condition of various springs, all while checking on the cattle. We had more stock than we could adequately manage, and I worried we couldn't feed them all or protect them if their numbers increased in the spring as predicted.

I surveyed our ranch and squinted against the sun as I rode, my anxiety growing as I traveled farther from home. Something niggled at the edge of my mind, and I twisted in my saddle, peering over my shoulder as if looking for someone trailing me.

Finally, I glanced up at the blue expanse, the wind rustling ceaselessly through the swaying grass. "Lord, is it you making me uneasy? Paul's gone, and now we have a wounded rider, and Ma's acting odd. You know I don't cotton to Ma and Paul's idea about an adventure. Seems too hard for me to just step back and allow you to take over. I can't see you've done an all fired great job so far, with Pa dead and the ranch tumbling down around my ears. What about the stock and the hay and the lack of money? Maybe our quiet little corner of Texas doesn't rate very high on your list, but it's all I've got."

A scowl tugged at my mouth, and I pressed my lips tight, my face pinching as I dropped my gaze and stared far ahead. "Wish you'd just tell me what to do," I grumbled.

As I scanned the prairie, it became apparent we had no way of cutting all the hay we required for the amount of stock we owned. Paul was no hand with a scythe, but he tried hard.

Glancing to the south, I searched for signs of his return. Surely he'd be back soon, I hoped.

What if he didn't return? My scowl deepened as I considered this. "Where are you, Lord?" I growled from between clenched teeth. Would God ignore our plight despite our needs?

Hours later, shadows stretched across the plains and gathered in the folds of the land when I rode back into the yard. Chickens scattered as I dismounted and led my mount into the gloomy barn, startled how quickly the temperature dropped as the autumn sun slid behind the western hills. A chilly wind had arisen, and I hadn't thought to bring my coat with me. Although Indian summer lingered, I knew winter was not far off. A chill numbed my fingers as

I unsaddled, and I knew that for another season, I would not leave the ranch yard again without a coat. With the last rays of sunlight, I saw the clouds had banked in the north. Maybe a storm brewed.

As I rubbed the little mare, I considered rotating the riding stock for the next day, allowing each horse a respite as I worked every animal. We had too many stock horses for just one rider, and no one who'd buy the extras. Everyone lacked cash money. Putting the brush back on the shelf, I hurried to the house.

My stomach growled with hunger, but the smell of fresh coffee drew my attention as I stepped into the dimly lit kitchen, a stub of candle burning on the counter and another on the table. The aroma of baking bread welcomed me as I closed the door, shutting out the autumn cold as twilight descended. Ma sat at the table reading her Bible, but she rose when she saw me.

"Hello, Johnny. Sit down and let me serve you." A wide smile creased her face, but I waved her back into her seat.

"Coffee first, Ma. I can get it." I stepped to the sink and pumped water over my hands.

She settled back into her chair, her smile never dimming as she watched me wash up and retrieve a mug from the cupboard. I squinted against the steam as I poured the hot drink, my stomach growling louder as I joined her at the table.

"How is our patient?" I queried as I lifted the cup to my lips. A shudder raced through me as my bones warmed. I glanced at the cooking stove, grateful for the heat after the chilling prairie winds.

Ma closed the thick book and leaned back, watching me. "Good. Tired. I think he has lost some blood, but he'll be fine. He just eats and sleeps."

I took another sip of the hot drink, soaking in the warmth. She stood abruptly. "You need soup," she commented as she moved to the stove and filled a bowl. I shrugged and smiled up at her, knowing she couldn't sit still long with someone to feed.

The rich smell of the thick stew wafted, and I remembered my incredible hunger. I dove into my soup with enthusiasm. The coffee tasted good, and the soup felt filling. Slowly, my tired muscles relaxed. After emptying the soup bowl and draining my mug, I leaned back in my chair and watched as Ma filled the cup again.

Reaching for the steaming mug, I noticed Ma's eyes on me, studying me closely. I frowned and gulped coffee. "What?"

Ma cocked her head, her brow furrowing. "Johnny, am I pretty?"

I choked on my coffee and wiped my mouth with the back of my hand. "Well, not that I'm a good judge of such things, but sure, I guess." I smiled reassuringly, but she frowned even more, clearly not satisfied with my response. I shifted uneasily. I'd never thought of Ma's looks until James's remark early this morning.

She turned and fussed over the stove, and I could tell something bothered her. Women were strange creatures to me. I've lived with Ma all my life but sometimes could not explain her moods. Once again, I remembered Hannah Tall Basket. What was the intent of her comments on our last meeting? I could not understand her either, but she was often on my mind.

James's compliment must've startled Ma's thinking, not having any other such attention in many years. Perhaps she now worried about her appearance with someone other than me and Paul around. If my thoughts filled with memories of Hannah, what did Ma think on? Pa had been gone over five years, dead for a while. Did she feel lonely?

I carried my empty dishes to the counter and stretched. "I'm beat," I said, yawning for emphasis. "See you in the morning." Ma nodded but said nothing, her hands busy with the dirty dishes.

As I stepped to my bedroom door, I glanced at her again, wondering why she'd asked me about herself. With no one else on the place, her options were limited, and I wished she had a female to talk to. Women valued such different things than men, and I felt sure she would've enjoyed discussing her feelings with another woman.

In my room, I draped the heavy gun belt on the back of a chair and sat on the edge of the bed to remove my boots. The gentle tinkle of rain splattered across my window, and I recalled the dark clouds that had massed all afternoon along the northern horizon. We had as much hay as we were going to cut, and the barn and sheds were tight and snug. I hoped it would be enough, although I knew we had more stock than we could feed through the winter. So, let it rain. There was nothing more I could do about it now.

My thoughts turned to Paul, and I wondered if I'd ever see him again. Were he and Lydia safe? I sent a heartfelt prayer skyward and hoped they'd arrive home soon, before winter truly set in.

Crawling into bed, I pulled the covers over me, grateful to not be out on a night like this. Shooting a glance at the closed Bible on my nightstand, I squinted before blowing out the candle, casting the room into darkness. God knew my fatigue, right? Surely, he wouldn't mind if I occasionally skipped my Scripture reading.

I went to sleep that night thinking of James and his wounds and Ma's sudden unease about herself. She'd never seemed overly concerned about her hair or her dress during the war, or so I imagined, although I couldn't ever recall really studying her. And why should I?

Still, my thoughts returned to James and Hannah, making me wonder if Ma ever felt lonesome like me.

CHAPTER 18

Rain spattered the roof as James and I ate our breakfast together. Gusts of wind pushed the slanting shower against windows, reminding us often of the storm outside. The cold, dreary day made a body appreciate a warm fire. Ma seemed especially quiet and kept her distance, hovering in the background as I talked with James. He sat across the table from me now after demanding to get up from the couch in the front room, despite Ma's concerns. His face had strained pale when we helped him to the kitchen, but he ate with vigor, I'll say that for him. At this rate, he'd be on his feet soon.

"Tell me about Red Bill," he said, pointing at my Colt with his coffee mug.

I pulled the big pistol proudly from the holster and laid the weapon on the table.

"Johnny Garret, you put that thing away. We don't lay guns on the table during meals," Ma reprimanded with a sharp tone that made me obey quickly.

James chuckled and glanced appreciatively at Ma. As if feeling his gaze upon her, she brushed loose hair from her crimson cheek and looked away. I tilted my head, unsure at what was going on.

Over our second cup of coffee, he told me stories of his time in the cavalry. He told me about various battles—some of the names I remembered from Pa's infrequent letters—and I listened eagerly, grateful to be talking man talk with this rider.

As he droned on, I became aware that Ma listened too, and I wondered whose benefit the war talk was truly for. After a while, his words faltered, as if his stories had reminded him of more than he cared to recall. He ran a hand across his face and smiled faintly.

"At Appomattox, we were turning in our rifles for food when this big Yank told us of the opportunities in the Union Army. At first we laughed, and then I got to thinking about what I was going to eat the next day. I had no idea what awaited me back in Alabama and no money to get there. They gave me travel pay and I swung by home on my way west, only to find my land had been taken for back taxes. As it turned out, I became a dispatch rider and never actually joined the army. Kind of dangerous sometimes with the Indians, but I eat regular and always get paid."

"I'm a rancher," I said stubbornly. "I don't know what I'd do without this place." My gaze drifted over the worn rugs and the shabby furniture, clean and serviceable, yet all had seen better days. But this was my home, and I remembered Ma's adventure, to keep us on the family place with the Lord's help.

My roaming gaze settled on Ma before lifting to the lined, plank ceiling. Did God know of our struggles? Did he care about Ma's constant prayers and deep faith?

"Well, you've done well, keeping the land," James said casually as his eyes drifted to Ma for the hundredth time. I frowned at his constant scrutiny of her, but appreciated his words, nonetheless.

I snorted and the pair of them looked at me. "We have the land," I agreed. "But we need cash money. I'm worried how we'll feed all our stock this winter. And I have no idea how we're to pay the store in town what we owe." Then, as if wanting to align the rider on my side, I offered another dig, knowing Ma listened.

"Besides, Ma's ideas aren't going to pay the bills. She thinks Jesus will step into this kitchen and deliver a stack of greenbacks into our hands."

I'd wanted the comment to make him laugh, but a scowl darkened James's features, and he shot Ma an apologetic glance, as if apologizing for me.

Ma narrowed her eyes as she studied me, but she didn't say anything. I could feel the shame wash over me, and I regretted my rude jest, my hurtful words surely hitting their mark. Then, James laughed. Small wrinkles in the corner of his eyes formed as if he enjoyed laughing, and I cringed, afraid he actually would join me in making fun of Ma's claim that God was with us on a grand journey.

"John, you make me think. You need money and you have too much stock. Your ma says Jesus brought me here. I ignored her belief, though, my own doubts nagging me like a foxtail weed in my sock. Then I remembered my dispatches."

He paused, a surprised expression spreading across his features that drew my interest. He seemed excited, and Ma left her place near the sink to take a step nearer, as if unable to resist his curious words.

"What is it, James?" Her voice held a note of an expectancy that irritated me, like she'd known all the time that this strange rider would share valuable information.

He looked up at her, eyes glowing. "Well, ma'am, you told me God brought me here, and I told you that's crazy. But now I wonder." He paused and gripped his empty coffee mug as if his next words startled him too.

"I'm riding dispatch over to Fort Marcy to report the necessity of beef at all the outposts, including the reservations in the Indian Nation." Looking from me to Ma, he shook his head and smiled. I could read the relief on Ma's face. Her eyes darted to the ceiling as she lifted her apron to her mouth to stifle a cry.

I didn't understand but didn't want to say anything to make me look dumb. I could tell my mother was thinking over what he'd said. "You mean the forts need cattle? Maybe our cattle?" She spoke quietly, afraid his news might not be true. I blinked, realizing for the first time that his announcement could benefit our ranch.

"That's right. The army has money to pay, but needs cattle driven immediately to the outposts and forts."

Ma took another step closer to the table, wiping the tears from the corners of her eyes. "How much will they pay?"

James shifted, his smile widening. "Twelve dollars a head."

I leaped to my feet. "Twelve dollars a head!" That was a lot of money.

He faced me. "They're offering twelve dollars a head to any rancher who will deliver cattle and risk the Indians. The army's desperate to get beef before winter sets in. If you can deliver stock, you'll be paid fair and quick." He turned soft, kind eyes on my mother. She stared, taking in his words and nodding, as if seeing something I couldn't see.

"You were right, Annie," he whispered. "The Lord did bring me here to tell you this news. God brought me here for a purpose. Maybe I'm a part of your adventure."

Rain continued all that day and the next, a gentle, continuous rain from a leaden sky. A hint of snow hovered with the cold rain, but I thought it felt too early in the season for snow. Yet weather was often unpredictable on the panhandle, and I knew winter crouched at our door.

I rode out early until late the next two days and found a lot of stock crowded near home. It would not be difficult to round up a small herd of cows to drive to a fort. We would wait for Paul to return, although I worried about his inability to ride a horse and doubted we could deliver stock anywhere, let alone a distant army outpost. Yet Ma seemed confident the deal would go through, as if she believed in the impossible.

James recovered quickly. He'd been used to hard living and was a tough man. Ma's cooking and kindness put him on the mend. By the third day, he was walking around the house.

Over supper that night, between furtive glances at Ma, James shared his plans. "I'll go on to Fort Marcy in a day or two. As a civilian contractor, I can quit when I choose."

He narrowed his eyes as he looked first at Ma and then me. "John, if you'll have me, I'd like to help drive the cattle. I know the routes and how to push cattle. You won't have time to dawdle if you intend to sell beef before the snow flies."

I could feel my eyes widen, then squint as a look of triumph passed over Ma's features. She'd been crowing about Jesus bringing this rider to our house with such great news, but I still felt the skeptic, not willing to allow the Lord to take credit for a wounded man trying to impress a woman. Even I could see the way he looked at Ma.

"You can leave the army when you want?" I demanded more information.

James shrugged. "I'm not really a soldier anymore. I ride for the army, delivering messages between the forts. I can go when I want." His face softened when he looked up at Ma as he went on. "And I choose to leave now. Hopefully, you'll allow me to return and help with the drive of cattle."

There was no doubt I needed his assistance, but his manner, his presumption that we needed him rankled me.

Of course, we *did* need him, but I couldn't help but wonder if he'd help us so eagerly if Ma weren't pretty.

I cleared my throat and glanced at Ma for approval. She smiled but said nothing, allowing me to make up my own mind. I felt she wanted me to make the decision, as if I were in charge of the ranch now. Even if Paul returned, he could not help until he learned to ride a horse, which might never happen. We needed money now and this man offered. Was he a gift from the Lord like Ma supposed? I shook my head, clearing my thoughts.

"We'd be grateful if you'd help us out," I said, not wanting to get my hopes up. Could we do it? Was it even real? Did the army really need cattle—our cattle—to feed the forts?

James nodded, a pleased look coming into his face. "I know where they all are, and I know which ones we can drive to easily, before winter really sets in. You push your stock near the house so when I return, we don't waste any time rounding them up."

I shifted on my chair as the plan came together smoothly. Yet something niggled in my mind. Life had become so difficult. Every decision had to be weighed carefully as a wrong move could spell destruction or failure for the ranch. Why would this man risk everything to help us?

I eyed James suspiciously. "Why are you so eager to help us? You have a good job. Why would you leave it for a chancy thing like delivering cows?" His proffered help did not make sense to me. "Anything could happen with delivering cattle. Weather, Indians, outlaws, or a stampede could leave you with nothing."

He smiled an infectious grin and I hated to admit I liked his attitude. "Let's just say I don't want to miss out on what God is doing here. I told you I had my own spiritual struggles in the war, and I don't think it's an accident I'm here now. I think your ma is right, something brought me to your ranch. I feel I should see it through."

Was there another reason? My mouth puckered as I peered at Ma where she stood, eyes shining as she smiled at me. James moved and drew my gaze as he took a piece of coal from the stove and traced a crude map of the area on the inside of an old cowhide. He filled in details as I offered suggestions, making the map as correct as we could while Ma poured more coffee and finished the supper dishes.

Our map included the corners of Texas, the Indian Nation, Colorado, and New Mexico Territory. He placed the names of forts and outposts with great care, making sure rivers where the outposts were located were clearly identified.

I tapped on a large section between the forts, my finger stabbing the smooth leather. "There's a big problem here. We'll have to cross Comanche lands to reach all of these forts."

He chewed his lip for a long moment and then shook his head. "I guess we could go around the Indian land, but that might take too long. Or we can just forget about the forts west of here and concentrate on the reservations in the Nation. But that means we sell less beef. I know for a fact that Fort Union is very impatient for cattle right now. We could push twenty head there in a little over a week if we can go straight west. If we have to go around the Comanche, it would simply take too long."

He stared hard at the old hide while we sipped our coffee. He'd shaved and his smooth face made him look younger than I'd first considered his age. He couldn't be much older than Ma.

"Let me worry about the Indians," I said, my hands squeezing my cup. "You deliver your messages and get back here as fast as you can. I'll gather cattle and be ready for your return."

I lifted my mug for another drink, hiding my fears behind my cup. I didn't know what I would do but thought maybe I could speak to Hannah. Perhaps she'd have an idea that would help. Besides, I wanted to see her again.

Our plans made, we all turned in early. By the way James moved toward his bed in the parlor, I could tell he was still a little weak from his wounds. Yet the decision to have him help push cattle to the forts had energized him, and he seemed eager to complete his mission and return to our ranch. He would leave in the morning.

I'd just settled beneath the blankets when a knock at the back door brought me up quickly. Slipping from bed in my long nightshirt, I shoved my bare feet into my boots, drawing my Colt as I raced to the kitchen. A dim moonlight streamed through the dark window, but I could see James with his drawn gun crouched beside the back door.

"Who is it?" I hissed as I pressed my back to the wall and peered out the window, seeing nothing. Our ranch lay on the main trail, and we never knew what manner of riders passed our house. Last spring and summer it had been returning soldiers, the war over and men wanting to locate missed loved ones. But tonight, perhaps a thief lurked in the yard. The war had made everyone desperate.

"I can't be sure," James whispered from his side of the room. "It looks like a pair of travelers. I think one is a woman."

"A woman?" I rushed to the door and flung it open. There on the stoop, soaked from the merciless rain, stood Paul and a woman, barely discerned in the dull light.

"Paul, come in, come in," I urged, dragging the grinning man inside and out of the rain. A candle brightened the room and James tossed the smoking match into the grate on the stove before he turned to face the newcomers. Ma appeared at her door, wrapping her faded robe around her as she hastened to wring Paul's outstretched hand.

"You've returned," Ma said with obvious delight. Then she turned to the woman cowering behind Paul. "You must be Lydia." Ma reached for the girl and dragged her into the light. I closed the door, shutting out the cold and the rain.

"This is my Lydia," Paul sang proudly as he pointed to his companion. The woman's eyes were wide with fear, and she glanced this way and that, watching Ma and me and then gasping when she saw the gun in my hand. Ma shook her head at me, and I hurriedly placed the pistol on the counter and covered the weapon with a dish towel.

"Why, you're freezing," Ma huffed, suddenly realizing the two travelers wore sodden clothes. They both shivered, although Lydia shook uncontrollably while Paul seemed to be filled with an excitement that warmed him.

"Let's get you into dry clothes," Ma said and indicated her nearby room.

Lydia shot Paul a desperate look, but he smiled. "It's all right. You go on now with Miss Annie."

The two women disappeared into Ma's room with a stub of candle James handed her while I poured Paul a cup of coffee from the cooling pot atop the stove. We hadn't been in bed long and I hoped the drink was still warm.

I introduced James and the two men shook hands. "James thinks we can drive cattle to some army forts and sell beef," I explained after telling Paul how the wounded rider had come to be with us.

Paul's eyes grew large, and he gulped another sip of the drink. "I won't have to ride a horse, will I? John, you know I'm willing, but riding a horse ..."

His voice trailed off and I grinned. I assured him we would not need his services on the trail.

"How was the trip?"

His happy face shifted to a scowl, and he drained his cup, handing the empty mug to me before he replied. "They weren't happy to see me back there, and even less when I announced I was there to take Lydia away. Then Lydia was scared to go with me, although she wasn't happy on that farm. In the end, I convinced her to come away with me. We jumped the broom and started north."

"You're married?" I glanced at James, but he only squinted thoughtfully.

"Yes," Paul laughed. "I'm married, John, and happy to be back here."

Ma heard the last as she ushered Lydia into the kitchen, the woman now wearing a dry dress. "Congratulations, you two. I will not expect to see you tomorrow until you're hungry. Come any time and I'll fix you a meal. You probably should get some rest."

She shot Paul a knowing smile that was completely lost on me, and Paul nodded shyly as he rose, taking Lydia's hand, he led the girl to the door. The frightened woman still hadn't spoken to me, but I allowed she was probably scared to death with the lot of us asking questions and overwhelming her.

"We'll see you folks tomorrow," Paul said as he opened the back door to go to his cabin. "Thank you for everything."

"I'll say my goodbye, Paul and Lydia," James said as he rose from the table. "I hope to be off before dawn."

The room quieted after the couple left and I noticed Ma's bedroom door closed softly. James and I stood alone in the kitchen, and I yawned. "Goodnight again," I said as I walked to my room. He glanced at Ma's door, a frown creasing his features, and then he blew out the candle and moved toward the parlor.

At breakfast the next day, Ma seemed quiet. Making sure James had all he needed for his journey, she'd packed food and extra blankets for him. We'd only known James four or five days, yet he'd become part of the team so quickly.

He laughed when he saw the thick pack Ma handed him. "This will be a heavy load for my horse," he observed doubtfully. Then he grinned when he caught Ma's worried expression. "But I surely appreciate your kindness. I wouldn't have made it if John and you hadn't saved my hide."

Ma blushed and fidgeted with her apron. "Hurry back, James," she whispered and then turned to busy herself at the sink.

"See you soon," he said as he shook my hand. He glanced at Ma's stiff back before he opened the door and vanished into the morning gloom. Dawn was not far off, but not even a hint of gray hovered at the eastern horizon.

Closing the door against the autumn chill, I faced Ma. She dunked her hands into the warm water and briskly scrubbed dishes, ignoring my stare. "God is with us, Johnny. You have to see that now. James will prove a real help, and Paul and Lydia are here too. The Lord is providing, just like I said."

I wanted to nod, to agree with her, but something stilled me, and I crossed my arms over my chest. Was this all a pipe dream? Would James return? Did Paul and Lydia's arrival just mean two more mouths to feed? I still felt the concern heavy on my shoulders as I moved toward the door to begin morning chores.

CHAPTER 19

Trudging to the barn as the sun tipped the eastern horizon, my shoulders sagged, despite the promise of a new day. Shadows reached across the yard, casting the hard-packed dirt with dark, familiar patterns I'd grown accustomed to. This was my home, the only home I'd ever known, and changes came swiftly and slowly. The land appeared the same, yet something different hovered in the autumn air, a sense of expectancy that worried me, as if something loomed in the distance, just out of sight.

A chicken cackled when I reached the large barn door, announcing another egg to the world. I paused, scanning the familiar ranch with its outbuildings, corrals, and weathered little house. What was God doing here? Was he doing anything? Was James Casey's arrival just a coincidence, like I believed?

My sweeping gaze lingered on the foreman's cabin where Paul and Lydia now lived. I figured they might not be seen for hours yet, resting from their arduous journey. Heat stole up my neck as I recalled the couple had only recently been married. Perhaps they might not be seen for many hours.

Turning away from the quiet cabin, I glanced again at the house where Ma's shadowed form flitted across the kitchen window. James had been gone less than an hour, yet

I acutely felt his absence. While he'd been here, he'd offered a man's presence, a sense of leadership I appreciated. Did Ma miss him too?

Now, only a fool couldn't have noticed the way the dispatch rider looked at Ma. Strangely, I wasn't nettled that a man other than Pa paid attention to my mother. Pa had been gone a long time, and she was a lonely woman. I figured she deserved happiness as well as anyone.

After saddling a wiry looking gelding, I returned to the kitchen and packed grub into my saddlebags, formerly Red Bill's. With a pair of heavy blankets, I figured to rough it for a day or two, depending on how long my trip west might take.

"Where are you going?"

Her voice didn't stop me from shrugging into my coat. I patted the heavy gun on my hip, reassuring myself the pistol hung comfortably at my belt. Taking up my rifle—another of Red Bill's gear—I turned to the door, but Ma stopped me with another cup of coffee, the steam rising. She smiled, a question in her eyes as I accepted the mug.

I sipped the hot drink as she pushed her tangled hair into place, her sharp scrutiny following me as she bunched the long tresses and secured them with a ribbon. Her rumpled dress told me she'd been up for hours before James departed, probably praying as she often did in the early mornings. I couldn't ignore the dark circles under her eyes.

"I've got to visit the Comanche camps, see what I can learn. You heard James. We need to take the shortcut across their lands if we want to sell beef before snow flies."

Ma nodded and leaned against the wall, her hands slipping to her sides. "You be careful. I want to sell cattle too, but I want you alive more than anything."

I nodded with a grin and placed the empty cup on the counter. "I'll be careful. See you in a day or two."

Draping the filled saddlebags over one shoulder, I moved toward the back door, but Ma stepped to me suddenly, taking my shoulders in her hands before she kissed my cheek. For the second time that day, I blushed with embarrassment. "Ma," I protested, frowning at her unexpected show of emotion. "See you in a couple days."

She smiled up at me, but I read the fear in her eyes. Sometimes riders never came back, and I wondered if she was thinking of Pa like I'd done earlier.

She followed me into the morning chill and watched as I tied my saddlebags into place and thrust the rifle into the scabbard. The saddle creaked as I stepped into the stirrup and seated myself, taking the reins firmly in one gloved hand. Ma stepped even closer, peering up at me with an agitated expression.

"Don't worry. I'll be safe," I said gruffly, trying to reassure her that I wasn't a little boy anymore. At seventeen, manhood had been thrust upon me, but I felt as ready for the responsibility as I was going to, or so I figured.

She shook her head, her long hair dancing across the top of her shoulders. "It's not that. I want to ask you something before you leave." She paused and I could tell this was something difficult for her to get out. "What do you think of James?"

I felt my lips tighten. "Ma, I think he's a nice man, but we don't really know much about him. Patience and prayer." That was a favorite saying of hers, and I said it now to comfort her. She smiled knowingly and patted my knee.

"You're right. I love you, Johnny. Come home soon. God bless you."

I left her standing in the yard, a lonely, frightened woman with feelings for a stranger. Anger stirred in my gut as I realized how much God had asked of her. All alone she had kept a ranch together and kept me fed and safe.

Did he have a plan for our ranch, as Ma supposed? I shook my head, unsure as I walked the gelding into the trail and turned north before leaving the road at Clover Creek and heading west toward the high plains and the distant Comanche camps.

Before departing the cover of the creek, I studied the trees, the cottonwood and elm leaves painted in glorious colors of crimson and amber. Fall lay upon us, and we would have to hasten if we hoped to deliver cattle anywhere soon. Herding a pair of particularly fat young steers ahead of me, I pushed the unbranded cattle onto the mesa and trotted after them, my thoughts wandering.

Pa had always taught me you don't go asking for favors without bearing a gift. If we were going to ask for safe passage across Comanche lands, I figured to sweeten my chances with these two steers. Winter would be upon us soon, and I hoped fresh beef would taste good to any reluctant Indians.

The Teyuwit band of the Comanche were only one group or village. The land would only provide enough game and firewood for a village of about a hundred and fifty people, so the Comanche bands had separated and lived in different locations within Comanche territory. My thoughts settled on Hannah Tall Basket, and I shifted in my saddle, uneasy with her memory. Would she be glad to see me?

My gaze shifted from the two trotting cattle to my horse, my insides tightening as I recalled the Comanche were not only great hunters, but also exceptional horse thieves. They often made daring raids as far south as Mexico to plunder horses from enemies. I patted the gelding and hoped I'd be riding home again soon.

I'd been to this camp before. Although nomadic, following the vast herds of buffalo or occasionally moving to better grazing, the Indians often returned to favorite places, and I hoped they'd returned to this preferred winter spot located beneath a protective bluff and out of the wind. A stream meandered along the base of the bluff, and there seemed to be plenty of firewood and water, although ice would have to be cut from the stream throughout the winter to get to the water below.

The rainstorm had passed, and now only a few scattered clouds dotted the gray sky. A bitter wind blustered from the north, heralding the coming winter, but colorful leaves clung tenaciously to trees along the few waterways, and I knew I still had time.

I scowled and glanced up at the skittering clouds. "I still have time, right?"

Although I doubted God cared about me or our plans or this chance to save our ranch, I still worried he watched me, silently observing me. He'd been quiet for so long.

But if James returned in time, and if the Comanche allowed us to drive cattle across their lands, and if winter held back, we just might make a successful drive.

I squinted, studying the vast sky and the few darting clouds and the ceaseless winds buffeting me and the long prairie grass. "Are you with us? Do you care? The Bible says you love us and are always with us, never forsaking us, yet I've felt forsaken."

I paused, biting my lip as I nudged the pair of steers on. I felt foolish speaking with the Lord if I truly believed he wasn't aware of our plight. Or maybe he was aware and didn't speak because of some other unknown reason. Whatever the truth, I had to admit I wished he were with us, like Ma claimed.

What of James Casey? My horse lunged to block the escape of one of the steers as my thoughts turned to the dispatch rider. We knew little of him and yet he'd already made an impact on my small family, filling us with a hope we hadn't held for years. Had Ma set her cap for him?

I peered into the distance, searching for signs of the Indian camp, and shrugged. Well, why not? We lived in a hard time, in a hard land. Relationships came and went. I worried for Ma, not wishing her to get hurt, but I'd felt loneliness too.

The day wore on and I tugged the collar of my coat higher, picking cornbread crumbs from my lap as I nibbled a chunk of johnnycake. Off to the south, I glimpsed a line of buffalo, a small herd moving away from the wind.

Toward late afternoon, chilled and tired, I drove the pair of steers from a creek bottom when I saw the brave on horseback, watching me. His dark eyes bore into me, but he didn't move as I faced west and kept pushing the steers. Keeping a hand on my thigh, near my gun handle, I figured this was probably one of the Comanche I searched for. I had no illusion I would just ride into their camp unobserved, but a shiver wormed down my spine. There was no doubt more than this lone brave watched me. I licked my dry lips and hoped they'd let me come visiting.

By the time I traveled another mile, there were three more Indians on different hills watching me. A few minutes later, I drove the steers to the edge of their camp where a crowd had gathered to view my entrance. The quartet of riders had converged to escort me into their village, riding all around me, letting me know they were near. One false move would mean my scalp.

A lean-faced, bronzed warrior positioned his horse in front of me, halting my progress. I recognized Dark Cloud and frowned when I saw Red Bill's scalp tied to his lance. I nodded at his cold stare, waiting. Shrieks and screams made me turn to watch the two steers being chased toward the creek, a line of ragged children and women on their heels.

More warriors peered at me from beside their buffalo skin tents, but the quartet of riders seemed adequate to hold me, trying to frighten me. As they stared, one would occasionally bump my horse with his own. I ignored the provocation as best I could, knowing any reprisal would be fruitless.

A sigh escaped me when I caught sight of Hannah marching through the village, coming toward us with an impatient, angry scowl on her face. Long black hair waved on the wind, and I blinked, trying to remember the small girl I'd spoken with as a young boy. Like the day I found Red Bill's body in the trail, I could see the high cheekbones and delicate features of the beautiful girl and marveled at the transformation of the youngster in pigtails to this Comanche princess coming to meet me.

My gaze shifted from her form-fitting buckskin dress to the lowering clouds above. The storm had passed, yet a residual chill remained behind, promising that colder weather loomed.

"Johnny, I must apologize. I was only now told of your presence. These men wanted to make you wait, to test or provoke you." Her scowl deepened as she glowered at the four silent braves around me. I sensed their deference to her and wondered anew at her authority within the tribe. Her pa was a chief, I knew, but I speculated at the power a young woman possessed within the Indian tribe. She said something in Comanche and three riders turned their mounts and rode away. But Dark Cloud didn't move, his hawk-like gaze riveted sullenly on me.

With a flounce of her head, Hannah lifted her chin and turned her back on the lone warrior, moving toward the center of the village as if she hadn't noticed the taciturn young man.

I shot Dark Cloud a look and followed Hannah, nudging my horse forward. When finally out of his presence, I slid down to the ground and held the reins as I trailed the slender girl.

"They tell me you brought two cows." She glanced at me over her shoulder, a shrewd, curious look that made me ponder. Did she guess the intent of my visit? I didn't have long to wonder as she weaved a path between tents, countless Indian faces peering at us as we passed. "The cows are a good gift. Is there something you want from the Comanche?"

Her boldness unnerved me a little, but I walked on, leading my horse through the noisy village as onlookers pointed and whispered loudly about me. They knew me, or at least they knew Pa, yet my presence among them must have caused some concern. Only a tentative truce existed between the settlers and the Comanche camps that occupied western Texas. Land ownership had become a major issue on the plains. With more pioneers encroaching onto Indian lands, some massacres and attacks had occurred, although we hadn't experienced any hostile attention.

I narrowed my eyes, recalling the lone warrior who had stared me down when Hannah found me in camp. Dark Cloud certainly seemed hostile, although he hadn't done anything to me. Still, if looks could kill ...

I hadn't answered her inquiry, wanting to speak first with her pa, but she glanced at me again as she led me to a larger tent on the edge of camp. "It will be dark soon and it is too late to ride home tonight. You will be my guest."

A small cluster of children tagged along behind us, watching the spurs on my boots with fascination. As we stopped before the large teepee, I ground-hitched my horse and glanced back at the pressing crowd as Hannah lifted a flap and stepped into the tent. Dark Cloud caught my eye, the brave who'd ignored Hannah's instructions, and crossed his arms over his powerful chest, a challenging look chiseled into his stern features. I nodded at the fierce warrior and pulled my rifle from the scabbard as I followed Hannah into the teepee.

CHAPTER 20

Behind me, the thick tent flap fell into place, cutting the biting wind, and I stared about me, allowing my eyes to adjust to the gloom of the spacious room. A lance and two bows with a quiver of arrows hung on strings along the walls. Two women moved from the fire in the middle of the room to sit in the shadows. Only an aged man sat near the small blaze, his gaze fixed on the dancing flames as I listened to Hannah announce my presence.

Her father seemed to not hear, but when Hannah finished her speech and sat down beside him, he glanced over his shoulder and signaled to the silent women. One of them hurried to pour from a water skin and handed the tin cup to me before hastening to her seat once more.

Gratefully, I sipped the cold water as my eyes continued to roam the interior. The buffalo-hide walls had been painted with colorful designs, marked indications of the chief's status and achievements. Piles of furs and blankets lay about the floor, and I wondered if Hannah still lived here with her father and his wives. Surely, she was a maiden of marrying age and no doubt Dark Cloud had been a champion of hers.

A chill knifed my chest at the unexpected thought that he might even be her husband. Was Hannah Tall Basket married?

After a long minute, the old man spoke. His words flowed with a melody I enjoyed, the language beautiful to hear. But Hannah's pa never smiled as he talked.

Hannah nodded and looked at me, gesturing to the elk hide below me. Slowly, I lowered to the ground and placed my rifle beside me. "Buffalo Horn wants to know what has brought our neighbor on this visit."

Pa always taught me to be honest with Indians. They respected honesty and bravery and little else. "I have brought two cows as gifts for my Comanche friends. I hope this gift will be received well. I would like to ask my neighbors for a favor."

Hannah must've sensed my nervousness, for she smiled encouragingly before turning to translate my words. As far back as I could remember, Hannah had always been our interpreter when Pa and I visited the Comanche. I recalled a tale of her being sent away to learn English, a story I promised to verify after this meeting with her pa.

The old chief motioned to my rifle and pointed to the pistol at my belt and said something. Hannah bit her lip, and her worried look made me even more nervous.

"Father ..." she began and then hesitated, glancing at her pa before starting again. "Buffalo Horn asks if the rider you saved is well? Your guns are loud and strong against the Comanche braves who chased him."

My stomach clenched. So, they knew about my rescuing James. Well, what was I thinking? Of course, they would know. Would my scalp soon hang in a Comanche lodge?

"Yes, the rider was hurt, and I saved him." I thought it best not to apologize for the dead or wounded Indians. Maybe my coming was not such a good idea.

Hannah interpreted quickly and Buffalo Horn nodded. He said something that made Hannah grin, her white teeth flashing in the gloomy room.

"He says you are brave, Johnny Garret. Brave like a Comanche who joins a battle not his own for the joy of the fight. To have victory in battle is strong medicine."

The old man and Hannah nodded, their dark eyes intent on me. I shrugged, not sure how to feel. Was I brave for rescuing James? I didn't feel brave.

Buffalo Horn spoke again, and I studied Hannah. "My father says those young braves were not wise tackling a seasoned warrior. The rider had arrows in him and still fought. You rescued him from the braves, but my father thinks maybe you rescued the braves from the rider."

I tilted my head, startled as the old man nodded sagely.

The door flap opened, and Dark Cloud stood there, glaring at me, waiting for permission to speak. The tent lapsed into silence, and I waited as anticipation swelled within me. Surely his arrival didn't bode well for me.

At a gesture from Buffalo Horn, the young man broke into rapid speech, gesticulating wildly as he pointed at me and ranted. I gripped the tin cup tightly with one hand and laid my other on the pistol at my belt. When he finished, he seated himself next to Hannah, a little too closely, I thought.

Hannah looked at me and I read worry in her eyes. "Dark Cloud says you stole an enemy from his friends. They were not through with the rider, and you stole him away, robbing the braves of a scalp. He wants your scalp in return."

No one spoke for a long moment, and I gripped my pistol tighter. If the chief allowed Dark Cloud to take me, I wasn't going without a fight. I glanced at Buffalo Horn, wondering what he might decide.

The old chief lifted his eyes to Dark Cloud and said something that made Hannah stiffen, but she made no move to protest. I waited, hoping I still had a chance to plead my case with the chief. We needed permission to take the shortcut across Indian lands if we expected to arrive at the military forts before snowfall.

Hannah leaned close to me and whispered, "Father says that if a man saves another man's life, it is good. If the braves had strong medicine, your rescue would never have happened. He says the Creator is with you."

I felt my brow furrow. Was God with me? Certainly Ma and Paul thought so. Even James surprised me with his declaration he would throw his faith into the adventure that enveloped our ranch since the war ended.

Where did I stand on the spiritual aspect of events? Surely God lived, I knew that. But I'd felt cheated by the unending challenges that smothered us. Would we never catch a break?

Then I recalled the arrival of Paul and the finding of Red Bill. Surely the Lord was looking out for us, right? Still, I wasn't sure.

The old chief spoke, and Hannah turned to me with an anxious look, as if warning me that my answer might decide my fate. "Buffalo Horn wants to know the favor you ask of the Comanche."

I drew a deep breath and gathered my courage. "I've come this far," I muttered. Clearing my throat, I went on. "I wish my neighbor to allow me to drive cattle across his land. Safe passage for me and a friend. I will give you beef for this permission."

I held my breath, waiting, wondering if my life were about to end. Would I die in this Indian teepee, in front of this pretty girl? I glanced at Hannah as she translated my request, but she only stared at the dying fire, not meeting my searching gaze.

Before the old man could respond, Dark Cloud howled and interjected with a loud tirade. He pointed at me and yelled with an accusing note.

Hannah leaned toward me. "He says this is bad what you ask. Why should the Comanche allow you to cross our lands and sell food to our enemies? He does not give you permission."

Suddenly Dark Cloud shook his fist at me, his face darkening in the shadowed light of the murky tent. He rose to his feet, standing tall as he crossed his arms over his broad chest. He spoke, his eyes locked on Hannah as he said his final words. With a grunt, he shoved the tent flap aside and left the teepee.

Hannah dropped her gaze and Buffalo Horn narrowed his eyes, but neither spoke for a long moment.

"What is it, Hannah? What did he say?" I could tell his words hurt her deeply and she seemed reluctant to reply. With a glance at her father, she shifted on her elk hide cushion. "Dark Cloud says you do not have the protection of the Great Spirit on you. He says he will kill you if he finds you alone on the prairie." Here she lowered her eyes again and continued softly. "He also says that I am to be his wife and you had better not try to interfere."

Cold blood chilled my veins as I studied her in the dim light, the low blaze casting a ruddy glow on her copper skin.

"You're to marry him?"

She lifted her face and a wide grin spread across her troubled features. She shook her head. "No, no. Dark Cloud wants to marry me because my father is chief. It will advance his position in the tribe. But father will not allow it. He says he knows who I am to marry, and it is not Dark Cloud."

I held up a hand, stilling her speech. "Wait, wait. He knows who you are to marry?" I paused and my gaze shifted to the old man. Buffalo Horn tugged at the deer hide that draped his shoulders, wrapping the cover closer as he stared back at me, stoic. I wondered at the amused glint in his eyes.

"Who is it?" I persisted.

Hannah giggled, and my gaze shifted once more to the girl, her sadness gone now as she laughed. "He'll never tell," she said with a note of pride. "He says he has known for years, but cannot tell. The man I am to marry is a secret."

I leaned back, suddenly aware I'd been holding my breath.

Hannah tilted her head. "Why, Johnny? Why do you care who marries me?"

Shaking my head, I leaned forward once more. "I don't know. I mean, of course, we're friends. I'm just curious, that's all." I studied her, enjoying the way the firelight danced upon her smooth skin. The glowing blaze reflected in her gaze, and I felt myself pulled toward her, as if about to fall into a great depth.

Buffalo Horn grunted and I jumped, forgetting we were not alone. He watched me closely with a gleam in his sharp eyes as he spoke. Hannah listened attentively to the old man and then nodded, rising as she motioned for me to follow.

She slipped first through the tent flap, but I hesitated, not sure I'd presented my case adequately to the Comanche chief. I nodded at Buffalo Horn and followed Hannah into the gathering twilight.

"Father says," Hannah faltered, stumbling over the confusing titles for her pa. "I mean Buffalo Horn." She sighed and strode into the thickening gloom, her statement unfinished.

I glanced all around, saw the previous crowds had vanished, and tagged along with the Indian princess. I'd presented my case to the old chief, but I felt pensive, unsure

I'd done so effectively. What would we do if the Comanche refused passage across their lands?

I shot a hurried prayer heavenward and stalked after Hannah, seeing she walked toward my horse where the animal had been picketed on a tuft of grass a short distance from camp. She halted alongside the animal and stared out over the darkening prairie as I unsaddled the weary horse, dropping my gear in a pile.

"I'm Buffalo Horn's youngest daughter," she shared suddenly.

I arranged my saddle beside my bedding before retrieving a brush from my saddlebags, prepared to curry my horse after my short trek from home. Slow arcs of the brush warmed me as I worked, a gentle breeze drifting across the plains. Overhead, I caught sight of the evening star, the first of the night. Soon, the sky would gleam with countless pinpoints of such glittering lights.

"No sons?" I ventured, liking the sound of her voice and not wanting her to fall silent.

"My mother was his youngest wife. She died when I was born. He has no sons, and he has told me I was born to herald something new to him. In a vision, he saw a message he has kept secret, but he says a part of the vision was to send me north to the missionary school in the Nation, the school for Indian children on the reservation. He told me to learn English and I would speak with white visitors."

My hand stilled and I leaned against the gelding. "He knew he would have white visitors?"

Hannah took a step toward me, her arms dropping to her side. "The others didn't like his prophetic message, but it soon came true when your family delivered cattle to our camp that winter, saving us from starvation. Since then, a cloud hangs over us, a feeling that something is to happen to us with the white settlers."

My hand moved again, brushing swifter now, for I hated her words. Pa had said something similar to me the day after we delivered the cattle to the starving Comanche, years ago. He'd said the Indians had seen their best days, and with the killing of the buffalo and the coming of the pioneers, soon the Comanche would be pushed off the prairie. I hated the impending demise of our neighbors, and what it might mean for Hannah. We were just friends, but I'd been thinking of her a lot lately and wondered if there were more I could do for her.

"Father says I am to marry a man who will take care of me, protect me. I am to wait for him, but he is not Dark Cloud." She scratched the horse's ears, and I watched as the gelding nuzzled her neck, her black hair ruffling in the evening breeze. I almost pushed a rebellious tendril into place, then shook myself, startled at my unexpected thoughts.

"Buffalo Horn says he will think on your request and tell you his answer in the morning," she added, as if suddenly remembering the purpose of my visit. I nodded and shoved the brush back into my bags. As I straightened, I caught her stare before she looked hurriedly away, dropping her gaze. Shyly, she looked at me again and grinned. "Now, Johnny Garret, you are my guest. Would you like to enjoy the beef you delivered?"

Large fires blazed around camp and the smell of roasting beef filled the air. When I nodded, she took my hand and led me to the nearest fire. For the next few hours, we talked.

I felt surprised how easily the words came. I'd never been a hand at talking with girls, but with Hannah it seemed different. I found myself telling her of Pa dying in the war and not coming home. I spoke of Paul and Lydia, our plan to sell cattle to the forts, and eventually of James and Ma. For some reason, this was the part that most interested her.

"Do you think they love each other?" Her eyes glowed with an excitement I didn't understand while the firelight cast shadows dancing across her bronzed cheeks. I found it difficult to concentrate with her sitting so close.

I snorted. "No, of course not. They've only just met."

Hannah smiled mischievously, a knowing glint in her dark eyes. "What do you know of a woman's heart, Johnny? You do not know what lies in a woman, ready to blossom when the time is right. Maybe your mother is ready to love again."

"It is too soon," I protested weakly, a little irritated that she might comprehend Ma better than me. "They've only just met," I repeated, but I remembered the longing in Ma's eyes when she asked about James.

Hannah only smiled and shrugged as she gnawed at a rib bone. "We will see," she said with a prophetic note that made me uneasy.

CHAPTER 21

The chill of a Texas autumn morning awakened me, and I snuggled deeper into my blankets, studying the dark blue expanse above. Only a few stars remained as I stretched and laced my fingers behind my head to watch the sunrise.

The previous evening with Hannah had left me with a sense of wonderment I'd never experienced before, nor identified. Why this complete feeling of excitement and anticipation, like I couldn't wait to see her again? Of course, I figured it out as I watched the sky turn a deeper blue and then gray before a pink tinge hovered on the eastern horizon. I'd rarely had friends, certainly no one I'd seen often. Hannah was the only person my age I could call a friend, someone I'd seen occasionally. Yet the way she filled my mind surprised me.

Something niggled at me, and I frowned as my happy memories of Hannah fled. Buffalo Horn's assertion that the Creator was with me annoyed me, and I squinted at the fading stars.

"Are you with me?" My whispered plea lifted quietly from the vast Texas prairie. I couldn't help but wonder if the Lord heard me.

"Ma prayed for help, and you sent Paul, although you certainly took your sweet time about it. We've needed help for so long. And I can't deny Red Bill's body surely helped."

I paused, enjoying the frank conversation with Jesus. Of course, he wasn't saying anything, and I savored the opportunity to say what was on my mind without opposition. I know if Ma or even Paul were here, hearing my prayer, they'd have choice arguments about God's perfect timing and how the Lord worked all things to the good of those who loved him. But for right now, I relished the chance to state my case before God of the universe, if he were truly listening.

"I counted on Pa coming home after the war. Now, I'm burdened with a weight that feels too heavy for me. Is this your will for me? To crush me?"

I paused again, then sighed. "Ma thinks we're on a great adventure. Well, you know I'm skeptical."

Something moved in camp, and I turned, watching as tent flaps opened to the east to allow the morning light to enter. The Indians stirred. I stretched again before tugging on my boots and rolling my blankets.

When I'd finished packing, I saddled the gelding. Nearby, women pegged skins to the ground and worked at scraping the flesh and sinews from hides, preparing them for bedding or tent covers. Children scampered after barking dogs that now ignored me, my presence no longer a novelty. The feasting of last evening flashed again into my memory and I grinned, recalling the smiles and comradery of the friendly people. Especially Hannah. Why was it so easy to talk to her?

Leading my horse to the stream, I allowed him to drink while I washed my face and hands. Hunger evaded me after last night's feast, but I dearly wished for a cup of coffee. After returning to camp, a brave motioned for me to follow him. With a gesture, he indicated Buffalo Horn's lodge.

I entered and allowed my eyes to adjust to the dimly lit room. Several men sat around the small fire in the center of the teepee. Hannah was there too, and she gestured for me to take a seat beside her. Dark Cloud glared at me across the little blaze, but I scanned the circle, supposing the other men were elders of the tribe.

"The council has made their decision about your request for crossing Comanche land with your cattle," Hannah whispered.

I nodded, not taking my gaze from the circle of men. Then, as if pulled by an unseen hand, I looked into her eyes, searching for some indication of the council's decision. Hannah said nothing and dropped her gaze to study the smoking fire.

Buffalo Horn shifted, drawing my attention. The old chief spoke and then motioned for Hannah to interpret.

A dark shadow crossed her smooth features, but she held her head high. "Buffalo Horn says the Comanche have fought hard for many years to take and protect this land from many enemies. If everyone were allowed to cross our lands, they would soon lose respect for the Comanche. They would think it is open land and the Comanche would have nothing left. You, Johnny Garret, do not have permission to cross our lands with your cattle."

My shoulders sagged under the weight of her words. Our plan to sell cattle and make money was finished. What would we do now? Angrily, I scoffed, knowing I'd been right to be distrustful of the Lord. He wasn't with me. Despite Ma's great faith, there was no sovereign plan for us or the ranch.

My mind whirled with anxious thoughts. How would we eat and buy things and pay our property taxes next time?

I glanced around the small fire, hoping against hope that I'd heard her words incorrectly. But the stoic faces that peered back at me confirmed I'd heard correctly. Only Dark Cloud's features held a note of triumph.

Hannah's father spoke again, and his words were quick where before he'd spoken slow and deliberate. A twinkle glinted in his old eyes, and he stared at Dark Cloud as he talked. With a motion, he indicated Hannah translate.

"Johnny," she began, and the way she said my name made me look at her. Her wide eyes shone in the dim firelight. "Father says that in the winter, the Comanche like to stay near their fires and inside their lodges. For the winter only, the Comanche will not travel north of Yellow Creek. Come springtime, Comanche lands will again include all the land far to the north."

I glanced at Dark Cloud and felt pleased to see the look of triumph had vanished, a look of surprise and anger creasing his scowling face.

For a long moment, no one spoke or moved. Was I hearing this right? Was the chief letting me have travel rights if I stayed north of Yellow Creek? I looked at Dark Cloud openly now and grinned. His threatening glower rewarded me that I had indeed heard right, and my spirits soared.

"I can't believe this is happening," I breathed as Hannah walked me to my horse. A sense of incredulity hovered around me.

"Why not?" She shrugged as I shoved my rifle into the boot. "The Lord is with you."

"You too?" I frowned as I stepped into the saddle, seating myself as I tugged my collar higher. Despite the faded blue sky, a brisk gust blustered from the north.

"What do you mean?" She looked up at me, shielding her eyes from the sun.

"Ma is always talking like that, telling me we're on a spiritual journey or something."

Hannah nodded, her eyes glowing with interest. "Perhaps you are. I have seen the way you have grown. Maybe Jesus is asking more of you than you feel comfortable giving."

I tilted my head. "Huh? I don't even pretend to understand that."

Her laughter lilted like a melody. "I mean, I've seen you step up and take charge now that your pa is gone. It was you who found the dead man on the trail and you who rescued the rider from the braves. And it is you who asked Buffalo Horn for safe passage."

I shrugged as I gathered the reins. "So?"

She smiled and her teeth dazzled in the dull sunlight. "So, we are growing up. We are not children anymore. You are becoming a leader and a brave man."

My eyebrows arched at her encouraging words. "I didn't look at it that way." I thought of Ma's claim that God was doing something great with our ranch, and I wondered. Despite my reluctance, was I a participant of her unwanted adventure?

"As you look to the Lord, he will deepen your faith," she added with a serious look on her pretty face.

Now it was my turn to laugh. "You *do* sound like Ma," I accused with a grin. "But things have been so difficult. We've had really hard times. Sometimes I doubt if God is with us."

She stepped back from my prancing horse, the gelding impatient to get moving. "Hard times come when we least want them. Storms blow, and the wind breaks weak branches from the trees. But the tree that still stands is stronger because of the storm."

CHAPTER 22

Topping a nearby ridge, I reined in the gelding and looked down at the Indian village below the bluff. Hannah still stood there, her long hair blowing gently in the morning breeze. I stroked the buffalo hide robe that lay across my knees—the Comanche's parting gift for the pair of steers I'd delivered—and lifted my hand to wave.

As she watched my departure, my heart swelled. I'd come asking favors and had left with great news. Also, an old acquaintance had been rekindled into something more than I dared hope for. And what had Buffalo Horn wished to convey to me by allowing safe passage across their land during the winter?

I turned the gelding and galloped to the east, eager to return home. A dull blue sky stretched overhead, and I knew the long hot days of summer were behind me for another season. But autumn lingered with vibrant, rich-colored leaves clinging to the trees along the streams. Gratefully, I realized winter was not upon the plains yet.

I raced across the prairie, my thoughts swirling with questions and ideas. Why had Buffalo Horn allowed such a kind offer? Was it to help my family for our generosity over the years, or was it to infuriate Dark Cloud, to let the young brave know his attention to the old chief's daughter was not appreciated?

My heart warmed as I thought of Hannah, our time together, and her final words. Was there a purpose in the storms of my life? Would they make me stronger as I leaned into the Lord?

Without cattle to push, I made quick time. Paul came to meet me as I rode into the yard.

"John, I see you still have your hair." He grinned as I handed him the buffalo robe and swung down from the saddle. We shook hands. I'd missed him.

"Paul, I want to hear all about your trip to fetch Lydia. How is she?"

Before he could reply, Ma stepped through the kitchen door into the yard and hugged me tightly. I felt embarrassed at her open appreciation for my safe return, but I felt pleased too. Although I was the man of the place now, I still needed a mother.

"I'm all right, Ma," I said into her hair before she stepped back and studied me.

"You look older somehow, Johnny."

I grinned, wondering if my time with Hannah had affected me in any way. Just then, Lydia peeked around the corner of the house, her eyes wide with curiosity as she watched me and Ma.

"I'll make fresh coffee," Ma said as she returned to the kitchen. Paul held my gelding's reins as I nodded at Lydia.

"Good afternoon, Lydia. You were wet and tired last I saw you."

She only stared at me, like I was a two-headed calf. Paul took a step closer.

"It's okay, Lydia. John won't bite. Come over here and meet him proper." He motioned her forward and she grasped his hand.

"I hope you find our ranch comfortable. I'm glad you've come to live here." I spoke softly, not knowing exactly what to say, but wanting her to relax.

Paul shifted. "She sure is happy to be here. She keeps telling me she feels like it's a dream."

"Well, it's no dream," I said in a gruffer tone than I'd intended. "Lots of hard work and long days."

I hoped she couldn't hear the bitterness in my words. Abruptly, her brow furrowed, and she glanced at Paul before she spoke. "I'm surely used to hard work, but I appreciate your kindness to me and Paul. And we're excited to join your adventure with you and Miss Annie."

A scowl tugged at my jaw, and I nodded again before turning to the kitchen. "I'll see you at supper," I mumbled as I stumbled to the kitchen, suddenly tired.

My journey to the Comanche village had been taxing, yet a different weariness settled in my bones. I felt tired of talking of our adventure, the unreasonable nature of the situation annoying me as I sat at the table and stared at the hot cup of coffee before me. Ma bustled around the kitchen, telling me of the countless eggs the chickens were laying, but all I could think of was the Lord. Had he blessed me with the permission from the Indians? A nameless sensation hovered around me as if I were being watched by unseen eyes. Steam wafted from the hot mug and warmed my chilled face, but I had forgotten the cool fall afternoon. Buffalo Horn's final words played in my mind, and I eagerly looked forward to James's return.

Ma came to join me. As a rancher's wife, she'd learned to let hungry men eat before information could be shared. Priorities. Finally, I pushed my empty plate away.

"Well, Johnny, I'm dying to hear." She carried my dirty dishes to the counter and refilled my coffee mug. When she brought the steaming cup to the table and resumed her seat, I could read the look of hope and anticipation on her face. "Tell me what the Indians said."

As I blew on the hot drink, I eyed her over the rim, not able to keep my good news from her any longer. "Hannah's father said we could cross, but only during the winter, as long as we stayed north of Yellow Creek. That gives us almost a straight shot to Fort Union and the reservations in the Nation. I'm sure we can drive small bunches of cattle that far." I paused to take another sip. "I don't know why we can't start as soon as James returns."

Her face stiffened at mention of the army dispatch rider, an anxious look crossing her features. "Oh, Johnny, do you think he'll come back? I think I scared him off. He is a free riding man, and I sort of hinted he'd be welcome on the ranch."

I shrugged, hoping beyond hope that James would return, but wanting to clarify Ma's expectations. "No telling. He might think we're too much of a gamble. His dispatch job provides monthly pay he might not want to give up. Can't blame him," I concluded, my sour words discouraging even to me.

Ma drew a deep breath and lifted her chin. "No, I won't believe that. It's no accident he came to our ranch, and no accident you saved him from the Indians. The Lord brought him here for a purpose. I believe that. I must believe that."

Again, she looked doubtful but then shook her head. "Do you really think this could work? We've had such a run of bad luck. For years, we lived off wild onions and beef and a few vegetables from the garden. We almost lost the ranch."

"I think you're wise to consider all options, all challenges. I hope this works, but it might turn out to be nothing."

She shook her head again. "I can't allow myself to think like that. I need to have faith. The battle belongs to the Lord. If God is for us, who can stand against us?"

I sighed. I'd heard Ma say these words a thousand times, but now she believed they were coming true. Did I? I glanced at the ceiling, still not sure. God had disappointed me too many times before. Ma said the Lord's timing was not our timing, and a truer statement never existed. If I were God, I'd never have us suffer as we had.

What had he been waiting for?

Walking to the barn, I saw Lydia had returned to the laundry, and Paul was feeding the chickens. I watched him for a moment as he scattered the feed over the barn floor. The chickens ran to gobble the seeds, their necks stretched comically.

"Lydia seems like a wonderful girl but a bit shy. Is she going to be all right?"

He tossed another handful of feed. "Yes, I think so. She's having a hard time trusting this can be real." He gestured to the house, the yard, and the outbuildings. "We never had a place of our own."

He told me of their trip to the ranch, starving as they walked in the cold rain. "She worries this might be too good to be true. But she loves our cabin and the glass window. Our own fireplace and books on the mantel. I promised to teach her to read as I learn myself. I'm getting the hang of it."

"You will, Paul. Give it time." I shifted and glanced over my shoulder, making sure Ma wasn't close. "We're in a bad way. We need money. I'm hoping to drive small bunches of cattle to the outposts with James, if he comes back."

Paul chuckled. "He'll come back, don't you fret. Did you see the way that army man looked at Miss Annie?"

"I don't want him to come back just for her," I snapped. "I need to make the ranch a real business, producing an income. Winter is soon approaching, and we need to stock a store of supplies."

My mind went over the additional folks added to the ranch, possibly including James. We would need a lot of supplies to feed this crew.

"The Lord is our strength. Trust, John, and lay your fears on him. God is faithful. He's started a mighty work here and he'll see it through."

Paul's words fell on deaf ears, and I sighed. Clenching my teeth, I returned to the house, the buffalo robe under one arm. The large hide made a welcoming cover to the worn leather couch, and I stared at the skin and remembered the Indian camp.

Footsteps behind me made me glance over my shoulder. Ma stood in the hallway, studying me. Her gaze darted to the buffalo skin and then back again as she crossed her arms over her chest and leaned against the wall.

"Did you see Hannah when you visited the Comanche?" She eyed me innocently, but I shifted, sensing something more to her inquiry. She knew I needed a translator to communicate with the Indians.

"Ma, you know she was there. How could I talk to them without her?" I felt a little annoyed at her question, almost defensive.

"Well, I just wondered. You should invite her to dinner sometime."

I snorted. "How can I invite her to dinner? She doesn't live nearby."

She smiled. "Ah, but you would if she did." She patted my arm before turning to her bedroom. "I want to pray before I turn in. I'll say goodnight now, Son," she said softly as her door closed, and I wondered what all that was about.

CHAPTER 23

For the next five days, I rounded up cattle, moving them closer to the house. I even did a little branding. I wanted to make sure I pushed the stock onto pieces of ground that provided good grass and easy access to water. I didn't want them drifting far from the ranch house when the time came for the cattle drives.

Pa told me once that people back east had fences all around their land, keeping their animals from straying. I couldn't believe it. Out here in Texas, none of our land was fenced and the cattle roamed where they wished. I remember asking Pa where the easterners got all the wood for their fences.

"Vast forests cover much of the Atlantic seaboard—tall trees used for houses and fences and barns. But they don't have the cattle herds we do, nor the extensive, open plains," Pa had explained, his eyes shining as he surveyed our immense land holdings.

On the evening of the fifth day since my return from the Indian village, I saw James talking to Paul beside the barn as I cantered into the yard. A chill descended as the sun slipped behind the western horizon, and I felt pleased to come home after a long day on the prairie.

James lifted his hand in greeting. A cloud of dust hovered around me as I halted near the hitching rail, and I swung down, tossing the reins over the rail as I watched James approach. He'd shaved and his face looked tanned and smooth. His rugged features were shadowed in the fading glow of the day. Instead of the faded blue army jacket, he now wore a new red flannel shirt and a cowhide vest, but still wore his cavalry hat.

"John, I'm glad to see you." We shook hands. "Paul told me about the Indians." His grip felt firm, and I grinned, appreciating the way he treated me like a man.

"When did you ride in?" I glanced toward the kitchen door.

He saw my quick look at the house and shifted as he kicked at a rock with the toe of his boot. "Oh, an hour or so, I guess. I would've been here sooner, but I had to pick up something special in town."

He shot another look at the house and then slapped me on the shoulder. Taking my reins, he led my horse to the barn, talking nonstop about the impending trek planned for Fort Union. I followed, feeling like he'd changed the subject abruptly.

While I unsaddled in the barn, James leaned against a pole and listened as I gave the details of the arrangement with the Comanche. "Buffalo Horn only will allow passage during winter, north of Yellow Creek."

The former dispatch rider nodded and thrust a piece of hay between his teeth, chewing thoughtfully. "Why'd the old chief do that? Is he or the girl a Christian?"

My hands stilled as I brushed my horse. "A Christian?" I glanced at him over my shoulder. "What makes you say that?"

James was silent a long moment as I continued brushing. When I reached for the grain bin to retrieve a bit of corn, he spoke.

"I've been angry for a long time, tossing my faith aside. Or at least wrestling with the Lord, blaming him for everything."

Kernels rattled loudly in the feed trough, and I strained to hear him above the noise, eager to hear his response more than I cared to admit.

"When those Comanche jumped me and you rescued me, I'd been praying, wondering where God was in all of it. Then I came here and met your ma and felt challenged to turn to the Lord again."

I slapped the horse on the rump as I stepped from the stall and faced James, curious but not wanting to show my interest. I glanced toward the milk cow, feigning indifference, but I held my breath to catch every word he shared.

"I'm convinced there is a great event going on here, and I'm honored to be a part. I don't feel up to the difficulty of this situation, but the Lord is." He paused and lowered his voice before going on. "And so is your ma. I've never met a more faithful woman. She is committed to watch Jesus solve her problems in any way the Lord chooses."

I drew a deep breath and looked at him, tired of the spiritual hullaballoo that surrounded our ranch these days yet intrigued by this rider's insight. God challenged James's faith. Was the Lord challenging me to trust him more?

"Why did you wonder about the Comanche being Christian?" I wondered, bringing him back to the topic at hand.

James smiled and then nodded. "Sorry. Kind of strayed, didn't I? I only wondered because this whole thing feels covered in the Spirit, as if the Lord is trying to do something mighty here. Whether to grow my faith or have believers gather in force to accomplish something good, I don't know. But the Indians are clearly playing a part. Why would the old chief allow us to cross their lands? That seems like God is involved, right?"

A scowl settled on my face, my brows bunching. Buffalo Horn had been unexpectedly kind to us. Was it the Lord's doing?

"Hannah said she'd been sent to the missionary school to learn English. She might've been told of Jesus while she was there," I suggested, angry I hadn't asked her of her stay at the distant school. Instead, I'd taken the time around the feasting fires to fill her ear with my worries and concerns. I felt ashamed of being so self-absorbed.

James led the way out of the gloomy barn and into the fading twilight. With his imminent return, I'd asked Paul to fix up one of the bunkhouses for him. Lydia had cleaned the old cabin and delivered blankets, a wash basin and pitcher, and a box of matches.

That night at supper, Ma was silent and pale as she scurried to serve everyone. Lydia helped, but the mood seemed strained, and Ma wouldn't meet my searching gaze. I informed Paul that I counted on him to watch the place in my absence. He beamed under the responsibility.

After supper, Ma disappeared into her bedroom when Paul and Lydia left for their cabin. James and I drank coffee while discussing the route we would take to Fort Union. His finger traced the path on our cow skin map, and I painstakingly sketched the military post on the Cimarron River. Carefully, I added Yellow Creek and the Pecos River.

"We'll gather our bunch tomorrow and be ready to depart the next day," James advised, sending another glance toward Ma's door. He'd been shooting sidelong glances that way all evening. "The weather is holding, and if it stays mild like this, we can complete a few more deliveries before snow flies."

His manner filled me with confidence, an assurance I hadn't felt in years. Could this really work? I felt reluctant to allow excitement to build within me, afraid of being disappointed.

"Do you really think we can push cattle to more than one outpost this fall?"

He seemed to study the map and then glanced again down the hallway. I pursed my lips, not liking his lack of attention. These cattle drives were important to me and would mean the difference between having food to eat this winter or possibly starving. The concept frightened me.

"James," I urged when he didn't respond.

He looked at me. "Huh? Did you say something?"

I shook my head and rolled up the map. "No. Don't worry about it. I think we're tired. See you in the morning."

Chairs scraped as we pushed away from the table. He nodded at me as he went out the door, a cool gust of wind slipping inside as he stepped to the back porch. Winter was coming, and I hoped we'd make at least a single drive to sell cattle.

I lowered the wick on the oil lamp and then lit a candle, prepared to go to my room when I noticed a dim light in the parlor. Ma leaned close to a candle, threading a needle into a sock.

I leaned against the door frame, watching. "You didn't have much to say tonight. We're going to gather cows tomorrow and then take off the day after." I spoke to her as if she hadn't heard our plans a dozen times, but I knew she had something on her mind.

"Oh?" She speared the needle into the sock and leaned back, her gaze lifting to mine. "I hope things work out," she mumbled softly.

"Work out?" My words sounded sharper than intended. "We've hoped for something like this for years. Why are you suddenly not interested?" She'd been praying for this, right? Wasn't this her adventure, her amazing opportunity? Why the abrupt disinterest?

She dropped her mending into her lap, her shoulders slumping as she stared at me. I thought I detected a glisten in her eyes, but the lighting wasn't good. "You wouldn't understand," she whispered.

I squinted and crossed my arms over my chest, my empty mug dangling from one finger. "Try me."

She sat up, her back straightening. "I'm afraid I'm losing my focus."

I squinted harder. "What does that mean?"

She looked away. "It's not fair to dump my worries on you. You have enough responsibility without me adding more fears."

I huffed impatiently. "Ma, we've been through a lot these past few years. You can tell me anything."

But she only stared at the wall. Her hand lifted slowly, as if very heavy, and she scratched her ear. The dim candlelight cast shadows over her features, but I read the worry there, etched into every line of her face.

She looked at me, and abruptly her eyes glowed with renewed purpose as she drew a deep breath. "I'm sorry, Johnny. I feel like the scales have fallen from my eyes and I see things clearly again. The cattle drive is everything. The Lord has ordained this, and we will remain faithful, ever sensitive to the Holy Spirit. I will pray for your success."

Puzzled, I nodded. Her familiar words of spiritual fervor comforted me as I turned and strode to the kitchen, depositing my mug on the counter. With the candle, I stepped into my room and undressed for bed.

Ma was always telling me how God would do this and do that, the wonders of the Lord never ceasing, but tonight I'd detected a chink in her divine armor, as if something else were on her mind. Something other than the adventure she had prophesied all summer.

CHAPTER 24

"Johnny, we'll need supplies before you and James leave tomorrow." Ma's call made me hurry, shoving my feet into my boots. I slung my gun belt around my waist as I stepped into the kitchen. The oil lamp burned brightly on the table, and the dark mantle of dawn lingered outside.

"I'm supposed to help James first thing, Ma," I protested, taking the steaming cup of coffee she offered.

She gestured to the seat at the table where a plate heaped with potatoes and a thick slice of cornbread waited.

"We're out of meat," she explained as she slid into a vacant seat across from me. I read the worry in her eyes, dark rings indicating she hadn't slept. I dropped my gaze and fell to breakfast. When I glanced to the back door, expecting to see James at any moment, Ma lifted her chin. "He had his breakfast an hour ago."

"Who?" I asked stupidly, for we both knew of whom she spoke.

"James came in early, while you slept." A crimson wave crept up her neck and she looked away, fidgeting with her apron. "We need supplies," she repeated, trying to change the subject.

"I doubt Mr. Anderson will give us more credit," I mumbled around a mouth full of cornbread.

The worried look had returned, and her cheeks paled as she leaned forward. "You must try. Go to town immediately and see what he says. If it doesn't work, I'll go in a day or two. Without supplies, we won't last until you return with cash money."

The desire to lash out and accuse her of failing faith niggled at the edge of my mind, but I bit my tongue. A freezing rain had fallen last week, reminding me that winter could come swiftly to the north Texas plains. I needed to push cattle to the forts quickly, and Ma would need stores in my absence, enough food for three hungry folks. James and I would have some supplies, but we'd have to stop and hunt to supplement our meager stores. I nodded, not wishing to delay our trip any more than necessary. Besides, the look of apprehension in Ma's face had deepened into dread. Her adventure was testing her resolve, and I didn't want to take this moment to remind her I'd been the voice of reason, telling her God didn't care if we failed or succeeded.

Her fear frightened me. Before, I'd leaned on her relationship with Jesus, heckling her while at the same time drawing strength from her faith. Now she seemed genuinely scared, and I knew I needed to talk to Mr. Anderson before James and I headed for Fort Union.

I hurried to the barn, congratulating myself at avoiding an argument. There would be no winners in this fight if we didn't have enough food to get through the winter. But I felt nettled, blaming Ma for getting us into this adventure, this test of faith I wondered if God would honor.

Paul worked in a stall, a lantern casting a soft glow on the gelding he saddled for me. I checked the cinch before shoving my rifle into the scabbard and swinging into the saddle.

"James said to tell you he's on the north meadow, bunching cattle and preparing for branding. He'll expect you in a couple of hours."

I felt my eyes narrow as I nodded. So, Ma had talked to James about my errand to town. He was a stranger to us, but he'd worked quickly to get into the business of the ranch. What was his game? Did he truly seek to build his faith, or did a pretty widow have anything to do with his eagerness to help?

Spurring the gelding, I rode for town. Cold wind buffeted me as I galloped the few miles, slowing to a trot only when I saw the outbuildings of the small prairie town.

A rooster crowed from the livery as my horse walked down the main street, only a single light glowing in the café when I passed. Drawing rein in front of Anderson's mercantile, I swung down, shoving my gloves into my pockets as I pushed through the front door.

"Wait a minute," Mr. Anderson boomed from the back counter as he lighted a lantern. Wind whistled through cracks in the door behind me, and I shivered. Soon a halo of light stretched around the smiling clerk.

"Ah, Johnny Garret. Come in, come in," he greeted warmly.

I moved toward him, maneuvering a path around piles of dried goods, heaps of blankets, and barrels of flour. The storekeeper grinned as I approached, and I had to admit his sincerity surprised me. We'd owed this man money for months.

"Morning, Mr. Anderson," I began. I'd tried to rehearse a speech on my way into town, but all my prepared words vanished now that I stood before the clerk.

"Morning," he nodded. "And how is your ma?"

I shifted, his kindness unnerving me. Last time I'd come to his store, he'd lamented loudly about giving credit to folks who don't pay their debt. He'd swore that would be the last time, yet here he smiled at me. Surely, he could guess the mission of my visit.

Figuring the best approach was to just spit it out, I stepped forward. "Mr. Anderson, I'll need credit for more supplies. We're making a cattle drive that should provide some cash money, if all goes well. But I'll need credit for now."

He nodded and slipped an apron around his neck. Taking a pencil from his pocket, he licked the point and pressed the tip to a note pad. "Go ahead." He tapped the pencil on the paper.

I gave him my order, afraid he'd stop me at any moment and tell me I'd gone too far. But he didn't interrupt except to offer suggestions on amounts of flour and coffee and other staples.

Finally, he tallied the amount in his book. I thanked him as I gathered the supplies and headed for the door.

"I met your new hand yesterday."

His unexpected words halted me, and I glanced over my shoulder. "James?"

The storekeeper nodded. "James Casey, that's right. He paid your tab and bought a silver comb."

Well, you could've knocked me over with a feather. I stared, unable to speak. Gripping my purchases a little tighter, I walked out onto the boardwalk where the morning chill enveloped me, reminding me we needed to hurry if we intended to beat old man winter.

It took only a few minutes to pack my supplies, all the time my mind whirled. So, James had come by the store and paid our bill. I chewed my lip and swung into the saddle, wondering why the dispatch rider would do such a thing. How should I feel about another man paying my bills? Grateful, I supposed.

Yet something rankled in me, making me uneasy as I spurred the gelding into a trot and left town. As I rode across the windswept plains toward home, my mind kept coming back to Ma. Did James pay our bill because of her?

My cold cheeks pinched when I narrowed my eyes, feeling awkward about a man showing Ma attention. She deserved new friends, and I appreciated the developing alliance the adventure had fostered, but what were James's intentions?

I tugged my hat lower. I was the man of the ranch now. True, Pa wasn't coming home, but I was a man, and James needed to talk to me before undertaking such decisions on his own.

As I trotted into the yard, Paul came to meet me, wearing Red Bill's sheepskin coat. I tumbled the supplies into his arms before turning the gelding toward the gathered cattle on the north side of the house. With knots coiling in my gut, I rode to meet James, knowing I had to confront him.

His gaze lifted from the branding fire at his feet when I approached. He stood there, a tall, rangy man in his cow skin vest and battered cavalry hat. A dented coffeepot simmered in the coals. I reined in, peering at him. He had to guess I'd found things out when I rode to town, but he didn't say anything as he tilted his head, just watching me, waiting.

"Is there any coffee?" I leaned one hand on the pommel, wondering how to begin.

He filled a blackened tin cup and handed the mug to me. I nodded my thanks and shifted, my saddle creaking in the morning breeze. Cattle bawled noisily, and I glanced at the cluster, the small herd of twenty head of stock looking at me as I sat my horse.

Sipping the scalding coffee, I studied James over the rim of the mug. He appeared casual, his gaze scanning the bunch of cattle and the distant prairie, but I sensed his unease. Perhaps he knew I needed to talk to him.

Different approaches came to mind, ways of sharing what I'd discovered in town, but I shook my head of them. "You paid our tab," I blurted, pleased to get it off my chest and toss it on the table for all to see. I hated beating around the bush anyway.

James picked up a stick and tossed the kindling on the fire. A sigh escaped him as he glanced at me before studying the cattle. "Didn't mean to upset you."

"I just want to know why you did that. If you were being kind, I'm grateful. I'll pay you back when we complete this drive. But ..."

As I paused, he looked at me again. "But?"

"Well, Ma," I said, not wanting to say something stupid.

He nodded. "I see what you mean."

When he didn't elaborate, I pressed. "Well?"

James smiled. "You saved my life, John. I appreciate what you've done for me. Your tab wasn't much anyway."

"Is that all?" I demanded, wanting to learn his plans where Ma was concerned.

He sighed again. "No, now that you prod me. I guess I'm amazed at what I've found on this quiet corner of Texas. I'm just a man from the war with a tattered faith in Christ. I get shot by Comanche and thought my days were over. I made my peace with God, and then you came along, saved my bacon, and brought me here."

He paused and dropped his head as his shoulders slumped. I sipped my coffee, watching him, knowing he wasn't through yet.

"Your ma is a special woman, John," he whispered so I could barely hear him. He lifted his face and I saw the crooked smile etched there. "But there's more going on, and you know it."

I blinked. "What do you mean?"

James kicked at the fire and watched sparks flutter as he chuckled. "The adventure. Your ma prays and Paul comes to the ranch, a dedicated Christian with a gift for prayer. Then you find the dead outlaw and pay your taxes. Then me, a man haunted by demons I can't shake. Yet my faith is renewed here, and I deliver the missing piece of the puzzle. What to do with all your stock? I know where a market is and how to tap into it. Then the Indians give you a pass on their land. Don't you see? Everything is falling into place, and I want to be a part of it. I don't want to miss what Jesus is doing on your ranch."

CHAPTER 25

That night after supper, bone tired and ready for bed, I helped Paul and Lydia with the dishes. During the meal, James had appeared pensive and restless. His usual confidence had seemed missing this evening, our last night on the ranch before the trek to Fort Union. I glanced at the dispatch rider where he sat with Ma in the parlor. What ailed him?

Paul and Lydia retired for the evening, promising to see us off after an early breakfast. As I closed the door behind the couple, I glanced down the hallway where the first fire of the season blazed merrily in the parlor.

I'd packed my gear inside my bedroll and spent the evening cleaning my guns. Eager for the next day's trip, I promised myself I would go to bed soon, when I'd completed all preparations. Yet something badgered at me, and I shot another worried glance toward the parlor where Ma and James conversed in low tones. I felt a little surprised they had so much to talk about.

Spinning the cleaned cylinder, I loaded the gun and shoved the pistol back into my holster. My boots stood ready near my bedroom door, and I padded softly down the hallway in my socks to say my goodnights. At the doorway to the front room, I froze, my eyes widening as I stared at James sitting beside Ma, peering closely at something she held. Their heads almost touched as they whispered about the object in her hands, clearly oblivious of my presence or that I was even in the same house as them.

When I cleared my throat, they jumped back like children caught with their hands in the cookie jar. A guilty look crossed James's features, while Ma's cheeks stained pink. I acted like I didn't notice.

"Goodnight, Ma. See you bright and early, James."

Ma nodded but wouldn't meet my gaze. James scowled like I'd interrupted something. He stood and moved toward me. "Yes, I'd best be getting to bed too."

He paused beside me and glanced over his shoulder. "Goodnight, Annie," he said softly.

I felt my eyebrows arch at his easy way of using her first name. Ma didn't reply, just sat staring into the fireplace where the blaze crackled merrily. James slapped my shoulder as he passed me and walked outside without another word. I wanted to say something to Ma but didn't know what. Chewing my lip, I went to my room.

The sound of bustling in the kitchen awakened me the next morning. Not even a tinge of gray showed in the east when I stomped into my boots and strode into the lighted room, swinging my gun belt around me.

"Morning, Lydia," I greeted, reaching for a mug and the coffeepot bubbling on the stove.

Lydia turned at my step. "Good morning, John," she said shyly, still not completely at ease in my presence. I tossed my hat on the floor and slid into a chair just as she placed a heaping plate of potatoes and eggs in front of me.

She hesitated a moment and then let out a long breath. "You'd better eat up. Nothing but beef and beans for you for a while."

She whirled and retreated to the stove once more. I grinned, appreciating her attempt at familiarity.

"I'll surely miss your cooking, Lydia." She lifted her head at my praise, but not turning to look at me. I hoped a good foundation for friendship had been laid between us, knowing the young woman was a huge help to Ma around the house.

The thought made me ponder as I recalled James's comment of the previous day, that the Lord was assembling a team to complete the adventure he'd initiated, the adventure Ma had prayed for.

Paul was a prayer warrior like Ma and Lydia—a great support for the two of them. James provided the contacts we needed to sell cattle. Where did I fit in? What skills did I contribute? Even Buffalo Horn had allowed us to cross Comanche lands during winter, a blessing I couldn't deny.

Without coming up with an answer as to my role, my thoughts turned to Hannah as I ate. She'd been sent to the missionary school years before to learn English, a gift now utilized in my dealings with her father. Was this another sign of God's intervention?

I shook my head, clearing my muddled thoughts. The Lord was active, I agreed, but was he with us? Did he care if we failed or succeeded?

The back door burst open, and Paul entered carrying a pail of milk. He nodded as he slid into a vacant seat across from me. Lydia poured him coffee and topped off my mug. Ma entered the kitchen and frowned when she surveyed the room, her glance straying to the back door.

As I sipped my coffee and listened to Paul talk of the milking and the latest batch of eggs from the barn, I covertly studied Ma over the rim of my cup. Although her eyes seemed tired, rimmed with dark circles, her brown hair had been worked into a tight bun above the nape of her neck. I squinted when I noticed an unfamiliar silver comb gleaming where it held her tresses in place. An anxious air clung about her, probably due to my leaving, but I wondered as I recalled Mr. Anderson's report that James had purchased a comb like the one in Ma's hair.

"My reading is improving, John," Paul said suddenly, drawing my attention again. I nodded, proud of his hard work, but something niggled at the edges of my mind, something about Ma.

"Well done. Keep at it," I advised and stood, my chair scraping loudly. I picked up my hat and headed for the door. There'd been no sign of James, and I figured to visit his cabin and check on him. Our trek west needed to begin, and I felt in a hurry, a sense of anticipation filling me as I shrugged into my coat.

As I touched the doorknob, James pushed into the kitchen. I caught a nervous look on his face as he dropped into my vacant chair and thanked Lydia for the plate of potatoes and the steaming coffee the woman placed before him.

Intrigued, I leaned against the wall and watched as the former army rider kept his face averted, intent on his breakfast as Ma's gaze fixed on him.

He scraped his plate loudly and drained his second cup of coffee before leaping to his feet, mumbling his thanks as he moved toward the door.

"You eat so fast," Paul commented with a chuckle. "I think I saw sparks fly from your fork."

James paused beside me and turned. "I'm sorry, folks, but we need to be going." His gaze darted to Ma, the first time I think he looked at her this morning. A grin creased his taut features when he glimpsed the silver comb in her hair.

I frowned as he shifted, twirling his hat in his hands. For a moment, they looked at one another, and then, he tugged on the doorknob. "Be seeing you all soon," he said as he stepped onto the back stoop. "May God bless our venture," he called over his shoulder.

My frown deepened as Paul and Lydia murmured their amens, but Ma stared after James, not even seeing me beside the door.

What was going on? I shoved my hat on my head and leaned to kiss Ma's cheek before trailing James into the darkness. Two hours later, our small herd pointed to the northwest, and I still wondered if James's role on the ranch was merely his idea to sell cattle.

Stars lingered dimly when we'd started, and dawn had soon burst glorious and fresh in the chilled autumn air. Now, a vast blue sky stretched to the horizon as an eagerness rode with me, urging me on as we pushed the twenty head of stock. Across the backs of the cattle, James's strong voice sang hymns to the endless sky. Occasionally, he paused and tried again, obviously fixing lines he'd butchered, incorrect words he hastened to repair.

I knew these hymns, having been raised with the familiar songs, but I pressed my lips, unwilling to participate. Ma's words came to me, reminding me of the Scriptures about training a child in the way they should go, and I cringed. Unbidden, the hymns danced across my mind, although I didn't speak any aloud.

Why had God surrounded me with these devout people? Ma and Paul loved the Lord in ways I couldn't fathom, their faith deep and committed. James had allowed his life to be guided by a renewed fervor for Jesus I couldn't comprehend. I felt the Lord had ignored us for so long as Ma prayed unceasingly during the war. I blamed God for our struggles rather than trusting and believing the Lord heard Ma's pleas. And now we were launched on a great adventure I still doubted. Was there something wrong with me? I wished I could share their hope, but fear of possible disappointment filled me. I felt my spirit warring within myself.

We covered over seven miles before the sun warmed our shoulders enough that I shed my coat, tucking the garment behind my saddle.

We'd each brought two spare horses, hoping to save our mounts from exhaustion. Noon came and went, but still we pushed the cattle on through the long afternoon. The cry of a hunting hawk made me study the soft blue canopy above, marveling at our brazen attempt at selling cattle. With renewed anticipation, I quit my daydreaming and went back to work.

Finding a hollow with a little water in the bottom, we bedded the cattle down for the night as the sun lay far to the west. The cattle lowed wearily as they spread along the trickle of water and grazed.

After tying a rope between two cottonwood trees, I secured the horses to the line and spent time brushing them down and checking their hooves while James gathered wood and built a fire. By the time I walked to the bright blaze, darkness surrounded us, and a few early stars shimmered above, twinkling in the deepening black sky. The aroma of fresh coffee and cooking meat made my mouth water. I accepted the plate of food from James and sat down as he dove into his own supper.

Silence lingered as we ate with only the slight scrape of utensils on tin plates and the distant bark of a coyote marring the quiet. When the meal was completed, I cleaned the dishes while James walked out to check on the herd. After his return, he grunted with satisfaction when I handed him a steaming cup of coffee where he sat propped against his saddle. Firelight played on his features as he drank, a relaxed look on his face, but I studied him over the rim of my cup, wondering how to begin.

All day long, my thoughts had been filled with the memory of that silver comb. I didn't want to confront him, but a responsibility rested on me I refused to ignore. I was, after all, the man of the house.

"I guess you gave it to her last night." My words fell like rain on a pleasant day, unexpected and unwelcome. He hadn't been avoiding me, but he hadn't told me of his gift either. Now it was time to throw my concerns on the table, out in the open.

You would've thought I'd kicked him the way his head jerked, as if he'd been waiting for my attack and yet seemed unprepared when my words came. But I needed to know where he stood.

He narrowed his eyes as he studied the leaping flames of the small blaze, and I noticed his white knuckles where he gripped his cup. "I reckon you mean that silver comb," he muttered darkly.

"I do."

"How did you know? Did she tell you?" There was a wistful note in his voice I ignored.

"Mr. Anderson told me you bought it. I saw it in her hair this morning."

He shifted and looked at me. "Mr. Anderson has a big mouth." He paused and then arched one eyebrow. "How do you think it looks on her?"

I had to admire his nerve. He wasn't crowing like a boy over a captured frog or bragging about the new shine in Ma's eyes, but I understood his question. He wondered how I felt about the gift to Ma, my mother.

Now, I'd been thinking on that very thing all day, recalling the kindness in his voice when he spoke with her, the smile she had for him when he entered a room, and the way he asked me about my feelings on the situation. I remembered it all and nodded slowly.

"I think she's a special woman."

"So do I," he agreed swiftly, and I heard the eagerness in his tone.

"Then go slow. Her heart needs time."

"Her heart needs time? What does that mean?" He looked at me sharply, and I read the concern in his eyes.

"It means she has a big heart, and I don't want it hurt," I snapped. "You be careful with that," I warned as I leaned back against my saddle.

A slow grin spread across his face, and I could tell he was pleased. A few minutes later, he crawled into his blankets.

I sat by the fire for another hour, drinking the last of the coffee while I pondered Ma and James Casey. Should I pray for them? Their friendship was so new, yet I wanted the Lord's guidance, although I'd been filled with doubts about spiritual matters. Jesus had lived in my heart since my youth, though sometimes he didn't seem like he was home.

I licked my lips when I stretched in my blankets and peered up at the night sky. "I know you're there," I whispered, hoping he would listen to me this time. "I need your help."

I blew out a deep breath. "Never mind. If you want to help, you know what I'm thinking about. If not, then it doesn't matter."

CHAPTER 26

"Quiet?" James asked as he blew on his cup, steam rising into the dark morning chill.

I gripped my mug with both hands, warming myself as I crouched beside the fire. A steer lowed plaintively from the blackness near the seep, and I pushed my hat back. "Yes, quiet except for a lone wolf I heard in the night. Weather looks to hold. We should have good travel."

He nodded, and I went on, wanting to let him know I held no grudge for yesterday's conversation. "Maybe he was howling at you. Perhaps he's offended at that terrible racket you call singing. I'm surprised the cattle didn't complain."

James grinned. "The cows like my singing. Besides, I think that wolf was howling because he's lonely. It's not good for a man to be alone."

My jesting froze into an icy ball in the pit of my stomach, and I tugged my hat low again. Finishing my coffee, I packed our gear and saddled the horses. We were becoming friends, James and me, and I think we'd reached an understanding about Ma, but he'd touched a raw nerve with his last comment. My thoughts turned to Hannah Tall Basket.

With a slap on a steer's hindquarters, I pointed the small herd and drove them north and a little west. We'd only brought cattle we didn't need for building the herd back home. Steers and older cows past their prime, no young stuff that had years of reproduction left in them. Our brand rode the flank of each animal, and a sense of pride filled me at the thought I was finally doing something good for the ranch. We surely needed the cash money.

We crossed the plains north of Yellow Creek and then swung due west, pushing the small bunch of cattle easily as we lolled along, ever nudging them but not wishing to run their fat off either.

Days blurred into one another as we worked hard, rising before sunrise and traveling until the sun leaned far to the west. We saw no one, or I should say I saw no one.

The night before arriving at Fort Union, James glanced at me across our small campfire. "We're being followed."

I blinked. "Followed? Who would follow us? I haven't seen anyone."

"A pair of Indians. They hang back and watch us."

"Indians?" I mused and nodded, comprehension dawning. "Dark Cloud threatened to get me." At his curious look, I told James of the angry brave and his demands for a scalp since I'd rescued their trapped prey. I didn't tell him about Dark Cloud wanting to marry Hannah.

James chuckled and I enjoyed seeing the wrinkles in the corner of his eyes as he laughed. "They surely weren't happy when you took me away from them." He stopped laughing and ran a hand through his hair, his cheeks paling slightly. "That was a close shave."

We sat silent for a moment and then James tossed another log on the fire. "You better watch yourself, John," he warned.

I glanced over my shoulder into the darkness, agreeing with him.

The next day we drove the final distance to Fort Union. I held the small bunch of longhorns on a grassy spot outside of town while James rode in to talk to someone he knew. Within an hour, three soldiers rode out with James.

I watched the blue clad troopers with a sour taste in my mouth but held my tongue, remembering the war was over and we needed this sale. Yet I also remembered Pa and didn't answer their calls of greeting as the soldiers rounded the herd and drove them away. With only our riding stock, we trailed behind, glad to be rid of the slow-moving cattle.

We rode to a squat log structure on the edge of the parade ground, the level land ringed with transplanted trees sporting withered leaves. Several buildings rimmed the parade ground, and I suspected barracks and businesses made up most of the structures of Fort Union. In the distance, a line of trees marked the Cimarron River.

Pausing to stomp the dirt from our boots on the rough boardwalk, James showed me the document he'd signed for payment on twenty delivered cows. Despite the cold autumn day, I felt my palms sweat as I followed him inside the building.

"Let me do the talking," James whispered as we approached a counter. A soldier asked us our business, and when James told of the delivered cattle, we were quickly ushered into another office.

The trooper behind the desk looked at James's document with a sharp glance, then he looked up at us. "You two just delivered twenty head of cattle?"

James nodded, acting cool where I struggled to conceal my excitement. Were we really about to be paid?

The soldier rose and rummaged under the counter. I heard the tinkle of coins and my palms grew even wetter.

"Well, you boys are entitled to twelve dollars a head, times twenty. If you have more stock, keep them coming. We need more beef and no one else will hazard the Indians."

He counted twelve double eagle gold coins into James's outstretched hand. "That's two hundred and forty dollars, in case you're bad with sums." The soldier guffawed. "Will you rebels know what to do with all that money?"

James pocketed the coins and took a step toward the door. "There's no rebels here today, you ugly little toad. We're just men trying to make a living."

The soldier's face fell, but we were out the door and heading for our horses before he could reply. "We'll ride out of here to bed down," James instructed as we turned our mounts from the fort. "This kind of money will be talked about, and there are men around who would kill for far less than this. Cash money is scarce."

I glanced longingly at the crude sign above one of the buildings, the word café scrawled in red letters. "Leave now?"

At the tone of my voice, he turned and saw my meaning. A slow grin parted his weeks' worth of whiskers.

"Good idea," he said as he swerved toward the eating house.

We sat at a long table with benches on either side. A man in a greasy shirt brought us a coffeepot. Plunking the steaming container on our table, he wiped his hands on his shirt. "What'll it be?"

"What do you have?" James reached for the blackened pot.

"We have deer and beans or antelope with beans. Your choice."

"We'll have the antelope. Do you have any pie?" James ordered for me, and I didn't mind. Excitement bubbled within me at the thought of the gold he carried. We had money, and for the first time in a long time, I realized we would make it through the winter.

Relief flooded through me, and I relaxed, holding my hot coffee cup with both hands as we waited for our food to arrive.

While we ate, a pair of rough looking men entered and sat against the wall, not eating as they tried to discreetly watch us. But James noticed them first and nudged me with an elbow, indicating the pair of louts. I felt my shoulders tense as I remembered we carried gold and were not safe in this unfamiliar outpost. Draining our cups, we stood and hurried outside.

We left the fort by late afternoon, a brisk wind chilling us as we trotted up the slope to the east, leaving Fort Union behind. The pair of men watched us from the café porch, but made no move to follow, yet we were wary all the same.

Riding fast for a couple of hours, we stopped to change mounts and then kept going. We rode until long after dark and still we rode. James seemed to be tireless while I sagged in the saddle, but I kept thinking of the supplies and dress goods Ma could purchase now.

When James halted on a knoll to study our back trail, moonlight shimmered across the plains, revealing nothing stirring except us. Wind blustered gently, gnawing with cold teeth at my ears and neck. I tugged my collar higher and listened to the horses pant and heave in the shrouded moonshine.

"You know, we tempted fate, pushing this herd this late in the season," James said softly as he stared at our back trail.

I nodded, watching my breath come in little white puffs. "Lucky," I agreed.

He pushed his hat back and squinted at me. "Luck had nothing to do with this." His face shone pale in the night light and I felt his scrutiny pierced my soul, as if he could read me clearly. He shook his head. "You need to remember Jesus rides with us."

"I want to," I grumbled. "But I need to see more success. Things have been too tough for too long, and I need to see God working."

James chuckled as he tugged on his reins and started on. "You sound like doubting Thomas. 'Blessed is the man who doesn't see and still believes'," he quoted. "If you haven't seen the Lord's hand in this adventure yet, you never will," he called over his shoulder as he led off again.

I hesitated, watching him leading the spare horses as he trotted down the trail again. It was long past midnight, but James didn't show any sign of letting up. Yet, my fatigue had vanished at his scathing observation. Was I unable to see the Lord's hand? Was I so hard hearted that I couldn't see Jesus working in our situation?

I continued to ponder my lack of faith while we covered another ten miles in the dark. Finally, James rode along a little stream for a mile before stopping beneath a large elm tree, a few leaves still clinging tenaciously to naked limbs. The moon leaned far toward the horizon, and I knew dawn was only a few hours away.

"The horses need rest," James said as he unsaddled his horse. Dropping our gear in a heap, he led the horses to water and then brushed each weary animal before stretching out in his blankets, not even bothering to remove his boots.

Exhausted, I staggered after him, working with him until I stumbled to my own blankets. With a sigh, I laced my hands behind my head and peered up at the glorious sky, stars stretching overhead as far as the eye could see.

"This was a good day," he said suddenly from his nearby bed. "Thank God."

I squinted into the night, wondering why I couldn't see what he saw. Had I allowed misfortune to harden my spirit? I recalled one of Ma's favorite verses, "Rejoice in hope, be patient in tribulation, and constant in prayer," and knew I had not measured up. I'd been a follower of Christ since I was a young boy, but my heart had been broken by too many disappointments, and now I felt a skeptic of the Lord's intervention.

I attempted to pray, to ask for God's guidance and that Jesus might show me mercy for my heart of stone. Somehow my prayers seemed fruitless, and with a sense of futility seeping into my bones, I fell asleep.

CHAPTER 27

"John, what will you do if you sell more cattle? What do you want the money for?"

James's question made me shake my head, to dispel the anger and annoyance that settled within me at not being able to connect with Jesus. I didn't understand this chasm that yawned between me and the Savior. I felt his presence, as if he watched me from a distance, displeased with my shallow attitude. He loved me, right? Must I own a strong faith before I could see his hand?

Sure, even I could see the strangers that assembled at our ranch these past months, but the war was over, and folks returned home. Or, like Paul, Lydia, and James, they sought new homes. But was this proof of God's involvement?

I shook my head again and considered James's question. "Well, I'd like to give Paul and Lydia something. Sure, Ma would appreciate new dress goods." My glance lifted from the bedroll I tied to meet his gaze. "And you, James. This is all your idea. I'd share with you."

He grinned. "Nope. This is all for you, leastways this drive. I owe you my life."

My thoughts darted to Buffalo Horn's words, that saving a man's life was special. I think I understood a little of what he meant, although I'd saved James without thinking about any reward.

"How about you? What would you do with money?" I tossed a saddle on my gelding and drew the cinch tight as James poured cups of coffee from the boiling pot resting on the coals. We'd only made a small fire for brewing coffee while we nibbled on cold sourdough biscuits. We were both eager to get home, although we'd agreed to take a longer route, far north of Yellow Creek to avoid any chance of running into Dark Cloud. If we could avoid conflict with the Comanche, we hoped to deliver a few more small herds of cattle to distant outposts before winter truly set in, including the Indian reservation across the Texas border in the Nation.

James lifted his cup as he eyed me over the rim. I kept packing our gear, waiting for his reply as I kicked dirt over the glowing coals. As the hot embers hissed, I glanced at him, wondering at his hesitation.

As we stepped into our saddles, he turned to me. "I've thought often of a dream. It kept me going during some tough times in the war. I would think out every way to improve a ranch, making it a better place to live, better ways to make it pay. I've pondered that dream so long, I feel I know exactly what I would do if money ever came my way."

"Maybe it will now that we're selling cattle," I suggested, appreciating all of his work to help me and Ma survive.

He shook his head as he kicked his mount into action. We walked a dozen yards before he went on. "This is your dream, John. Your ma has gathered a team to work the Lord's will for the Garret ranch. I will not intrude with my ideas."

Mulling this over, I spurred after him. Without the cattle to slow us down, we should be home in a couple days, swapping tired horses for our spare ones along the way. Yet something niggled at my mind as I thought of James and his dream of a ranch of his own. Did Paul and Lydia have dreams too? I hoped the Lord would take these good people into consideration if he chose to bless us one day. For now, I felt content to have money to see us through the winter.

Two days later, we came to a dugout carved into a hill. I'd never ridden this far off the main trail as our detour around Yellow Creek demanded. This homestead must be our nearest neighbors to the north. Only a blue column of smoke alerted us of the vicinity of the crude shelter. A wagon leaned precariously at one side of the hard-packed dirt yard. Broken tools and scrap pieces of leather harness lay scattered beneath a cottonwood tree. In a nearby lean-to, which served as a barn, two gaunt horses stood, heads down against the chilly afternoon breeze.

At a call from James, a rifle protruded from a gap in the plank door. I glanced at the lone window in the front wall of the sod shack, but only a piece of burlap billowed in the wind.

"What do you want?" an old man replied. A shock of white hair rumpled above his thin face.

"I'm James Casey. This is John Garret. We're your neighbors to the south."

The man took a step from the sod cabin, but his rifle never wavered. "John Garret? Are you son to Vince Garret?"

I nodded, a wistfulness filling me at mention of Pa. "My father. Never came home from the war."

He nodded, and I thought I noticed his rifle barrel lower a mite. "Too many men never come home from the war, including my two boys. I thought you were those no-account tax collectors, come to take our land."

"No, sir." My gaze swept the run-down homestead once more.

"They've been hounding us for months," the old man went on. "Had to take a shot at them last time." He chuckled sourly, and I got a better look at him. He couldn't have been much older than James, maybe a decade older. But the rifle he held gleamed brightly from much use. I kept my hands on the pommel, where he could see them.

"We're no tax men," I said again.

The old man shifted. "Well, pardon my rough talk. I'm Henderson. Get down and water your horses. Come far?"

We swung to the ground, and James stepped forward, making sure the homesteader could see him. James must've noticed how easily the old man handled the rifle.

"We're coming home after riding to Fort Union, over in New Mexico Territory. Sold some stock."

A too thin woman stepped from the dugout and stood beside her husband, listening to what James said.

"You buying stock?" Her unexpected words made us hesitate as we led our horses to the water trough beside the lean-to barn.

A sharp glance passed between the old man and his wife before she continued. "We haven't seen cash money in two years."

Things had been rough for Ma and me for years, but we'd always eaten. I read the defeat in their faces and knew they'd missed more than one meal.

"I didn't plan on buying." At my words, something like fear or desperation passed through the old man's eyes, and he squinted, his bushy eyebrows bunching.

The woman nudged him, and the old man raced on, as if in a hurry. "I have fifty odd cattle and the best water in the region. Good grazing too."

I shot a quizzical glance at James and he shrugged, letting me talk. I turned to face the homesteader. "You mentioned back taxes."

His shoulders sagged as a sob escaped from the woman. He looked at his wife and blinked. "My boys didn't come home from the war. We're done out here, the prairie's beaten us. I'll need to keep my horses to take us away, but I'll give you my cattle and the land for a hundred dollars. You're getting the better of the deal. I have nothing."

I couldn't ignore the pleading in his voice. I thought again of the hard times we'd endured and nodded, almost as if an unseen hand had moved my head.

"Let's take a ride and see what you've got," I suggested. A look of relief filled the woman's face, causing her knees to buckle. She stumbled backward to sit on a bench against the sod shack, holding a faded apron to her face.

James walked to the woodpile and wrenched an axe from a stump. "I'll cut wood while you survey the place," he said casually, but I caught the significance to his intention. These folks needed all the help they could get.

Henderson and I rode for an hour. I counted at least fifty unbranded cattle and suspected there were more hiding in the brush. A small stream meandered across his land and when he showed me the spring bubbling below a nearby bluff, I knew I was going to buy his ranch. When I told him so, he nodded slowly as his gaze scanned the bleak landscape.

"We've been here for six years and have nothing to show for it. Lost my children, and my wife's health ain't good. We'll go back to Louisiana where I hope my brother still lives."

Back at the dugout once more, we shook hands on the deal, and I nodded to James. I watched as the man held out his trembling hand while James counted five gold pieces, the coins clinking loudly in the gathering dusk. The woman cried.

CHAPTER 28

Henderson signed a bill of sale and outlined his land holdings to us before we rode south for a few hours. We pitched camp sometime before midnight. We'd ridden in silence, each full of our own thoughts. I couldn't stop thinking about the lonely homesteaders living off squirrels, beef, and squaw cabbage. Ma and I'd lived off beef and vegetables from our garden and a little credit from Mr. Anderson's store for coffee, flour, and beans. Compared to the Henderson's, we'd done all right.

A knot coiled in my gut as I rode, my anger rising at how unappreciative I felt at what the Lord had done for us. I blamed God for our struggles, and yet others had it worse than us. Certainly I had lots to be angry about, plenty to complain about, but did I take the time to count my many blessings?

Without a fire, we curried the horses and turned in, working by the dim starlight. Neither of us seemed to want to talk, yet much needed to be said. Besides sympathy for the broken homesteaders, we needed to discuss the ramification of buying their ranch. In the twinkling of an eye, our ranch had expanded.

Was the Lord behind this newest development? I'd been so excited to sell a few cattle and the thought of gold made me giddy, realizing for the first time in years we would survive the winter without fear. I felt grateful and wondered too about my prayer from last summer. I'd asked the Lord to show me his hand, to prove his provision and love. Had he heard my prayer after all?

Yet something nagged at me, as if God held up his end of the bargain but something lacked on my end.

We rode into our yard late the next evening, the sun just vanishing behind the western hills. The house loomed dark when we arrived, but a welcome glow streamed from the kitchen window as we stabled our weary horses. Paul brought a lantern and helped us feed and brush the animals, telling us the little news he possessed. We were glad to learn nothing untoward had occurred in our absence.

By the time we shambled into the kitchen, Ma and Lydia had prepared a meal and fresh coffee simmered on the stove.

After embracing Ma, I unbuckled my gun belt and dropped into a chair, pleased to be home once more. I saw Ma glance at James, a small smile creasing her pensive features. She nodded to the tired cowboy and took his hat from him as he moved to sit across from me. She couldn't take her eyes off him and backed into Lydia, who delivered cups to the table.

"Sorry, Lydia," Ma mumbled and moved forward to sit between me and James. Paul took a seat across from Ma and we briefly told of our ride to Fort Union, leaving out the part about Dark Cloud trailing us.

An anticipation hovered in the room as James and I talked of the drive to the fort.

"How much did you get paid?" Ma's inquiry made me laugh. Surely the underlying interest was in the gold I carried in my pocket. James had given me the remainder of the coins after paying Mr. Henderson. Now I jingled them before dropping them one by one on the table. All eyes locked on the six yellow coins, the seventh having been divided among supplies at Fort Union and the meal at the café.

With my finger, I dragged one of the gold pieces to the place in front of Paul. "It's not much, but I want you to have this. We hope more is to follow."

Lydia stood beside her husband, and I saw her eyes shine with tears as Paul hefted the coin and held it up for her inspection. The newlyweds stared at the gold piece, eyes bright as they clasped hands.

"Thank you, John," Paul murmured, turning his gaze on me.

"And thank you, Jesus," Ma said loudly as she stared down at the small pile of coins I pushed before her. Then she tilted her head and peered at me. "How much did you get?"

"We sold for twelve dollars a head," I explained, shooting James a hurried glance. Had I done right, purchasing the smaller ranch to the north?

"This surely doesn't come near two hundred and forty dollars," Ma said quietly, a note of curiosity filling her words.

I shifted in my seat, the chair scraping loudly in the still room as everyone leaned forward to catch my explanation.

"On our way home, we stopped at a homesteader's place north of us. Henderson was his name. He was eager to sell out and go back east. I bought his land and cattle for a hundred dollars, although he still owes another eighty to back taxes."

"A hundred dollars," Ma breathed in a whisper, and I couldn't tell if she thought I'd made a good deal or if she lamented the loss of the money. Her eyebrows arched. "Back taxes?"

"John made a wise purchase," James interjected. Ma turned to look at him, and I felt grateful for his support.

"Do you really think so? We need the money to get through the winter."

James grinned. "Don't you worry, Annie. Give us a day or two to rest up, and we're pushing another herd to the Indian reservation in the Nation. We'll pick up Henderson's cattle on the way. With that money, we'll be sitting pretty."

His confident words seemed to mollify Ma. She nodded and her smile returned. "I'm proud of you, Johnny," she said as she placed a hand on my arm. "The Lord is with us. All of our success is because of him."

I wanted to believe her, truly I did. Yet something pestered me, reminding me of our hardship and the incredible amount of work we'd accomplished to bring this cattle sale to fruition. Was God with us, or were we simply the hardest working, luckiest folks in Texas?

My thoughts whirled as Paul and Lydia said their goodnights, the gold coin clenched in Paul's hand. He gave me an appreciative glance before stepping through the kitchen door to vanish in the darkness. No doubt, there were not many hours until dawn, and we were all tired. James lingered over a third cup of coffee, but Ma didn't seem to mind.

Stretching out in bed, promising myself a hot bath on the morrow, I wondered at Ma's words. Were we lucky, or was God blessing us? I'd begged the Lord to show me his hand, and yet my doubts persisted as success piled atop one another. Could I not believe what lay before my eyes? Had my skeptical heart betrayed me, not only demanding a sign from Jesus but not believing when the Lord provided? What did God have to do to convince me he cared for us?

With light streaming through my window, I crawled reluctantly from my warm bed. I'd never been afraid of hard work, but the idea of gathering another herd to push north in a Texas November didn't excite me, although making money did. Any cash we could obtain would keep the wolf from the door for another day.

James and Ma were sitting at the kitchen table when I entered, conversing in low tones. James greeted me with a casual air that didn't fool me. Ma's rosy cheeks shone guiltily, and I knew they'd been talking about something they didn't want me to hear.

"John, ride to town and file on Henderson's land. I don't think we should attempt to pay the taxes yet. Let's wait for this next drive to the Indian Nation. Then pay. Also, pick up these things at Anderson's." He handed me a list.

I studied the slip of paper while Ma filled a plate with potatoes and eggs. On the edge of the dish, a mound of butter melted on a thick piece of toast. I relished good cooking, especially any cooking I didn't have to do over a campfire.

"You'll be branding?"

He nodded at my question as he sipped his coffee, his gaze on Ma where she stood near the sink. His eyes dropped and he shifted. "Yes. We'll want the Bar G slapped on every head we deliver to the reservation. I don't trust the Indian Agent there, but we need money, and he needs beef."

"So, we won't pick up the Henderson cattle on our way?" I ate heartily, watching James as I cleared my plate. He seemed distracted by my questions and Ma's presence, but he blinked and turned to face me, suddenly realizing the business at hand.

"We'll brand his stock this spring. Right now, I want a herd of forty branded cattle to drive north before winter sets in. November has already arrived, and that means

December will be here before we know it. Snow will blow soon if we don't get a move on."

I held my coffee mug for Ma to refill. She scurried away to the counter once more, and I frowned at her indecision. Since James arrived on the ranch, she seemed unsure of herself and yet interested in everything he did, as if she hung on every word he uttered.

I liked having James on the place, liked his leadership and business savvy, but I wondered at Ma's reaction to his presence. No one could doubt his fervor for discussing Scripture or his desire to study the Bible, but something more drew his attention to the Garret ranch, and I had my suspicions. His renewed faith in Christ had ignited something within him, a willingness to work hard to build our ranch that went beyond merely the adventure he'd signed on for. I wonder if I might've been content with his newfound level of trust, the unexpected faith he'd discovered, yet I sensed he prepared for something deeper.

Did his motivation have anything to do with Ma? Even I couldn't deny their obvious attraction to one another. And Ma didn't seem so lonely with James around.

My thoughts turned to Hannah, not surprised I couldn't keep my mind from her for long. A sense of intimidation filled me when I considered the beautiful Indian princess. She was the daughter of a respected Comanche chief, and I was just a poor rancher trying to build a life for myself on the Texas plains. Her long, dark hair and her dancing eyes filled my mind, and I remembered how we'd played together as children so long ago.

I jumped when Ma shook my shoulder. She scowled when I glanced up to meet her gaze.

"I called your name three times," she chided, bringing the coffeepot once more to the table. James stared at me, and I felt the flush creep up my cheeks as she filled our cups. "What were you thinking of?"

"I was thinking of ... I need to ride to town for supplies." My cheeks burned warm as I leaped to my feet, almost toppling my chair. Buckling on my gun belt, I grabbed the steaming coffee mug and moved toward the kitchen door, eager to make my escape.

CHAPTER 29

My thoughts of Hannah troubled me as I walked to the barn. Did Ma suspect?

Paul met me in the stable as I saddled my horse. He teased about the late hour and me sleeping in. Then his face grew somber, and he leaned against the stable wall, his eyes piercing in the dim light of the murky barn.

"I want to thank you again for the gold coin," he said softly. "We ain't never had money, and I agreed to work here for room and board."

I slapped his shoulder as I drew the horse from the stable. "You deserve it." I mounted and settled into the saddle as I tugged on my gloves. "Ma swears the Lord brought you to the ranch. I wish I could give you more. You've proven a great help."

He tilted his head as he looked up at me. "What do you think, John? Did the Lord bring me? Did God bring James?"

I shook my head and lifted my reins, preparing to go, but Paul grasped the bit and held firm.

"I'm serious. What role does Jesus play in this adventure Miss Annie prayed for? Is it chance we've all gathered to watch God work?"

I shifted, making my cold saddle creak in the late morning. I shrugged, trying to dispel his heavy mood with indifference, but he would have none of it.

"Tell me, John," he urged. "Is Christ working for this family, guiding this adventure?"

Again, I shrugged. "I don't know. Maybe. Some good things have happened," I conceded weakly.

"Such as?"

His persistence annoyed me, and I bit my lip as I considered my reply.

"Well, Ma prayed and you arrived. Then I found Red Bill on the trail and paid the taxes. Then I saved James and he knew about selling the cattle to the forts."

"That's right," Paul agreed and released my bridle. "I have seen the Lord work, but I sense your doubts. I wonder what worries you."

"Worries me?" I repeated, feeling my eyes widen in disbelief. "Are you kidding? We owe more tax money on the ranch I purchased. We need supplies to see us through the winter. There's a lot of things I worry about," I snapped.

He took a step backward, nodding slowly, and a look of pity crossed his features. "I see now. You have a small faith."

At first, I felt offended. I'd been a Christian most of my life. But then I realized he was right. I spurred my horse, dust kicking up as I left the yard.

I felt my stomach clench at Paul's accusation, knowing he'd spoken the truth. But I couldn't be angry with him for something I'd suspected about myself for months.

"Why don't you work with me?" I pleaded, shouting at the skittering clouds shoved across the sky by a northern breeze. I felt winter in the air, and knew James was right to hasten our trip to the Indian reservation.

"Do you even hear me? I want to please you, but I feel cheated by you. Pa died and the ranch nearly collapsed, not to mention the endless hard times we endured during the war. Did you hear my prayers?"

My demands went unanswered, and I slowed my horse, not wanting to run the gelding unnecessarily. I ground my teeth until my jaw ached. Did God care about us out here on the Texas prairie? Ma believed he did. So did Paul and James, believing God had begun an adventure for us to follow.

Did I belong in this journey? My hands gripped the reins tighter and I spurred into an easy trot, covering ground while not pushing the gelding. Did Jesus want something from me as Hannah suggested? I'd begged for help those dreary days Ma and I toiled alone. Now, Ma declared the Lord's intervention. I saw his hand in some ways but struggled to trust him. He could pull the rug out from under us at any moment and we'd be right back where we were before.

"I think that's it, Lord," I whispered into the chilled breeze, tugging my hat lower. "I wonder if I can trust you. I see you providing in amazing ways, but wonder if it will last. I've been disappointed too many times before."

To trust. The concept, the action filled me with terror, and I knew Paul had seen my small faith.

My accusing observation didn't bring lightning down upon me, and thunder didn't peal angrily from heaven, yet I felt I wasn't alone. Glancing around, I surveyed the vast plains, noting each familiar landmark on my way to town. I waited apprehensively, perched on my saddle as if something would leap at me from the gullies and attack me, but nothing did. I waited, still sensing an unseen presence.

Patience. The word filled my mind, crowding out all other thoughts. Unbidden, the command spoke to my soul. Patience? What did that mean?

Town loomed on the plains, and I slowed the horse, the animal heaving as we walked down the main street. Reining before the land office, I tied to the hitching rail and stepped inside the little building, grateful to be out of the cold.

A man I didn't recognize leaned against the counter, picking at his fingernails with the point of a knife. James had informed me a lot of new faces were around town, men from up north, carpetbaggers rushing to the south to pick our carcasses clean.

"Can I help you?" His question lacked any interest, and he didn't bother to look at me.

I unfolded the bill of sale and laid the paper on the counter. "I bought the Henderson ranch. I want to transfer title to my name."

Suddenly, I had his full attention. His gaze came up and he studied me for a moment before knocking at the glass window beside him. "Boy, come in here," he called to someone unseen on the front boardwalk. The clerk scrawled something on a scrap of paper and handed the slip to the boy when the youngster entered. "Run this to Mr. Richards at the hotel," the clerk ordered.

Completing the necessary signature and filing fee took only a few minutes, then I hurried to see Mr. Anderson. The storekeeper beamed when I paid what I owed him and hastened to fill my order as I leaned near the front window of the mercantile, watching the two tax men loiter on the boardwalk in front of the hotel. They stomped their boots and turned up their collars against the cold before thrusting their hands deep into their pockets. I grinned at their discomfort, guessing why they waited in the cold.

When I carried my purchases to my horse, I wasn't surprised when the pair of neatly dressed men hailed me.

"Mr. Garret, a word, if you don't mind. Will you have coffee with us?"

I didn't particularly wish to talk to them, but I admit my curiosity. They probably wanted to tell me of the back taxes Mr. Henderson owed. But the allurement of coffee drew me, and they ushered me into the hotel lobby, out of the cold once more.

"Mr. Richards," I said as I shook hands with the blood sucker. "And Mr. Dalrymple," I went on as I turned to his partner. They stared at me not so covertly as we found seats at a table and waited while a servant poured coffee. I smiled at the vultures through the steam as I lifted my cup. I could tell they didn't remember me from our meeting last summer.

Mr. Richards glanced at his partner and then cleared his throat. "We understand you lately purchased the Henderson ranch. We didn't know anyone was interested in that parcel."

"Butts up to my land," I explained, not caring if they were upset or not at my taking land they expected to confiscate soon.

"You know he owed taxes on the property," Mr. Dalrymple said abruptly, leaning forward. "You would have to pay them, as new owner."

"Certainly, gentlemen," I replied as casually as I could muster. "Mr. Henderson informed me of the debt upon purchase."

"Then, you have the money?" Richards gestured to Dalrymple and the two men searched stacks of papers until he held a sheet up to the light. Dalrymple snatched the paper from him.

"Henderson owed eighty dollars," Dalrymple stated triumphantly. The portly man glared at me. "You have eighty dollars?"

I shrugged and took another sip. These men were scoundrels, of the worst kind, living off the misery and misfortune of others. "When do I need the funds?"

The two men exchanged glances, and I could tell I had a little time to produce the necessary money. They squirmed on their chairs, trying to figure out how much time to give me.

"We couldn't give you more than sixty days," Richards said with a sly smile tugging at the corner of his mouth. They didn't think I could get the money and I tensed, wondering if I could. Did a cattle drive to the Indian reservation guarantee anything? I hoped James knew what he was doing.

I pushed back from the table and stood. Draining my cup before setting the empty mug on the table, I nodded to the two swindlers. "I'll see you after the New Year."

Doubts filled me as I cantered home. Black, ominous clouds hung low in the north, and I feared a storm brewed, right in the direction we intended to go. Would we make the trip and pay the taxes on the land I'd purchased? Oh, why had I bought the Henderson place? An expansion was a risk right now when we had so little working capital.

As I approached our ranch, a cluster of cattle grazed to one side. I saw the smoke from the branding fire before I spotted James. With a wave, I let him know I would drop off the supplies and come to help.

"What's wrong?" Ma's direct query made me sigh as she sensed my unease when I delivered supplies. She could read me like a book.

"We owe taxes on that land I bought. Was that a dumb thing to do?"

She smiled as she took the packages from me and stepped onto the porch. "Have faith. This adventure is unfolding all around us in exciting ways. I trust the purchase of that land was for a purpose."

"I'm tired of faith," I snapped as I held my prancing mount with an iron hand on the reins. My anger surged and

I scowled at Ma, sick of hearing how I just needed more faith. What I needed was more money, then I wouldn't have to wait and pray and hope. Why couldn't the Lord just give me what we needed so I didn't always have to worry?

Ma's happy look vanished and she narrowed her eyes, one hand on the kitchen doorknob at her back. "You just completed a drive to Fort Union and sold cattle. Jesus has provided, and all you say is it's not enough. He brought us Paul and James and allowed you to buy more land, building for the future. And all you can say is you're not satisfied."

She paused while we glowered at one another. A chill breeze gusted, reminding me I was supposed to be with James, branding mavericks. "I have work to do," I said sullenly.

Ma went inside without another word, and I spurred my mount to the gathering herd beyond the house, my anger burning in my guts. Would God never make things easy for us? Now I needed to brand cattle in the cold for an arduous trek to the north in late November with foul weather pending. I clenched my teeth as I pulled in beside the little fire where James stood.

"What's got you in such a stew?" His sour greeting made me want to spit.

"I don't want to talk about it," I barked.

He held up both hands in surrender. "Calm down. I was just curious."

"What are we doing here?" My gaze shifted to the bawling mob of cattle, most of them wearing the Bar G on their flanks. I noticed only a few unbranded.

"Are you referring to this branding party, or does your question have deeper significance?"

I squinted at him, confused. "What?" I knew I wasn't thinking clearly as my anger burned against the Lord. I felt weary of always struggling, always worrying, and the cold wind from the north wasn't helping matters.

James gestured to the small herd behind him. "We have a few more head to brand. I tried to gather mostly branded cows. We don't have time for much more." He kicked the red-hot branding iron thrust into the coals and then looked at me again. "Is that what you meant?"

"I guess so," I grumbled, not wanting to explain. But as I spent the rest of the afternoon dragging unbranded cattle to the fire, I wondered if my question had deeper meaning, as James suggested. What was I doing out here, on the empty plains of Texas? Sure, this was my land, and I'd just bought more. Ranching was in my blood, and I couldn't see myself doing anything else. But … my discouraged attitude made me consider. Were things never going to get better? Perhaps the Lord was prompting me to pull up stakes, leave the hard life of the Texas prairie as Henderson did. Perhaps that old man was the wise one.

I dragged the final unbranded cow to the fire where James wrestled the beast to the ground. I grabbed the hot iron from the fire and held the brander to the cow's flank, hair sizzling as the Bar G burned into the hide. With a lunge, James released the bawling cow and scrambled to his feet, coiling my rope as he tugged the line free from the animal. He squinted as he handed the lasso to me, but I turned away, not wishing to hear any of his insight. Cold wind blustered as the dull sun lay far to the west. Fatigue and cold lay heavy in my bones as I walked my horse to the barn while James put out the fire and stalked to the house.

I'd worked hard all my life. Tired and cold wasn't new to me. But now something nagged at me, and I suspected the Lord worked on my heart. I hated the way Jesus wouldn't speak but allowed my thoughts to wrestle with him, chewing on his hard truths as he taught me, grew me, developed me.

I knew the Lord loved me, but we'd struggled for so long, and now I wanted an easier road. God could just bless us and make things easy, but I sensed he had a purpose I couldn't grasp. There was something happening on our ranch, and I couldn't understand its meaning.

As I approached the barn, eager to escape the chill, I glanced at the setting sun. Dull rays faded across the prairie, filling folds and swales with shadows. "What do you want from me, Jesus?"

A word or a feeling filled my mind, like a mist rising from a bog. *Patience.* The sensation was the same I'd felt earlier today when I left town. I paused as I dismounted, leaning against my horse. Patient about what?

CHAPTER 30

The second day after leaving home, we arrived at the Henderson place. The burlap piece blew in the dugout window, confirming the place had been deserted. The wagon and team of horses were gone, but articles of clothing and unnecessary utensils had been cast aside, revealing a hasty departure.

As the small herd grazed nearby, we spent a few minutes tidying the little dugout and stowing usable items. Perhaps this cabin could be utilized as an outpost of our ranch, for future inspections to this distant range. The Hendersons had abandoned the small potbellied stove, and soon a fire crackled merrily in the grate as James got supper simmering.

I took care of the horses and glanced out at the darkening plains as twilight gathered.

"I can use a chair in my bunkhouse," James announced as I entered. I looked at the few pieces of furniture the Hendersons had left behind and nodded, appreciating anything we could use on our place. He grasped the back of a chair and shook the wooden piece, testing its sturdiness. "It won't be long and we'll be snowed in, with days of playing cards and checkers. It'd be nice to have a chair in my cabin."

"Not that I suspect you'll spend much time there," I said slyly, grinning.

He looked at me sharply and then shrugged. "Sure, I hope to spend hours this winter in your house." He arched an eyebrow and studied my reaction, curious what my response would be.

I nodded and reached for the steaming coffeepot. "Why not? I think Ma likes you."

He pressed his lips together and waited for more, but when I didn't add anything, he shrugged again. "I think she does too."

We ate in silence, the way of hungry men who appreciate a hot meal out of the cold. Wind whipped over the plains and guttered down the stovepipe, scuttling the flames with fresh air. Only the small blaze and a single candle lit the dreary dugout. The back wall of the cabin was bare earth, and I wondered how folks could live in such a drab, ramshackle abode. I felt blessed to live in a house.

James pushed his empty plate from him and looked up. "Well? What do you think of that?"

I blinked, confused. "Think of what?"

He shifted and then reached for the pot to fill my cup again. "What do you think of your ma liking me?"

"Do you like her?" I countered with my own question, wanting to know his intentions. I sipped my coffee and studied him while James squirmed.

"I do," he said at last. "She's a beautiful girl, but there's more to her than that."

I tilted my head. "Go on," I urged, curious at his assessment.

"She has a faith I envy," he rushed, as if he'd given her virtues much thought. "She loves the Lord and seeks his will. I've never known such a kind and devout person."

I nodded, pleased with his observations of Ma. But I sensed there was something more he wanted to say. "Go on," I urged again.

He hesitated, the ruddy firelight playing over the lines on his rugged features. "I don't know how to say this," he confessed softly.

"Oh, you've done pretty well so far. Don't stop now," I said cheerfully. I liked James and wanted Ma to be happy. Even I'd noticed she didn't seem so lonely since his arrival.

"It's something I feel," he said in a low, unsure tone. "As if I have a role to play on your ranch. Almost as if I were supposed to be there. Ideas come to me about ways to improve the property, develop the ranch. Ideas I don't feel are from me."

I frowned, not understanding. "Then where do these ideas come from?"

He shrugged and stared into the fire, not saying anything more.

The storm we'd sighted to the north had unleashed only scant snowflakes, blown before a bitter wind. We'd pushed on, leaving Texas and entering the Indian Territory. A few of Henderson's mavericks had tagged along, despite our attempts to dissuade them. We didn't want the agent at the reservation to question our cattle's ownership, but more than a dozen head followed behind our little herd, as if unwilling to be left behind. We decided to not fight them and waste precious time. We felt cattle rich but money poor, and this last drive before winter descended would ensure our survival through these next months and the payment of taxes on the land I'd purchased. Time was important, not to be taken lightly as we drove our herd north, eager to beat the storm that bore down on us.

The blowing snow turned to freezing rain. At first, the cattle were game, allowing us to drive them against the gale. Sharp drizzle like needles pelted our unprotected skin, making my ears burn with pain before numbing completely. Soon, however, the cattle wanted to hide in draws and turn their backs to the wind. We drove them mercilessly, making them trot to stay warm as we neared the reservation James knew.

"Are we getting close?" I shouted above the wind when I next passed James. He nodded and then grabbed my coat sleeve before I could ride past.

"Someone trailing us again. A lone man," he yelled and then gave chase to a steer that darted for the brush.

I glanced over my shoulder at the empty prairie behind us, seeing nothing. Dark Cloud? Did the bitter Comanche brave follow us to kill me?

I shook my head and pushed the cattle on, committed to this crazy ride in a storm. We hadn't gotten any sleep the night before, exchanging horses for fresh ones as we held the herd together in the lee of a steep bluff. Exhaustion threatened, but James thought we'd arrive the next day.

Sleet showered us as a faded sun lifted in the east. Freezing and teeth chattering, we pushed the cattle all morning until we topped a rise and halted, stunned to see weather-beaten buildings sprawling on the plains.

"You hold the herd here on the flats. I'll ride in and make arrangements," James called before cantering down the slope.

I slumped in my saddle and wiped a gloved hand across my frozen cheeks. Pa's old slicker barely kept the cold out, yet I still sat my saddle. A feeling of triumph filled me as I huddled beneath a naked elm tree, my eyes locked on the listless cattle. Above me, bare branches rubbed together like skeleton bones. Had we really made it?

Six Yankee soldiers rode out to drive the cattle away. I watched closely, not trusting them. A few blanketed Indians had left their teepees and braved the cold to watch the cattle's arrival. James and I counted the cattle herd as a burly sergeant counted aloud. "Fifty-seven," he announced gruffly.

I'd counted fifty-eight, but James nodded and tugged his collar higher as the sergeant handed him a scrap of paper and pointed to the Indian Agent's office.

Tying our six horses to the hitching rail, we stomped inside the little building, glad to escape the freezing wind. Snow drifted on the gale, but hadn't increased in the last two days, the full fury of the storm holding off.

A slight, balding man sat behind a desk, peering over wire-rimmed glasses as we entered. He rose and moved to the counter, his face pinching when he caught scent of us.

"Cattle? You've delivered cattle in this storm?" His nasal voice declared him a northerner, and I felt my palms moisten.

"Mr. Hastings?" James question ignored the man's inquiry. At the agent's nod, James tugged off his gloves and handed the scrap of paper to him.

"Fifty-seven head of stock, at twelve dollars a head," James said. I enjoyed the ring of pride in his words.

Mr. Hastings read the sergeant's note and sniffed. "The cattle are ten dollars a head."

James shifted and shot me a glance before he opened his coat and retrieved the army document of purchase price.

The Indian Agent snatched the paper and scanned the document quickly, his eyes narrowing as he read. He handed the paper back to James. "I'm sorry. That is an outdated price sheet. The price today for your stock is ten dollars a head."

I cringed at the obvious swindle but felt pleased to learn we'd at least make ten dollars a head. Five hundred and seventy dollars was a lot of money, but James shook his head, and I knew he wasn't going to take this lying down.

"You're cheating us. The document clearly states twelve dollars a head. I just sold stock at Fort Union for that amount. I won't take less."

Mr. Hastings gave a curt nod, and a thin smile creased his pale face. "I'm sorry. I can only pay ten dollars per cow. Take it or leave it."

My stomach fell at thought of leaving with nothing, and I wanted to shout at James to accept the offer.

James tugged his gloves on as he turned to the door. I felt rooted in place, not believing we'd driven those cattle all the way here for nothing.

"Let's see what the army has to say about your Indians starving this winter because you tried to cheat us," James warned as he moved to the door.

"Wait, wait," Mr. Hastings called when James gripped the doorknob. "Be reasonable. You can have ten dollars a head or nothing, if you allow your stubbornness to get the better of you," Hastings countered tersely. "Don't be a fool, man. You'll get no better offer this season."

James shrugged and pulled the door open. A gust of freezing wind filled the little office, scuttling the blaze that burned in the small stove in the corner. When he stepped onto the stoop, Hastings called after him again.

"All right, all right." Mr. Hastings leaned over the counter and gestured for James to return. Outside, the wind shrieked like a banshee after James slammed the door once more. Hastings scribbled a bill of sale for fifty-seven head of cattle, no mention of brands, and I understood Henderson's mavericks were not an issue.

"Will you buy more cattle from us this spring?" James stepped closer, waiting to be paid.

Hastings shook his head. "No guarantee. We really only need the cattle to see us through the winter. The Indians hunt more in summer, and prices fluctuate when I can get beef from other sources."

As the crooked agent counted the money into James's outstretched palm, I peered at him, my curiosity getting the better of me.

"Mr. Hastings, where are you from?" My question seemed to startle him, and he tilted his head as James pocketed the cash.

"From the proud state of Pennsylvania," he said with a lift of his chin. I nodded and followed James to the door. With a glance over my shoulder, I saw the carpetbagger still watched as we stepped into the driving wind.

There was no mention of a hot meal at the café, the reservation only having the army mess hall to serve its soldiers. But I didn't say anything as we mounted and turned our horses to the south, toward home and warmth.

CHAPTER 31

The storm teased us for two days with the threat of impossible travel and drifting snow. Although the cold wind pushed us down the trail, I felt grateful the thick snow held off, as if restrained by an unseen power. For the remainder of the third day, we traveled swiftly, despite the chilling storm on our heels, and then camped within the two remaining walls of a tumbled down adobe house. The horses stood heads down behind the sheltering wall while we huddled in front of the fireplace, a blaze burning brightly made from the rotted poles of the broken roof.

James reached into his pocket and drew out the money. With a grin, he handed the bills to me.

"I don't mind if you carry the money," I protested, but he shook his head.

"Your money. I don't know why I carried it last time." He paused as I stuffed the cash deep into my shirt pocket.

"Why did you hold out for the twelve dollars?" My question didn't seem to surprise him, and he filled our mugs from the blackened pot before replying.

Steam wafted in thin wisps from the tin cup he held, and he grinned, his hard features softening in the firelight. "I kind of wondered the same thing." When I frowned, not understanding, he went on. "I knew he was cheating us, but I couldn't prove it. Part of me just wanted to take less and be content with what we got, but another part told me to hold fast, to not buckle to the bald little swindler."

"You knew he'd give in?" I prodded, not comprehending.

James sighed and sipped his coffee. Wind whipped the canvas tarp we'd stretched overhead, and I shivered, grateful for the slight shelter the tumbled house provided.

"Ever since I talked to your ma," he began, and then he shook his head. "John, I believe her. It's like we're on this great adventure to see what God can do, if only we have faith. I knew Hastings was lying, and I figured if Jesus had us drive those cattle north in horrible weather, it was for a purpose. I didn't figure that purpose was to get cheated."

He laughed when he saw my scowl. "Don't you agree? You've known Annie longer than me."

I ignored the way he casually used Ma's given name and shifted, unwilling to disclose too much. Yet I wanted to tell someone. Since the beginning, when Paul arrived and Ma presented her idea of wholehearted trust in Christ, a journey to watch the Lord provide and work through difficult challenges, I'd been the hold out. My skepticism had kept me from seeing the Lord's hand in everything, sometimes thinking I'd seen Jesus do something miraculous and other times filled with doubts. Could I trust God with everything? We'd suffered so much and for so long, I struggled to believe the Lord was with us even when things weren't going our way.

"Is blind faith so easy for you?" I sipped my coffee and tugged my collar higher, listening to the wind howl. Or was that a wolf? And where was Dark Cloud? Had the storm made the Comanche warrior give up his attempt at catching us unaware and doing away with me? Something told me he was still out there, watching for his chance.

James chuckled. "Blind faith? Maybe. I admit I've thrown my trust into this deal. Something about your ma inspires me, encourages my faith. I feel she is closer to the Lord than I am, and I want to be a part. Paul too. He knows the Spirit, you can tell. My prayer is to grow my faith so I can see the Lord in everything like they do."

I shook my head and scowled. "I've been a Christian all my life, and I believe the Bible is truth. But I can't just make myself believe coincidences are the workings of God. I need facts, a plan I can understand, then I'll throw my faith behind an idea. I'm afraid to risk everything on a feeling that might be nothing."

James said nothing for a while as we stretched out in our blankets, pushing sticks from our gathered pile of wood into the little blaze. The wood crackled merrily as the storm threatened to unleash its full ferocity, but only bitterly cold wind and a few scattered snowflakes drifted beneath the tarp.

"I was like you," James spoke abruptly, and my gaze lifted from the scuttling fire. "I only believed what I saw. Good things were a blessing, bad things a punishment. I never realized the Lord uses all things for the good of those who love him. God is sovereign, the Lord of good and bad. He uses all circumstances to grow us, to stretch our faith, and to develop our character."

At my continued scowl, he chuckled again. "Can God use a dead outlaw on the trail for good things? Can God use a Comanche arrow in my shoulder for good things? You rescued me when I'd given up, and the Lord has brought me into an adventure I'm excited to be a part of. I'm eager to see what he'll do next."

My frown deepened as I considered Ma and what part she played in James's excitement. I could tell they were attracted to one another and wondered how much of his commitment was due to a lonely widow on the Texas plains.

I huddled in my blankets and listened to the wind as the canvas tarp snapped and whipped overhead while I wrestled my doubts. I wanted to believe—I really did. Sometimes I felt the Lord's blessing, like when we received the reward money for Red Bill, or when Paul came to our ranch. But when things weren't easy, I struggled to believe the Lord was with us, guiding us, blessing us. If I were God, I wouldn't make things so tough for those who love and follow him. What purpose could there be in difficulties other than to suffer and struggle?

The tarp flapped in the gale, broken loose from its moorings. The temperature had dropped even more, and I blinked awake, trying to discern figures in the darkness. Dawn must not be far off, but the fire was reduced to gray ash. I shivered as the canvas shuddered in the wind, wondering what I should do.

"John," James called above the roar of the wind. I glanced at the dark heap of blankets where his bed lie and blinked again. "This storm has only just begun. It's going to open up today and it'll be difficult, not to mention dangerous, to continue on. Should we ride into the storm and back to the reservation? We can sit out the storm and wait for better travel weather. Or should we push on and make a break for the Henderson place? With the wind at our back, I think we can be there by nightfall."

I considered our options and didn't want to ride into the storm again, back to the Indian reservation. I knew James was allowing me to make a man's decision. Even though it might be safer to return to the reservation, I felt eager to get home. I worried about Ma and knew she worried about us.

But something else nudged me too, something unnamed, prompting me to go south.

"James, if you're game, I'd like to head for home."

"I was hoping you'd say that." His words held an eagerness that surprised me. In a minute, we'd stomped into our boots and rolled our blankets. As I loaded gear on the horses, James handed me a few leftover biscuits from the night before and a thick piece of jerked meat.

"No time for a fire this morning," James explained as we stepped into the saddle, turning the horses to the south. "We need to get going if we want to beat this storm."

I would've loved a hot cup of coffee, but I felt the need for haste. James obviously did as well. With the wind driving us ahead, we started riding toward home. A few hours later, a dull gray hovered in the east, but there was no sign of the sun.

All day we moved on, exchanging horses when they tired. We never stopped to rest except when we watered the horses.

The sleet drove at us from all sides, piercing our exposed cheeks like burning needles. Still the wind pushed us on. Late in the morning, the scattered snow turned to freezing rain. Two hours later, the snow returned as the temperature dropped even more.

Grabbing James by the shoulder, I leaned close. "How far to the Henderson place?"

James scanned the surrounding landscape as the horses pranced nervously, frightened by the worsening tempest. "A couple of hours still, I figure," he shouted above the wind.

"We'd better make it soon," I replied as I shrugged deeper into Pa's old slicker. "We'll freeze if we don't find shelter soon."

Without a reply, James plodded on, the horses walking with heads down. It was truly a miserable day, but we held our course, and the miles slipped away behind us.

The horses trudged obediently, trusting there would be warmth and maybe some grain at the end of the ride. We saw no one, nor any animals. Again, I wondered if Dark Cloud had been foolish enough to follow us. I grinned, knowing that if he did, he'd be as wretched as us.

All afternoon the storm grew worse. The snow had become a wall of white that made identifying landmarks difficult. Drifts crisscrossed bare places, making travel more difficult on the horses. As the blizzard strengthened, my fears increased. Had God given us the two cattle sales only to have us die in the storm? Was he punishing me for my lack of faith?

"You could fix this," I muttered behind my scarf, glancing expectantly at the lowering sky. "If you're with us, you could turn this snow into sunshine."

I jested, realizing again my doubts were too great for me to overcome. God might be with us, but I felt despair seep into my bones. Would things always be difficult for me? Why would the Lord torment me with challenges too great for me to bear?

My skepticism soared, and I wondered if I'd allowed coincidences to get the better of me. Perhaps I attributed too much to Jesus. Perhaps the storm had nothing to do with God.

As I topped a rise, I looked to the west, surprised to see a dull glow in the white canopy lean toward the far horizon. Frozen to the bone, shivering so hard my chattering teeth made my jaw ache, I knew the twilight neared and we still were not near camp.

Finally, rounding a copse of bare-limbed trees, I saw the dugout. Pounding a fist on James's shoulder, I pointed to the ramshackle abode as the fading light darkened the windswept prairie. White drifts resembling creamy butter snaked every which way. Without a word, James angled toward the dugout with the last of the day's dim light.

The wind slowed and allowed us to push the weary beasts into the lean-to barn. Nearly falling from my saddle, I pushed James toward the dugout. "Get a fire started. Make coffee," I ordered. He nodded as he stumbled toward the cabin, the canvas bag of cooking gear slung over one shoulder.

I unsaddled each horse and brushed them carefully before draping blankets across their backs and securing the covers with pieces of rawhide. After pulling hay and a little grain into the feed bins, I turned to make my way toward the dugout, my feet frozen like blocks of ice. Then I saw the Indian horse, a hackamore over the animal's muzzle and a blanket tethered to its back. The horse took a tentative step toward me, and I reached for the leather reins.

I frowned when I noticed only a little snow lay across the blanket. Someone had ridden this horse very recently. The third stray horse I'd encountered recently reminded me of the events that surrounded the other two, and I wondered if this were to be an equally significant situation.

Tying the animal to the corner of the cabin, I stomped my boots before pushing inside. A small fire blazed in the potbellied stove and a coffeepot simmered atop. James hovered above the little fire with outstretched hands to the flames, warming his numb hands. He turned when I entered.

"You'd better thank God we found this place. Another hour and we'd be dead."

I scowled at his bold confidence. What made him think God helped us survive the storm?

"There's an Indian pony tied to the dugout. It just wandered into the yard." I tugged my gloves from my frozen hands and held them to the fire.

James tilted his head. "Indian horse? In this storm? Most Indians like to stay near their fires in bad weather. Must be Dark Cloud's horse. He must've fallen off. No doubt he's dead by now, frozen like us."

"I don't think so," I added. "Little snow on the saddle."

"Ah? He's close then," James agreed. Then he shrugged. "Too bad. There's little hope for him now."

"He must be very close." I chewed my lip, wondering why I wanted to search for him. No doubt he'd wanted to kill me and remove a possible competitor for Hannah.

I almost laughed at the foolish idea. I certainly was no competitor for Dark Cloud, although Buffalo Horn said the young brave had no chance with his daughter. Did I?

I almost laughed again. Hannah had no interest in me.

Tugging on my gloves, I stepped to the door. "Have coffee ready when I return."

"You're not going out there," James protested. "We barely made it here ourselves. You'll freeze."

"He must be close," I repeated as I tugged on the door. "I'll be right back."

Night had fallen. The wind had died down, but snow fell in heavy flakes now, piling thickly on the ground. Leading the Indian's horse to the lean-to barn, I made room for him among the others and then followed his trail onto the prairie. Dim tracks lay outlined in snow but were filling quickly.

My boots crunched in the fresh snow as I strode into the night, glancing over my shoulder occasionally to keep my bearings. The dugout soon vanished in the gloom, but I kept walking.

"Am I stupid?" I glanced up at the starless sky. "I know he wants to kill me, but if there's a chance I can find him, I'll give it a try." I remember the mysterious urge to attempt the trek to this dugout, and I wondered if the Lord had guided me here. Was I supposed to find Dark Cloud?

I remembered the sensation I'd felt on my ride from town when I felt someone whisper into my head. Was that real? I wanted to save Dark Cloud, if I could, but I was shivering again and knew I needed to turn back soon.

"Fifty more steps," I said aloud as I started counting softly to myself. The horse tracks had petered out. Fear niggled within me and I knew I needed to turn around.

Rounding a thicket, I stopped, having counted my fifty steps. "Well, Jesus, what do I do now?"

Snow layered on the shoulders of my coat, and I brushed the little piles away. My tracks would be buried soon if I didn't turn around now. I knew I could easily back track myself if I went before snow filled my prints.

But like the ride home from town, a sensation prickled at the back of my head, prompting me on a few more steps. I frowned, not liking the feeling of going farther than I deemed safe. Yet I trudged on, urged by something unseen.

Another thirty steps and I halted again. "Lord, we're playing with fire here. I won't be able to find my tracks in the snow." But I walked on another twenty steps, foolishly thinking a feeling impelled me.

A dark heap lay in the trail, the figure almost hidden beneath a thin layer of snow. Eyes widening, I hurried to the slumped form and rolled the body over. By the dim light, I recognized Dark Cloud.

CHAPTER 32

Snowflakes swirled around me as I peered closely at Dark Cloud. The Indian slumped in the trail, his head lolling to one side, and I feared he was dead. Placing my fingers to his throat, I sighed with relief when I found a faint pulse.

A low growl near at hand made me glance over my shoulder. There, not more than eight feet away, crouched a wolf. His eyes gleamed, and his jaws trembled as he snarled at me, cords of saliva swaying from his curling lips.

Moving ever so slowly, I let go of Dark Cloud and reached for my Colt. I kept my eyes fixed on the rigid creature and drew the weapon from beneath my coat. When I pulled the hammer back, he leaped.

The bellow of the pistol boomed and then was swept away on the wind. The wolf sprawled in the snow, his glittering gaze still looking at me from sightless eyes.

As I shoved the gun back into my holster, I heard James calling from the dugout. Bending to lift the senseless Indian over one shoulder, I staggered and started down the trail.

When James called again, I corrected my steps to take me toward his voice, the trail gone now as night enveloped me and snow concealed my former path.

"Here, James," I called as I trudged closer to the unseen cabin. What had I been thinking to wander into the snowstorm as night descended? I shivered as I realized how close I'd come to getting lost in the storm. Yet *something* had beckoned me on, and I wanted to believe the Lord had brought me safely back to the dugout.

James hurried from the gloom, skidding to a halt when he saw the man's form across my back. "It's Dark Cloud. He's hurt," I explained as I staggered on, suddenly feeling very tired.

"I heard a shot," he said as he matched my stride.

"A wolf found him too. I shot the varmint."

James nodded as the outline of the cabin loomed in the murky light. He kicked the door open and followed me in before slamming the door in place. The little room felt warm after the cold of the trail, but I still shivered as I placed the Indian on the bed in the corner and stepped back. Heaving, I stared down at Dark Cloud while James inspected the injured man.

"I think his leg is broken," he mumbled as he felt each limb. "Probably fell from his horse and struck his head. There's a bump on his noggin above his ear," he added as he tossed a blanket over the still man.

He stood beside me, and we stared down at Dark Cloud. "He wanted to kill you."

I nodded, still not saying anything. This man was my enemy, yet I wasn't angry with him. He'd done what he thought was best for him, and now he lay injured in the bed of the little dugout.

"Funny, right?"

James's question made me glance at him. "What?"

He shrugged and then pointed at the silent figure. "He wanted to kill you, and here you are the one rescuing him."

I didn't reply and James shifted. "I'll need splints." He squinted at me. "I still haven't had coffee," he grumbled as he moved toward the door. "Be right back."

When he pulled the door open and stepped into the night, he shot me a warning glance over his shoulder. "John, don't turn your back on him."

I sat on a chair near the stove and watched Dark Cloud. Nothing stirred outside but the wind, and I worried James was taking a long time to return. When he finally entered, he nodded when I handed him the steaming cup of coffee. We drank in silence for a moment before James spoke.

"I cut splints. I think he'll be all right. Then I fetched that wolf and skinned him out."

My eyebrows arched. "Why'd you do that?"

He shrugged and drained his mug. Taking his knife, he split the Indian's buckskin pants and fitted the splints to the broken leg. Thankfully, the damaged bone had not pierced the skin.

As James shoved more fuel into the small stove, the Indian stirred. Dark Cloud blinked and then tensed when he saw me.

"Here," James said as he handed the injured man a steaming mug. Only the ceaseless wind broke the stillness of the little room while the Comanche brave sipped the hot drink and watched us closely.

I leaned my chair against the wall and observed Dark Cloud inspecting his doctored leg. The pain must have been fierce, yet the stoic Indian stared sullenly at us while he sipped coffee, never taking his gaze from us. As the storm blustered outside, we rested after the arduous trek from the tumbled adobe of last night. That we'd pushed our luck was evident to both of us, not to mention we'd been tracked by a relentless warrior who wanted me dead.

Why? I frowned, trying to puzzle Dark Cloud's motives. He didn't like the temporary pass Buffalo Horn offered us, but there was something more. My scowl deepened when I remembered Hannah Tall Basket. Did this fool think I was any threat to his plans to marry the Indian princess? According to Hannah, he didn't have a chance with her anyway.

My thoughts turned to the beautiful girl and then I froze, uneasy with my wandering ideas. We were friends, nothing more, yet I wondered if I wished for more.

When Dark Cloud made gestures indicating the whereabouts of his horse and weapons, James pointed outside to the crude barn. The former dispatch rider picked up a stick from the woodpile and snapped the small limb in two, grinning as he pointed at the Indian's leg.

"You tried to kill us, and you almost died." James pointed at me. "He saved your lousy neck. The man you wanted to kill, saved you."

Dark Cloud's dark eyes revealed nothing, and I wondered if he understood anything James said. But he rested on the bed without a whimper, and I felt grateful I didn't have to meet this warrior in battle.

Through that long night, we took turns keeping watch on the injured man and feeding the hungry fire. Dark Cloud dozed fitfully, but never spoke. In the morning, I filled the wood box and checked on the horses. Another four inches of snow had fallen in the night, and I knew we weren't going anywhere for a while.

The silver pelt of the big wolf lay stretched across a broken barrel. Not yet properly tanned, the large skin still revealed the enormous wolf that almost got Dark Cloud. The animal must've been starving to hunt in the storm. Had I been a few minutes late, the wolf would've killed the Indian.

For two days we stayed put, taking turns reading from the Henderson's Bible they'd left behind. While Dark Cloud grudgingly accepted our food and drink, I searched the

Scriptures for messages on faith while James worked over the wolf skin.

Scraping and twisting the gray pelt, James worked as he whistled or softly sang hymns. I lounged in the corner and occasionally replenished the small fire as the wind raged without. Last summer, I'd determined to believe the Lord's presence in Ma's adventure only when I saw his evident hand. But the more I studied the Holy book, the more I learned Jesus pointed to his miracles and interventions to prove his identity, to validate he was the Christ. Later, when the Lord confronted doubting Thomas, he accused Thomas of believing only because he saw the resurrected Jesus. "Blessed are those who have not seen and yet have believed."

As if slapped, I lowered the heavy book and leaned my head against the wall. Have I sinned in asking Jesus to perform for me? Who am I to demand the living God do my bidding?

Shamefaced, I pushed the piece of burlap from the window and peered out, eager to strike for home. I felt bored and confined but also convicted. Desperately, I wished to go home.

I turned to watch James work over the silver pelt. "That thing smells," I grumbled as I tossed the Bible on the table. "When can we get out of here?"

My gaze shifted to Dark Cloud, where the Indian studied me from beneath his bushy brows. He watched me like a hawk, and I was sick of his scrutiny. As soon as the weather broke, I wanted to leave this dingy dugout.

As if reading my mind, James ran his hands over the gleaming hide and peered at me. "We'll leave in the morning. We all need to get out of here."

The next day, as Dark Cloud followed our horses without complaint, I read the strain on his taut features. His injured leg must've caused great discomfort, but he said nothing as he sat his Indian pony, the miles slipping by as we neared home.

Snow lay scattered in drifts, some of the land windswept and bare. A lowering sky threatened, but patches of vibrant blue peeked through the gray canopy as we hurried toward home. The money we'd made from the sale of our cattle felt heavy in my pocket, and I wanted to tell Ma and Paul of our great success. Even with paying the taxes on the Henderson place, we had more than enough money to make it through the winter.

But something else whirled in my thoughts. My lack of faith had begun to glare at me. Like the snow-laden clouds that hovered above us, I felt my doubts hovered around me, making me uneasy with my glaring lack of trust. What kind of a Christian was I to doubt the Lord's presence? Sure, I'd felt abandoned and disappointed when Jesus was silent, but even I had to admit he'd been active on our ranch these past months. Had I lost my connection with God altogether? Fearfully, I glanced up at the steel gray clouds and prayed.

James slowed until my horse matched his pace. We walked on together for a moment before he spoke. "I've been considering how Buffalo Horn must've gone against many of the braves in that Comanche camp when he gave you permission to pass on their land."

I nodded when I realized he was probably right. "I'm sure that's true. Perhaps many of them didn't want me and my cattle on their land."

He hooked a thumb over his shoulder to the silent Indian behind us. "I think you should take Dark Cloud to his camp and show them Buffalo Horn was wise. Only your presence on the prairie saved this Comanche's life."

I squinted and pressed my lips into a thin line. "But he wouldn't have been out in that storm if it weren't for me. He'd be safe back in his teepee."

James chuckled. "Well, don't tell them that." He glanced at me from the corner of his eye. "I can tell something will come of this. I can feel it. Ever since I backed Annie and threw in with her adventure, I swear I sense things more clearly."

"What kind of things?" I asked eagerly, recalling my concerns with my own spiritual shortcomings.

He peered at Dark Cloud before he replied. "I'm not sure. I used to have a close relationship with Jesus, before the war, before I felt he'd turned his back on me."

I felt my eyes widen at the sound of my very own words coming from James. Did other believers struggle as I have? Did others feel Jesus was absent when he was silent?

"And now?" I prodded, needing to know more.

James let out a long sigh. "I'm a weak man. The Lord never left me. I mistook his quiet for being preoccupied elsewhere, as if he didn't care about me. Now I realize he was always at work, shaping my faith. It's no accident I delivered dispatch for the army all the way out here."

He paused and then looked at me sharply. "It's no accident the Lord had you rescue me, in more ways than one. There's something big going on here, and I was intended to play a part. My faith is ready for this deal. I see that now."

A scowl settled on my features, making me squint into the dull sun that hovered above the distant horizon. We'd be home in a few hours, and I couldn't wait to see Ma, but something James said worried me even more.

Was I ready for the deal James hinted at? Was my faith big enough to handle what the Lord had in store for me? Sadly, I worried Jesus would find me unprepared.

CHAPTER 33

James, Paul, and I took turns watching Dark Cloud as the Indian stretched on our parlor floor. Lydia refused to come near the Indian, her eyes wide with terror as she argued he might kill us all in our sleep. Paul assured his wife the men would guard the Comanche until he departed for his own camp the next day. Only I would go with Dark Cloud. I don't think I could've dragged James from our house if I wanted to.

All evening, the army veteran circled moon-eyed around Ma as the women scurried to put a late supper on the table. Everyone seemed glad we were home safe, but Ma and James had eyes only for one another.

At dawn, I helped the warrior onto his horse as James and Paul looked on. His sullen countenance helped further explain his name, but he seemed curious as we bundled him with my buffalo robe the Comanche chief had given me. His injured leg must have pained him, yet he gave no indication the injury caused him concern.

I stepped into the saddle and peered down at the two men who braved the cold to see us off.

"There is purpose in this," Paul muttered prophetically. I frowned and then shook my head, trying to clear my routine response. My constant doubts irritated me, and I began to understand why Ma felt annoyed by my negative attitude.

"Maybe," I shrugged, pleased I'd not said something adverse to the adventure they'd all believed in. Was Jesus with us? Did a great undertaking yawn before me?

"The Lord is definitely doing something," James agreed. "Be safe and hurry back." He took a step back from our horses and shoved his hands into his pockets, glancing over his shoulder to the house. I sighed, knowing he wanted to hurry back into the warm kitchen.

"Wait, I almost forgot." He tugged a rolled object from under his arm. I recognized the wolf skin as I shoved the pelt into my saddlebags.

"Something to remember us by," James said, gesturing to the surly Comanche brave beside me.

As I rode from the yard with Dark Cloud on my heels, I wondered if perhaps there was something else that drew James back to the house. I snuggled deeper into my coat, the raw prairie wind blowing frigidly across the quiet plains. How serious was James about Ma? He'd given her a silver comb and helped ensure her survival on the ranch with the drive to the army posts.

My thoughts turned to Hannah Tall Basket. I'd surely been considering her more than I should, thinking about her smile and her long black hair more than was good for a young man. I liked the way we enjoyed each other's company and the easy way she talked to me, but she was an Indian princess, spoken for, according to her pa.

My jaw ached as I clenched my teeth. Who was Hannah to marry, and why did the idea worry me so much?

As we moved to the west, Dark Cloud seemed to quicken his pace. Perhaps he recognized familiar landmarks, for soon he trotted his horse. I felt safe enough alone with him. Would I feel so secure if he were well and healthy? Perhaps he longed to get back to Hannah. I felt a stab of jealousy but waved it off.

When his face screwed with pain, he slowed once more and walked his horse, an impatient look resting on his strained features.

When I indicated we should take a break and eat the small lunch Lydia packed for us, the Indian shook his head and pointed to the west, never slowing his marching horse. A thin layer of snow covered everything except the low places where it had drifted deep. We avoided the creek bottoms and floundered through ditches until the sun lay far to the horizon and I knew we were close to the Comanche's winter camp.

Dark Cloud sagged atop his horse. He must've been in real pain, but he never complained. As twilight descended, we caught sight of a watchful sentry and the drifting smoke of campfires.

Barking dogs and shrieking children met us as we walked through camp. Women pointed at Dark Cloud's injured and braced leg, but the warriors only watched with stoic faces. When we halted before Buffalo Horn's lodge, two braves helped the Indian from his horse and carried him away.

The crowd surged around me, yet I felt very alone. They peered up at me with curious glances while I stayed on my saddle, unsure what to do. When Hannah appeared beside me, I let out a sigh. "Oh, thank God," I breathed when I saw her smiling face.

She placed a hand on my horse's neck and tugged her deerskin cape tighter around her. "Johnny, I'm glad to learn Dark Cloud was with you. He left days ago, and we feared him dead. I am glad to know he is alive."

I don't know why her words riled me, but a stab of jealousy pierced again as I felt my brow wrinkle. "You were afraid for him? Did you miss him?"

She shrugged as she stepped back, giving me room to dismount. "Sure. He is a good hunter. We would miss him if he were dead."

Her noncommittal reply didn't make me feel any better as I stepped from the saddle, stiff after the long day on horseback. I pulled the wolf skin from my gear. "He trailed me, hoping to kill me," I snapped, hoping to dash his standing in her eyes. "I saved him from this." I thrust the silver pelt into her hands.

Again she shrugged, absently stroking the soft fur. "You look fine to me."

As she turned to lead the way into her father's lodge, a man called from the outer edge of the surrounding throng. A path cleared through the crowd, and one of the braves who'd carried Dark Cloud away stepped close to Hannah. He whispered excitedly to her, gesturing repeatedly to the hide she held, and I watched her eyes widen. With a grin at me, she pulled the tent flap open and motioned I enter the lodge.

Warmth welcomed me, and I stepped aside for Hannah to enter while my eyes adjusted to the gloom. The old chief was seated before a small blaze and indicated a piled elk hide for me. Together, Hannah and I sat across the fire from Buffalo Horn. I blinked when I noticed three more elders sitting in the shadows, all watching me intently. They ignored me when I nodded at them.

Hannah spoke in Comanche, her rapid words floating singsong in the room. No one interrupted as she talked, but all the men exclaimed with grunts of satisfaction when she lifted the silver wolf skin for all to see.

Surprised, I glanced from Hannah to the elders and Buffalo Horn. The men nodded solemnly before the old chief spoke, gesturing to the unfurled wolf pelt his daughter held.

Hannah nodded when her father finished. She turned to me, a wide smile wreathing her beautiful face. "Father—I mean Buffalo Horn—says you are guided by the Creator.

Dark Cloud vowed to kill you, and instead, you saved his life. You rescued him from the wolf and fixed his injury, although he wanted your scalp. You are a great warrior, John Garret, and the Comanche thank you for returning Dark Cloud to us and visiting our camp."

I felt my eyebrows lift as I glanced at Buffalo Horn once more. The chief nodded solemnly, but a gleam in his eyes made me squint as I searched for a deeper meaning in his scrutiny.

When he nodded and said something to Hannah, she rose and gestured for me to follow. Handing the wolf pelt to her father, she stepped out of the teepee and wrapped her deerskin cape around her as I placed the tent flap over the doorway.

She smiled, and I felt my head swim. "You are a hero, Johnny. You bested Dark Cloud, one of our fiercest braves, and you fetched the wolf that almost killed him. Father says your bravery shows he was right to give you passage across Comanche lands. The elders agree."

I shifted, not sure what to say. But standing near Hannah made me realize how much I'd missed her.

Hannah led me to a bonfire near where my horse had been tethered at the edge of camp. A carpet of stars littered the night sky, and not even a breath of wind stirred. The night felt cold but somehow pleasant with the crackling fire and Hannah's warming presence.

As she sat beside the blaze, she eyed me from beneath dark eyebrows. "Buffalo Horn says you have the heart of the wolf, a great fighter. He says you will fight for your people." She paused before she went on. "Those you love," she added shyly, glancing away.

I couldn't take my eyes from her and continued to stare, enjoying the lovely view. When she sensed my gaze, she nudged me with an elbow. "Don't look at me that way."

"What way?"

"Like the men who want a wife. You know I can only go to the man my father chooses for me."

Her candor unsettled me, and I peered up at the immense sky, craning my neck to study the canopy of countless stars stretching to the horizon. Certainly, we weren't in any position to discuss marriage. What about love? What did I feel for Hannah?

"I have a question for you," I said abruptly, eager to change the subject.

My buffalo robe, which Dark Cloud wore earlier, lay heaped beside my saddle. Hannah draped the heavy hide around her shoulders. "Good. I want to talk to you too."

Poking a stick into the dancing flames, I kept my eyes from her, wanting to concentrate. "I know you went to the missionary school on the reservation."

She chuckled without humor. "I hated it at first. All the other children were mean to me. They called me a wild Indian. The Cherokee, Choctaw, Chickasaw, Creek, and Seminole felt I didn't belong among them."

She straightened and I glanced at her, watching her clear profile outlined by the stars overhead. "I am Comanche, daughter of Buffalo Horn."

I nodded, wanting her to see I agreed with her. "Your pa is a great chief."

Hannah's shoulders slumped and her chin dropped. "We are a proud people, but father says we are not long for the plains. The elders disagree, but Buffalo Horn has worked to prepare me for what is coming. That is why he sent me to learn English."

I chewed my lip, considering. As I struggled with my own doubts and challenges, I hadn't worried about the changes coming to the Comanche. Hannah had her own issues. Perhaps this wasn't a good time to ask my question.

She nudged me again. "Hey, the seasons come and go. Life is change, right? Thank God he knows what he's doing."

My eyebrow quirked. "Does he? I mean, that's my question. I feel he's been silent and distant, not hearing my prayers. We've suffered so much without his help."

A bitter grin flashed across Hannah's face, and she frowned, her brow wrinkling in deep furrows. "I know how that feels. After my mother died in childbirth, I was raised by other nursing women. But a rumor circulated that I was cursed." She shrugged and tried unsuccessfully to grin again. "Perhaps the tale was started by a jealous girl, for the men of the tribe didn't seem to mind. Buffalo Horn eventually sent me away for my education."

"Is that where you learned about God?"

She shook her head. "Of course not. The Comanche are a very spiritual people. We know of the Creator. But at school I learned about Jesus." She lifted her chin. "I have read the Bible."

Her declaration made me shift, wondering if she knew more than I did. Remembering the purpose of our conversation, I pressed on. "You must've learned a lot about God at the missionary school."

Hannah nodded.

I licked my lips. "How does faith work?"

She tilted her head and I tried to ignore the amused look in her eyes. "How does faith work? What do you mean?" Her eyebrows arched with interest.

Pushing another stick into the glowing coals, I considered dropping the subject. I felt foolish asking Hannah about Christian faith. I'd been a believer all my life, yet Ma's adventure forced me to look at my personal convictions, and I didn't like what I discovered. Overwhelmed by doubts and a pessimistic attitude, I'd become the sour note in the team of good people the Lord had assembled at our ranch.

I looked up at the glittering stars and squinted. *You brought me here, right? For this precise moment, I am here because of you. Please speak to me.*

"After the war, Pa didn't come home. Ma and me had a real hard time, and I didn't know what we were going to do. Then Ma prayed for an adventure."

I paused, my throat tightening. Hannah squeezed my arm, but I rushed on, not allowing my emotions free rein. "Ma prayed and Paul came, a good man, a man of God. He loves the Lord, and you never heard such praying. He knows Jesus like a close friend. Then I found the outlaw and we paid our taxes with the reward money, but still, I couldn't see the Lord's hand. I kept thinking bad things were sure to follow every good thing God allowed. Then he brought James."

"The rider who loves Annie?" Hannah's interjection made me smile.

"I don't know if he loves Ma, but I suspect something is going on between them."

Hannah's dark eyes glowed. "Oh, I just knew it. He's here to love Annie." Her eyes narrowed as she studied me in the firelight. "It's not good to be alone."

I shifted and kicked at the burning logs, making the sparks flutter skyward. "Hannah, listen, I need your help. Why can't I have their faith? James told us about the army posts buying cattle and we're making money. Why can't I just see God's hand and be happy?"

When Hannah laughed, I scowled, wondering if I'd been a fool to share my spiritual struggle with the Indian girl. But when she squeezed my arm again and drew my attention, I leaned close, eager for any insight she might possess.

"You need Texas faith," she whispered seriously.

"Texas faith?"

She nodded. "When I was at school, a map of the United States hung on the wall. Texas is big, the biggest state. You need to let your faith grow big like Texas."

"I can't just snap my fingers and make my faith grow," I growled, starting to regret sharing my dilemma with her.

"That's right, not a snap of your fingers." She flicked her fingers for emphasis. "Prayer, Johnny. Pray sincerely for your faith to grow," she said. "I can tell you Jesus uses the tough times we endure to build our faith, to prepare us for challenges that lie ahead. The more you read the Bible, the more you see how God works."

I shook my head, not liking what I heard. "I don't want to be prepared for challenges ahead. I want good things to happen all the time. We've had our share of tough times."

I knew I sounded petulant, like a spoiled child, but I felt I deserved some easy answers. I'd endured enough struggles. God wanted good things for me, right?

Hannah smiled again, her copper-colored cheeks gleaming like burnished bronze in the ruddy glow of the campfire. "That's foolishness. Jesus loves you enough to prepare you for what's ahead. But faith and trust take work. The Bible says the world is tough, but Jesus has overcome the world. With his help, you can persevere."

I waved a hand dismissively. "I know all that. But how can I grow my faith now?"

For a long minute, she remained silent, considering, and I wondered at her next words. Did she hold any truth that might help me? I didn't want to be the cause of failure for my family's ranch.

Hannah shifted, drawing my attention once more. "Prayer, of course. Bathe every endeavor in prayer. And read your Bible. It also helps to be in the community of other believers."

"I do that already," I grumbled, hoping that wasn't her best advice.

"Take captive every thought," she said abruptly.

My ears pricked. "What?"

"You know. Set your mind on things above. Don't focus on negative things. Look for the Lord's hand everywhere and count your blessings. I believe the Lord will honor a sincere desire to grow your faith, but this will take discipline. You must master your doubts."

I nodded, seeing her point. I *had* allowed my foul mood to taint the Lord's work at our ranch. "Take captive every thought," I repeated, recalling the familiar Scripture. I thrilled at the written Word of God speaking directly to me, directly to my circumstance.

Hannah's eyes danced with excitement. "Your ma believes she's on a great adventure? And so are you. A personal spiritual adventure with Christ. Whether you see it or not, you are becoming a strong man. Have faith, Johnny, and look for Jesus amidst the journey. Have Texas faith."

CHAPTER 34

As I rode for home the next day, the buffalo robe spread across my lap, I prayed about Hannah's advice. Could I grow my faith if I stayed focused on the Lord? I'd let my skepticism paint everything sour, tainting each of the recent events. Finding the dead outlaw, adding strong Christian believers to the ranch, gaining access to the Comanche lands during winter, and selling small bunches of cattle to the outposts were all blessings I'd looked at unfavorably. I hadn't even considered what significance the purchase of the Henderson place might have, but my initial thought was of more responsibility and work rather than the Lord's guiding hand. Perhaps God was growing our ranch. And me.

The sudden positive concept made me realize how much of an obstacle I'd become to Ma. She needed support and prayer from me, not the additional stress I'd piled upon her already burdened shoulders.

Shaking my head, I cleared my muddled thoughts and tried to focus on good things. With a growing sense of excitement, I tried to see each event through God's eyes, each blessing laced with spiritual meaning.

Was Jesus with us? My initial response was to discount every experience with a practical and realistic explanation of everything that had happened in the past eight months. Then, I shook my head again.

No. To start fresh, I needed to think differently. Patiently, I considered each event and tried to look at them with a spiritual measure that truly challenged me. I felt frustrated at how difficult this proved for me. Was my faith so small?

When another disruptive and destructive thought came to me, I took the idea captive, studying the concept from a biblical standpoint. Slowly, I worked on being less cynical and more optimistic.

Something else Hannah mentioned niggled at me. Was Ma's adventure my adventure too? Was God reaching out to me, trying to accomplish something intentional in me? As I looked back over this past year, I wondered. Perhaps he'd heard my long-ago prayer for spiritual maturity.

By midafternoon, I rode into the ranch yard, the sun westering behind me. My mental exercises had made the day fly by, and somehow I felt my spirits lift, as if the Lord were working inside of me. Perhaps a glimmer of Ma's adventure peeked through the storm clouds of my mind, allowing me for the first time to perceive what God might have in mind for our ranch. And for me.

Could good things be in our future? For so long, I'd only waited for the other boot to drop, always looking for negative outcomes. Maybe Jesus had a purpose in every trial I faced. I resolved to wait on the Lord and surrender my contrary will to his divine control. What harm could come from my surrender? I'd certainly found no success with my way of doing things, only frustrating myself and those around me.

A light glowed in the kitchen window, beckoning me from the darkness as I rode to the barn where I dismounted and led my horse into the gloomy building. Cold wind whistled across the prairie, but the barn felt warm and dry.

I stabled my gelding and rubbed him down with a piece of old sacking. My thoughts whirled as I worked, wondering what God would do if I gave him a willing heart to work with.

Another glance at the house revealed no one in sight. I walked to an empty stall and knelt, lifting my eyes to a dark corner in the loft. "Are you with me, Lord?" My whispers barely made a sound and I listened as the wind buffeted the old building, making the boards creak and groan.

I licked dry lips and tried again. "Father, I want to be close to you. I have such worries and your Word tells me to be anxious for nothing. Yet I struggle with the responsibilities piled at my feet. The ranch, our future, James and Ma, and ... well, Hannah. I feel ... something."

I cut off, not knowing what to say. Hannah and I had been friends for years, but something had changed, and I sensed we both felt the difference.

"Well, Jesus, I don't know all what to say, but you know my heart. Let my faith grow. Let me be part of this team you've put together on our ranch. I want to serve you and trust you have something mighty you want to accomplish. Let me be patient to see your hand and allow me to praise you always, even when I don't see you working. Let me see life through spiritual eyes, always seeking to see you in every action, in every situation."

Pausing again, I scowled into the darkness of the old barn and waited, wondering if God might reply. When nothing happened, I nodded. "All right, Lord. Let my adventure begin as I look for you in everything. Give me strength to persevere and wisdom to discern your desires. Give me discipline as I read your Word and learn more about your love. I guess what I'm asking for is your guidance as I want to live for you, trusting you all the time, even when I can't see you."

I scrambled to my feet and moved toward the house. When I reached the big barn doors, I hesitated, peering over my shoulder into the shadows of the dark building. Was I a fool? Did the Lord really meet me in the murky barn where the milk cow chewed her cud and horses swished tails while chickens cackled?

For an instant, I wondered at my sanity. Then I squared my shoulders and lifted my chin. "No, Father, I will not doubt. You are with me. Do mighty works through me that bring you joy and glory."

With a nod, I walked to the house.

CHAPTER 35

"I'll bet the Indians were thrilled to see Dark Cloud again," Ma said. Steam rose as she poured coffee, but I caught the look of pride on her face through the mist. "Truly a man's errand, taking him home," she added, patting my arm.

Paul nodded, nursing his own cup of coffee from across the kitchen table. I grinned, remembering his first taste of the strong drink so many months ago.

"The Comanche were pleased for his safe return. Hannah's father believes I was guided by the Creator." I dug into my supper as the others watched, me being home so late. But I noticed how Ma stood beside James near the stove where the dispatch rider sipped his own drink. They seemed natural together, like they'd spent time talking and getting to know each other. I thought of how much I enjoyed Hannah's company and then ducked behind my mug, embarrassed at thinking of the Indian princess.

"Hannah?" Ma's eyebrows arched as she replaced the pot on the stove and glanced at James. He only nodded, his gaze resting on Ma with a curious gleam.

Lydia hummed softly from the rocker in the corner of the kitchen where she darned socks. "Not good for a man to be alone," she said softly with a smile at her husband.

Paul chuckled and shook his head. "No, Lordy, not good at all. I reckon the best day of my life was marrying you, woman."

Lydia beamed and I frowned, not wanting to discuss any more love talk. I had my own thoughts on the matter and didn't want to focus unnecessarily on them. My faith needed help, and I resolved to direct my attention in that direction.

But Ma wouldn't be put off. "Did you see Hannah when you were at the Indian camp?"

"Sure." I nodded. "We talked some."

"I'll bet she's a real pretty girl now. She always had such a kind look in her eyes."

I felt everyone stare at me, waiting for my response to Ma's observation. I gulped, not sure how much to share. I thought Hannah was kind, no doubt of that, but I also thought she was the most beautiful girl I'd ever seen.

Heat crept up my neck and I looked hastily down at my plate.

James laughed. "What are you blushing at, John?"

No one else seemed to notice, and I shrugged, gesturing to Paul with my mug. "I saw you cut the dead limbs from the cottonwoods near the corrals."

Paul nodded and leaned back in his chair as I sighed, knowing my ruse had worked. Everyone seemed pleased to recount the many improvements the men had completed around the ranch, and my visit with Hannah was soon forgotten.

"Until recently, the garden has kept us busy. The corn crib is half full," Paul said as he sipped from his cup.

James shifted near the stove, pulling his gaze from Ma to face me. "We'll plant more corn in the garden next spring. More of everything, and the girls preserve the extra at harvest."

Again, I saw how the ranch was shaping up. But these enhancements had nothing to do with my developing faith.

I peered at James. "What's next? Do we make a drive to another army post?" Eagerly I craved a test to my newfound resolve. Surely with my willing heart, the Lord would bolster my flagging faith with opportunities to show off his abilities.

James glanced at Ma before he spoke. "We'll lay low for now, rest up after this last drive. We have enough cash on hand for a while."

I couldn't tell if his decision was based on the inclement weather or his desire to stay close to Ma. I scowled at the thought of not allowing my faith to be stretched, wanting to see God do something. My scowl deepened when Lydia turned the topic back to Hannah.

"This Indian girl? She interprets for you?"

I nodded slowly, reluctant to change the conversation back to our neighbors, especially Hannah.

Lydia continued. "I'd be so afraid in an Indian village. Why, I once helped care for a man whose entire family was killed by Indians. I'm sure I wouldn't know what to do if an Indian spoke to me." She shuddered and turned to Paul.

"You'd trust the Lord as John does when visiting the Comanche. Nothing to fear, wife," he soothed.

Lydia scoffed and clucked her tongue. "I don't know," she persisted as she speared the toe of another sock.

After a while, Paul and Lydia went to their cabin, and I was left alone with Ma and James. I nursed my third cup of coffee while Ma washed the few dirty dishes, James drying and putting away. Something different about Ma drew my attention, and I discovered the worry lines around her eyes had vanished. All through the war, I'd seen those worry lines deepen and grow, yet now they seemed as if they'd never existed. Ma's face seemed younger, and her cheeks glowed in the lantern light. I figured I had James to thank for her lessening workload.

I tilted my head and wondered at that. James or Jesus? Surely Ma had handed this spiritual adventure to the Lord, watching what God might do with our rundown ranch, but James had been a part of that journey. I knew the Lord had delivered the wounded dispatch rider into our midst.

Ma pulled the stopper on the sink and dried her hands on her apron as she turned to me. "Does Hannah have a young brave courting her?"

My scowl returned at the mention of Hannah's name. Wouldn't Ma let the subject drop?

I shook my head. "Her pa has already chosen her mate. She doesn't even know who he is."

I realized the exclusion from Hannah's future annoyed me. I certainly had no hold on her, but with our reintroduction this past summer, I'd been entertaining more thoughts of her than I should. Now that I possessed a genuine interest and liking for her, it irritated me she was already spoken for.

Ma shifted, a frown creasing her features, as if she were about to say more. I sighed when James stepped forward and interrupted.

"John, I know it's late, but can I see you in the barn? I want to show you something."

"Can it wait until morning?" Ma seemed anxious, probably worrying about my weariness after the long day. But my chair scraped as I pushed away from the table and reached for my coat, eager to make my escape from her interrogations.

"I've got a minute before I turn in," I offered, grateful.

James said goodnight to Ma and followed me outside. Only a faint glow from the kitchen lantern streamed through the window, casting a dull path to the barn.

Neither of us needed a light to show us the way, although a couple candles sat atop the grain bin if we needed them. Our boots crunched on the frozen snow as we made our way to the big structure and stepped inside. Warmth from the gathered animals welcomed us into the gloom, and I halted just inside the door, waiting for James to explain his concerns.

When a match flared, my eyebrows arched. He didn't require light any more than I did to navigate the dark interior, and I wondered at his intention as he stared at me over the glowing tallow stick.

"I need to ask you something," he began as he stood stiffly near the stalls. His coat hung open as if too preoccupied to properly dress for outside.

I shrugged and strode to the stalls to check the stock once more before bedtime. "Shoot," I called over my shoulder, not really paying attention.

"John, this is serious," he growled in a tone he usually reserved for commands.

I faced him, shoving my fists deep into my pockets. "All right, I'm listening."

The rider shifted uneasily and then stalked across the barn floor, pacing as he drew a deep breath. "John, you've only known me for a few months, but I've shown myself to be a hard worker. I'm responsible and I see the potential in this ranch."

"You want to talk about the ranch? Plans for the place?" I prodded after he paused, his pacing making me nervous.

He shook his head. "No, no. I love this place, but I want to talk to you about Annie."

I frowned. "Ma?" And then, like a lightning streak in the night, it hit me. He wanted to discuss Ma. A warm glow filled my chest.

He stopped pacing, faced me, and dragged a hand through his hair. "Yes," he whispered. "I've gotten to know your ma and I feel—well, I mean to say, er, I mean. I love her."

Well, you could've knocked me over with a feather. As I wrestled with the Lord about our future and my weak faith, Ma's adventure had taken an unexpected turn. Still focused on saving our ranch, she nonetheless had been nurturing an unforeseen friendship with James, as if the Lord were blessing her on all fronts as she leaned on Jesus.

"John, I figure with your pa gone, you're the man of the house," James went on hurriedly. "So, I want to ask you for your ma's hand in marriage."

I stared at him, stunned. Had I seen this coming? Maybe so, but not this soon. I cleared my throat. "Have you spoken to Ma about this?"

He shook his head again. "No. I wanted to talk to you first. You deserve that."

It was my turn to shift uneasily. "Do you think she expects this?" I was trying to think quickly but my mind felt sluggish. How was I supposed to respond? I knew Ma was still young enough to catch another man's fancy, but so soon? I felt our adventure had only just taken off, as if the Lord had to be coaxed to get on board. Now, things seemed to be moving faster than I could keep up.

"I don't know. I've made suggestions, but nothing has been said plain or out in the open. I don't think she'd be surprised, but I don't know. I wanted to talk to you first."

I tilted my head, studying James. A brave man, no doubt. Kind and considerate. He seemed intelligent and patient, but more importantly he loved the Lord. I could tell Ma liked him and she would have the final word on the matter, so I nodded, a smile creeping to my face.

"I appreciate you asking me first. It shows you're a thoughtful man who does things right. The decision is Ma's, but if she says yes, I have no objections." I squinted at the dispatch rider. "But you must promise to be good to her."

Relief swept across his features, and he nodded eagerly. "Of course," he said as he stepped forward and shook my hand. "I'll take good care of her, John. I promise."

CHAPTER 36

Moonlight gleamed brightly on the thin layer of snow that blanketed our yard. I listened as James made his way to his cabin, his boots crunching on the frozen ground. With a glance at the dim lantern light glowing from the kitchen window, I shoved my hands deeper into my pockets and walked toward the house, my thoughts still lingering on our conversation.

Ma lifted clean dishes to the cupboard as I stepped inside. She turned to me, her gaze darting past me to the empty space behind me. I read the disappointment that flickered across her features, and I pursed my lips, trusting I had the answer to my question for her.

"What did James want to show you in the barn?" She lifted the coffeepot from the stove and shot me an inquisitive glance. I nodded and watched as she filled two mugs and brought them to the table. Our chairs scraped loudly in the quiet house, and we sat silent for a long moment while we blew on our hot drinks, both of us lost in our own thoughts.

Ignoring Ma's inquiry, I blurted. "I think I love Hannah Tall Basket."

Her face broke into a wide grin. "Is that all? I've known that for some time. Did you just figure it out?"

I blinked at her casual response. "Ma, I'm serious."

"I am too, Johnny. Hannah's had her eye on you for years. I'm glad God's opened your eyes at last. Your father and I used to speak of it."

"Pa? He knew?" I frowned. How could everyone know but me?

Ma sipped her coffee and then nodded, eyeing me over the rim of her cup. "Yes. He wondered if she'd be your wife one day."

"Well, that's not going to happen. Her father's already chosen her husband. I thought it might be Dark Cloud, but she said Buffalo Horn did not choose him."

I paused, sipping my drink. What was God doing with me? I felt I'd just given my heart completely to him, a willing heart for the Lord to guide. Yet my spirits careened even more as I worried about our future and my growing feelings for Hannah.

"What am I going to do?" I grumbled quietly.

"You're going to pray to a faithful, loving God. We've embarked on a big adventure, and God hasn't let us down. Don't let him down. Every tear, every breath, every thought, every heartache flows through his hand. He knows who you will marry. Do not be afraid, do not worry. He has good things in store for you. Pray. Trust. Love."

I gripped my cup tighter and wanted to argue, yet I knew she was right. I'd agreed to seek the Lord with faith, and now when a trial swirled, I wanted to run for the hills. Pensively, I stared at her, my worries swelling. Then I shook my head and remembered Hannah's words. Texas faith.

Lifting my chin, I nodded. "You're right. I need faith. Don't allow the worries to get me down. Trust. God loves us, right?"

"Right." She smiled, her eyes glowing. "I love you, Johnny. I love to see you develop into the man of God I've always prayed for."

I nodded, suddenly embarrassed at her comment. "What do you think of James?" My sudden question startled her, turning the discussion away from me.

She shifted. "He's a good man. I think he cares for you a great deal. I trust him." She looked away and tucked a loose strand of hair behind her ear, as if not wanting me to see her expression.

"That's not what I mean. Do you like him?"

She shrugged, still keeping her eyes from me. "Oh, I guess I like him. He seems to fit here with us."

I leaned my elbows on the table, watching her closely. "Ma, do you love him?"

She shot me a sharp look. "Why do you ask?"

"Do you love him?"

Her shoulders slumped, and she looked down at the table. "Yes, Johnny, I love him," she confessed in a whisper. "I love him desperately."

I reached across the table and gripped her arm. "I love you, Ma. Goodnight."

The next morning, breakfast seemed awfully quiet. Lydia prepared the meal, and Paul said the flowery, flowing blessing, thanking God for his provision. Ma kept her eyes on her plate while James shyly cast glances her way, not speaking but clearly captivated.

"I've got chores to do," Paul declared as he pushed away from the table and went to the barn. Lydia busied herself at the sink while the three of us sipped coffee, somehow reluctant to separate.

"I've been praying," James announced bluntly. Ma and I looked at him. "This adventure is stalled. We need a new direction. I feel things need to be shaken up a bit."

I glanced confusedly at Ma. "Things have gone well. We've sold stock to the army posts and should continue when spring comes."

James shook his head. "Not good enough. I feel restless, as if the Lord wants to do more."

My brow puckered and I glanced at Ma again. Was he talking about them? "I'm satisfied with our success. We've done well."

"That's just it," James persisted. "I don't know we should be so content. What if there's more Jesus wants us to do?"

I shrugged, unconvinced. But Ma nodded, her eyes glowing as she studied James. "Yes," she said softly. "We should not limit the Lord. Whatever you feel God is telling you, let us know. This adventure is ongoing."

He smiled at Ma and then winked at me. "I agree. Keep praying. I feel we're on the cusp of something big. Perhaps Jesus will tell us what he wants us to do next."

I followed James to the barn, leaving Ma to help Lydia with chores around the house. As we saddled our horses, I bumped the shelf above the stall and the Comanche arrow I'd placed there before tumbled to the floor.

When I held the feathered shaft aloft, he narrowed his eyes and took the arrow from me. "Such a small, useless thing on its own. But with a good bow, this little spear can do mighty things."

I nodded, thinking how faith can accomplish so much with the right tools, the right attitude. Again, I resolved to think big, to allow my ideas to expand and not be hemmed in with limiting boundaries. With Christ, all things were possible—great things. And I eagerly wanted to see them happen on our ranch. Abruptly, I wanted to share these ideas with Hannah. After all, she was the one who told me of Texas faith.

He placed the arrow back on the shelf and peered furtively toward the barn doors before he tugged a small package from his pocket. After pulling back a scarf covering, a golden ring lay in his palm.

"So soon?" I wondered if Ma was ready for this, but then relaxed, recalling last night's conversation.

"I picked this up in town," James explained. "Christmas is in three days. I figure that will be as good a time as any."

I nodded, agreeing with his assessment. Ma seemed ready for the next part of her journey. Suddenly, I knew what I intended to do. With James moving forward with his plan, I would do the same with mine.

"James, I'm going to drive a few head of cattle to Hannah's people and check in on Dark Cloud. I'll be back in a day or two."

His wide grin split his face. "Really? Check in on Dark Cloud?" He winked and then chuckled knowingly.

I dragged my horse's reins after me as I led the gelding to the door, annoyed James could see through me so easily. Stepping into the saddle, I tugged my hat low and pulled on my gloves. "See you in a day or two," I growled, my irritation mounting. His laughter trailed after me as I trotted from the yard.

Rounding up a trio of mavericks took little time, and soon I started pushing them to the Comanche camp. But my impatience increased as the nettlesome, ornery set of cows attempted to scatter at every opportunity. As my eagerness to see Hannah expanded, so did their pigheadedness, stretching my nerves taut the closer I drew to the Indian village.

A gentle breeze blew cold across the plains, but excitement warmed me as I herded the cows westward. A growing sense of anticipation drove me on, and the hours passed, swelling to a crescendo when I caught sight of a lone brave standing guard on a hilltop.

The Indian sentinel returned my wave. I thrilled when I topped a rise and looked down into the basin where the camp lay nestled behind the steep bluff, surrounded by trees and the small stream along one side of the village. Dogs barked as I pushed the bawling cows the rest of the way into camp.

As Indians emerged from their teepees at the raucous commotion, I scanned the gathering crowd, searching for Hannah.

Relief surged when I caught sight of her. Relinquishing the cows to the celebrating onlookers, I walked my horse toward the grinning Comanche princess.

All the Indians greeted me with welcoming waves and smiles. I relaxed in my saddle as Hannah stood beside my horse, looking up at me with a radiant glow to her cheeks. I smiled down at her, a gladness in me for the gifts I brought the girl I loved.

"Johnny, it is good of you to bring cattle to my people. I wondered how long you would stay away."

Her manner annoyed me, as if I stayed away because I wasn't interested in her. My smile slipped and I felt my brows bunch. "I see no reason in being here often. What I want, I cannot have." I hoped she understood my meaning.

She glowered at me, her pretty face darkening as she crossed her arms over her chest. "I know what you want. You want my father to extend his permission for you to drive cattle across Comanche land. Well, that will never happen. You're lucky he gave you this winter."

"That's not what I came for," I snapped. "Nor what I wanted. I wanted to see how Dark Cloud was getting on." Now that wasn't totally true, but her impertinence threw me off balance, and my anger roiled.

She tilted her head, eyeing me suspiciously. "Was that all you came for?"

I nodded sullenly. Tears brimmed her dark eyes, looking hurt and forlorn as she lifted a trembling arm and pointed back the way I'd come. "Then leave, Johnny. You are not wanted here."

With a tug on the reins, I jerked my horse around and walked through the crowd of cheering Indians, my back as stiff as a board.

I glanced over my shoulder in time to see Hannah stomp to a teepee on the edge of camp. I also saw Buffalo Horn, the old chief watching me. With a shrug, I indicated the confusion and disappointment I felt. He smiled encouragingly, as if attempting to communicate something.

But I spurred my horse and headed east, my longed for visit lasting less than ten minutes.

CHAPTER 37

Why could women be so bothersome? I only wished to spend time with Hannah, share my thoughts on my growing faith, and see how she fared. Of course, I planned on checking on Dark Cloud, but he seemed small in my concerns now. My heart hung heavy in my chest as I crossed the frozen plains and headed home.

The chilling wind pierced my coat and made me shiver as I lifted my trot to a gallop to warm both me and the gelding. Yet my lack of comfort dimmed as I continued to consider Hannah. Why did she have to marry another man? Why couldn't I talk with Buffalo Horn and explain my intentions toward his daughter? We'd known each other for years, and I knew I loved her. Then I recalled her grim look as she pointed my way from camp. The determination etched into her features surprised me, as if she were truly disappointed to see me. Perhaps I was a fool to think anything existed between us. Surely, I was a fool to pursue a woman claimed by another and definitely not interested in me.

As twilight descended over the prairie, I snuggled deeper into my coat, burrowing my chin behind my collar. My horse traveled swiftly without the cumbersome cattle to slow us down. Soon, I'd be home, sitting by a warm fire with a hot cup of coffee. Yet my thoughts drifted to the welcoming Indian village where bonfires warmed laughing people as they roasted meat and shared time. And my mind filled with images of Hannah.

Shaking my head, I cleared my muddled thoughts. *Focus. Take every thought captive.* I needed Texas faith to ponder our next move. James had suggested something big might be on the horizon. I marveled at his limitless faith as we searched for new ways to grow the ranch. To find a secure way to make an income from the ranch seemed to be his bent. I felt satisfied with the small drives of cattle to army outposts, but I sensed James had a much larger scheme in mind. Perhaps Jesus did too.

Bitter wind buffeted me as I rode, but I forced myself to ignore the cold and ponder a bigger picture than my immediate discomfort. What did God want from me? I trusted he had a plan for my life, but would that plan fit into my desires? Laughter bubbled from me at the absurdity of my thoughts. "Forgive me, Father. Your will, not mine. Ma says you have a plan, and I want to give you my willing heart. Do what you wish with me. May I bring you joy. Don't allow my stubborn or small ideas get in your way."

I paused when a picture of Hannah flashed into my mind, and I grinned, enjoying the image. "And Jesus, let me have Texas faith. Grow my faith so I can be used by you, for you, whatever that looks like. I love you."

With a warmth filling my chest, I rode on as the sun dipped behind me. Long shadows settled into the folds of the land, and the temperature dropped even more, but I'd be home soon.

Tomorrow, I would ride into town for supplies, and for the first time in years, Christmas gifts.

A lantern glowed in the window as I approached the house. None too soon, as my gelding struggled to maintain a quick pace. Chilled to the bone, we slowed to a walk, allowing a cool down as we neared the barn.

"Johnny," Ma called from the back door. "Didn't expect you home tonight. Coffee's on."

Despite my eagerness to get indoors, I brushed the weary gelding and tossed hay into the manger before heading to the house. Ma sat alone at the table, two mugs in front of her, steam rising invitingly.

Leaving my coat on, I tugged off my gloves and unbuckled the heavy gun belt around my waist. After laying my hat and the pistol on the counter, I dropped into a chair and tried to grin at Ma, my frozen cheeks protesting. We sat silent for a long moment and sipped our hot drinks.

"Hungry?"

I shook my head at her inquiry, but shifted uneasily, sensing she would ask about my hasty visit to the Comanche.

"Did you see Hannah?"

I frowned at her persistence, knowing she would wheedle the truth from me if I weren't careful. "Why are women so difficult?" I hoped my turnabout would throw her off my trail. But Ma was canny like a hound dog, sensing which way her prey moved.

"God made us that way to test a man's love and determination. Only a truly committed fellow would be patient to discover a woman's real feelings. A woman's heart can be a mystery to those who don't take the time to think."

I blinked, surprised at her wisdom. Was she telling me to be patient, or was she saying I don't think?

"I'm glad you're home safe." She rose and kissed the top of my head. "Goodnight." She made her way down the hall. For a moment, I considered calling after her and telling her about my trip to see Hannah, but I slumped in my chair and nursed my coffee instead. I needed to get over Hannah and follow God's path. I wanted to stay the course with my developing faith. God had a plan, and I wanted to be part of it. Paul, James, and Ma were all in step, and I didn't want to be left out because I couldn't get my affairs in order. Texas faith, I reminded myself. *Stay focused. Stay faithful. Think big.*

With a sigh, I trimmed the wick on the lantern and drank the last of my coffee by candlelight. After placing the mugs in the sink, I stoked the fire in the stove and shrugged out of my coat before walking to my room. Slowly, I undressed and prepared for bed.

Stretching under my blankets, I shivered, waiting, wondering at God's intentions. "Something big?" My whispers made little sound and I listened as wind moaned beneath the eaves. A board slapped the barn, and I reminded myself the loose wood needed a nail tomorrow.

Hannah's smiling face shimmered in the darkness, and I pursed my lips. Yes, Texas faith. I agreed with her. The Lord was trying to grow my faith. But what else?

Clearly, we could no longer drive cattle across Comanche land after winter. And the thought of pushing a small herd to a distant army post seemed more than dangerous now that real weather had set in. There must be something else.

My thoughts drifted back to Hannah, but I shook my head. *Stay on track.* We had plenty of cattle, but where to sell them? James knew many of the soldiers at the outposts. We could simply continue driving small herds to them come spring, but I sensed something bigger loomed, like the Lord wanted me to wait for Ma's adventure to unfold.

"All right, Jesus," I mumbled sleepily as my blankets warmed. "I'll wait on you, let you tell us what to do. I sure hate this not knowing, but you're God and I'm not. Let me trust in you."

I hesitated and then quickly added, "And give me Texas faith."

After breakfast the next morning, I saddled a different horse to give my gelding a rest. James came to the barn, a scowl creasing his whiskered face.

"I've gotten my Christmas shopping done, but I want to pay the taxes on the Henderson place before the county tax folks get itchy feet and try something underhanded. I'll ride to town with you and see those gents in the hotel while you're at Anderson's."

With a bright sun glittering on the scattered patches of thin snow, we rode for town. I enjoyed James's company and wanted to put his mind at ease about asking Ma to marry him. He seemed nervous.

"Bought the ring at Anderson's?"

He nodded at my question and shot me a sidelong glance, testing my interest. I grinned and he relaxed. "Bought it soon after I got the silver comb for Annie. Anderson made some smart remark and I told him to mind his own business."

Chuckling, I peered across the frozen plains, pleased we didn't have any cattle drives planned soon. A bitter wind whipped, and I hunched my shoulders inside my coat. But what were we going to do? My gaze drifted to the skittering clouds rushing across the sky, and I said a silent prayer, asking for guidance.

"Something big?" I mused, squinting against the sharp sunlight glinting from snow.

James pursed his lips and then nodded as he caught my train of thought. "I feel the Lord is prodding me to a bigger deal, but I can't guess what."

"You're not satisfied with how things are going? I mean, we have a handle on the ranch for the first time in years."

"Nope, I'm not. And neither should you," he replied quickly. "This journey we're on is not for the faint of heart. I think God wants to do a mighty work here. I feel it."

"But things have been so rough for so long," I grumbled, still trying to be faithful as I warned him from gambling beyond what we might recover from.

"It's no gamble when you trust in Jesus. When you and Annie struggled all those years, the Lord was shaping your faith, building your patience and trust."

"He almost failed," I snapped as anger surged. "We almost lost everything."

"You mean *you* almost lost everything," James corrected as town loomed into view. "Your faith about collapsed while the challenges drove Annie closer to the Lord. Jesus uses trials to build our character, not to crush our spirit."

"Bold words from a man who almost gave up on the Lord," I mumbled.

James laughed. "Yep, my faith took a beating. But in his wisdom, Jesus led me to your ranch." He sighed deeply. "The Lord loves me despite my stubborn heart."

I pondered his insights as we slowed our trot to a walk when we entered town. James pulled rein before the blacksmith's shop. "I need to ask when he'll be open again for me to bring a horse in for shoeing," he announced as he dismounted before the little shack. "Meet you at the hotel."

Smoke lifted in wisps from the smithy's fire, and I studied the blazing coals for a moment before I turned back to my own errand. "See you at the hotel." I waved and then made my way to Anderson's General Store.

I waved again when Mort Caffrey peered at me from the café window, but I didn't stop to chat. I needed to get my shopping done, and this was the first year in many I had cash money to do so.

I spent a few happy minutes buying things for the people that mattered most in my life. After about a half hour, I tugged my hat low and stepped from the mercantile back onto the boardwalk. Cold air blasted me as I walked to the hotel, my boots thudding on the wood.

When I stepped into the empty lobby, I tucked the package containing my newly purchased gifts tighter under my arm before strolling into the sitting room. Only a little bigger than an average parlor, the room boasted its own fireplace and several small tables and chairs, only two of which appeared occupied. I recognized Dalrymple and Richards, the tax board crooks, at one, but didn't know the man sitting with James at another table across the room.

James waved me over when he saw me enter, gesturing to a chair while motioning to a waitress at the same time.

The hotel did not have a proper dining room, only serving sandwiches and coffee in the spacious sitting room, but coffee sounded good to me. With a nod at the serving girl who poured the hot drink, I listened as James introduced me to the stranger. "Mr. Brisbane, this is my partner, John Garret."

"Vince's boy?" the rancher queried gruffly, eyeing me from beneath bushy eyebrows.

I nodded again and shook hands before lifting the steaming mug to my mouth.

"I knew your pa," Brisbane continued. "I heard he didn't make it back."

I pursed my lips. "A lot of good men didn't."

He nodded and James shifted, drawing my attention. "John, Mr. Brisbane has a ranch south of town, about fifteen hundred head of stock. He's here to pay his taxes—"

"Only I can't," the rancher broke in, indicating the tax men at the table across the room. "Those vultures will not give me an extension, and my wife is ill. She needs a high, dry climate. We're leaving for Arizona immediately if I can sell my ranch. I'm not paying the taxes."

I quirked an eyebrow at James, curious why we were here. This man's problems were certainly not uncommon, but how did they affect us?

James glanced at the ceiling, as if beseeching guidance from someone unseen, and then turned to Brisbane. "Well, sir, we might have a proposition for you. We sold some stock recently and have a little money."

I chuckled as I leaned back in my chair, taking another sip of coffee. James must be teasing. We surely didn't have anywhere near enough money to buy this man's ranch.

"Why's he laughing?" Brisbane pointed at me.

"I don't know what James is talking about." I waved a hand dismissively. "But we haven't any money to purchase your land. I'm sorry he got your hopes up."

James glowered at me and then nodded. "He's right, Mr. Brisbane. But it's hope I'm talking about."

"What do you mean? Spit it out," the rancher growled, suddenly suspicious.

"I mean John's right, we have no money right now, only a little. But perhaps we can make a deal."

"What kind of deal?" Brisbane narrowed his eyes while I frowned. We had barely enough money to see us through the winter. What was James thinking? But a gleam shone in his eyes as James leaned forward, as if about to share something significant.

"You need to leave for Arizona immediately to help your wife, right?"

"Yes, but we have no money. I'd hoped these carpetbaggers would give me an extension to pay my taxes until I could find a buyer for my ranch. They gave me the horse laugh and informed me my ranch would be confiscated and sold at public auction unless my taxes were paid today."

James rubbed his hands together. "All right. Just hear me out. What if we pay your taxes and give you a little cash to get you to Arizona? If you give me some time, say until end of summer, I can give you five thousand dollars for your ranch."

I stared, my eyes bulging as I considered James's words. Where did he intend to get that kind of money? And he suggested giving our little cash to this man and his taxes.

Brisbane looked clearly flustered. "My ranch is worth more than that."

James lifted a hand. "Maybe at one time. Surely not now. And you stand to get nothing if you don't listen to me. My proposition might be your only chance at getting anything."

The rancher leaned back in his chair, eyes fixed on James. "Go on. I'm listening."

"With the taxes paid, the tax board will get off your back. If I don't give you five thousand dollars by end of summer, you keep your ranch. Perhaps you can find a buyer next year. But my idea is to sell your cattle and pay you the money I owe."

It was Brisbane's turn to chuckle. "There's no market for cattle in Texas."

I leaned forward now, resting my elbows on the table. We'd already sold some cattle. Perhaps James *did* have an idea.

Think big. My eyebrows arched at the unexpected thought, and I remembered Hannah's words. Texas faith. Did James have a real plan?

"Sell me your ranch. I'll pay the taxes now and give you a little money to get you to Arizona. Two stage tickets should cover that. If I don't pay you five thousand dollars by end of summer, you keep your land. If I can sell your cattle, I keep your land."

Brisbane squinted, pondering James's deal. "Either way, I have something. If I don't trust you, I have nothing." He glanced at me. "Vince Garret was an honest man."

"So is his son," I said hurriedly, hoping James knew what he was doing.

Brisbane hesitated and then stood, sticking out a hand, first to James and then to me. We shook and he rubbed a hand across his face. "All right, boys. You've got a deal."

CHAPTER 38

"Are you sure about this?" We pointed our horses into the wind and made our way home. Steel gray clouds scuttled across the dull sky, and I could tell a storm brewed. Absently, I wondered if we'd have a white Christmas, as much of the snow had already vanished, leaving occasional drifts in sheltered places. I turned my gaze from the lowering canopy above to study James.

The former dispatch rider nodded as he pulled his hat low and leaned into the gust. "I've been praying, sensing the Lord wanted us to tackle something great. Kind of like a test. I didn't know what it could be until I overheard Brisbane and those land robbers at the hotel."

He grinned at me, and I scowled, not sure I agreed with his spiritual sensitivity.

"I'm sure this is what God wants. Don't you feel the Spirit moving?"

Well, I did in a way, I guessed. I'd been praying too, ever since my talk with Hannah. Yet how was I to know this was what the Lord intended for us? My scowl deepened, and I chewed my chapped lips.

"Sounds like a reckless experiment to me," I complained. "It would take dozens of small drives to army posts to gather the five thousand dollars you promised Mr. Brisbane." I felt like I'd tossed my growing faith aside as a new challenge came upon us. Scornfully, I pondered my lack of strength when trials loomed. Fear niggled in my mind—fear of failure, fear of disappointment, fear of hardship. Would my faith never grow into maturity?

James laughed and I started, surprised at his easy manner. "This venture is what we've prayed for. The Lord is doing something grand, and I want to be along for the ride."

I nodded, still not convinced as I gripped my reins tighter and rode the remaining distance home in silence.

"Paul," James called to our friend as we came into the yard. He'd come from the barn and set a pail down, watching us approach. "Gather the troops. We need to pray," James said with a lightheartedness that baffled me.

Paul nodded as he hefted the milk pail and hurried to the kitchen. Later, with a steaming mug before me on the table, I listened as James outlined the proposal he made with Mr. Brisbane. No one seemed upset with the idea of giving this rancher money we didn't have. I squinted when James asked us all to join him in prayer, asking God to guide this opportunity, although he didn't have any answers to my many questions.

I gritted my teeth and bowed my head as first Ma and then Lydia lifted their petitions aloud, seeking discernment and God's guidance. When Paul began, I closed my eyes tight, willing myself to pay attention as his supplication flowed, drawing me almost to heaven's gate with his fervor and intimacy. I longed to know Jesus that well, to know his heart and to connect with God in a deep fashion. I sensed Ma, Paul, and Hannah were closer to Jesus than I was. Lydia still seemed shy around us, although her faith reflected in prayer impressed me. Even James appeared to be progressing faster than me in his spiritual development. Was there something wrong with me?

Again, I resolved to throw myself into the adventure. I'd balked for so long, dragging my feet with negative comments that seemed to hold me back rather than admit God's provision. When I considered all the Lord did since word of Pa's death arrived, I knew I had to give God the glory. Despite my lack of trust, he was with us, supplying the ranch in the most unexpected ways.

James shifted when Paul finished and began to pray earnestly. When he asked for blessing in the project with Mr. Brisbane's ranch, I squirmed, battling my own doubts with a strength I'd never felt before. As if my willing heart to allow God to work had given me a newfound ability to lean into God, to trust him, and to permit him to do mighty things, ignoring my resilient temperament. Gratefully, I realized God didn't need my permission to work around me, but my desire to trust him let me see his hand.

James prayed humbly, but with an excitement my prayers lacked. The adventure seemed to be going on around me, and now I wanted to be a part. As James ended his requests, I shifted uneasily, wanting to please the Lord with my intentions and spirit.

Leaning my forehead on my folded arms, I hunched over the table and concentrated, wanting to connect with Christ. What if God didn't sanction this impossible sounding drive of cattle? The ramifications of God's refusal to bless us were crystal clear, and I shuddered to ponder what would become of us if this crazy gamble didn't pay off.

But this was not a gamble if the Lord guided our endeavor. With resolve, I chose to trust, to hope Christ maneuvered events to present this opportunity to us. Surely the finding of Red Bill and the reward money was not chance. Undoubtedly James's arrival to the ranch was no accident, or his timely presence at the hotel today.

Hannah's words drifted across my mind, and I smiled, feeling her support and encouragement as I started to pray.

"Lord, you know me. You know how I blocked every good deed you gave us, trying hard to find fault with everything you did. Forgive me and search my heart. See that I want to serve you with a faithful spirit. Let me be a part of this adventure, to see you do impossible things and praise your name. Whether you bless us or not, let me trust you in all things, searching for the purpose you have in every situation. I know you love me and want to grow my faith, so let me learn lessons that will shape me into the man of God you desire."

I paused and drew a deep breath. "Please guide us in this purchase. You know how little we have, but I want to trust you can multiply a little into much if we give you our trust and wait patiently on you."

I ended but didn't raise my head, cherishing the connection with the Savior. I loved being in his presence, my heart exposed to him as I worshipped and prayed. An overwhelming sense of peace and surrender filled me, and I knew the Lord heard our prayers. Although he didn't promise me success in our project, I promised him devotion and obedience. I knew I would accept whatever outcome we experienced, knowing the trials we might face would grow my faith and develop my character. Hope swelled, and an eagerness to begin made me look up into the smiling faces of my family and friends. Together, we committed ourselves to the undertaking, and I silently thanked Hannah for my newfound desire to trust God, albeit reluctant in inception. I thanked God his accomplishments were not dependent upon my willingness.

"We stand to lose everything." My warning to Ma on Christmas morning seemed to have no effect at all as she stirred potatoes and eggs in a skillet. She glanced at the steaming coffeepot and then shifted her gaze to me where I sat at the table, dawn's darkness only beginning to fade outside.

Doubts warred within me, despite my resolve to cling to the Lord. Would my weakness ruin everything? Although I wanted to see the Lord's hand in this situation, I worried we were making a big mistake. For the first time in years, we had a little cash money. Should we risk losing a good thing for a bigger, uncertain prize? Perhaps Mr. Brisbane's ranch was a smart purchase, but perhaps we were being foolish. I feared losing the small comfort I'd experienced at the couple cattle drives we'd completed.

"God is a big God," Ma said simply, smiling at me. "Don't forget the story of the foolish servant who took the master's talent and buried the coin. The Lord rebuked his lack of effort. Faith in God is reflected in our actions."

I bristled, feeling like she patronized my fledgling faith. I was a Christian like her, but I felt small, as if the Lord had not given me a great abundance of belief. Yesterday, hope surged within me, while today my inexperienced spiritual sensitivity seemed to wane.

"I know he's big," I snapped. "But what if we're biting off more than we can chew? Perhaps James thinks we can accomplish more than we should attempt. We've had some success with the small cattle drives. Let's stick with that for a while, build our surplus slowly, our reserves against coming troubles."

I paused as I bit the inside of my cheek. "You know we're going to have more taxes next year. Better get ready."

Ma chuckled and I tensed even more, knowing I was losing this battle. Ma had been the initiator of the adventure last spring, and it suddenly felt foolish to try and talk her out of anything where God was given an opportunity to show his might. And James had come up with this crazy Brisbane proposal, her eyes sparkling whenever she looked at him. With a huff, I knew I wasted my breath.

"God is with us, Johnny," she said softly as she filled two mugs with coffee. She returned the pot to the stove and sat across from me, her chair scraping in the early morning gloom.

A sigh escaped me, and I nodded, resigned to the tenuous situation. I felt like the people of Israel who saw the Lord work, praised him, and then turned away. Was my faith so fickle, so precarious? Desperately, I wished for a big faith, solid and strong.

"All right, Ma. Forgive me. I want to believe, honest I do," I mumbled as I gulped my hot drink.

"Taste and see the Lord is good," Ma quoted, and I nodded again, remembering James intended to propose today. I smiled, pushing my misgivings aside and silently wishing Ma well. She sure deserved something good.

After breakfast, I joined James in the barn. He seemed nervous, his gaze darting restlessly as I helped him with the stock. I tried to ignore his agitation, but Paul huffed at the veteran's ill behavior.

"It's Christmas Day, James. A day to celebrate Jesus. Settle down. You're as jumpy as a newborn calf."

I slapped James on the shoulder as I passed him, loaded down with the fresh milk for the kitchen. "Don't hold his jittery mood against him. He has big plans for today."

"Plans?" Paul's eyebrows arched. "What kind of plans?"

I looked expectantly at James, and he sighed as he pulled the ring from his pocket, a crimson wave creeping over his whiskered cheeks.

Paul chuckled, nodding as his eyes glowed. "Good luck, James. Marriage has been the best thing for me. I love Lydia."

As I reached the big doors of the barn, I glanced over my shoulder, sensing their eyes on me. Both men were watching me. I hesitated, letting the pail down as I blinked. "What?"

They grinned and James nudged Paul. "Well, John, we have special ladies that make life interesting and full. We wonder about you, not that we doubt you have a special lady."

I blinked again. "Special lady?"

"Sure," Paul added with a twinkle in his eye. "Miss Annie says Hannah Tall Basket is sweet on you. James tells me you drove cattle to her people. Surely there's more going on there than you let on."

I frowned and hefted the heavy pail once more. "You don't know what you're talking about," I muttered as I stepped from the barn into the dull gray day. "Hannah is—"

"Hannah is what?"

I whirled, searching for the familiar voice that spoke from near the front porch. Mounted on ragged ponies sat Hannah and Buffalo Horn, flanked by half a dozen Comanche braves.

CHAPTER 39

I stared, my gaze locked on Hannah. Her cheeks glowed in the morning light, and her smile flashed before she looked away, a long strand of dark hair waving across her face. She dropped her eyes to the frozen ground and hastily tucked the rebellious locks into place. Buffalo Horn grunted and slipped from his horse as the other warriors dismounted. Only Dark Cloud needed assistance from the saddle.

Ma hailed the visitors from the porch, calling excitedly to Hannah, wishing her a Merry Christmas Day. Buffalo Horn strode stately up the steps and into the sitting room where Dark Cloud had limped and now stretched on a pallet in a corner. The five remaining braves retreated to the barn as Buffalo Horn spoke, gesturing wide as he offered a blessing over our home.

"Father is grateful to share the Savior's birthday with the Garret family," Hannah announced, her eyes darting around the room, wringing her hands. She frowned and glanced from the old chief to Ma. "I told them all about Jesus, his birth and his death on the cross. When Father learned Christmas is Jesus's birthday, he insisted on celebrating with you." With a sweep of her buffalo robe, she tossed the covering aside and straightened her dress.

I felt my eyes widen as I took in her white gown, her slim form outlined perfectly in the soft material.

"Of course, you are welcome, Hannah. Merry Christmas," Ma repeated cheerily. But my attention remained riveted on the slender girl.

"Do you like my dress, Johnny?" Her shy inquiry made me want to laugh. How could a beautiful girl ask such a silly question? "I made it when I was at the mission school," she explained as Ma made much of the fine stitching and simple style.

Buffalo Horn smiled proudly when he caught me studying Hannah's lithe form. I felt my neck heat and turned away to hurry the milk pail to the kitchen.

Although the day's feast tasted delicious—thanks to the addition of the venison haunch the Comanche brought along—the after-supper conversation proved the more interesting as the men discussed cattle drives to distant markets. Ma and Lydia inspected their red woolen scarves I gave them while Paul and James tossed my gift of new gloves aside as the conversation heated.

"But where will you drive so many cows?" I demanded hotly, wanting to know particulars about James's plan. Mr. Brisbane's ranch would give us an additional fifteen hundred head of stock we didn't need if we intended on making several smaller drives to distant military posts or Indian reservations. "With that much stock, we'll be busy driving cattle all the time to various posts. And we need more riders to manage the ranches if we are to keep what stock we own."

My sour outlook on the purchase of the new ranch had kept me up at night as I considered all options. Like a ship tossed on the waves, I wrestled a firm conviction we were doing the right thing against a flailing belief we were gambling unnecessarily. Any way you sliced it up, this pie made little sense in light of the successful deliveries we've had so far. Still I attempted to take captive every thought, and make my mind focus in the direction I demanded. I wanted a strong faith, really I did. Yet something warred in my spirit, making me cantankerous and taciturn.

James nodded. "I agree this makes little sense if we continue to do things the way we've done them. But I believe the Lord has something different in mind. Not just more little herds to army posts. I think we should figure on bigger drives."

"Bigger drives?" Paul frowned as he glanced at me. Finally, I felt I had a comrade in doubt. Perhaps someone else worried about God's intentions as much as I did.

"We would need more riders, like John said," Paul added, and my spirits bolstered. Had we tried too much too quickly? Perhaps slow and steady should be the recipe of the Garret ranch.

I opened my mouth to voice my opposition for the tenth time when Hannah spoke.

"Maybe James is right."

My lips snapped shut into a thin line. Leaning back in my chair, I eyed her. "Why do you say that?"

Hannah didn't seem uneasy with everyone staring at her, and I suspected her role as tribal princess might account. Surely, she was used to lots of attention.

"I mean, maybe the Lord is trying to show you something new, something different, something beyond what you can understand."

I scowled at her assessment of me, as if my concerns were limiting and shortsighted. Then my scowl deepened as I realized she'd pegged me correctly. The Lord was moving in ways I struggled to comprehend. Was my lack of faith getting in the way again?

I shifted uneasily, and yet something urged me on, unwilling to completely release my stubborn thoughts. "We've already found a way that works," I protested, trying to explain why we didn't require another way.

She glowered at me. "Perhaps this new way is better," she replied with narrowed eyes, and I sensed her disappointment at my obstinacy.

I glanced at James. "Do you have new ideas to offer?"

A sense of smug satisfaction filled me at his silence. But when he grunted and straightened in his seat, my eyebrow arched.

"A different idea?" she asked James while shooting me with a challenging look.

"Well," he began hesitantly. "When I rode in the war, our cavalry unit passed through Sedalia, Missouri. Lots of stock pens, right on a railroad spur. I'll bet they could ship cattle from there."

I frowned while Hannah crossed her arms over her chest, my smug expression fleeing from me to her. Buffalo Horn chuckled, his dark eyes twinkling as he lifted his chin and looked lovingly at his daughter, sensing her victory.

"Railroads would carry cattle like they carry cotton or rice," Paul agreed, glancing at James. "But how do we get them there?"

The smug look returned to me, although I felt a little like a traitor as my doubts resurfaced, knocking my flip-flopping faith sideways.

As if Hannah could read my conflicting thoughts, she leaned her elbows on the table and studied me. "Johnny, whatever happened to Texas faith?"

"What's that?" Ma asked quickly, her ears pricking to anything about trust.

I shook my head. "Nothing, Ma," I answered swiftly before Hannah could explain. "Just a plan on how to build faith. Not sure it works."

My heart squeezed at sight of the hurt that flashed across Hannah's features. I didn't want to argue, but she seemed so confident where my confidence had completely slipped, leaving me unsure.

"Well, Scripture says not to doubt, or you will be tossed like a wave on the sea, blown by the wind," Ma said.

"Only with a strong faith did I believe God would lead me to a wonderful place like this," Paul admitted honestly. Lydia reached across the table and clasped her husband's hand, her eyes glistening.

"Only through faith can we mature as believers." Hannah's eyes bored a hole in me. Abruptly, I felt miserable, as if I'd let her down. Again.

Lydia stood shakily and cleared her throat. "You know I don't like to speak before crowds, but I have a Christmas gift for Paul I want to share with you all." She smiled at her husband, her lips trembling. "We're going to have a baby."

With a whoop, Paul leaped to his feet and embraced Lydia, swinging her around as he continued to howl merrily.

"Well, I have a gift for Annie," James announced, not to be outdone. We watched as he dropped to one knee and looked at Ma.

I felt grateful the attention had been drawn away from me and stole a glance at Hannah, startled to find her staring at me with a pained look in her eyes.

As my gaze shifted to Ma, my heart lifted at the look of surprise and pleasure in her eyes, warming me and shaking me from my self-absorption. James made a show of pulling the ring from his pocket.

"I love you, Annie. I feel the Lord brought us together. Will you marry me?"

At Ma's quick assent, tears sprang to her eyes, and James embraced her. I wanted to be happy for James and Ma and for Paul and Lydia, although my heart felt suddenly heavy as I looked at Hannah again. She watched me through narrowed eyes, a look of wonder and sorrow penetrating me to my soul. She could read through me and guess my struggles as I wrestled with God. Would my faith never grow?

After supper, Paul read the Christmas story aloud, closing the Bible on his lap when he finished. Lydia stood beside him, a hand on his shoulder, proud at her literate husband.

Hannah excused herself quietly to deliver plates of food to the braves in the barn. Jumping to my feet, I hurried to help. She ignored me as I accompanied her outside, my arms loaded with platters.

Gray clouds hung ominously low as I followed her across the yard, her slender form concealed beneath her warm buffalo robe. Sunset hovered, as if reluctant to go down on this significant day, and I vowed not to allow the day to pass without redeeming myself in Hannah's eyes.

The Comanche men grunted with approval at our delivery, and Hannah spoke quietly with them, continuing to ignore my presence. As we walked back to the house, a single snowflake drifted from the murky sky and landed on her dark hair. I reached for her elbow, pulling her into the deeper shadows beside the house as the last of the dull sun dropped behind the western hills. Deep twilight settled over the land as I stared into Hannah's questioning eyes, and my heart lifted to my throat.

For a long moment, I couldn't speak. More snowflakes swirled and I remembered my question at a white Christmas.

"I have a lot to learn," I began, wanting to unburden myself, to apologize for disappointing her. Her oval face peered up at me, and I stared at her beauty, the tiny white flakes catching in her hair and melting on her cheeks.

She smiled up at me. "You *are* learning, but you fight the Holy Spirit. Lean into the Lord, Johnny. Trust him. He will not let you down."

I nodded, knowing she was right. Why did I have to struggle so much? Why couldn't I have a strong faith like the others?

"Texas faith," I said at last, and she nodded, her gaze shifting to the falling snow.

"I am happy for your mother," she went on softly. "James is a strong man. And I am happy for Lydia. Children are a blessing."

I felt pleased to move the conversation away from my glaring shortcomings. "I know he loves her. I believe they'll be happy," I agreed.

She shifted beside me. "You know, some men have asked me to marry."

I froze, suddenly terrified. "But I thought you couldn't marry."

She chuckled dryly, a bitter note in her voice. "Yes. Only my father knows who I am to marry."

"Then ... then you told them no?"

She smiled up at me over her shoulder, nodding. "Only Buffalo Horn knows when I am to marry."

"You could always choose your own mate," I suggested, holding my breath.

Hannah shook her head, her raven black hair shimmering in the dim dusk. "I would never go against my father."

We stood in the silence as the snow carpeted the ground, covering the land in a white blanket. "You know, I didn't come to your camp to ask Buffalo Horn for an extension to cross Comanche land."

"No? Why did you come?" Her inquiry held a note of wistfulness, as if she wanted to hear something special.

"I wanted to see you," I confessed in a whisper. Her eyes rounded as I tugged on her elbow, pulling her against me, and then they fluttered closed as I kissed her. My lips gently pressed against her own, and I felt her melt into my embrace as heat coursed through me.

A loud grunt pulled me from my whirling thoughts, and I stepped back, startled to not be alone.

Five Comanche warriors stood in a half circle around us. I read the disapproval in their stoic features and released Hannah, taking another step back. With downcast eyes, Hannah hurried from me and rushed into the kitchen while I faced the silent onlookers.

CHAPTER 40

Only a few tense moments passed as the Comanche braves watched me. Then I walked to the house, waiting to see if they attempted to stop my escape. Nothing happened, and I breathed easier when I stepped inside the warm house.

For the remainder of the evening, Hannah kept her distance from me, never meeting my searching gaze as I followed her everywhere with my eyes. Ma smiled at me once when she placed a hand on my shoulder, as if telling me she understood my dilemma.

The Comanche slept in the barn, despite Ma's protests there was plenty of room in the house. Lydia's eyes widened when she realized the Indians would sleep at the ranch this night, and she hurried Paul to their cabin.

James said a whispered goodnight to Ma as he left to help settle the Indians. I shook his hand and nodded as he smiled at me, a pleased look on his face. I remembered the nervous morning he'd spent in the barn, and I nodded again, happy for him and Ma.

"You're all right?" I asked my mother after everyone had left the house.

Ma sighed, her eyes shining. "So happy. Thank you, Johnny. James told me he asked you first."

"He loves you, Ma," I answered simply. My chest tightened when her eyes narrowed as she studied me.

"I saw you go to the barn with Hannah. You were gone a long time."

I remembered the kiss and it was my turn to sigh. "I wanted to talk with her," I admitted.

"Talk?" Her eyebrow quirked. "What about?"

I felt the heat rise along my neck and glanced away. "Oh, you know. About faith and Jesus and her father."

"Her father?" Her eyebrows bunched and I shifted my boots. "Why would you talk about her father?"

I waved a dismissive hand as I led the way into the kitchen. "Want more coffee?" Without waiting for a reply, I lifted two mugs from the cupboard.

"Johnny, what about Buffalo Horn?" She persisted as we sat at the table, blowing on our hot drinks.

Ignoring her question again, I rose to stoke the stove fire, but her glowering look made me tense anew as I returned to my seat. "Her pa says who she can marry. Even Hannah doesn't know who the chief has for her."

Ma nodded sagely, eyeing me over the rim of her cup. "The Comanche have specific ways of doing things. You would be wise to accept their practices."

"What does that mean?" I fumed, not wanting to accept their methods. I loved Hannah and suspected she loved me.

"God has a plan," Ma went on. "Accept and do not kick against the traces. A stubborn heart will not go well with God's plans."

As if Hannah whispered in my ear, I knew Ma was right. When would I grow up and lean into the Lord? My pigheaded ways had gotten me nowhere. I felt as if I were being tested, and I straightened my shoulders, firmly fixing my eyes on Jesus.

"I know." I sighed again. "And I want to do things the right way. I'll pray and trust the Lord. Only he can move the old chief's heart."

"Or not," Ma countered swiftly. "Whether God answers your prayer the way you want or not, you must surrender your will. Trust God has good things for you, even if they don't include Hannah."

Three days later, James and my mother were married in a simple ceremony in our sitting room. The silver comb sparkled in Ma's hair, and her cheeks glowed radiantly. She couldn't keep her eyes off James, and I grinned all day, pleased for the both of them.

The preacher rode out from town for the event. James moved into the house and the bunkhouse he'd briefly occupied was empty once more.

As 1866 dawned, a pair of cowboys rode into our yard, looking for work. Carl and Ronnie Krefeld needed to earn money to feed their ma and sisters. Rumors had spread throughout the countryside that the Garret ranch needed more riders. Soon after this, Steeple Mason joined the outfit, and moved into the bunkhouse with the brothers. He must've stood over six-and-a-half feet tall. Antonio Morales joined next. One of his uncles had died at the Alamo, thirty years before.

Like the Lord bringing animals for Noah's ark, young men arrived at the ranch, hunting jobs, as we began to build a great herd.

Although a Texas winter is no time to gather cattle or brand mavericks, we didn't have a choice. Work progressed as we built our herd, branding all the animals we could find—including the young ones that we wouldn't sell but would increase our numbers for next year.

Once again, Mr. Anderson gave us credit at the general store. We'd proven our reliability to him, and he agreed to supply us with the promise we would pay him after the drive to Missouri was completed.

All this time, I worked like a dog, driving cattle from the draws and creek bottoms and helping brand the mavericks. Slowly, the herd grew, all the boys doing the work of two men.

Paul agreed to drive the wagon and act as cook for the outfit on the trail. With the war over, everyone seemed eager to get back to some level of normalcy. Everyone in the outfit worked hard to achieve our goal, to build a herd ready to push to Missouri once winter released its icy grip on the plains.

After a month of hard riding, we'd gathered some twelve-hundred head of stock, letting them drift over the prairie while keeping an eye on them and not allowing them to stray too far. James rode his horse toward me where I'd helped brand the Bar G on a heifer's flank. Bawling, the young cow ran off a dozen yards before turning to stare round-eyed at us as I coiled my rope.

James reined in near our fire as Carl and Ronnie rode off to fetch another animal. I nodded at him and pointed to the battered coffeepot shoved amid the glowing coals.

"Thanks," he said as he tugged off his gloves. He pushed his hat back and wiped at his brow with his sleeve, watching me.

"John, I think we've gathered all I want from your home range. We even brought some of Henderson's stock." He paused to take a sip of the mug I handed him. "I think we should go to Brisbane's ranch and take the rest of our herd from there."

I nodded, knowing he was right. We didn't want to deplete our breeding stock too much. We still had to think of the future.

Thinking of the future always made me sour. I loved Hannah, but she wasn't for me, and I felt my future lacked any real joy. Why would God build my faith without the one who'd taught me so much about my spiritual journey?

I shook my head, resolved to not question the Lord. I wanted to obey God and serve him faithfully, though I disagreed with his methods. I knew he loved me and wanted good things for me, although I couldn't comprehend his ways.

Working in a saddle all day allowed me to think and pray. I'd already agreed to work with Christ rather than against him, reminding myself constantly that he knew the big picture of every event while I saw only a sliver of the situation. Yet, disappointment dogged at my heels, reminding me incessantly that I would never marry Hannah.

"You seem lost, like your thoughts are a hundred miles away."

James's sharp observation made me straighten my shoulders and lift my chin. I would not be the weak link on this adventure. I felt God growing me as I studied my Bible nightly. Praying unceasingly had drawn me to the Lord, and I vowed to allow God to work in my life, whether I liked the outcome or not. I hoped his refining fire would produce the results he wanted for me. God is the potter, I'm the clay, I reminded myself often.

"Nothing to worry you." I shrugged. "Jesus is with us, right? Keep our eye on the prize." I grinned, feigning a casualness I didn't feel.

Leaving the Krefeld brothers behind to manage the herd, the rest of the outfit rode for Brisbane's ranch the next morning. His land lay a long day's ride to the south, but we arrived at dusk as a storm broke, forcing us to stay indoors for two days.

When we arrived, we found only one man still at the ranch. Clyde Meyers looked more like a farmer than a cowboy.

"I'm from Ohio," Meyers reported. "The other hands all quit when Brisbane sold to you."

"Well, I'll be quitting too, boss," Steeple Mason announced, shooting Meyers a sharp glance. "I'll not ride with a Yankee."

James shook his head. "No one's quitting. We need every man to pull this off." Mason grumbled but stayed on, his need of a job outweighing his prejudice.

An argument developed over which brand to slap on the Brisbane cattle. Technically, they belonged to our ranch, but if we couldn't deliver the five thousand dollars we owed Mr. Brisbane, he would still own his land. In the end, we decided to use his brand. We burned the Double Triangles on over six hundred head of stock, leaving a fair number of young cows and a few strong bulls behind to build the depleted herd. Three weeks later, the outfit pushed our mob back to the Garret ranch.

By mid-March, we'd gathered our herd of about seventeen hundred head of stock and were ready to begin the trek to Missouri. Sedalia lay almost due east of the Texas panhandle, and despite the cold weather, we all felt impatient to begin.

One more rider joined us that last week as we made final preparations for the drive.

"What's your name?" James eyed the wiry cowboy suspiciously, the young man refusing to meet our curious gaze.

"Call me Lee," he replied evasively. "That'll work as good as any."

"Are you wanted by the law?" I shot a sideways glance at James as the newcomer shifted from boot to boot.

"Yes," Lee answered honestly. "But not around here."

"We're heading for Missouri," James added, quirking an eyebrow.

Lee nodded and drew a deep breath. "Missouri, huh? I guess that'll do."

As Ma and Lydia worked feverishly to prepare every meal for the outfit, the rest of the men worked tirelessly. Paul helped the women, learning better techniques that would aid on our trip. From before sunup to after sundown, we worked.

For me, I prayed all the time, stealing precious opportunities to study Scripture. With mounting fervor, I believed God had initiated this adventure and excitement simmered within me. Ma's teaching and Hannah's encouragement bolstered my faith as I leaned into the Lord, learning to trust he guided us and this expedition. Like a young boy who follows a treasure map to incredible wealth, I threw myself into each detail of the trip, making sure I understood each aspect of the journey.

The bitterly cold weather, the rowdy herd of wild cattle, or the endless list of preparations could not daunt my courage or anticipation. With determination, I resolved to trust the Lord and see what God could do when I gave him a willing, faithful heart.

CHAPTER 41

Before mid-March arrived, all of us were getting antsy, anxious to start. Paul outfitted the wagon so he could cook from the tailgate and carry all the bedding and necessary supplies. Also, he would carry my rifle, practice with the long gun making him a passable shot.

Not knowing what to expect, we prepared for anything. Paul carried food for nine men and medical supplies in case of injury along with tobacco for trade with the Indians. We hoped the trip would only take two months one way. Ten to fifteen miles a day would be average, notwithstanding storms or difficulties, which would put us in Sedalia by early May.

We discussed waiting until April, but a mild day with gentle breeze convinced us not to delay. We agreed to risk the early spring start. Paul encouraged us to begin immediately, wishing to be home when Lydia gave birth. Besides, every day we lingered, the herd had more opportunity to stray.

I hadn't seen Hannah since Christmas. I told myself this was probably for the best, but I couldn't keep her off my mind. When James announced we would leave in two days, a feeling of relief and resignation filled me. This trek had become a sort of test for my faith, and I embraced the challenge, pleased with how well I'd accepted the impending journey and the expedition's many struggles.

Come what may, I sensed I'd turned a corner on my flailing trust of the Almighty, and now felt more mature about my relationship with Jesus. Slowly, my connection with the Savior had deepened.

Scanning the horses in the corral, I surveyed the cluster for fitness and vigor, making sure we had healthy horses for the drive. But my thoughts continued to drift to Hannah. What was the beautiful princess doing right now? Did she think of me as often as I thought of her?

When clattering hooves drew my attention, I straightened from the buckskin gelding I inspected to watch a rider approach, an Indian I suspected, judging by the long black hair streaming in the wind.

When I recognized a woman's long buckskin gown, I tensed, fearing Hannah came with bad news. With a grip of the top rail and a leg over, I vaulted the corral bars and stood, waiting as her horse skittered to a halt. Gravel scattered as she brought her mount to a halt beside me. I laid a hand on the heaving animal's neck and peered up at her.

Hannah panted and her dark eyes flashed. "Oh, Johnny, I'm so glad I caught you before you took off. One of the men spoke with James and he told him your cattle drive begins tomorrow."

I nodded, my chest tightening, as I realized for the hundredth time I wouldn't see her again for months. We'd always been friends, but our relationship had developed unexpectedly into something more, something I felt sure we shared. I loved Hannah, and yet the Lord kept her from me, holding me back as my faith grew and matured. With an ache in my heart I dreaded, I leaned into the comforter, my Savior, and hoped my obedience pleased him.

"We leave tomorrow," I agreed, unable to take my gaze from her. I drank her in, etching her image in my mind forever. Perhaps she'd be married when I returned.

She glanced hurriedly over her shoulder and then licked her lips. "Run away with me."

I blinked. "What? What are you saying?"

A shadow flitted across her taut features. She leaned to take my hand, squeezing tightly. "Buffalo Horn has told me to prepare for my marriage. I am to be married this summer," she whispered.

Icy fingers clutched at my throat, closing my windpipe, and I struggled to breathe. "Marriage?" My croaking query made me shift, filling me with an uneasiness I'd expected for weeks. Here it was, the horrible thing I'd feared. Hannah was to marry another man.

"Come away with me," she repeated, pleading. "We can go west and leave everything behind. You can get a job anywhere, maybe a cowboy for another ranch. I will work for you, love you, and we will make a new life for ourselves far away."

"What of your people?" I stammered, wanting to leap at this chance to pursue my own wants. Was God giving me the desires of my heart?

"At Christmas, you suggested I disobey Buffalo Horn and not marry the man he chose for me. I have wrestled with that idea for weeks, and now I am certain. Let's ride away together. I love you and I want to marry you."

As if a tidal wave of emotion swept over me, tumbling my thoughts and longings, I felt overwhelmed with choices. Should I agree to flee with her? Life would be so much simpler with Hannah by my side. The two of us together forever—the girl I loved, the girl I wanted to build a family with, the girl I wanted to grow old with. I clenched my hands into fists, allowing my yearnings to course eagerly through my veins. I could be so happy with Hannah.

Then I remembered our families, the Comanche people and Buffalo Horn and their expectation of a tribal princess. Could I be the cause of such destruction and disappointment? Our selfish flight would destroy the ties with her loved ones. And my family, James and Ma, Paul and Lydia. We're supposed to do the right thing. To love God above ourselves and not pursue self-centered ideas. With a groan, I stepped back from her lathered pony and shook my head.

"No," I said softly. "We can't."

She narrowed her eyes. "Why not? This is what we want."

"That's just it. This is bigger than the two of us, Hannah," I reasoned. "We walk with the Lord. He's given us the faith, the strength to do the right thing. I will not disgrace you because I want you as my wife."

She glared down at me as she lifted her chin. "I thought you loved me. I thought you wanted to run away with me."

"I do. But I will not dishonor your family, and I will not dishonor God. My faith has grown, and I want to serve Christ more than anything else. I love you, but I choose to follow Jesus." I paused, feeling miserable as I clung to the Lord, giving him my heart, soul, and mind once more. "I want to do the right thing."

She scowled and tugged at her reins, preparing to ride away. "Then this is goodbye, Johnny Garret. You will keep your faith, and I will marry another man."

With a shout, she kicked her pony into flight, dirt flying as her horse galloped from the yard. I watched her go and knew I'd been tested. Did I do the right thing? I loved God, but perhaps this had been my chance to be with Hannah. Or was my faith tested to see if I would choose God over my heart?

Regardless, Hannah was gone, possibly forever, and I'd never felt so lonely in all my life.

The cattle had been held for weeks and were ready to move. Despite the cold, the herd seemed eager for the drive to begin, as eager as all of the outfit. Except me.

As if walking in a daze, I went through the motions of preparing for departure in the morning. I couldn't even remember my final words to Ma. She seemed happy, though, as she stood on the back stoop and waved to us as we rode away in dawn's gloom. I'd seen James kiss her and squeeze her tight, her early morning hair tousled, and a wide grin plastered on her pale face. Paul patted Lydia's swelling belly and laughed, promising to be home soon.

I watched all this activity with a heavy heart. Would I ever be happy again? Yet I clung to truth, knowing I'd struggled with a challenge and passed. Like Jacob wrestling the Lord, I felt I'd been beaten hollow, tied in knots, and come out the other side as a better man. My beliefs had been cooked in the fires of trial and found strong, durable, solid. Although I suffered from losing Hannah, I felt stronger somehow, more resilient. I'd developed, and I knew I'd pleased the Lord. Come what may, I'd chosen God over myself.

With an effort, I faced the eastern sky where a gray light hovered on the horizon. Snuggling deeper into my coat, I drew a deep breath. "You're with me, aren't you, Lord? Thanks for helping me. Give me strength as we begin this crazy drive to Missouri. May I walk with you and may others see Christ through me, through my actions, and through my faith. I love you, Jesus, and want to serve you with my life."

The cattle bawled as they struggled to their feet and started walking into the rosy sunrise. Shouting and galloping back and forth, the cowboys forced the herd on, the vast Texas prairie stretching before us. With God's help, we hoped to sell this mob and build our ranch. With Henderson's place north of us and Brisbane's range far to the south, we intended to go into ranching on a grand scale. But first we needed money and to sell cattle in a large number. We needed to arrive safely at a market where we could attain the type of funds to pay our debts and build our holdings.

I clenched my teeth and nodded, convinced all things were possible with Christ. "All right, Father, I'm yours," I said aloud to the morning light. "I've thrown into this adventure, and I trust you have a plan. I follow you," I whispered. "Take me where you want, do with me as you will. Your will, not mine."

I gripped my reins and spurred after another cow attempting to turn back. There was no turning back for any of us now, and I guided the stray back into the herd and faced east once more.

CHAPTER 42

James rode everywhere all day, checking with each cowboy, offering suggestions how to push the herd without rushing them unnecessarily. Although March loomed cold and endless before us, I knew every rider felt the excitement I sensed. The incredible drive had begun, and we were as thrilled as James to be a part of the amazing journey.

A bitter wind gusted all day, shoving at us from the north. But we pointed the mob eastward and trailed, allowing the cattle to amble leisurely. Grazing occasionally at the brown grass that crusted the frozen ground, the herd moved slowly.

At one side of the vast herd, Paul's wagon lumbered noisily, hanging pots clanging as the wagon lurched over ravines.

Late afternoon found us on a narrow creek. The cattle lined along the watercourse as the dull sun leaned far to the west. Paul had parked beneath the bare branches of a huge cottonwood where a cheerful fire glowed brightly in the gathering gloom.

"Good thing the water's not frozen," James called as he rode by, intent on reaching the inviting blaze. I knew Paul would have coffee going, but my responsibilities remained, and I circled the cattle where they bunched into a mass on an open plain beyond the creek.

The cowboys greeted me as I passed them and promised they'd be relieved soon to go to supper. Darkness descended and a peacefulness settled within me as I realized the die was cast. I'd given up on Hannah and the great trek to Missouri had begun. We'd only traveled about a dozen miles this first day, but I felt grateful we were on our way.

In groups of three, we took turns guarding the herd at night. Paul took charge of all camp duties, from fetching water to splitting firewood. He cleaned all the dirty dishes and made sure hot coffee was available all night for the guards.

Before sunrise, we rolled our bedrolls and stowed our gear in Paul's wagon, a new day dawning. A cycle of long days ensued where the cold weather couldn't hamper our progress or the knowledge we were doing something great. If Texas cattle could be driven overland to distant markets, the flagging economy could be bolstered. Every man needed work to provide for their families, and perhaps cattle drives would give them hope and allow them to recover after the war. Perhaps even the future of Texas depended on this unbelievable event.

Again, I believed my actions carried weight beyond myself. God saw the big picture while I could only see a sliver of a situation. I sensed things bigger than my own wishes and wanted to be a part.

Like all the cowboys, James and I took turns on guard duty. Day after day, we rode tirelessly to prod the herd on, leaving Texas to enter the Indian Nation, east of the panhandle. As the days passed, the weather warmed, melting snow and swelling creeks and rivers. We made dangerous water crossings where cattle floundered in rushing currents, and riders risked to push the herd across.

A snowstorm in late March didn't stick to the ground, white patches vanishing as a chilled sun rose over the endless plains. But the cold followed us relentlessly, like hounds nipping at our heels, ruthless in pursuit.

Steeple Mason proved cantankerous and rude, and not to Clyde Meyers only. The tall cowboy complained ceaselessly, a constant drag on any campfire conversation.

"My pa told me he killed more Yankees than anyone else in his regiment. He said Yankees were cowards," he announced one evening at supper, his gaze fixed on the hapless Clyde. We ignored Mason, although I could tell Meyers hated the jibing.

Spring rains drenched the prairie, making the plains a muddy mire that bogged the cattle. We pushed on, never letting any obstacle impede our headway.

Paul's cooking garnered loud acclaims. Ma and Lydia had trained him well—his food tasted good, his coffee always hot. We let the cattle drift throughout the day, only stopping for supper each night and breakfast the next morning.

Miserable weather and exhausting days made me want to complain, but something wonderful had happened after my talks with Hannah. Although I still thought of complaining about every difficulty, I turned the idea into prayer and praise. With a grateful heart, I counted each of my many blessings. It didn't take long to recall the many men and families who suffered more than we did. The war had taken a toll on everyone, but God had been faithful.

"Lord, I see how Red Bill helped pay the taxes, how James's arrival gave us the idea of selling beef to the outposts, and how the Comanche permission to cross their lands allowed us the money we made," I whispered to the scuttling clouds as I sat my horse, watching the herd slowly pass. "You've been with us throughout, guiding us with heartache and suffering to build our faith and to grow us, molding our character. May I become the man of God you see in me."

An image of Hannah flashed in my mind, her long hair waving in the wind, and I tensed. She was not for me. When given the opportunity to flee with her, I'd chosen to wait on the Lord. Was I a fool when the girl I loved offered to run away with me? We could be married now, and I would have what I wanted.

Yet relations with the Comanche would be strained, and I would've dishonored her father if I'd done as she asked. I sensed the Lord wanted me to do things the right way, regardless of my personal feelings.

Sighing, I nudged my horse forward and walked beside the moving herd. We had a job to complete, I reminded myself doggedly. I needed to focus, to stay the course and cling to my beliefs. A smile tugged at my lips when I thought of Texas faith, and I shook my head as the image of Hannah haunted me again.

At the Arkansas River, we made camp on the banks of the great waterway. Spring floods had not swollen the current yet, and with luck, we'd cross the herd in the morning. Thunder rumbled in the distance, but I didn't think the storm would come near us. Nonetheless, the herd milled restlessly and all the cowboys rode night guard.

With a dull gray in the east, we pushed the cattle across the frigid river. Paul waited while the herd wore down the steep banks, making a passable road for his wagon to ford. As the last of the cattle swam the muddy water, I stopped beside his wagon. Worry filled his eyes as he gripped the long leather reins, and I realized this was his first river crossing.

"Afraid?" My question seemed to startle him from his own thoughts, and he nodded.

"Yes, I'm afraid. But when my fears surround me, I know Jesus surrounds me more." He gave me a weak smile and lifted the reins. "We're not alone on this drive to Missouri, are we, John?"

I stared as he slapped the long reins and his wagon lurched, the horses plunging down the plowed bank to splash into the river. He crossed without incident, and I knew Paul was right. We were not alone.

I thought about this all day as we pushed the herd deeper into Indian Territory. That night I approached Paul where he worked beside the bright campfire. Light danced across his weary features, but he sang hymns as he filled platters of beef and beans for the cowboys. The men stood as they ate or squatted on their haunches, silent while they consumed supper. But Paul's words had wormed in my mind, and I wanted to know more.

He stopped singing long enough to grin at me as he poured coffee into my tin cup. "Paul," I began, glancing over my shoulder to the others before going on. "What did you mean about your fears surrounding you?"

His grin broadened as he handed me another biscuit. "I get afraid sometimes, but I know that's when the Lord wants me to be strong. He's looking down on me, saying 'Paul, do you trust me?'" He chuckled as he shook his head. "Jesus doesn't want me to be a baby believer forever. He wants me to grow up and walk with him in faith."

I frowned, trying to understand. "Is that what the Lord wants from us? To grow up and surrender our will?"

"Love the Lord your God with all of your heart, with all of your mind, and with all of your soul," Paul phrased. He drew himself up proudly and beamed. "I just read those words from Jesus yesterday. I'm really enjoying the Bible, John. God's Word speaks to me."

I stepped aside as Morales stuck out his cup for a refill. Hannah's words came back to me, and I chewed the inside of my cheek. Yes, I began to see what Texas faith meant for a follower of Christ.

The next day, I rode my horse alongside James and asked him the same question. "What does God want from us?"

He shot me a curious look and then nodded. "I used to ask myself that very question. The Lord commands us to seek justice, love mercy, and walk humbly with our God. But there was little justice or mercy in the war, and I fell away, feeling God wasn't involved. Yet I cannot deny how the Lord led me to your ranch and guided my every step as we sold cattle to the army outposts. It was as if God had prepared me for this very moment in time, as if I had to experience everything I did to make me the right man for this job."

He paused and his face broke into a wide smile that made him look younger than his years. "And now I feel blessed beyond reason. The Lord is with us. I sense his hand upon us, and I feel we're doing something great, something beyond us."

"A grand adventure," I whispered, recalling Ma's words from so long ago.

"Annie's a wise woman," he agreed with a nod.

"She told me to keep an eye on you." I grinned, lightening the moment. He chuckled as I nudged my horse away.

"She told *me* to keep an eye on *you*," he called from behind as I cantered off, needing to think and ponder on the sage advice of wiser folks.

With a start, I realized I played a small role in this journey we'd started months ago. Whether I liked it or not, God was moving among us, and I was invited to participate or get out of the way. There was no room for slackers or doubters in God's plan.

Then I laughed, knowing I was often both of these. Clearly, there was room for the spiritually young and skeptics, but God yearned for us to mature so we could experience his goodness completely.

As I trailed along with the other cowboys, watching the cattle graze as we pushed them east toward Missouri, I continued to see how Hannah understood so much more than I did. Although I'd been raised in a Christian home, I'd allowed dour circumstances to shape my faith rather than waiting patiently on the Lord, seeking his will for my life while enduring life-crushing situations. The Lord's refining fire scorched, burning away the useless and the weak to reveal the true strength of those who persevere. Could that be me? Did I possess the Texas faith demanded for spiritual maturity? Would Jesus be patient with me as my fickle feelings ebbed and flowed like the tide?

Clenching my teeth, I determined once again to seek Christ first, walk in faith, and watch the Lord work. Each day was a new day, with new mercies dawning. Despite my weakness, I resolved again to be strong and lean into the Lord.

We encountered wild storms and wide rivers on our trek, but each obstacle we met with fortitude and grit. Once, a band of Shawnee braves demanded ten head of stock to cross their lands. James bargained for only eight cattle and some tobacco, and the drive continued.

April arrived and then passed into May, the cold nights fading into pleasant spring days. In the distance, the Ozark Mountains loomed, and we knew we approached Missouri. That afternoon, dark clouds clustered on the northern horizon and a stiff gale blustered.

"Every man in a saddle tonight," James ordered after supper. "Paul, keep the wagon packed, ready to move."

As we'd neared our destination, a sense of anticipation had descended, almost making me believe we'd arrive safely in Sedalia. But the brewing storm hovered just out of reach, making the cattle bawl restlessly as the cowboys circled the milling herd.

With a clap of thunder that boomed like an explosion, the entire herd stood stiff-legged, eyes wide as they stared into the gathering twilight. The thunder echoed across the plains, fading into the distance. When a jagged lightning streak stabbed the earth near camp, horns knocked as the cattle tensed, the nervous animals shoving against one another. But when another forked lightning bolt zigzagged across the black sky, accompanied by an ear-splitting thunderclap, the herd raced into the gloom.

CHAPTER 43

Wind rushed across the prairie, and I pulled my hat low as I galloped after the herd, cattle bumping my stirrups. A wall of rain drenched me as the storm opened up, and I hunkered over my saddle as the animals ran heedless of direction. As the squall continued, I gripped my reins tight and followed the cattle, hoping my horse wouldn't lose his footing and pile up. To stumble now would spell disaster for a horse and rider, surrounded by hundreds of wild cattle with flailing horns.

At first the herd stayed compact. As the miles passed and obstacles diverted sections of the mob, I found myself with a cluster of cattle that slowed as the storm waned. By midnight, judging by the stars peeking through the ragged clouds, I trotted after a hundred head of stock. Slowing even more for a swollen creek running bank full of noisy waves, I called to the cattle and halted them in a clearing below a wooded knoll.

Alone, I listened into the night as I rode among the gathered little herd. Heads down, the tired beasts stood, unwilling to rest upon the sodden turf. The sudden rainstorm had passed, but the herd scattered across the countryside, and I wondered what damage we'd incurred. How had the other riders fared?

When a faint gray appeared in the east, I rode my exhausted horse up the hill to peer around. Not a mile distant, a rider tagged behind a small group of cattle. Shouting and waving my hat, I soon caught his attention. With a whistle, the cowboy swerved the small cluster of stock and drove them to join my mob. I grinned when I recognized Ronnie Krefeld.

"I thought I was the only man alive on these endless plains," he grumbled as we shook hands. There was a bit of congratulation and greeting in the gesture, and I felt sure he wondered as I did if we'd find other survivors.

"Did you see anything of the others?" I ran a hand across my unshaven jaw, wishing for a cup of coffee and a bath. What would we do now? Everyone from the outfit was lost, and the herd scattered to the four winds, but I was alive. Where did the Lord fit into this catastrophe?

"I think I saw someone go down when the herd broke," Ronnie admitted softly, as if reluctant to say the words aloud.

"Any idea who?" I persisted, wondering. Had others died in the stampede?

He shook his head. "I don't know. I think Carl was on the other side of the herd, but I'm not sure." At mention of his brother, he turned away, but not before I caught the glisten in his eyes.

For the next several hours, loose stock drifted into the clearing, swelling our small gathering. We took turns circling the mob and scanning the surrounding area from the nearby high knoll. My heart leaped when I caught sight of a canvas-topped wagon in late afternoon, the vehicle lurching over rough ground. With a shrill whistle, I caught Paul's eye and he turned the wagon toward our meadow. Within the hour, we had a fire burning brightly, a coffeepot shoved among the glowing coals.

"Did you see anyone else?"

He frowned at my question and then grimaced. "I found what was left of someone. By the fancy spurs and high boots, I figure it was Morales." My stomach clenched at his news, but he went on. "Hard to tell after a thousand cows ran over him."

I gritted my teeth and went to search for more firewood. When I returned, Steeple Mason stood beside the fire, a steaming cup in one hand.

"Thought I alone survived," he greeted as I dropped my load of sticks near the cheerful blaze. I never liked Steeple, but I felt pleased others were alive. The three of us riders took turns watching the herd as the night passed.

Early the next day, Ronnie called from the summit of the knoll, waving his hat. With a shout, he raced to camp, never slowing as he passed.

"It's Carl, about a mile out," he yelled as he rode away, his horse kicking up wet grass. By afternoon of that second day, we had about eight hundred head of cattle, bunched in a loose herd. The stampeded cattle seemed content to graze on the rich grass. Spring had come to the prairie, the long winter behind us for another season. Luxuriant grassland waved gently in the breeze under an azure sky, and the awful events of a day ago seemed far away and long ago. But where were James, Lee, and Meyers? Were they dead like Morales?

On the third day, a rider in a dark suit coat rode into camp. He studied the herd with a knowing eye before dismounting. "Is John Garret here?"

Startled, I stepped forward. "How do you know me?"

He hooked a thumb to the north. "I'm Dooley. A pair of riders are holding a small herd to the north, about five hundred head. The lead man is James Casey. He said to keep my eye out for you on my way back to town."

So, James was alive. I let out a long breath and nodded, wondering who the other rider was. I felt glad for Ma that James lived. He'd become a significant part of our ranch in more ways than one.

"What town is that?" I queried, knowing Paul was running low on supplies.

"Sedalia. A Shawnee Indian told me that a cattle herd was coming, across the Nations. I rode out to meet you, make you an offer on your stock."

I thought of the Shawnee braves who'd traded passage across their lands for eight of our cattle and I smiled, wondering if our deal had been more fortuitous than we could've ever imagined. "Did you tell this to James?" I glanced at Paul. This was what we'd risked so much for. Paul grinned in return, sensing my relief at being near the end of the drive.

The cattle buyer nodded. "Yes, I told him, but he said he had to discuss my offer with you. Said the herd is yours."

I blinked, startled, and I glanced at Paul again. "Well, Mr. Dooley, what's your offer?"

He straightened his shoulders. "I'm prepared to give you fourteen dollars a head, delivered to the stock pens at Sedalia."

I felt my breath catch, unable to figure the sum in my whirling thoughts. Fourteen dollars a head was more than we expected.

I shifted again. "Let me join our herds and talk with James. I should have an answer for you by tomorrow."

Mr. Dooley nodded and mounted his horse. "I'll see you tomorrow," he said as he rode from camp.

For the remainder of the day, we scouted for James and then pushed our herds together as he told me about Lee. "When the cattle stampeded, we were together, riding fast within the running herd. I saw a break in the mob and swerved for the gap just as Lee's horse went down, throwing him to the ground."

By nightfall, the cowboys took turns checking on the mob while James and me discussed the offer on the cattle.

"I didn't figure on fourteen dollars a head," I confessed.

"But we also didn't figure on a stampede that cut our herd by four hundred head," James growled. "That's a loss of over five thousand dollars. We'll need every dollar to pay Brisbane and begin ranching on a large scale. We have the makings of a good outfit, but we'll miss Morales and Lee."

I would miss the wiry vaquero and the evasive rider too, but we both admitted things could've been worse. Eagerly, we accepted Dooley's offer and drove the remaining herd into Sedalia.

James demanded cash money, so we loafed around the café while Mr. Dooley gathered the funds. Paul ordered supplies for the return trip.

After receiving our pay, Steeple Mason stepped forward, stuffing his money into his pocket. "Well, boys, this is where we part ways," he drawled. He shook hands all around, even with Clyde Meyers, but I felt pleased at his departure. His negative, argumentative attitude grated on my nerves.

"Will you go back to Texas?" Carl Krefeld asked as we gathered around Steeple. The tall cowboy stepped into the saddle and looked down at us, ginning. "Nope, nothing in Texas for me. I think I'll head west, see what I can find. So long." And with a wave, he rode down the dusty street.

Clyde Meyers and the Krefeld brothers agreed to return to our ranch. We would need more riders, but we were beginning with a few seasoned hands. Others would join us when news of our success got out. Now, Texas ranches would have a market for their cattle. Despite the war, things were looking up.

Still, as we headed our horses and Paul's wagon west on that quiet May day, I couldn't help but feel something lacked within me. A hollow sensation filled my gut, and I knew with the arduous drive over, my thoughts would return to Hannah once more. I remembered her encouraging words and the way she smiled at me, her dark hair in the falling snow as I kissed her last Christmas. Although I'd grown as a believer, maturing me more and more into the man of God the Lord desired, my heart ached. Would sorrow be my companion as my faith developed?

Regardless of our ranching success, I felt lonely.

CHAPTER 44

Before leaving Sedalia, James sent a telegraph to Mr. Brisbane, wiring the rancher his funds. He handed the reply to me as we stalked to the edge of town where our outfit waited.

James and John Stop Thanks for the money Stop The ranch is yours Stop God bless.

We outfitted our wagon and when the second load of five hundred head shipped out, the cattle buyer assured us he could now handle the remaining cattle and released us. We started for home.

With no cattle to slow us down, we made good time, keeping pace with Paul's wagon as we ambled back through Kansas and into the Indian Territory.

The plains blossomed with rich, green grass and vibrantly colored patches of wildflowers. Late May provided mild weather for our journey home, weather we appreciated after the storms of spring that nagged at our heels on the trek east. Now, meadowlarks whistled from the thickets and locusts whirred along the riverbanks. At night, we slept to the chorus of coyotes howling at the night sky. With no night guard on a herd of cattle, the trip seemed leisurely and restful.

Yet my heart felt troubled as we approached Texas. I wanted to see Hannah again. Was she married now? Had

Buffalo Horn disclosed her impending husband? An ache filled me I couldn't shake, although I prayed unceasingly, laying my heavy burden at the Lord's feet. Shouldn't a sense of peace overwhelm me when I obeyed God? I'd pursued faith with a fervor I now realized had grown and developed me as a believer, yet I still loved Hannah. Would I always suffer for being submissive?

Buffalo, antelope, and deer covered the grasslands of the vast prairies. One day, a herd of wild horses trooped along a nearby ridge, whistling to our horses and making them prance nervously.

Despite the beauty and grandeur of the landscape, my mind revolved upon the details of the risky cattle drive. We'd pushed seventeen hundred head of stock across six hundred miles to a distant market. Only thirteen hundred head were delivered, but no one could deny our victory. Or was our journey the Lord's victory?

Our success would have a long-lasting impact on every cattle rancher in Texas. I thought of our small corner of the panhandle and the incredible adventure Ma had initiated last summer when the rider had brought the news of Pa's death and Ma had thrown herself at the feet of Jesus, launching an adventure I'd been so reluctant to join.

Looking back, I saw clearly how God had caught me up by the scruff of my neck and shaken me, shaking the doubts and cynicism right out of me as I submitted to his will. I shuddered to think what would've happened if I'd persisted in being an obstacle to the Lord. Of course, he can do anything, and my unwillingness would only have caused more difficulties for me. His plans cannot be thwarted, yet my maturity as a believer could easily be delayed if I allowed my skepticism to persist.

Still, I struggled. With God's blessing, the future of our ranch seemed secure, yet I missed Hannah. She'd taught me so much about faith and allowing God to work in my life. And she'd become a special friend. Would I see her again?

Sometimes, I tied my horse to the tailgate of Paul's wagon and rode beside him on the hard wooden bench. He told me of his Lydia and the baby he longed to see, and my heart ached even more for Hannah.

James often read his Bible at night around the campfire. He talked of the responsibility of a family and being a landowner, and his eyes glowed with excitement. Would I ever know the excitement of fulfilling the life Jesus had for me? As my spiritual awareness deepened, would I ever discover God's purpose for me?

When I left the cavalcade to gallop far from the slow-moving wagon, I sought the Lord in prayer. "You know my heart, Jesus. You know what is best for me, but I long for Hannah Tall Basket. Let me trust that you have something wonderful for me, *someone* wonderful. I surrender to you and give you a willing heart. Do with me as you will, and may I praise your name forever."

Topping out on a rise, I sat my horse and watched the outfit pass below. From here, I could faintly hear the wheels creaking above the constant wind as Paul's wagon jostled over the prairie. James and the other riders loafed in their saddles, enjoying the respite before we returned home to the tough work that awaited a fledgling ranch eager to blossom. Steeple Mason wanted to drift and see new lands. I did not. The ranch my father had started was now mine, and I yearned to see the land develop into a prosperous business. I wasn't afraid of hard work, but I didn't want to face the future alone. I knew God was with me, but would he give me a partner as he did Paul and James? And not just any partner. I wanted Hannah.

Pushing my stubborn heart aside, I shook my head. "Forgive me, Lord. Your will, not mine."

After crossing the Arkansas River, the swollen river running bank full with snow melt, James noticed a dust cloud on the horizon. At first, we feared a dust storm, but as we came on, we saw cattle.

Pulling off the road to allow the herd to pass, we silently watched the cattle drift along, grazing as they moved to the east. When a cowboy hailed us, drawing rein beside the wagon, he wiped his brow with a dirty sleeve.

"I know you must think we're crazy to push cattle to Missouri, but if the Bar G can do it, so can we."

I glanced at James, and he grinned, nodding. "No one thinks you're crazy, cowboy. Good luck."

Each night on that ride home, James pushed us to cover a few more miles until twilight forced us into camp. Each morning, we rose early and started on before dawn, all eager to get home.

Three weeks after leaving Sedalia, we rode into the ranch yard, Lydia smiling broadly as she held a baby up for Paul's appraisal. Ma hurried from the barn, her eyes wide as she watched James dismount. Without a word, she rushed into his arms, but I saw the tears on her cheeks. When she whispered in his ear, he whooped before patting her belly, and I knew Paul and Lydia's baby would not be the only child on the ranch.

"I named her Annie," Lydia announced proudly as she handed her daughter to her husband.

Paul beamed as he took the squirming bundle into his arms. "A perfect name," he mumbled as the cowboys dismounted.

Soon the wagon was unhitched, the gear stowed, and the men settled once more in the bunkhouse. Ma poured coffee for James, Paul, and me, and I sighed as I leaned back in the kitchen chair, pleased to be home.

"By the way," Ma said with a smile that hadn't dimmed since our arrival. "Happy birthday."

I blinked, suddenly startled to remember my birthday had come again. In the hustle and bustle of the cattle drive and our return home, I'd forgotten. In a flash, I recalled my last birthday when the rider had conveyed the message concerning Pa. How much had changed in a single year.

Before I could reply to Ma's acknowledgement, a clatter of hooves drew me to the window. A group of Indians trotted into the yard, and I recognized Hannah among them, her long hair blowing in the wind. Dark Cloud was there too. He dismounted in a fluid leap, his leg healed.

We all moved to the back stoop to greet our neighbors, but I had eyes only for Hannah. If possible, she was even more beautiful than ever, and her eyes danced mischievously when she caught my gaze.

"Dark Cloud insisted on coming to share his happy news. He has married one of my best friends," she announced with a gesture to the Comanche warrior. The brave stood tall when Hannah indicated him, and Dark Cloud nodded at me as he said something in Comanche.

"Dark Cloud says he remembers when his enemy became his friend, when his friend saved his life," she interpreted. Dark Cloud clasped my forearm and looked into my eyes with a grunt, conveying much.

"Friend," I agreed with a firm grip on his forearm. Yet my gaze shifted curiously to Hannah. "He married one of your friends?" I muttered from the corner of my mouth as Dark Cloud turned to greet James.

Hannah giggled. "Well, when Buffalo Horn announced who I was to marry before the entire tribe, Dark Cloud realized there was no point in waiting for me any longer. He quickly married Sweet Grass."

My heart sank and I narrowed my eyes. "Your father made his announcement? Do I know the man?" I couldn't hide the bitterness in my words, but Hannah only smiled as Ma grasped her elbow, pulling Hannah toward the kitchen, chattering away.

Laughter pealed over her shoulder as the two women mounted the back stoop. I scowled while James led the Comanche to the corrals to inspect the horses. Was Hannah to marry another man soon? I loved her, but I knew God would do anything to bring glory to his name. I bowed my head as I slipped around the corner of the house to be alone.

"You are God, and I am not. Let me accept what you have for me. Your will, Lord, not my own." I paused and squeezed my eyes shut. "But I love her, Jesus. You know I love her." I bit my lip and nodded, surrendering once more. "Forgive me, Lord. Your will be done."

Later, as the afternoon passed, Ma and Lydia shared baby stories with Hannah who sat with me at the kitchen table. The young woman stole sidelong glances at me, smiling wistfully as if she held a secret she longed to share. When Ma blushed at the mention of her baby's arrival at summer's end, Hannah rested an elbow on the table, leaning close to me. The intoxicating scent of prairie and sunshine wafted from her long hair.

"I have an announcement too," she whispered so only I could hear.

"I know," I grumbled. "You are to announce your marriage. So, who is the lucky man your father saw in his vision so many years ago?" Did I really want to know?

"You, Johnny," Hannah said softly, her dark eyes shining as she reached to take my hand. Her face peered up at me, and I studied her, too overcome with joy to speak. Her copper cheeks glowed with a crimson blush, and her smile trembled as I bent to kiss her.

EPILOGUE

"Happy Birthday!" Everyone shouted as Ma placed the cake on the table, all eyes on me. I smiled gratefully and leaned back in my chair, the small kitchen crowded with those I loved. My gaze shifted to Hannah where she sat beside me, her shoulder brushing mine as she cuddled our small baby. I felt my throat tighten, and I tried to swallow the lump as I lifted my mug of coffee, hiding my unexpected emotions behind the cup.

"Are you all right?" At Hannah's quiet question, I squeezed her arm, unable to reply as the back door banged open. Paul and Lydia laughed, following Little Ann while their toddler weaved onto the back stoop, the small girl's eyes riveted on the chickens scratching in the yard.

"Go get those chickens," James called merrily as he trailed the others. Lydia swung the tottering girl to the hard-packed dirt yard and released her once more, feathers flying as the birds scattered before the flailing child.

Laughter drifted on the warm summer afternoon, but I tensed, feelings reeling as my family gathered to celebrate another birthday before I departed the next day. At nineteen, I felt stunned at God's faithfulness and provision. Our ranch flourished, and the business of raising cattle seemed strong. Although the railroad still hadn't made its way into Texas, the temporary hub for buying and shipping cattle in Sedalia, Missouri, had been replaced by fresh rails stretching across the Kansas plains, just to the north of us. Our second large cattle drive was planned to launch tomorrow, and I wanted to relish this last day with Hannah and my daughter before I left.

"Are you all right?" Hannah's repeated inquiry made me nod, although I still worked at the lump in my throat. Ma caught my eye and winked knowingly before turning to follow James outside, her arms wrapped tightly around my little brother. Soon, I expected Jimmy to be chasing Little Ann across the yard.

I drew a deep breath and sighed, regaining something of my composure. "I'm all right," I mumbled, squeezing Hannah's arm again.

She pulled the loose blanket from the baby's face and hummed softly. "Faith is a perfect name for our girl," Hannah said.

"Uh-huh." I blinked the moisture from my eyes and studied our daughter. For so long, I'd grappled with struggles and feelings that threatened to overwhelm me. Yet so much had changed this last year.

"I don't deserve any of this," I muttered. At Hannah's searching glance, I gestured to the sleeping baby she held and the cluster of loved ones outside, the crowd chuckling while they encouraged Little Ann's chicken hunt.

"This," I repeated, still waving my arm to indicate everything. "You, the baby, our ranch succeeding." I paused and drew another deep breath.

"God feels you do," Hannah said with an assuredness I didn't feel. "But not because of your goodness, Johnny."

I shifted my boots beneath the table. "Well, no, of course not," I agreed. My mouth puckered and I leaned closer to her, inhaling the fresh scent of her long hair. "Why has the Lord blessed me?" I whispered before gently nibbling her ear.

Hannah giggled and pushed me away, her dark eyes dancing.

"You have worked hard to discover a deep faith, a deep relationship with our Savior. But his rewards are not so you can boast and become puffed up, like a strutting rooster, as if you did something remarkable."

"Oh, no?" I teased, trying to pull her close once more for a stolen kiss while the others lingered outside.

"No," she laughed, holding me back at arm's length. Her smile flashed, her teeth dazzling against her bronzed cheeks. Her grin softened as she became serious once more.

"I am proud of you, Johnny. Proud to be your wife, to have your children." Her gaze dropped to where our child nestled in her embrace. After a moment, she looked at me again.

"God has worked in you. True, you allowed his shaping hand through trials and doubts that didn't sour you to Christ. But he is not through with you yet."

My eyebrows arched as I considered my wise partner, my best friend. "He's not done with me yet?" I shifted again, my chair creaking. "Well, no, I don't suppose he is."

I hesitated before I went on, not sure I wanted to hear the answer. "What do you think the Lord has in store for me?"

She laughed, the rich sound filling the small kitchen. "How should I know?" Then she quieted, her gaze piercing me as if she looked into my soul. "But I trust you will meet whatever comes your way with the faithfulness you've cultivated. With trust, hope, and the great strength Jesus has given you. You will be an example to our family, to our children, and to their children. You will be expected to take your legacy seriously, as others watch you lead in a godly manner. Much is expected of a mature Christian man."

"Me?" I almost gasped at the severity of her words. "I still have so much to learn," I protested, not sure I wanted such a heavy weight upon my shoulders.

Hannah shrugged, her grin returning. "You can do it. I've seen your sensitivity to the Spirit develop as you wrestled with the Lord. But not only to grow your faith."

She paused and glanced again at the silent child in her arms. "No, Johnny, God doesn't only want to grow your faith so you can endure challenges, be a leader, and point others to Christ."

"Then what?" I frowned at her meaningful words, deeper than I'd wanted, as I tried to enjoy a special moment alone with the woman I loved more than my own life.

Hannah shook her head, but her smile never faded. "Through a deep faith, forged in tough times, we come to know our Lord cares for us with an everlasting love. Only as our faith deepens do we really see how much he loves us, which grows our faith even more, allowing us to trust him through difficulties."

"Texas faith," I breathed softly, glimpsing a little of how much I still had to learn.

Hannah nodded. "With a big faith, we see a bigger love," she said, drawing close to me with a twinkle in her dark eyes. "God loves you, and so do I. Through good times and rough. As God matures us into the people we are to become, I want my faith to grow as I've seen you grow. Into the man of God I love."

The lump returned as my throat swelled again. I didn't fully understand the Lord's love for me, but as I draped an arm around Hannah's shoulders and peered down at Faith, I pondered her prophetic words. God wasn't through with me yet. Perhaps Ma's adventure wasn't over, and the next part of my journey only beckoned on the horizon.

I bent to kiss Faith's forehead and knew I wasn't alone. Two years ago, Ma's prayers had encompassed the entire ranch, bringing all of us into a spiritual expedition I'd not soon forget. Through knowing Christ, we'd all grown in some measure. My family surrounded me, supported me, and I knew the adventure wasn't over yet. And Jesus rode the prairies with me as I grew in Texas faith.

ABOUT THE AUTHOR

ANDREW ROTH taught American History for twenty-two years at the middle school level before beginning his literary career. He lives in Bakersfield, California, with his wife and is a proud father and grandfather. A native of Kansas, Andrew was raised with a deep love and appreciation for history, particularly the Old West. Andrew has been a Christian for more than three decades, and his hope is that his writing will encourage readers and rebuild lives. The passage he feels is his guiding verse is Jeremiah 31:4, "I will build you up again and you will be rebuilt." Andrew's website is: http://andrewrothbooks.com.

Renewed Redemption

ANDREW ROTH

Train to Laramie

ANDREW ROTH

Mercy Again

ANDREW ROTH

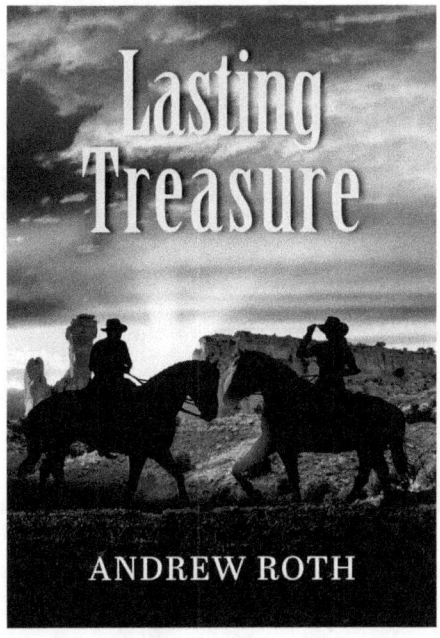

Lasting Treasure

ANDREW ROTH

www.ingramcontent.com/pod-product-compliance
Lightning Source LLC
Chambersburg PA
CBHW071155020726
47502CB00002B/418